Blood of the Sun

Blood of the Sun

The Path of Ra Book 3

Dan Rabarts Lee Murray

Published by Raw Dog Screaming Press
Bowie, MD

First Edition

Cover Image: Daniele Serra
Book Design: Jennifer Barnes

Printed in the United States of America

ISBN: 978-1-947879-26-3

Library of Congress Control Number: 2020943325

www.RawDogScreaming.com

Acknowledgements

Normally, this is where we write a long list of thanks to our beta readers, our publisher, our kids, and our spouses. We send our compliments to our lawyer, coo over the cover design, and make tongue in cheek remarks about how great it's been to work together again. Dan asks if it's wine-o'clock, and Lee whines about Dan's explosions.

This time, though, things are different. Times are different. Because on 15 March 2019 at 1:40pm, a gunman entered two Christchurch mosques and shot and killed forty-nine people. Another victim died later in hospital. A further fifty were injured. Families were shattered. As the city went into lockdown, and emergency services proved their mettle, New Zealanders responded with shock, grief, and utter disbelief.

"There is no place in New Zealand for such acts of extreme and unprecedented violence," said our Prime Minister, Jacinda Ardern, in a press conference at the height of the conflict. And yet it happened: a deadly massacre on New Zealand soil. The youngest among the victims, Mucad Ibrahim, was just three years old.

Well, bad stuff happens every day, right? Take a look at the news. The world is full of sadness. Why make such a big deal of this?

The reason is because up until that moment, we were blithely writing massacres into our near-future fantasy, setting the landscape alight with illegal firearms and frantic life-or-death car chases in a murderous complot masterminded by a cold-hearted zealot. And we did this smug in the knowledge that it could never happen here in New Zealand.

We were wrong.

Unlike the small boy in this story, there will be no second chance for Mucad Ibrahim.

So, here, where we would normally sip wine and blow kisses to the wind, we would like to acknowledge the Muslim community for their devastating loss. We acknowledge the long-suffering people of Christchurch, still bruised and broken from the 2011 earthquake, emergency services personnel, and our fellow New Zealanders for your resilience and your compassion during these dark times. Kia kaha. Stand strong. We have never been so proud to be Kiwi and call Aotearoa our home.

Dan Rabarts and Lee Murray, October 2019

Publisher's Note

Because the region this novel takes place in is so much a part of the story, we have chosen to retain the British spelling conventions that are the standard in New Zealand. This work also incorporates New Zealand phrases and words from the indigenous Māori people, so we have included a brief glossary in the back for anyone not familiar with these terms.

- Prologue -

Leaning forward, Anaru cuts the black water with his paddle and heaves, the muscles of his back straining as he drags the wooden blade through the swell, the movement as powerful as it is silent. When he lifts the paddle out of the water, he takes a second to glance at the men around him. His companions' mouths are set in grim determination. Their eyes, though, shine with fervour, their pupils reflecting the neon glow of the ancestors' fires, tāhu-nui-a-rangi, which shine in the sky to the south, the luminous rifts of green and gold so bright they have turned night into day. Anaru knows it is no coincidence. The fiery streaks are a message from the gods, proof that tonight's crusade is just and true, that Anaru and his companions have the old ones' blessing as they glide across the harbour to take the power of Ra from their enemies.

Yes, it's fitting. It's as it should be. Are they not children of Aotearoa, too? Cast-offs come together to make their own tribe, not through birth, but of choice. Raised up under their chieftain Hanson, and then, when Hanson died, under their new chief, Kingi.

Plunging his blade into the water again, Anaru smiles despite the effort. Like a sign in the local dairy window that reads 'Under New Management,' Simon Kingi has changed the gang. With Hanson at their head, they'd been little more than a nest of thieves, a rag-tag band of pickpockets and shysters. Not anymore. Kingi is a force of nature, a true taniwha-chief, whose wairua-spirit walks with the gods. Where others saw a bunch of low-life scum, Kingi recognised their worth. Saw them as more than dogs and whores. He raised them up from the filthy streets, taking just weeks to transform them into a fearsome warrior-battalion. Even now, Kingi's voice trembles in Anaru's ear like the rustle of pingāo grass far off on the beach. Fragments of the century-old war-song pulse in his head:

Ka hīkoi mātou ki te hoariri...[1]

We will march to the enemy...

Mo te kingi!

For Kingi!

With the southern lights guiding their route, the warriors glide on across the harbour towards the shipyards. The spikes of golden light lend strength to Anaru's

1 Lyrics of the Māori Battalion Marching Song, by Cpl Anaia Amohau, written for the Te Arawa Treaty of Waitangi Centennial celebrations in February,1940.

muscles. They spur him on. Ra urges him on too; the metal hei-tiki pendant of the sun god slapping against Anaru's chest with every stroke of the paddle.

A massive ship looms to their right. *Yongyang –The Eternal Light.* They are close to the docks now. It's as Kingi said it would be. The power awaits them, theirs for the taking. As if anticipating their arrival, the *Yongyang* moans softly at her berth, the lap of the ocean's waves gentle against her hull.

Suddenly, there's a shout and the man to Anaru's right points upwards. On the deck of the ship, men are running.

"We've been seen," someone breathes.

No, not just seen; betrayed. Their enemies are gathered on the wharf. They've come to steal the power from under Kingi's nose.

Yet Kingi's voice is calm and sure. He murmurs in Anaru's ear, the words working their way into his mind, the way an octopus reaches its tentacles into the crags of a rock. "Warriors! Prepare yourself for battle. We march to the enemy!"

Hair rises on Anaru's nape. Men will die tonight. Perhaps he will be among them.

In the sky, the ancestors in the south sit forward to watch the coming battle. The rustle of the pingão keeps cadence with the pounding of Anaru's heart. He breathes deep. These moments before the battle are a mixture of exhilaration and resignation. It's like lying with a woman in that instant before release—when there is no turning back.

Lifting his eyes to the sky, Anaru dips his paddle in the water once more.

CHAPTER 1

- Pandora -

A pair of bulked-up officers carrying semi-automatic rifles stop them at the entrance to the Port of Auckland. One of them steps out of the milky wash of the headlights and approaches the vehicle. He raps his knuckles on the windscreen.

Penny's heart skips. *This isn't normal.*

In the driver's seat, Penny's brother Matiu is as cool as a cucumber. He lowers the window. "Officer?" he says, his tone unctuous. It's the voice he uses to get one over Mum, one he's perfected through years of trying to get out of the dishes.

The man lifts his face-shield, revealing a five o'clock shadow. Impressive, since it's barely four AM. "You'll have to turn the vehicle around, sir," he says, raising an eyebrow, a decided lack of sincerity in that 'sir.'

Penny hasn't got time for their pissing match. Tanner called her forty minutes ago. He'd expected her in ten. She leans over the console, ducking her head to speak to the man across her brother. "You need to let us through."

"Yeah, it's not going to happen, lady. This whole area is off limits." The officer waves his rifle casually towards Bledisloe Wharf. "It's a crime scene."

Penny resists the urge to roll her eyes. "Yes, exactly. A crime scene. That's why we're here. Detective Inspector Tanner called me expressly. I'm Dr Penny Yee from Yee Scientific Consultancy. This is my…driver, Matiu Yee, and in the back is my technician, Beaker, I mean, Grant Deaker."

The officer sucks air in over his teeth and shakes his head. "Sweetheart, you could be the twenty-first Time Lord with her Companion, I still wouldn't be able to let you through. My orders are not to let anyone in without the proper authority."

Penny bristles. She's no one's bloody sweetheart, least of all some Neanderthal toting a gun. She has a doctoral degree, close to a decade's-worth of post-doc experience, and she owns her own business—the parts the bank doesn't own, anyway.

"I assure you, I have the proper authority," she says sweetly. As sweetly as she can through gritted teeth. "Detective Inspec—"

"It's all good, mate," interrupts Matiu, buzzing the window up to half-mast. "This time of the morning, you won't get any argument from me. I'm just as happy to go back to bed." Stamping on the accelerator, he lurches the car forward, barely missing the squaddie out front, then slams the vehicle into reverse.

"Matiu!" Penny jabs the ignition switch.

The Holden jolts to a stop, whiplashing them all back and forth. In the rear, there's a nervous squawk from Beaker, followed by a yelp from Cerberus, the dog's nails scratching the leather upholstery.

She glances backwards. “Sorry, guys.”

Her lab technician shuffles his feet to one side, allowing the Labrador Retriever to clamber out of the footwell. “No problems. We’re all fine here, aren’t we, Cerb?” Beaker’s voice, and his own blaze of red hair, disappear behind a wall of golden fur.

In the half-light, Matiu glares. “Pen, c’mon. Let’s just go.” He reaches for the ignition.

Penny stops his hand. “No!”

“Pandora—” Matiu says, and Penny’s teeth ache. The only name she dislikes more than ‘sweetheart’ is her given one.

Matiu lowers his voice. “I don’t know if you noticed, but the Mutant Ninja Terrorists in black out there, the ones sporting the HK MP5s, those guys are from the Armed Offenders Squad.”

Penny blinks.

“Which means they only get called out when the *offenders are armed*,” Matiu says slowly.

“Well, yes. It’s a multiple homicide, Matiu,” Penny says, equally slowly. “That’s why Tanner asked me to bring Beaker. My guess is a couple of wharfies had a set to or something…”

“A *couple* of wharfies? Open your eyes, sis. Have you seen how many squaddies there are out there?”

Penny squints through the haze of pre-dawn humidity. Her breath catches. Between the teetering stacks of containers, there has to be at least fifty squaddies shuffling like zombies in the eerie light of the aurora.

The upholstery squeaks as Beaker leans forward. “There do seem to be a lot of men with guns…”

Cerberus lets out a low growl.

Penny nibbles her lip. *Definitely* not normal.

“Let me get Tanner on the phone,” she says. While she’s fumbling in her satchel for her cell, knuckles rap the window again. “Give me a second, will you? I’m trying to get your bloody authorisation for you,” she mutters.

“Um…Penny,” Beaker mumbles from the back. “It’s Officer Clark.”

Clark? Penny’s head whips up. “For goodness sake, Beaker. Why didn’t you say?” Gripping her satchel, Penny throws open the passenger door and gets out of the car. “Officer Clark. Sorry we took so long. These men won’t let us through.”

“It’s OK,” Clark tells the gatekeepers. “Dr Yee is our science consult.” He smiles stiffly, giving them a thumbs up and the squaddies fall back, their black uniforms melting into the shadows.

Penny wants to scream. A century and a half of women’s suffrage and a man’s word still carries more weight. Still, they’re in, which means the job—whatever it is—is hers, so maybe this isn’t the time to kick up a fuss about the state of women’s rights.

"Matiu, you might want to pull the car in over there," Clark orders. He signals to a parking bay off to the right. "Come this way, Dr Yee. And you too, Mr Beaker."

While Matiu parks the car, Penny and Beaker follow the constable, who weaves them through the containers towards the end of the wharf, where a single ship is berthed on the northern quay. Beaker lopes alongside Penny, the on-site sampling kit bumping against his thigh. Clark hurries ahead.

"Clark? What's happened?" Penny calls. "Why the rush?"

Shaking his head, Clark says nothing.

"I reckon his blood 1,3,7-trimethylxanthine titre is low," Beaker quips.

Penny gives Beaker a wry smile. Clark isn't the only one who missed their morning dose of coffee.

They pass under a stack of containers, its bulk momentarily blocking the streaks of green and violet rippling in arcs across the sky, and Penny shivers in spite of the humidity. It's only the fourth geomagnetic storm in a month. When auroral lights appear this far north of the geographic pole, and in the Auckland CBD where light pollution is high, it can only mean one thing: the solar winds coming off the sun are nothing less than colossal. When the second storm occurred, Penny had looked it up on Auroralert, a real-time solar wind and geomagnetic data mapping service. It was alarming. They were reporting planetary indices as high as Kp8 and Kp9. These guys aren't crackpots either, their data streamed via NASA's ACE spacecraft. Huge geomagnetic storms coming in thick and fast.

And so far north.

Hardly surprising then that certain scientists are saying that this marks the start of the Earth's magnetic pole reversal. Penny's inclined to agree. After 780,000 years since the last one, a flip is long overdue. But some people—the end-is-nigh doomsayers—are calling it the end of the world. With Auckland's recent blackouts, the quakes, the ongoing heat wave, and now a weekly southern light show, it's easy to understand why. Either way, over the past few months it's resulted in an epic crime wave with people throwing caution to the wind, settling old feuds, or looking for a quick score so they can tick off all those items on their bucket lists before civilisation disappears from the face of the planet. Desperate times. Last week, someone told Penny that Tanner's department had forty homicides on the books.

Forty!

"It's a bloody shitstorm," Clark says, echoing Penny's thoughts.

Penny frowns. It's not like Clark to swear, though.

"Er…what exactly do you mean by a shitstorm?" Beaker asks.

But by now they have reached the end of the stacks. Penny stops dead. She gasps.

"Oh my God," Beaker whispers.

The bodies. So many bodies. Charred and mutilated beyond recognition, they lie in blackened broken heaps. Bledisloe Wharf has become Danté's Plain of Burning Sand.

Penny stands up, her gumboots slipping in the slick of blood and gristle in spite of the the elevated plates the police had laid down to prevent contamination of the crime scene. She swallows the saliva that is welling in her mouth. Please, no. Not again. She's already vomited twice in the past hour. Surely, there can't be anything left in her stomach. Pulling the surgical mask away from her mouth, she lifts her chin, searching for a thinnest waft of cool air off the ocean. It's a mistake. Without the mask, the greasy stench of petrol, urine, and spilled intestinal contents is cloying. The chemoreceptor trigger zone in her medulla oblongata goes into overdrive. She swallows again, fighting back the peristalsis in her small intestine.

It's then she catches sight of Noah Cordell—former lover and boss Noah—in conversation with Detective Inspector Tanner on the other side of the wharf. No wonder she's feeling queasy. Why is he here, then? Isn't his lab still out of action after that little explosion in his DNA sequencer a month ago?

Cordell lifts his eyes to look in her direction.

Quickly, Penny raises a sample bag in front of her face, pretending to scrutinise its contents through the plastic. Her stomach roils again. No, no, no. She refuses to vomit while he's looking. She'd never hear the end of it. In fact, she can almost hear him now, lecturing her on the importance of universal procedures for ensuring sample integrity. Once upon a time, she'd thought Cordell's nitpicking was meant to improve her skills, a senior scientist taking his new graduate under his wing. She definitely learned a few things from his mentorship; mostly, that the man loves the sound of his own voice. *Ugh.*

Turning away from Cordell, Penny closes her eyes while she waits for the wave of nausea to pass.

Yat, yee, sam, sei, ng, lok, chat, bot, gau, sup, sup-yat, sup-yee...

By the count of twelve, her emetic centres are sufficiently under control for her to return to work. Crouched by the corpse, she speaks into her hands-free. "Subject #14. Height, around two metres, and weight, approximately 95 kilos, suggest the subject is male. Of solid build with limbs intact. No evidence of gross trauma."

Other than the fact that the poor man's flesh is seared almost to the bone, you mean.

Thinking like this isn't going to stave off her nausea.

Choking back chyme, she continues her report. "Cause of death unknown, but it's likely to have been the result of an explosion: the initial impact of the blast and subsequent fourth and fifth degree burns to around 80% of his body. Clothing minimal, possibly blown off in the blast. No piercings or tattoos evident. Hair colour, unknown. Eye colour, unknown. Finger pads..." She picks up one, then the other, withered hand. Not even a partial. "...obliterated. Shoe size: looks like it might have been a ten. Sole is too melted to tell. The jaw is intact, so dental records might be a possibility when we get the subject into the lab. I'm taking tissue samples for DNA and blood analysis now."

Collecting the tissue, she seals up the samples and slips them into a cooler bag, then waves an arm to hail one of the uniformed police constables waiting at the edge of the carnage. "This one can be bagged and set aside."

This one. With no idea of a name, age, and only a guess at the gender, what else can she say? She steps back as the two men approach, their plastic decontamination suits rustling. They grasp the body at the shoulders and knees. But as they lift it, the blood-encrusted clothing shifts, revealing the blackened muscles of the victim's chest wall…

"Wait. What's that?" Penny asks.

"Looks like a pendant," says the officer at the head of the body. "You did well to spot that. Looks like it's cooked right into the poor bugger's chest."

"I'm sorry. Would you mind putting him down for a moment?"

Penny examines the item. The officer was right; it is a pendant, although the metal ridges have softened, liquified in the fire that killed its owner, leaving the details so blurred that it is difficult to make out what it might have been. She turns the disc in her hand. It looks a bit like that painting that used to hang in her aunt Mārama's bedroom, the one of the Māori sun god, Ra, but it could be any number of things. A starfish for example, or perhaps a sunflower? Hard to tell. Still, someone might recognise it. The victim's parent. Or a partner. When the shock and grief of his death has passed, they might be pleased to have it.

Taking a pair of disposable tweezers from her satchel, Penny lifts the trinket from around the victim's neck and places it in a plastic sampling bag, dropping the tweezers in on top before sealing it. Then, using a marker pen from her pocket, she labels the bag #14—pendant, and includes the date and time. That done, she nods at the officers to continue.

"Another one here when you're done with," Brendan Mather calls. Pulling down his face mask, the pathologist picks his way over to Penny, stepping gingerly over a dismembered hand and something grisly that might have once been an ear. "You OK?" he asks, handing her a bottle of water.

Dropping her own mask, Penny screws off the protective cap and takes a small sip. "Thanks. I've been better."

"Yeah." Mather drinks from his own bottle.

They survey the gruesome scene.

"How many are there, do we know?" Penny asks.

Mather wipes a droplet from his beard with the back of his sleeve. "Hard to say, given the state of the bodies. A leg here, a leg there, everywhere a leg-leg," he chants to the Old MacDonald nursery rhyme. He pulls a crooked smile then steps aside while the officers carry away the charred remains of #14.

"I guess some of the victims might have been immolated in the explosions," she says.

"Don't forget the ocean. Seems at least some of today's body-count came in by boat, so we'll have to see what the divers bring up. Evidently some of the victims were mowed down as they disembarked. Like the Allies landing in Normandy. As an initial count, Clark and Tanner think there could be anywhere from sixty to ninety corpses."

"So many," Penny murmurs, her eyes following her brother crouching near the line of victims that she and Mather have already processed.

Mather rolls his shoulder. "Good thing you're here. Less than half the bodies examined and already my back's killing me. Don't even get me started on the smell."

The bottle still in her hand, Penny wraps her arms across her chest. "Do we even know what happened here?"

"Other than three cars exploding and lots of people dying, you mean? Whispers are, it was a gang war."

A gang war? Penny snaps her head up, checking on her brother's whereabouts, but Matiu has moved away from the bodies and is leaning on the bonnet of the car, Cerberus' doggie face pressed up to the windscreen behind him. Penny lets out a breath. Honestly, she's as bad as everyone else, jumping to conclusions the minute anyone even mentions gang involvement. So Matiu had gotten himself caught up in one of the gangs. Well he'd paid the price for it, hadn't he, with that stint inside. Thank goodness, he was out of that life now and making a clean break.

Penny turns back to Mather. "A gang altercation holds with what we've observed so far—with the victims being mostly young and male." Amongst the bodies—those whose features are still recognisable—more than a few are of Asian descent, many carrying the scars of previous brawls.

"Some of them were known to the police," Mather says, leaning in conspiratorially. "I overheard Tanner mention the Han Triad."

Penny nods. "But what were they fighting over to warrant this kind of carnage?"

"The usual, I guess. Money. Power. Women. Drugs."

"Out here? On the wharf?"

Mather shrugs. "Who knows? Maybe they just liked the view." Putting the cap on his water bottle, Mather steps over the might-be piece of ear, then calls back to her over his shoulder. "We should count ourselves lucky, Dr Yee. People don't tend to converge on the docks armed to the teeth at three AM unless there's a nefarious reason, so there's unlikely to be any innocents in this pile of offal."

There's no way of knowing, of course. Not until they've processed all the bodies.

Putting the water bottle in her pocket, Penny pulls up her surgical mask.

Better get on with it, then.

CHAPTER 2

- Matiu -

The morning sun is a hammer. Heat shimmers across the battered containers stacked on the city wharves like the toy building blocks of a bored childgod who forgot what he was making. Matiu rests his butt against the Holden's bonnet, arms folded, soaking up the heat through his leather jacket. It's barely over the horizon, but it's promising to be another scorcher. How long can he stand here looking tough before he has to bail and make a break for the shade? Maybe use the excuse that he needs to take the dog for a toilet stop, find a smoothie cart along the way. Has he even had breakfast? He can't remember.

But as long as Penny's working, he's on the clock. Especially when the place is crawling with cops and Armed Offenders Squaddies, toting their antiquated but reliable HK MP5 semis like war-trophies, and casting him more than the occasional glance from behind their polymer face-shields. Not friendly glances, either. The sort that beg the question what the hell business a dude who looks like he should be lying among the dead has hanging out here like he owns the bloody place.

But shit, if these puppet soldier-boys can handle the heat in full body-armour, Matiu can cope with a bit of sweat down his spine. At least he's not out there where Penny and Beaker are up to their armpits in corpses. Even from this distance, he keeps catching whiffs of copper, innards. Offal spoiling under the sun. So many bodies, so much blood. Not pretty at all. Cerberus lolls his head out the open back window, tongue panting. If Matiu can smell it, then the dog is probably swamped in the aroma of fresh meat.

His phone rings, and he slides it from his pocket, checks the screen. Damn. Pretty hard to look tough when you're talking to your mum on the phone. But she's called half a dozen times now. Better answer before she gives herself a stroke.

"Mum."

"Matiu, where are you? I've been trying to reach you for half an hour, and Carlie says your GPS must be glitching because it's placing you at the wharves and I've just heard there's been some police callout down there and why on earth would you be there? For goodness' sake, Matiu, don't tell me you've been caught up in that—"

"Really Mum? Why would you even think that?" He tries to keep the smirk from his voice.

"Oh, I didn't mean, not that you might've been… I meant, you might've been in the wrong place at the wrong time, because of the shipment."

"What about the shipment? What shipment?" The fun of putting her through the shredder over the suggestion he may have fallen in with his old gang ties is washed out by that one slip of the tongue.

"Oh, it's nothing. I'm sure if your father didn't tell you already then you don't need to know."

Matiu whirls, hunkering over so none of the uniforms watching might read his lips. Sneaky bastards can do that. "You mean this ship, the cars coming off it? This has something to do with Dad?"

"Oh, darling I really don't know—"

"Mum, people are dead. Not just a couple, but stacks, literally. They're actually piling these bodies up to move them."

"You *are* there!"

"Yeah, and so's Penny. She's working, helping process the bodies. It was a gang shootout." Not just any gang, either, not that he's going to tell his mother that. He's glimpsed some of the bodies being wheeled away from the scene. Recognised some faces. "There are people shot to pieces, cars turned to burned-out wrecks. If this has something to do with us, Penny could be in danger!"

"Matiu." A different voice.

Matiu catches his breath. "Dad."

"What's the status on the new fleet cars?"

He pauses, blindsided. He looks across the wharves, the smoking remains of at least three cars, a few more riddled with bullet holes or scarred by the blast of flashbangs. Painted with blood. "Dad, how many of these cars are ours?"

"Matiu, I need you to focus."

"OK, so this is a fleet renewal delivery. I can go with that. Does your insurance cover unexpected acts of terror and war?"

"Can you get on board the ship?"

Matiu glances around wildly, noting the positions of the uniformed cops, the AOS. All of them with one eye on him, the guy who looks like he should be laid out with the other dead gangsters. "It's a crime scene being controlled by the AOS, Dad. I can't go anywhere or do anything without a fracking sniper scope on me."

"Your sister, she's working there. On the crime detail."

Matiu draws a shallow breath. "Did you already know we were working this scene before Mum called?"

"Get Pandora. I need you inside that ship. Use your sister's position, do whatever you have to do. I'll call you back in ten. Matiu?"

"Dad?" He wants to ask what the hell? When did his dad get all cloak and dagger? The sun shivers across the containers, slides in cold black lines down the barrels of semi-automatic assault weapons which have spat their share of lead today.

"This is important, son."

Matiu's stomach twists, but he nods. "Give me fifteen. You know what Penny's like." He swipes off. Whatever just happened, another fragment of the sanity he clings to so tenuously has just broken away and splintered into a thousand confusing shards. He opens up the back door, and Cerberus bounds free. Matiu snaps on his leash. "Come on boy, let's go find Penny."

The dog barks in excitement, and they head off in search of his sister.

- Pandora -

Around eight, Penny, Beaker, and Mather down tools, a uniformed officer bringing them take-out coffee and a bag of bagels. Penny isn't hungry. Even if her stomach wasn't still churning, conditions on the wharf are anything but sanitary. But Beaker and Mather must have cast iron constitutions because they strip off their gloves and dive in.

"Are they all cinnamon raisin, then?"

"The one at the bottom is cheese and onion."

Leaving them to it, Penny unzips her hazard overalls and rolls them down to her hips, then leans against a container to make the most of the strip of shade. She sips her coffee and fans herself with a paper napkin. The coffee is awful, but the heat is worse. "I'm melting," she says.

"Yup. It's hot all right. Got to be ninety degrees in the shade," says Beaker.

Penny can't help it; she does the math in her head—ninety degrees minus thirty-two…times five ninths is…32.2° Celsius—and since adding 273.15 is easy enough, she converts to Kelvin, too—305.35K. Any way you look at it, it's hot, and the day has barely started.

"I wouldn't mind a swim." Mather speaks through a mouthful of bagel.

Picking a raisin out of his bagel, Beaker pops it in his mouth. "I don't recommend it."

"Right," replies Mather, nodding. "The bodies in the water."

"Not just that. The water's dodgy. Penny and I have the contract to monitor local water quality for the city council. Standard stuff, but it pays the bills. Anyway, ever since this heatwave hit, we've seen a rise in harmful algal blooms. The thermotolerant coliform counts are pretty high, too."

"This blasted heat," Mather says, rubbing a hand across the back of his neck. "Spoils everything."

The coroner's van pulls in, the driver hopping out to open the back and allow the uniformed officers to load up more bodies, the black body bags sliding into the van like loaves into an oven. While they're at it, the driver looks about, and, spying Mather, comes across to join them.

"Isiah," Mather says. "Care for a bagel?"

Beaker offers the driver Penny's bagel.

Isiah thrusts his hand into the paper bag, pulling out the last cheesey torus. "Thanks, don't mind if I do."

"How's it going back at the lab?" Mather asks while the man chews.

"Not good. It's what I came to tell you. The cool store at the morgue is full. We have capacity for one last load, and then that's it."

Mather put his hands on his hips. “What? No. There are still another thirty bodies to process. Get the technicians to move some about, make some space.”

Isiah slows his chewing and pulls a face. “Already done, sorry.”

“Well, what the hell are we supposed to do? We’re up to our elbows in cadavers here!”

Isiah backs away. “I don’t know, man. I’m just the messenger.” He turns and hotfoots it back to the coroner’s van, which is now loaded almost to bursting, two officers leaning on the doors to squeeze them shut.

Mather crushes his empty paper cup in his fist and throws it on the ground. “Well, this just stinks.”

Penny doesn’t like to point out that it’ll stink even more in an hour or two.

“I shouldn’t have given him the bagel,” Beaker says, morosely, while Mather paces back and forth, muttering.

The van pulls away, revealing Tanner. The detective is stalking across the wharf towards them, Cordell dogging his heels. Penny pushes away from the container. She shields her eyes against the glare, marvelling, not for the first time, how like a Wookiee the big detective inspector is with his oversized frame, crumpled tan suit, and a tendency to bellow if provoked. And although she hasn’t actually seen him pull anyone’s arms out of their sockets, she wouldn’t put it past him, either. Cordell, on the other hand, is more like Threepio: garish, garrulous, and über-annoying.

“What’s up with you?” Tanner asks Mather from ten metres out.

The pathologist throws up his hands in disgust. “We’ve just been told there’s no more room at the inn.”

“What?”

“The cold store at the morgue is full,” Penny explains. “We’re going to need somewhere else to store the bodies.”

“I’m sure Pandora’s little laboratory could accommodate them,” Cordell says, checking his fingernails with studied nonchalance. “You do have a cool store, I presume? I mean, you have to store your samples somewhere, don’t you?” He throws her a smile that is as sincere as a White House press secretary.

“*Of course,* I have a cool store.”

“It’s not very big, though,” Beaker says nervously.

“How many can you take?” Tanner demands.

Penny nibbles her lip. “Two?”

“Two!” Incredulous, Mather shakes his head. “Well, that’s a fat lot of use, isn’t it? What about the other twenty-eight? We can’t just leave them to marinate on the wharf. Cordell, you’ll have to take them.”

Adjusting the Windsor knot of his tie, Cordell gives a practiced cough. “Yes. Of course. LysisCo would be happy to assist. No question. We’ve always served the Auckland police, consistently delivering accurate and rapid results. The only problem is we’re carrying out an unscheduled upgrade to our facilities right now.

The result of a recent…accident. Some people are calling it sabotage. It's inevitable really. Being at the top of your game attracts a certain amount of attention. There are bound to be petty jealousies, some professional and some, well…"

For the millionth time, Penny wonders what she ever saw in the man.

"Can you help or not?" Mather demands, cutting across Cordell's infomercial.

"Unfortunately, no."

"What about schools?" Beaker says. "They have laboratories."

"Don't be ridiculous," Cordell huffs. "You can't store bodies in a school cooler. Imagine the outcry if little Johnny slips on a dismembered limb while returning the potassium permanganate to the shelf."

Penny shudders. The man is about as sensitive as a prophylactic made from bicycle inner tube. Embarrassed, Beaker shreds the empty bagel bag with his fingers, his face a wash of hot pink.

"Beaker was just offering a suggestion," Penny says.

"This is exactly what I meant, Detective Inspector," Cordell says "Now, were I appointed Consultant in Charge of Scientific Analyses, I could take care of these sundry aspects and free you up for more important investigative work. And while LysisCo is on hiatus, I have no conflict of interest. There really is no better candidate for understanding how to allocate resources…"

And how to clip the ticket every time! So that was his game. Cordell's own lab was out of contention, so he wanted to lord it over anyone else vying for a police contract by securing the role of project manager.

"Penny…"

Penny almost jumps out of her skin. She hadn't seen her brother move from the car. "Matiu, I really can't talk right now." She puts out a hand to fend off Cerberus, who is swarming around her legs sniffing eagerly at the human detritus smeared on her overalls.

"Pen…"

With the exception of Beaker, who is busy turning the paper bag to pulp, the men look at her with disdain. That's just great isn't it? They're going to think she's so unprofessional, bringing her brother and her fur-baby to a crime scene.

"Matiu, get Cerberus out of here now," Penny hisses.

He shrugs. "OK then. Have it your way. But I know where there's a cool store that's not being used right now."

"If you'll excuse me for a moment." Snatching up Cerberus' lead, Penny pulls Matiu out of earshot. "What have I told you about crossing the crime scene tape? Are you trying to get me thrown off this job?"

To her surprise, Matiu lowers his eyes and scuffs the toe of his boot against the side of the container. "Pen, you have to get us on that ship."

"What are you talking about? No, I'm not getting you on the ship. You need to take the dog and get back in the car. Go home if you have to. I'll call you when I've finished up."

"Pen, you don't understand…"

"Of course not, Matiu. I only spent eight years at university, how could I possibly understand?"

"No, that's not what I mean. Look, Pen, I can't really explain. I just know it's important." He stuffs his hands in his jeans' pockets.

Tilting her head to one side, Penny frowns. "If this is another one of your hinky *feelings—*"

"No, this is worse. This is Dad."

"And how do you suggest we might even do that?"

"More bodies."

She stares at him a moment. "I beg your pardon."

"Tell them there may be more bodies on the ship. The kaumatua's been and gone, he did his karakia, the whole site is tapu now, but he never went aboard. Tell them...tell them I can go up there with you, do a karakia if we find any more corpses."

"Victims, Matiu. We call them victims, not corpses!"

"Yee!"

Penny whirls. "Yes?" she and Matiu reply in unison.

Tanner closes the distance between them in a half dozen Wookiee paces. "What's this about a cool store?" he asks Matiu.

"Big place. Fingers in the horticulture sector. Familiar to the police, if you know what I mean." Matiu squints against the sun.

"Local?"

"Yes, Sir."

"Discreet?"

"Of course."

"How big?"

Matiu spreads his arms like a fisherman estimating his catch then glances at the piles of bodies, where the flies are beginning to swarm. "I reckon they should be able to cope with the overflow here."

"Excellent. Text 'em, will you? See if they're happy to lease us some space."

Matiu shrugs. "You can probably text them yourself. It's already under police jurisdiction."

Tanner looks at him sideways. "You mean Puketutu Island? That old villa where they were running that wheatgrass operation from? What's the woman's name, again? Carr? Corr?"

Penny's eyes widen. They can't be serious.

"Kerr. Sandi Kerr," Matiu replies. "And yeah, that's the place I mean."

Except, they *are* serious.

"Hang on," Mather says, muscling in.

Oh, thank goodness.

"Does this place have a generator?"

"Good point," says Beaker. "The frequency of these power outages is a real problem."

"Yes, I totally agree," Cordell chimes in. "Without a generator, we may as well leave the corpses to bloat on the wharf."

No. This can't be happening. You don't enter the gingerbread house just because the witch has stepped out for a moment. That's just asking for trouble. Penny shudders. Sandi Kerr is evil, pure and simple. The last time Penny had seen her, she'd been about to poison a pregnant woman. It was only by a miracle—and a well-timed kick—that she hadn't succeeded, crawling away while Penny and Erica were helping poor Charlotte deliver her baby. Kerr might be missing, but she'd resurrected herself before, hadn't she? So, what was to stop her from doing it again?

"Probably," Matiu says, and Penny wants to scream. "Get whoever's out there to see how it's all powered up. Probably has solar arrays, since Kerr would've been trying to keep as much of her shiz off the grid as she could."

Tanner's brows come together. "We'll check it out. Good thinking, Yee."

Penny sighs.

"Always a pleasure to serve the civic good, Sir," Matiu says with a grin that's as genuine as a mako shark's. Stepping to one side, he nudges Penny with his elbow. "Get us on that ship," he whispers.

"Right then," says Mather. "If you'll excuse me, I've got work to do." Replacing his mask, the pathologist trudges back to the bodies festering in the sun. With a quick nod in Penny's direction, Beaker lopes after him.

Penny pulls her overalls up over her shoulders, but rather than joining Mather and Beaker, she hangs back. She can't go once more into the breach of bodies until she's handed off Cerberus to Matiu, anyway. Besides, if Matiu's right—and as much as she hates to admit, there's usually something to his hunches—then they need to get on that ship. But will the cops really buy the ruse that Matiu can do a karakia? Guess she can only try.

While she's wracking her brains for an excuse, Clark appears at the end of a stack of containers. He waves his hand, attracting their attention, before jogging over.

"Clark!" Tanner bellows. "Where are we with the Port Authorities? Has that ship manifest turned up?"

"Not yet, Sir, but it seems we have another problem."

"Shit a brick! What now?" Tanner barks.

To his credit, Toeva Clark doesn't flinch. "The press is causing a ruckus at the entrance," he says. "There's a whole pack of them: TVNZ and RealEvent. Even *DishIt* has a crew out there. They're demanding a statement."

Tanner hitches his trousers over a sagging paunch. "The Armed Offenders Squad are manning the gates. Let them deal with it."

This time, Clark grimaces. "About that. They said they're willing to help us process the ordnance, and they've already pinpointed where the rocket launcher was fired from the deck, but they're drawing the line at crowd control. They say it's not their remit."

Tanner's nostrils flare, and Penny takes an involuntary step backwards, almost bowling over Matiu, who gives her a poke in the back in a not-so-subtle reminder.

"If you'll permit me to offer a suggestion," Cordell says. He smooths the fabric of his suit. "I have some experience with the press. In fact, I've represented the police on other matters…" He trails off.

Clark and Tanner exchange glances, then Tanner laughs, his shoulders lifting. "All right, Cordell. Since you offered. Here's the brief: you say nothing whatsoever about any gang involvement. On pain of death."

Cordell smiles.

"I'm serious, Cordell. When the gangs hear about this, there's going to be a race for power. The last thing we need is to precipitate a turf war. Instead, you tell the press there's been an explosion on the docks which has led to multiple casualties. No names as yet."

"And the cause of the explosion?"

"Unknown. You can tell them that it looks to have involved a number of vehicles, which would explain the severity of the event."

"An investigation is underway," Penny says.

"The police will provide more information as soon as it comes to hand," Clark adds.

"No comment," says Matiu.

Looking Matiu up and down, Cordell makes a moue of distaste and turns his back on him. "And the Armed Offenders Squad? What do I say about them? The reporters are bound to ask why they're here."

Tanner shrugs. "Tell them it's standard procedure in an explosion."

"Is it?" Cordell looks surprised.

The burly detective narrows his eyes. "It is today."

"Right," Cordell squeaks. "I'll get right on to it. Wish me luck." He adjusts his tie and hurries off.

"Detective Tanner!" The shout comes from one of the dive team further along the wharf. At that same moment, Tanner's phone rings. "Lion Sleeps Tonight" ringtone.

"Gotta go. Clark—I'm assigning you to organise the Puketutu cool store." He waves an arm in the direction of the senior constable before lumbering down the wharf, his phone held to his ear.

"Will do," Clark says, digging in his front pocket for his notebook.

Matiu looks at Penny, his eyebrows waggling in a *'come on, do it now'* way.

You better be right about this hunch, Matiu Yee.

"Um…Officer Clark?" Penny wipes her forehead with her palm. "About the explosion. If the rocket was launched from the deck of the *Yongyang,* I was wondering if we should check the ship? Make sure there aren't any other victims?"

So lame. No way he'll ever agree.

CHAPTER 3

- Matiu -

Clark gives the uniform guarding the vehicle ramp a nod, leading Penny aboard, with Matiu and Cerberus sidling along behind. They sweat as they ascend towards the hulking cavern of the ship's innards, which at least promises to be cool. Two cars have been abandoned on the double-wide ramp, the driver's doors hanging open from that fateful moment when the shooting had begun and the graveyard shift wharf staff, who must've been unloading the vehicles, had run for safety inside the ship.

Matiu fires Penny a quick look, warning her not to get curious just yet. Sure enough she was reaching for her sampling tape, maybe hoping to dust a fingerprint or two off the cars just to confirm who was really driving. She's thorough like that. But Dad wants them inside. He was very specific.

"Last thing we need," Clark mutters, about halfway up the ramp. "And the wife was planning birthday dinner for me tonight. Guess I'll probably be late."

"It's your birthday? Happy birthday."

"Thanks."

"At least you'll be getting the Cannibal Special for dinner when you get home."

"The Cannibal Special? What's that?"

"The cold shoulder."

Clark spares him a look that suggests he might really want to laugh, but the truth of it is a little close to home.

At the top of the ramp, an Armed Offenders officer watches the docks below, staring down the length of a serious-looking sniper rifle. The safety is firmly locked on, Matiu notes, but apparently the AOS aren't ready to believe this mess is over til it's over. From up here, this guy has a decent view of the immediate area, but with shipping containers stacked across so much of the wharf they'll be relying on the drones hanging in the sky, feeding visual back to the command truck, for their intelligence. If either gang tries anything else, they'll have another firefight on their hands before they've even begun.

They step into the ship's interior, the air cooler than outside but muggy, thick with the stink of old oil and that slightly sweet, burnt reek of heavy-grade biodiesel. Despite modern shipping's attempted migration to wind assistance, solar panels and electric motors, newer technologies have never quite been able to generate the range or the power to drive a leviathan like this across the ocean without that extra push from a combustion engine.

"Can you imagine spending your life holed up in one of these things?" Clark says with a shiver. "It'd drive me nuts."

"In ways that piles of dead bodies going rotten in the sun won't?" Matiu asks.

Clark flicks him a look, then casts his eye about for any sign of violence. "What do you think? We need to bless this place too?"

Matiu shrugs. "Won't hurt to give it a once over, eh?" He brushes past Tanner, words rumbling low in his throat. "*Tihei, tihei, tihei, mauri ora!*" With his right hand cast out to one side and trembling in time with his low chants, he wanders away from the others to inspect the remaining vehicles. They've all been unstropped, ready to be driven off the ship. They're unlocked, key tags sitting in the centre consoles. Business as usual. A mental count of the number of cars parked up on the wharf plus those in here tells Matiu this is a significant upgrade, enough to replace most the aging fleet in both Auckland and Wellington.

Clark is hanging back near the sunny opening in the hull, his phone pressed to his ear. Penny sidles over to Matiu, as they venture deeper into the ship.

"Would you mind telling me what we're really doing now?" Penny grates at him under her breath. "Because I don't for a moment believe that Dad would've told you to twist a policeman's arm into letting you wander around a crime scene unaccompanied."

Matiu shrugs. "The crime scene's out there. This is just like the stationery cupboard." He lifts his voice. "*Ka tangi te titi, ka tangi te kaka, ka tangi hoki au. Tihei mauri ora!*" Then, lower, "And I'm not unaccompanied. You're with me."

"*We're* unaccompanied. And don't deflect. For a start, you're not even doing a karakia; that's the opening of your whaikorero. I, personally, would like to get this job over with, but clearly you're not so concerned, since you're not the one leaning over a bunch of corpses that are about to rapidly go rotten in the sun."

Matiu cracks a door and leans in to check the dash. Standard hybrid biodiesel-electric. Since both resources are so stretched on this husk of a planet—battery raw materials and any sort of combustible fuel—let's just try to make it look like we're doing our bit by putting all the technology in one vehicle and hoping it looks responsible. Brilliant to be a part of such a cost-effective, environmentally destructive conspiracy. Matiu shrugs. Not like he's ever going to have children to inherit this wasteland when he's gone. Really not his problem.

"I told you," he says, closing the door, "this is all Dad. I reckon Clark over there is on the phone to Port Authority right now getting all the details of this manifest and it won't be long before he knows that all these cars belong to the Yee family and its associated interests, and we'll be swiftly escorted from the scene. So we don't have long to find what Dad wants us to find and get out of here. *Te hunga mate ki te hunga mate. Te hunga ora ki te hunga ora, tena koutou, tena koutou, tena koutou katoa!*"

"Belong to us…? What—?"

"Look around, sister. This is your inheritance."

He continues down the line of cars into the ever-deepening gloom, until the profile of a roofline strikes him as different. Matiu once prided himself on his ability to pick the highest black-market value of any one of a string of vehicles parked on a street at night, including how long it would take him to crack the sec and boost it, and that sense is suddenly tingling. In a fleet of matching white sedans, this one is the prize.

All the other cars are branded as Holden Chancellors, assembled in China but clinging to the legacy of their origins as a local product, despite the Chancellor being a recent addition to the range and never having been built in any English-speaking country, much less good old New Zealand. But the outlier has no branding on the bonnet at all. Matiu circles it like a bookie sizing up a racehorse. On the boot there's no make badge, only a single silver decal against the white paint over the space where a number-plate belongs: *Solaris.*

There are no more cars beyond this one. It was buried as deep in the ship as it could be. "This is what we're here for," Matiu says. "This is what Dad wants us to find. *Ko Arawa te waka! Ko Moehau te maunga!*"

"A car? Matiu, if you dragged me up here so you could play with a *car—*"

He gives her a look; the serious one he reserves for those moments when she's about to lose her rag at him and he really doesn't have the patience to talk her down. She trails off, scuffing her feet on the deck.

"It's not just any car," he says, as his phone rings. "It's some sort of prototype." He digs the phone from his pocket, giving Penny a nod. "Dad. Yeah, I found it. OK, we can manage that. Call you back when it's done." He swipes off and shoves the phone back in his pocket. Gives Penny his other look, the one that says, *I'm about to ask you to do something you're not going to like.*

"I need you to distract Clark, while I drive this car off the boat."

"You're going to *steal* a car right from under the noses of the police? Matiu, there are men out there *with guns* whose job it is to shoot people trying to steal cars! Have you been paying any attention at all?"

"It's ours, Penny. Yee Transport Enterprises owns all these cars. This one…this needs special treatment. It's why it was hidden down the back. There are going to be a lot of people sniffing around here who Dad would rather didn't get a close look at it. *Te hunga mate, haere, haere, haere, haere ki hawaiki nui!* I need to remove it from the scene in a discreet and efficient manner. Can you help me?"

"No, Matiu. I'm not going to be an accessory to grand larceny."

"Dad'll be cross."

Penny gives him her own look now, the one that says, *you're going to regret crossing that line, buster.* Then she turns and thumps across the deck, her footfalls echoing in the cavernous gloom. Matiu watches her go, then cracks the back door on the Solaris. "Hop in, boy," he mutters, and Cerberus clambers in the back, before Matiu slides into the driver's seat. It folds around him like they were always meant to be together. As his hands touch the wheel, the dash glows up and the headlights ping bright in the gloom. No motor sound, just the low hum of an electric system waking up. Not a hybrid then, but a full electric. "What's special about you?" Matiu mutters to himself, scanning the battery levels, the virtually nil mileage, the symbols on the dashboard. Available power sitting at 95 percent.

Full electrics had a brief span of popularity in the 20s, until the market collapsed due to a shortage of the rare earths required for battery manufacture, while demand on the power grid to keep all those vehicles charged up blew out the infrastructure needed to maintain it. Too much stealing from Peter to pay Paul in the energy markets, and the transport industry rolled back towards the most renewable source of energy they could sustainably consume, in the form of biofuels. Never mind the problems that arose from reprioritising massive tracts of farmland from growing food for people to growing fuel crops for vehicles. We feed the cars, but the people go hungry. Eventually, something has to break.

Matiu taps the accelerator, and the Solaris inches forward. Even under load the motor is barely audible. Proximity sensors glow, warning him of the car parked next to him, the bulkhead on the other side, the steering wheel twitching in his grip to allow more clearance. "That could get annoying," Matiu tells the car. Then he's in the main access and heading for the exit. He slows as Penny and Clark disappear around a corner, then makes his way gently towards the ramp.

- Pandora -

She can't believe Matiu is asking her to break the law. She won't do it. She won't. It's not right. People can't decide to flout the rules just because it suits them. That's not how civilised society operates. But while Penny's brain is telling her one thing, her feet have other ideas, striding her across the deck towards the constable.

Her treacherous mouth opens, and she calls out, "Toeva!"

Dammit. Her heart is somersaulting like a cheddar wheel in England's Downhill Cheese Chase. It's happening again; Matiu is getting her into trouble. Leading her into temptation. He's been doing it since they were kids. He'd get some ridiculous idea in his head—shoplifting lollies from the local dairy or pinching apples from the only tree in the neighbourhood—needling her until she went along with it. Well, what was she supposed to do? She's the big sister. He's her baby brother. Someone had to look out for him. When they inevitably got caught, she'd be the one who copped the blame.

There were never any external consequences. With the biggest vehicle fleet in the country and the ear of the Transport Minister, the Yees had too much influence for that. Dad would make a donation to the victim's preferred charity, smooth any ruffled feathers with a bottle of rare South Island wine, and they would go on. It was later, at home, that the real fallout occurred:

"Pandora, really, all we're asking is that you look after your brother and demonstrate some responsibility," Mum would say, and Dad would chip in with, "I'm disappointed, young lady. Highly disappointed. We expect better from you.

This kind of behaviour is never acceptable." It wouldn't matter that Matiu was the instigator.

Except this time, it's Dad asking the pair of them to steal a vehicle from a ship—and *without* following the appropriate customs procedures. Although, it's not exactly stealing. They'd just be removing it prematurely. It's technically Dad's car, after all.

Only, the ship and its cargo are part of a violent crime scene that is currently under investigation. The worst loss of life in an urban centre in over thirty years—ever since the Christchurch earthquake took 185 lives back in 2011. Penny's mind races. What if it isn't a coincidence? What if the fleet shipment has something to do with the showdown outside on the docks? What if the contents of this deck are the reason for the piles of men lying broken and burned on the tarmac outside? But that doesn't make any sense. It's just a bunch of cars. And anyway, Yee Transport Enterprises would never be involved in anything illegal. *Dad* would never do anything illegal. Of course not. There has to be some other explanation.

A trickle of sweat runs between her shoulder blades.

The thing is, Dad might do something like this to protect Matiu. If Matiu was involved somehow. The sweat cools on her back. Penny shivers. And Mather, Clark, Tanner…*everyone* is saying the massacre is gang-related…

Clark swipes his phone off and slips the device in pocket. "Dr Yee? Is there a problem?"

Penny flashes him her best movie star smile. "Yes, there most certainly *is* a problem, Officer Clark. You didn't tell me it was your birthday! Many happy returns."

There. This isn't her providing a distraction, so her brother can uplift a vehicle without authorisation; she's simply wishing a colleague a happy birthday. A perfectly legitimate thing to do. *Perfectly. Legitimate.*

"Thank you, Dr Yee. That's very kind."

"And, I might add, you don't look a day older."

Clark flushes, and Penny catches Matiu's reflection in his sunglasses. Matiu has pulled into the aisle!

"Well, that'll be because it's still yesterday." Clark chuckles. "I've barely slept."

"Birthday hug. Bring it in!" Throwing open her arms, Penny lunges awkwardly in his direction, hoping to turn him about-face with the momentum of her hug.

But Clark shunts backwards, his face crumpling in horror. "Dr Yee. You um…" He points at her overalls, which are slaked with blood and entrails.

"Oh," Penny says. "I was forgetting about that. I must smell like an abattoir."

She needs to think of something. Matiu will be driving past them any second.

In the end, the solution is simple: she steps around the constable, and Clark, too polite to do otherwise, is forced to face away from the gangway to maintain eye contact.

He tilts his head to one side. "Maybe I can take a rain check on that hug?"

"I think so!" She giggles. Not too nervously, she hopes. Just metres away, behind Clark's back, her brother is committing Dad-sanctioned grand larceny.

Penny swallows. If Clark turns and Matiu is caught, they'll toss her baby brother in prison and throw away the key, Dad's Ministry contacts notwithstanding. Even Erica, Matiu's probation officer girlfriend, would struggle to get him out of this one. Poor Mum would be distraught, but Mārama… For a moment, Penny thinks of their aunt, Matiu's biological mother, curled up in her hospital bed, her dark hair spilling across the pillow, and her mind as fragile as fluted glass. If anything happened to Matiu, it would send Mārama spinning over the edge. It might even kill her…

The vehicle—some sort of modified Commodore—creeps forward. Luckily, it's so quiet Penny, and by extension Clark, can't hear a thing. Whatever the manufacturers have done to soup up the engine, it's a step up on previous models. Still she's wary: Clark isn't the sort to miss a trick.

She imagines Matiu gripping the steering wheel.

"Earth to Dr Yee?" Clark says, waving a hand in front of her face.

Penny shakes her head. "I'm sorry. All of a sudden I was miles away."

"That will be the early start—that, and the legion of bodies still to be processed. So, how are we going up here, anyway? Your brother done with his karakia? I heard a bit of it, sorry I had to take that call, if you'll forgive the disrespect. Did you find anything amongst the cargo?" He twists his torso to survey the lines of vehicles strung out within the ship's hull.

No!

Quick! Penny hustles him around the corner by the elbow. "No, thank goodness. Nothing of note in here, but I wondered about the deck?" She waves her hand towards the stairs. "You know, where the perpetrators fired the rocket launcher." She grasps the handrail and takes two steps up the metal ladder, turning back to face him. "I should probably take a quick look."

Over Clark's head, she watches Matiu ease the vehicle onto the ramp.

For goodness sake, hurry up.

"Are you sure that's necessary, Dr Yee? In my experience, the AOS boys conduct a pretty thorough investigation."

"They might have missed something."

"I was up there myself earlier. No bodies. No puddles of blood. Just a lot of empty shell casings."

"Did they swab the railings?"

"I don't think…"

"What about the door frames?"

"Well, there are quite a lot of crewmen…"

Come on!

The rear of the car disappears from view.

Penny lets out a slow breath and jumps down to join Clark on the deck. She takes him by the arm. "You know what? I think you're right, Toeva. Not much point wasting time now that the AOS boys have stomped all over the site, is there? I should probably get back and help Dr Mather."

Bewildered, Clark lets her lead him to the head of the ramp. "Wait. Your brother came up here with you." Shrugging out of her grasp, he turns to scan the rows of cars for a glimpse of Matiu.

"Matiu? Oh no, when he saw there were no more bodies for the cool store, he left me to it and went back to the car. He said the dog was being too much of a nuisance."

"Oh? I didn't see him leave."

Penny's relief is like stepping out of a pair of pinchy heels after a day at the races. "You might have been on the phone."

"Ah, that'll be it."

Leaving the cool of the ship, they descend the ramp where a wave of glaring heat and the stench of waste hits them full in the face. On the dock, Tanner stares up at them, his expression about welcoming as Charon the ferryman.

"On second thoughts, maybe we should go back inside," Clark quips.

CHAPTER 4

- Matiu -

The sniper spares him a glance as he rolls out of the ship, and Matiu gives him a nod and a wave. He eases down the ramp, past the two abandoned Chancellors. At the gate on the street a fleet truck is pulling in, to start removing the cars from the dock. Some of them are well past the point of paint touch-ups though, and can be tagged as heading straight through the land of insurance claims and on to the kingdom of scrap metal. Matiu shudders. He's glad he won't be doing *that* round of paperwork. In the mirror, he glimpses Penny and Clark making their way down the ramp behind him. As he drives out of the shadow cast by the ship, a yellow icon lights up alongside the battery monitor. Weird. Making landfall on the dock, Matiu drives slowly and silently to where the aging Commodore they arrived in is parked. The Commodore is a weary old beast, his punishment of sorts for parking his last one in the harbour. This car, this Solaris, will fit nicely on him.

His phone rings again. "Yeah, Dad, I've got it. She's a tidy set of wheels. Care to tell me what the hell it is?" His eyes stray to the battery indicator, showing a healthy green. Available capacity reads 96 percent. Must need calibration. It was at 95 on the ship, it can't have gone *up* since he drove the car off.

"It's something you have to keep very safe, Matiu. This is something a lot of people want."

He frowns, scanning the fluttering CRIME SCENE tape, the chiller wagons, the piles of dead bodies. "Something they might want enough to kill for?" A cold knife twists through his belly.

Dad is quiet for a time. Then he says: "Don't let that car out of your sight. I want it back here, in the garage, as soon as you can get away."

The battery meter creeps up to 97 percent.

"You can count on me, Pops."

"Don't call me Pops."

"Righty-o, Daddy-o."

"Just get that car locked up as soon as you can." The line goes dead.

"See ya. Love you," Matiu says to the ether.

The battery meter rises to 98. What the—?

Someone raps on the window, startling Matiu. He whips around to confront whoever just tried to get him to soil his shorts, into a face he vaguely recognises, but from where he doesn't know. Cerberus yelps and whirls about on the leather, Matiu lowers the window. "Yeah?"

"You want us to load this one up, bro?"

Matiu scans the guy's overalls. Chand. "Not this one, I'm driving it. Who are you working for?" He opens the door and steps out, causing Chand to take a few steps back, his face growing suddenly paler.

"Yee Transport, I'm here with Old Pete. Sent to pick up the cars. I'm new."

"Why do I know you?" Matiu fixes him with a stare, trying to place the driver's face.

Chand backs away. "I…I think we met a few weeks ago… On the bridge. Not sure we were ever…introduced? Anyway, I lost that job with Wyatt Couriers. I tried to tell them it wasn't my fault, but I think…" Chand's bottom lip quivers. "I think they were looking for an excuse to lay off some staff and so they fired me, for what happened on the bridge. But my sister's a lawyer and she made some phone calls and now, hey, I work for Yee Transport."

"You got your sister to blackmail my dad into giving you a job?"

Chand takes another couple of steps back. "Blackmail's not a nice word."

Matiu grins. "Like your styles, bro. Go keep an eye on Old Pete, he's a bit of a leadfoot. I've got this one covered." He jabs a thumb at the Commodore. "If you can run the old girl back to base, that'd be the biz. Keys are in it. I'll catch you later."

Chand sags, tension uncoiling from him like a spring. He looks tired, haunted. Does he wake up in the night, seeing that thing on the bridge, that thing that used to be Simon Kingi? Like Matiu does? Chand shambles away, as Penny storms his way, leaving both Clark and Tanner behind, her face thunder. Oh boy, what has he done now?

- Pandora -

Penny stalks back towards the fleet car. "Beaker!" she yells. She doesn't slow. "Come on! Grab your kit. We're leaving."

Standing between the mountains of dismembered body parts, Beaker blinks. "But there are still—"

"We're going. Now!"

"Right." Beaker scrambles to collect up the sample bags. Too angry to help, Penny leaves him to it and storms up the wharf.

Not far away, Mather climbs out of the carcass of a car. "Hey! What's going on?"

She ignores him and charges on, her rubber gumboots thwack-thwack-thwacking on the concrete. She's being petty, she knows. It's not like this is Mather's fault.

"Dr Yee. Stop, please."

Ugh. Penny pulls up. She folds her arms across her chest and waits for him to reach her. Kicks away a dented bit of car fender.

"What's got you all het up?"

Penny puffs air from her cheeks. "Tanner's removed me from the wharves."

Mather pulls off his gloves. "What? Why? What's happened?"

"The ship manifest turned up, that's what. Seems the *Yongyang* cargo hold includes a delivery for the Yee family fleet."

Yes, Dad's name is listed on the manifest. It isn't the reason she's being chucked off. That's just a pretext. *A crap one at that.*

Blank for a moment, recognition finally shows on Mather's face. "Oh, I get it. You're *those* Yees."

Penny stomps her heel on the concrete. "I'm not actually," she sniffs. "Well, I am, but Yee Transport Enterprises is my parents' business. I'm not a director, or even a shareholder. I have no visibility on their activities. I didn't even know they had plans to upgrade the fleet. Not that it makes any difference; Tanner's still calling it a conflict of interest."

Pursing his lips, Mather slaps the gloves against the leg of his overalls. "Well, that's not going to fly. He can't expect me to process this lot by myself. I'll be here until next Christmas."

Beaker has finally caught up. Sweaty hair plastered to his forehead, he looks like a pack mule with a sample bag slung over each shoulder, one tucked up under his armpit, and both his hands full. "What's going on?" he asks, breathless.

"Tanner's kicked us off the case."

Beaker's eyes pop, and he almost drops the sample cases.

"Fuck this," Mather says. "You're not going anywhere, either of you. Give me a tick and I'll get this straightened out."

"Honestly, don't bother. Come on, Beaker. Let's just go." She slips the bag out from under Beaker's arm and slings it over her shoulder.

But Mather whirls, his finger raised in mid-air, like Montgomery Flagg's iconic Uncle Sam recruitment poster. "Dr Yee, I need you."

"Yes, yes. You're worried about Christmas. We heard you."

Mather's eyes narrow. "For your information, I don't give a fucking rat's arse about Christmas. I don't care who your family is, and I care even less if Tanner makes his case. None of those are my problem." Sucking in a breath, he sweeps a hand towards the mounds of bodies. "See this? This isn't a heap of blackened baby-back ribs served up on a burned-out car. These are *men*. Human beings. And it's our job to process them. To find out who they were in life and offer them some dignity in death. Whoever these men were, we owe it to them to return their remains to their families, so their loved ones can say their farewells."

Penny feels a slug of shame. Her shoulders slump. "You're right," she whispers.

"Maybe *I* could stay," Beaker squeaks.

Penny shakes her head. "Sorry, Beak. It's not up to me. The police have ordered us to leave and you're my employee, so as far as Tanner's concerned, that means you, too."

Mather really will be here until Christmas and it isn't even Easter yet.

"Well, I hardly think Cordell is going to help me. He might get his widdle fingernails dirty," Mather says.

They all glance towards the gates where Cordell is standing on a packing crate, holding court for the press. Beaker tries to stifle a fit of the giggles.

"Go and get yourself cleaned up," Mather says. "Have some breakfast. I'll talk to Tanner and see if I can get you reinstated."

Penny nibbles her lip. "He was pretty adamant."

"Better pray for a Christmas miracle, then."

Penny smiles.

"Go on. Get. I'll call you in a bit." He lopes off down the wharf to where Tanner and Clark are huddled with the port authorities.

CHAPTER 5

- Pandora -

"Where's the car gone?" Beaker asks.

Good question. Where is the car, Matiu? And more to the point, which car should we be looking for?

"Um, Matiu must have moved it," Penny mumbles. "Maybe it's up near the entrance." She rounds the stacks at the city end. Up ahead, the gates to the port are closed, several uniformed police officers patrolling the port side, while every card-holding member of the press is crowded outside on the street, their phones and recording devices pushed through the bars to capture Cordell's monologue.

For all the good that will do them.

A roar goes up. Whoops—someone spied her.

Penny jumps back behind the stacks. "Beaker, hang on. We can't go out there covered in blood and gristle. The press will be all over us. Tanner asked us to be discreet."

"Tanner threw us off the case."

"Beak, c'mon. We can't afford to burn bridges. Quite apart from your salary, I still have the Breadmaker to pay off." To be fair, since going out on her own, Beaker and the benchtop DNA sequencer have been her most astute investments.

Leaning against the stacks, Beaker uses the moment to take the weight off, dropping his shoulders to allow the sampling bags to rest on the ground. "We'd get to upstage Cordell," he says saucily.

She rolls her eyes. "Don't tempt me!"

Not content to take her word for it, Beaker peeks his head around the corner. A chorus of shouts goes up.

"Beaker!"

He swings back. "OK, so now what are we going to do?"

"We take off our protective gear. That way, at least we can leave in our civvies and if we get accosted, all we have to do is say 'no comment'. Right, get out of those overalls. I've got a bag we can put them in…"

Penny is bundling up the contaminated gear when Clark appears.

"Dr Yee." He rubs a hand across the back of his neck. "I'm glad I caught you before you left. I wanted to apologise for any offence during our discussion earlier. It's the optics of it really—with your parents' goods being on the *Yongyang*. Believe me, removing you from the scene has nothing whatsoever to do with the quality of your work."

"Hmm." Penny stuffs the soiled garments into the bag.

"In fact, Dr Mather is having a word with Detective Inspector Tanner right now."

"Give me your gumboots, Beaker."

"Mather is very strongly in favour of keeping you on…"

"Gloves." Penny rummages in the side pocket of one of the sampling bags for a carton of Benzalkonium Chloride wipes: 0.13 in 110mL. With an exaggerated flourish, she pulls out two, before handing off the carton to Beaker.

Clark shuffles his feet. "Anyway, we're about to finish loading another van, so I better head off. Tanner wants me to go to Puketutu to check out the cool store ahead of its arrival."

"Did you say Puketutu Island?" Beaker asks, while vigorously scrubbing his forearms to the elbow with the BZK wipes. "Would you go near Royal Oak?"

"A few blocks. Give or take."

"Awesome. Any chance you could drop me off at home?"

Her skin as tight as a peel-off facial mask, Penny stares at him. *Et tu, Beaker?*

"Sorry, Penny," Beaker says, balling up the wet wipe in his palm, "but Matiu could be ages. All I want to do is go home and take a shower. I've been up since three."

"Fine," Penny huffs. "Give me the stupid sample bags."

"About those…" Clark says, stepping between them. "Since you've been stood down from the case, I'm afraid they're going to have to go with me."

Penny gives him a glare that could melt tungsten.

He backs away. "Right, well, I'll let you carry them then, Mr Deaker," he says. "Come on, let's get you home."

Penny pulls the drawstring bag closed with a snap, and the two men scuttle away like a couple of cockroaches.

"Penny!" Matiu calls.

She swivels. *Finally.* He's off to her left, slinking between the stacks of rusted orange and blue.

He waves her over. "Car's this way. Come on."

She trudges after him.

All at once, she's overwhelmed with fatigue. Ordinarily, working homicides for the police is invigorating, sampling the scene and sifting through the analyses to reveal secrets that someone hopes will never see the light. There's a certain Hansel and Gretel logic to it, like a pulled thread on a jersey that must be teased out and unravelled until its inevitable end. But up until now, she's only ever faced one murder—one body—at a time. Nothing on this scale. Just thinking about identifying all those bodies is daunting. Maybe it's just as well she's been chucked off the case.

Penny looks up. They've been walking for ages. The crunch of Matiu's boots on the asphalt has set up a rhythm, mesmerising her. This isn't the way they came in. Gathering her bearings, she realises they're on Tooley Street; still on the docks, but at the other end of the harbour.

Her shoulders droop. "Are we there yet?" she says.

"Nearly. It's this way." Matiu ushers her into the carpark of the port's corporate headquarters. It's only half full—cars, or the biofuels needed to run them, are too expensive for most Kiwis to own one personally—but the port brings in essential goods from overseas markets, things New Zealanders can't do without, so their executives are some of the best paid in the country. Penny can't see the stolen car, which just goes to show if you want to keep something a secret, hide it in plain sight. Every vehicle in here is upmarket and expensive.

"Here we go." Matiu opens the door for her.

Sliding into the passenger seat, Penny slips her satchel into the footwell. Immediately, the car seat moulds to her fit her hips, the temperature adjusting to… perfect. She lies back. It's like resting on a cloud. She closes her eyes, vaguely aware of Matiu rounding the car.

When she opens them again, he's there beside her in the driver's seat, its contours melting to accommodate him. "Nice, huh?" He waggles his bum.

Penny sighs. *Puh-lease.*

Matiu places his hands on the steering wheel and the dashboard lights up like a spacecraft from a sci-fi movie. "Buckle up, sister." He pulls out of the park and into the service lane. "C'mon. You have to admit; this car is pretty cool."

Oh for goodness sake.

"That's it?" she blurts as she thrusts the safety belt into its socket. "You made me accessory to grand theft auto, from a *crime scene* no less, and all for the chip-warmer seats, some winky lights, and a bit of extra cushioning?" She folds her arms across her chest. "You have to be kidding me."

"Pen, it was nothing to do with me. This is on Dad. He's the one who insisted we go in and get it." Leaving the port, Matiu pulls the fancy-pants prototype into the Tamaki Drive traffic near Judges Bay.

"You could have told him no."

Matiu grunts. "Like you ever say no to the olds."

Penny puts her hand on the dash to steady herself, accidentally making a magnifying makeup mirror rise from the console. She slams it shut. "Don't go making this about me. I'm not the one on probation. What if someone saw you? Did you even stop to think about that? Do you *want* to spend the rest of your life in prison?"

"I'm fine, Pen. No one saw a thing." He pulls into the far lane.

A flash of silver draws Penny's attention to the dash-screen. "What about the Port CCTV, then?" she says.

"Will you relax, sis? I heard Tanner bellow at someone to have them turned off. Less chance of the press getting hold of the footage."

Ha! Just because there was no CCTV doesn't mean anything. There are so many blimmin' camera views on the car's fancy dash-screen, who's to know one of them hasn't broadcast the entire grand-theft incident into the police network? It's very distracting with them flicking all the time. How do they expect the driver to pay attention to the road?

Another flash of silver.

Wait a minute. Is that someone following them?

Penny checks the screens again. It's still there: three cars back, tucked behind a mobile pet-grooming van.

"Matiu. Quick. Turn here. There's someone following us."

"Where?" Matiu's head whips up.

"Behind us. A silver car."

"Great," Matiu says. "That narrows it down nicely; half the cars in the country are silver." Still, he turns sharp left into the next street. "Is it still there?"

"I can't tell. It's a few cars back."

"Can you get the registration?"

"I'm trying, but it keeps moving. Does this rear cam take photos?" She punches some buttons. The windscreen wipers come on.

"Penny, stop it!" Matiu shouts.

It's not raining, so the wipers go off automatically. Her heart in her throat, Penny checks the cam—and catches a glint of a silver-grey grill—just before a city bus pulls in behind them and blocks the vehicle from view.

"I don't know where I'm going," Matiu says. "See if you can find the GPS."

Penny doesn't dare look for the GPS. She might press the wrong thing and lose the rear cam. And if that happens, how will she keep track of the silver car?

"Penny? The GPS…"

Penny touches the dash and brings up the makeup mirror.

"On second thoughts, never mind."

Her palms bead with sweat. Someone is definitely following them.

"We're going to be in another car chase, aren't we? It's just like the time Simon Kingi followed us from that crime scene at Little Shoal Bay and then tried to drive us off the Auckland Harbour Bridge," she wails.

"Now, you're being paranoid. No one saw us take the car off the ship. No one even knew we were there. Most likely, it's just some random silver car that happens to be going the same way."

"Turn here!"

"Pen—"

"Turn! Hurry."

Matiu drags the wheel round, muttering, "This is crazy."

Penny grips the armrest as they swing into the side-road. "Do NOT tell me I'm crazy. That crapocalypse at the wharf is tied up with the gangs somehow. I don't need Tanner or Clark or anyone to tell me because I've been up to my elbows in intestines half the night. Some of those people were from Hanson's gang, Matiu. People who were once acquaintances of yours!"

Matiu lowers his voice. "OK, so you're not crazy, but you said it yourself, you've been up half the night. Let me take you home. You're exhausted."

"There!"

"What?"

"There. Pull into that little lane. There's a café. Let's pull over and have some breakfast."

Matiu shakes his head, but he does as he's told, turning into the lane and parking in a space right outside Bernie's Diner.

Penny drops her eyes to the screen. One…two…three cars later a silver Mercedes goes by. The driver turns to look into the lane. Penny nearly dies of fright when Matiu clicks the handbrake on.

"So? Did you see anyone?" Matiu asks.

Not just anyone but someone she knows. There could only be one reason he'd be following her and there is no way she's discussing it with Matiu.

"Must have been my imagination," Penny replies.

Matiu snorts. "Well, since we're here; I guess no one can begrudge us breakfast," he says.

CHAPTER 6

- Pandora -

The café is small, just eight tables running in two lines on either side of a central aisle with the kitchen and servery near the back. The walls are soccer pitch green and home to several Minecraft-style installations made from old batteries. Someone's idea of art. Two archaic heat pumps are doing their best to move the air about.

Matiu peels off the minute they get inside the door. "Get me a mixed grill, will you? I'm going to nab the table by the window. Dad told me not to let the Solaris out of my sight." He tosses his leather jacket on the back of the seat and slides into the booth.

Solaris. That figures. Even its name is pimped up.

Penny steps up to the counter.

"Welcome to Bernie's," the server says brightly. "Our food is made fresh, the way you like it. Today's specials are our Avocado Smash…"

Er no, thank you. Penny shakes her head. No squished avocado; she's vomited twice this morning already.

"…our Raspberry Acai purée in a bowl…"

Another no.

"And our famous Meatpacker's Blood Pudding and—"

Penny raises her hand, cutting them off. "I'll just have a side of toast," she says, "And a mixed grill for my brother. Plus, two Venti coffees. Double shot."

She waves her card at the machine, picks up a number, and makes her way over to the booth, sliding into the seat and propping her satchel against the wall.

Matiu is on the phone. "Still driving my sister," he says. Arching his back, he glances out the window, his elbow pointed at the ceiling and the phone pressed to his ear. "It depends. What about you?"

Penny's own phone is trilling. She fumbles in her satchel. Odd. She doesn't recognise the number. "Hello. Yee Scientific."

"Dr Yee. Mather here."

That was quick. Maybe it's good news. Penny straightens. "How did you get on with Tanner?" she says, fiddling with the knob on the pepper grinder.

"Yeah. No joy, I'm afraid."

"Oh. I'm sorry." She really is. Hours of potential work out the window just because her name is Yee.

"Not as sorry as me." Mather's voice is wistful. Penny imagines him scanning that oozing pile of blackened corpses.

"What will you do?"

There's a pause. "Tanner says there's an industrial lab out at this island setup your brother mentioned. Cordell's gone to check it out. Providing it's up to par, LysisCo are going to set up shop there in the short-term. They'll help me process the bodies."

Penny accidentally knocks the grinder over. "Right. Of course…that's good. His staff are very effective." A stray peppercorn rolls across the table. She catches it just before it spills onto the floor.

Mather grunts. "It's not his staff who bother me. Anyway, I wanted to thank you and Beak for your help this morning and apologise about how things turned out. If it was up to me…but Tanner said he couldn't take the risk, not with your brother known to have run with Hanson's gang—"

"Now look," Penny stammers.

"Dr Yee, I don't really care what your brother did or didn't do. I'm just telling you, so you know. It might be something you want to look at. Because I could really use your help, right now. Anyway, I better get on. Still a pile of work to do." His laugh is harsh.

"Thank you for letting me know."

"Sure." He cuts the connection.

Righting the pepper grinder, Penny sweeps the peppercorn into a serviette, then looks across the table at Matiu. What exactly did Mather mean *something to look at*? Matiu's her brother. It's a bit late to *un-adopt* him after all these years. Or did he mean she should get herself another driver? Her parents would never allow it. Not while she's working for the police. But then, from what Mather was saying, as long as Matiu is driving her, she won't be working for the police…

Penny studies the dark whorls of her brother's facial *kiri tuhi*. She wishes he'd never gotten those tattoos because when people look at Matiu, it's all they see. And while it's fine for Matiu's love life—some women are strangely attracted to the shadowy bad-boy branding—other people, like Tanner, seem to think he's at the bottom of every gang-related enterprise in the city, like he's the half-blood prince of the underworld or something.

Catching her watching him, Matiu lowers his eyes, shifts in his seat, and shows her his back.

Something you don't want me to know, brother dearest?

He needn't bother to cover his mouth. It's not like she can lip-read. And if he doesn't want to tell her his business, that's just fine; she won't tell him her business, either.

Like who was following them earlier.

"Mixed grill?" the server says.

"My eggs are here. Talk later," Matiu says into the phone. He points at the spot in front of him with his other hand, letting them know the eggs are for him.

"And a side of toast with two Venti coffees." By the time the server places the coffees on the table, Matiu is already sawing up a pair of breakfast sausages.

The smell of the coffee is intoxicating. Penny wraps her fingers around the mug and lifts it to her lips.

Suddenly, the ground rumbles and the lights wink out.

- Matiu -

Glasses jingle and clash, plates rattle, and the overhead lights are set to swaying madly. All across the café, salt shakers and pepper grinders tip over. Sugar bowls spill across tables in miniature snowdrifts. The building groans with the impact of the whip-jolt of several sharp shakes. In the kitchen, there's a metallic clatter of sliding pots and pans, and someone swearing.

Matiu sits rigid as Penny vanishes from sight under the table, her Drop-Cover-Hold instinct much stronger than his. He watches the flurry of panic wash over the café patrons, the wait staff, the pedestrians on the street as the earth continues to roll and shudder beneath them. Cerberus, clipped in the back seat of the Solaris with the windows down, leaps up and howls at the sky. The sound echoes off the alley walls, pounds against the glass like the roar of something deeper, infinitely more terrifying, something vast and full of hunger and rage.

Belatedly, his phone and several others across the café bell out a P-alert seismic warning, giving him a heads-up that there's an earthquake incoming. The shaking has stopped by the time the tones die out. Good old network lag. When everything stops rattling, Matiu is still seated, hands gripping the edge of the table to stop it wandering off. He listens hard, for the sounds of people hurt, injured. For the crackle of fire, or tumbling masonry. His every sense has switched to high alert.

"Good jolt," he says, peering under the table where Penny is huddled in the classic kiss-your-arse-goodbye pose generally reserved for passengers on doomed airplanes. "Doesn't look too major, though. You can probably come out now."

Someone's crying, someone else is yelling. Phones start buzzing all over. Car horns blare in the street. Cerberus continues to yowl. Matiu looks longingly at his breakfast while Penny extracts herself from beneath the table.

"Why didn't you drop, cover and hold? We've been trained to do this our whole lives!"

Matiu shrugs, standing and taking a handful of sausage off his plate. "Trained me to do dishes all my life too, doesn't mean I can do them yet." He exits the café, crossing the alley to the Solaris. Outside, the sounds of the city are oddly muted, and yet magnified. Like everything he can see and hear is passing through a lens of confusion. As if he's stepping out into an altered world. Cerberus leaps at him, nails rubbing on the paintwork. "Down, boy," he soothes, and lets the dog snaffle sausage from his palm. He ruffles his ears, pats down his flank. "Nothing to worry about. Just Rūaumoko farting."

His phone buzzes, and he swipes up the call. "Erica. You feel that? You all good?"

"I'm on the twelfth storey, of course I felt it! But we're OK, no-one's hurt right here, at least. We're evacuating the building now. What about you? What's it like at street level?"

Matiu glances around. Everywhere, people are streaming out of office and apartment blocks and cafés. Crunching through broken glass. Sirens wail closer. "About what you'd expect of Auckland in an earthquake. Panic and confusion, but no real harm done by the looks." Most everyone he can see is walking, not being carried. That's a good sign. "Lot of noise, few broken windows. Not much else."

"OK, that's good. I've got another call coming in, I'll catch you later."

"Right." He swipes off as Penny strides across the alley. Ever efficient in the face of crisis, she's managed to get their coffees transferred to paper cups and their breakfast into takeaway bags, even though the counter staff were probably just trying to evacuate. Can't let a good cup of coffee go to waste. Yet she denies she's anything like her mother. She thrusts his coffee at him. He opens the car door and slides in before swiping up his next call. The phone rings several times, a hollow echo in his ear. No-one answers.

"I just spoke to Mum," Penny says, climbing into the passenger seat as Matiu dumps his phone and presses the switch that engages the eerie low hum of the electric motor. "She wants us to go straight home, to the apartment, to prove we're OK."

"Sounds like Mum," Matiu says. "Shame about all the chaos on the roads, eh."

"What chaos? There aren't enough cars around for there to be chaos."

Matiu shakes his head. "Oh, you'd be surprised."

He backs out of the alley, reversing carefully into the growing crowds as the surrounding buildings disgorge their human contents. Clicking forward into drive, the car ghosts slowly down the road, bodies everywhere. He taps the horn lightly, judicious little warnings to the dazed pedestrians who have forgotten in the heat of the sudden crisis that roads are for cars, not people. It's not helping that the Solaris is so damned quiet. But he keeps it cool and calm, and soon enough the road clears, and he can apply some speed. Not a lot, because there are cars and vans and even old trucks filtering onto the main roads from every side street, clumping up the roads alongside the ubiquitous bio-diesel buses, not all of them as courteous or considerate as Matiu has decided to be.

"OK," Penny admits, looking at the congestion swelling around them. "You've made your point, but this isn't the way to Mum and Dad's."

Matiu nods, taking a swig from his coffee. "You've spoken to Mum, yeah?"

"I told you I have."

"So you know she's all right."

"Yes, of course she is."

"Good." He lets it hang there, as a gap appears in the lane ahead and he slides into it, finding open road and letting the Solaris stretch her legs. Leaves Penny to work out the obvious. He *could* just tell her, but where's the fun in that?

"Oh," she says, finally getting there. "You've tried calling Whaea Mārama, and she didn't answer?"

"Smart girl like you should work for the police or something."

"I think we'd better go check on her."

"Good idea. I'm so glad you thought of it."

"Don't get snippy with me. It's been a long day already, and it's barely breakfast time. Speaking of which..." She opens the paper bag and helps herself to a piece of toast.

Matiu bites his lip. Something gnaws at him. Like this is going to be a much longer day than either of them had planned on, and that there will be worse than just incinerated corpses and little earthquakes before it's over. "Where was the epicentre?"

Glad for the change of topic, Penny pulls out her tablet and swipes through a few screens. "Off Rangitoto. That's why the P-alerts didn't come through before the shaking hit. It was so close, by the time the servers could distribute the P-wave signal onto the network, the S-wave had already hit. When the Kaikōura Fault slipped properly in 2028, Wellington got 22 seconds warning off the P-wave before the 7.5 magnitude S-wave hit. The P-alert warnings saved hundreds of lives. Geology was faster than technology this time. Must've been shallow, but small, as quakes go. GNS is currently reporting it as a 5.8."

"But it was here. Close to home." Rangitoto, Aotearoa's youngest volcano, an island slumbering just across from all the fancy houses and cafés on Auckland's North Shore. Something's stirring. Something they've been waiting for. He glances at the breakfast bag and wishes they'd invented a good way to eat bacon and eggs while driving. Should've ordered a pie.

The drive to Mārama's is a special sort of chaos, distracted drivers cutting lanes and causing their own mayhem in their efforts to get out of the city or across town to check on loved ones or business interests. Hell of a wake-up call, a 5.8 rattler with your morning latté. Even down Mārama's low-rent suburban street, people are milling, gathered in groups on the corners, pointing in surprise at cracked footpaths. It's nothing as bad as Christchurch 2011 or Wellington 2028, not even on the same scale. Auckland, for all that it sits on one of the world's most active volcanic plateaux, has blissfully been spared a lot of activity from beneath the surface in its short history. Still, for most of the populace it's the biggest earthquake they've ever felt. There's a fear that comes with feeling the earth move under your feet and knowing you're nothing but a rag doll on a giant's trampoline, which can be hard to put into words. "Lot of people probably in shock," he says as they pull into Mārama's drive.

"There's no reports of anyone dying," Penny says, "or major damage to buildings or infrastructure. That's what natural disaster planning and building standards are for. I think Civil Defence can call it a win so far."

Matiu frowns. "Lot of scared people though. Going to be a bit of panic in the air."

"Quit being dramatic," she says, hopping from the car and letting Cerberus out. "People are much better at heart than you give them credit for."

He steps out and shuts his door. "Or they're not. We'll see."

CHAPTER 7

- Pandora -

Penny hovers on the back doorstep, holding tight to Cerberus' leash as she peeps into the kitchen. Trust Matiu to go running in without checking it's safe first. But then, there is Mārama to think about…

On the lead, Cerberus is uneasy, fidgeting and whining next to her. Patting the Lab up against her thigh, Penny gives him a reassuring hug before leaning into the kitchen to examine the interior. The roof and the walls appear sound. No sign of crumbling or cracking. She shouldn't be surprised. Built nearly a century ago during the State Housing boom of the 1950s, both the frame and the cladding of Mārama's house are made of wood—unlike the steel and concrete monoliths of the CBD. Ductile and with lots of connectivity, wood construction means these dwellings tend to sway on their haunches, like an old dog getting comfortable, rather than racking or sliding. Plus, in the old days, things were made to last, weren't they? Tradesmen took pride in their work, so you didn't need a fancy Master Builders' Guarantee to know the place was up to standard.

Although, the same couldn't be said for the kitchen cupboards! It looks like a SWAT team has swept the house for contraband. And in a hurry. There's stuff everywhere: the cupboards are hanging open and Mārama's ancient orange Tupperware containers are scattered all over the floor, spilled cornflakes adding to the busy pattern of the linoleum.

Whoops. Penny has inadvertently let the lead out and Cerberus is wolfing up the cornflakes. Full of wheat and sugar, they're really not good for him. She's about to pull him back, then stops. What the heck? Everyone's entitled to a bit of comfort eating now and then. Luckily there's no glass anywhere. For safety, Mum had cleared out Mārama's dinnerware some time ago, replacing it with vitrified brands. Fortified with magnesium oxide, and sometimes titanium, a monster truck could roll over it and your breakfast teacup would still come out with the handle intact.

Having made short work of the cornflakes, Cerberus squeezes past Penny, the leash getting away from her as he makes for the living room.

"Cerb—"

Damn. She'd wanted to give Matiu a moment to calm Mārama.

She peeks around the door. Whether it's the after-effect of the quake, or because he senses her aunt's anxiety, rather than his being his usual boisterous rambunctious self, Cerberus has elected to sit quietly in his spot beside her armchair. On the other side of the threadbare rocker, Matiu is crouched close to Mārama, speaking softly to her and stroking her hand, while she pitches back and forth, distraught. Look how white her knuckles are; the poor thing. She's holding on to Matiu like her life depends on it. And no wonder; all alone in the aftermath of an earthquake. A real bone-rattler, too. Penny decides to give them a bit more time. If anyone can settle Mārama, it'll be Matiu.

Where has the caregiver got to, anyway? Could she be injured elsewhere in the house, knocked down by the first quake, or perhaps in the aftershocks? After the big one, Penny hadn't felt any tremors, but by then she and Matiu had been in the car and with a large quake like that there were bound to have been some.

While Matiu is still murmuring to Mārama, Penny ducks down the hall to check the rest of the house. On the right, its windows overlooking the street, Mārama's bedroom is neat and orderly with its floral pink and green duvet and lemon scatter cushions—Mum's attempt to keep things cheery for her sister—although one of the table lamps has toppled. Penny switches it off at the wall before righting it.

No one in the bathroom either. Penny hangs the towels back on the rack and closes the cabinet.

The spare room is decorated with the vestiges of Matiu's teen years, a sports trophy on the dresser and a Van Halen III concert poster tacked to one wall, treasures left behind from those rare weekends when, needing to get away from Mum, he'd found refuge here. This room has fared better; only the sports trophy is on its side. Penny puts it back on its dust-free spot.

Had the caregiver run outside in a panic and was now too scared to come back inside? It's what the people in town had done, the nine-to-four office workers streaming from high-rises like water from a colander. Perhaps she'd been terrified for her family and wanted to get home. Surely, she wouldn't just leave, though? Not with Mārama as delicate as candy floss. Just in case, Penny pulls aside the net curtains to check the driveway. Only the Solaris. She didn't think she'd seen a vehicle, although that in itself doesn't mean anything since most people—those whose parents don't own the biggest car fleet in the country—are forced to use public transport. There's a bus stop a couple of doors down, one that's been in operation on and off for close to sixty years, from trolley cars all the way to the newer biofueled buses. You can see the shelter from here, the scratched Perspex smothered in faded pink graffiti. A bus is pulling away. She drops the curtain.

Just one last room. This one has been allocated for Mārama's caregivers. The door is closed. Penny knocks quietly. "Hello? Mrs Hamon?"

There's no reply.

"Hello? Are you OK?" Penny turns the rounded handle and steps inside. She gasps. Things are not OK. Not OK at all. All this time, she's been giving Mrs Hamon the benefit of the doubt. Well, there's no doubt about what happened. The cold-hearted cow has only upped and left. But not in a panic. Oh no. Mrs Save-Your-Own-Skin-Hamon has carefully collected up her things and packed them in her suitcase before abandoning her post. There isn't so much as a stray pencil left behind. No apologetic note. She didn't even bother to call Mum. Penny wonders if the woman had been on the bus she'd seen pulling out a moment ago. She wouldn't put it past her. If Penny could drive, she'd take the Solaris, flag the bus down, and tell the woman exactly what she thought of her. You don't just leave someone like Whaea Mārama on her own. It's close to criminal. Just wait until Mum and Dad hear. Mrs Hamon might want to take extra good care of her kneecaps.

Penny tiptoes back down the hall so as not to disturb Matiu and Mārama and lets herself out of the house to make the call.

- Matiu -

Matiu pushes through the open back door, glancing about for the familiar patchwork leather handbag Mrs Hamon always leaves on the counter. No handbag, no Mrs Hamon. Can't trust anyone these days. In the kitchen, cupboards hang open. The benches and floor are covered in tins, plastic packets, and spilled food. "Mārama?"

The only sound in the house is the creaking of a chair in the lounge. Matiu finds her there, rocking quietly back and forth in her armchair with its worn arms and faded blanket. She's holding a teacup, but it's empty. Toppled photo frames lie scattered along the hearth and hang in disarray on the walls. Mārama is staring ahead, into some empty space only she can see. He crouches beside her as Cerberus settles into his customary spot at her side. Gently, he removes the teacup from her hand and grips her fingers in his. She's cold, cold like she's just crawled up out of a deep, wet cave. Cold like the sun has not touched her skin in weeks. Cold as the sea.

"It's over," he says softly, hoping she can hear him, wherever she is.

"No," she whispers, gripping his hand so tight it hurts. "Not over. What has begun must be finished. This is part of it. The veil is breaking."

Matiu swallows hard. It's not that this is unexpected. Mārama sees premonition in everything. It would be easier to dismiss if her visions had not so often proved to be true.

"Just an earthquake," he says. "Nothing to worry about." His denial sounds hollow, like something Penny would say to soothe him, when they were children and their deepest worry was the invisible voice in his head. Before that voice took form, and stepped into the world.

Mārama twists to face him, her eyes so deep and clear he can see all the way into her soul, laid bare before him. "We chose to stay, *e tama*. We chose to face this. It's too late to turn away, too late to run." She sighs. "One way or another, the end is nearly here."

Matiu nods. "That's what I was afraid you'd say."

Penny appears in the doorway. She takes in the scene, worry lining her eyes, then she moves to the hearth and starts fussing with the fallen photo frames. "Bit of a mess," she says in the lightest tone she can, shooting Matiu a look loaded with questions. "Grab the broom would you, Matiu, and make a start in the kitchen."

Matiu holds Mārama's hand a moment longer, before rising. Cerberus whimpers a little, looking up at him with his dark, soft eyes. "We'll get through this," he says, but Mārama isn't listening. Her eyes are wide, bright with moisture. Whatever she can hear, it's not his reassurances. Not Penny's bright determination in the face of disaster. They're not out the other side of the disaster at all. They're still falling into it.

CHAPTER 8

- Matiu -

"I won't be long," Penny says as they pull into the parking space in the deserted basement of her apartment block. "Just grab a few things, then I'll be straight back."

"Why don't you have a shower?" Matiu says, screwing his nose up. "Honestly, those of us who've been stuck in a car with you for the last hour would really appreciate it. Am I right?"

On cue, Cerberus whines.

Penny wavers between being offended and clearly wanting to take the opportunity to clean herself up. The sun isn't making the stink of blood any more pleasant as the day heats up. "I'll be quick, I promise."

"Go," Matiu says. "Don't come back until they've removed the biohazard warning." Despite the unexpected stress of the quake, and Mārama's ominous vision, Matiu still hasn't satisfied his curiosity about the Solaris. Having driven from the ports to Mārama's house, and now back to Penny's apartment, the power level is still sitting at 98%. As if it has used no power whatsoever after an hour of driving around with the aircon on full blast. He looks over the back seat, where Mārama is idly rubbing Cerberus' ears. "You two OK here for a mo?" Getting no response, he pops the boot and steps from the car as Penny jabs a finger at the lift button. With a huff of annoyance, she heads for the stairs.

The boot is mostly empty apart from the spare tyre and the tools to change it. Moving to the front of the car, Matiu opens the bonnet. A compact electric motor and drive array, exactly what he'd expect from a new electric car. The only difference is a lack of heavy cables. Every electric he's ever tinkered with—which, admittedly, hasn't been many, preferring as he always has the power of combustion to the hum of batteries—has been fitted with thick copper conductors to carry the high amperage needed to operate without frying the cables. Induction, maybe? It would account in part for the lack of cabling, if the wheels were powered the same way a wireless charging pad works, but induction has never been very efficient for high-amperage applications, and the Solaris appears to be more than efficient. It's almost like it's *creating* power as it drives. Which is ridiculous, and flies in the face of all the laws of energy Matiu has ever learned. To be fair, those laws were usually to the tune of pump the gas, drive the car, then pump more gas, but he's pretty sure that feeding energy back into an electrical system from its own operation is the exception, not the norm. You need to put energy in to get energy out, and there is always loss. No energy system can escape losses through heat, friction, sound or other means. Either that, or the gauge is *patu*. Maybe it's a reverse meter, and the Solaris is on its last 2% of battery. It may be reporting an energy-used, rather than available, level.

That could be embarrassing, and a serious design flaw. Hopefully they make it to Mum's before the cells run flat.

Then again, two gangs had been out to kill for something on the *Yongyang*, and nothing made more sense than it being this car. Between that, and Dad's concerns for the car, Matiu is sure there's more to the Solaris than meets the eye. He cracks the cover on the electric motor, revealing a second series of covered compartments. In the centre, a symbol like a sun. For a moment Matiu's reminded of the sun and eye motif of Sandi Kerr's Touching the Sun cult, but a closer look reveals it is simpler, merely a technical representation of the sun over a positive and negative symbol with a lightning symbol between them. Photovoltaic, then. Interesting.

He unclips the cover, lifting it off to reveal a pair of batteries within. Each barely bigger than the lead-acids that fire up a motorbike from a key-switch, the unit itself is practically so small as to be utterly useless on a vehicle this size. The symbol indicates these two batteries are part of the photovoltaic system, so there must be a solar panel somewhere to keep them charged. Batteries this big would only be good for running the dash, locks, radio, mirrors. All the non-critical stuff. Nothing earth-shattering here. Still, he hasn't found the main battery array yet. They're normally under the back seat, and with Mārama and Cerberus so nicely settled in the back, he's not about to go digging around under there right now. He can have a closer look later. He snaps the covers down, and has just dropped the bonnet when his phone rings.

"Hey," he answers. "You back at work yet? Or still slacking off in the sun?"

"Whatever," Erica replies. "I'm slacking off in the shade."

"Joy of working in the public sector, eh? One little earthquake and you can shut up shop for the rest of the day. Probably on full pay, courtesy of honest hard-working taxpayers like me."

"Shut up. We can't go back to work until they've had an engineer inspect the building so I'm at a loose end until then, but anyway, I'm not calling about that. It's Charlotte."

Matiu presses the boot closed and rests his behind on it. "She OK?"

"She's really upset. She got a text. It's put her in a state."

"What do you mean? What sort of text?"

"It told her she had to go to the old Sandringham Community Hall. To check in."

Matiu shrugs. "So? She lives down that way. Probably a lot of community checks going on. People aren't all bad, you know." Can she hear him grinning down the phone at her? He expects so.

"Yeah, except the Sandringham Community Hall closed about four years ago. And the message came from Axel Weis."

"Who is?"

"He's the one who got her into the Touching the Sun cult in the first place."

Matiu's grin slips. "Did she go?"

"I don't know. Now I can't get through to her. They reckon cell towers are giving up all over the city and they won't be back up until they get the power back on. And I've got no way of getting from the city out to her place to check on her. Matiu, if she goes, if she falls back in with those people..."

"Not gonna happen," Matiu growls. "Nuh-uh. I'll do a drive-by, soon as my sister gets her arse out of the shower."

"Thanks hun," Erica says, and the line goes dead. More cell towers failing? Or batteries? How much of the city they rely on is falling apart as they speak?

Matiu slips his phone away. "Cerb, you watch Mārama and the car. I'll be back in a minute." Without looking back, Matiu strides towards the stairwell.

- Pandora -

The lights are on, but the power must have been out earlier because the basement is as hot as a freshly-dug hangi. Penny hurries across the concrete to the lift, keen to get out of the clammy heat. A piece of paper has been taped to the lift doors.

Awaiting post-earthquake city enginers audit.

Residents, please use the stairs until further notice.

She swallows her annoyance: the inconvenience she can understand, but the spelling mistake is inexcusable.

By the time she reaches her apartment on the fourth floor, her annoyance has reached tenth-floor proportions. To make things worse, the biometric lock fails, her thumb too sweaty to recognise her print, which makes her even crosser. She only has herself to blame; she should have added a wet version of her thumbprint when Matiu had added his, so he could let himself in and out when he dropped by to pick up Cerberus.

She juggles the empty coffee cup and her satchel in one hand, wipes the thumb of her free hand on her pants, and tries again. Success. Pushing the door open with her elbow, she stumbles inside.

Immediately, the apartment's smart technology kicks in: the air conditioning cranking up, the radio bursting into song, and the blinds raising to her preferred level—that is, low enough to let in the natural light and not so low as to give a ring-side seat to the nosy pair from the apartment opposite.

She breathes deep. Right, first things first: she kicks off her shoes. Then she pads across the lounge in her socks to the kitchen where she uses her hallux to open the recycling drawer and dispose of the cup. Then, grabbing some Decontaminase paper-wipes from the dispenser beside the sink, she sterilises the outer surface of her satchel, hanging it on its hook by the door when she's finished. Finally, she sterilises her shoes, and the marble floor tiles, before disposing of the paper wipes.

There. Done. She exhales, consciously breathing out the morning's stress. Now to get in the shower and clean off this crud. Matiu's right: she must smell like a slaughterhouse on a hot afternoon.

Penny heads down the hall. On the radio, the latest news has promoted the announcer to call a snap interview: "Some of our listeners are asking if experts should have recognised the recent appearance of the Southern Lights in the skies over Auckland as a portent of this latest 5.8 magnitude earthquake. Joining me at short notice to discuss this issue are some experts: meteorologist James Sang, and Dr Susy McPearce of Auroralert, the online geomagnetic data mapping service…"

Turning the radio off, Penny enters the bathroom. She turns on the shower mixer and lets the water run while she peels off her clothes and throws them in the hamper.

Stepping into the stall, she emits a small groan.

These acupressure jets are heaven.

She tips her head from side to side, savouring the effect of the water pummelling her neck and shoulders. Just thirty minutes of acupressure applied locally like this can reduce systolic blood pressure and increase arterial oxygen saturation. And while diastolic blood pressure and heart rate stats don't change much at all over a thirty-minute treatment period, they show significant decreases afterwards.

If only she had thirty minutes.

She sighs. Quite apart from the fact that city water restrictions won't allow her to stand here for more than twenty minutes, Mārama and Matiu are waiting downstairs. Penny pumps a kernel of soap into her hand. She'd better hurry it up.

She's barely finished sluicing off the stench of death when the power goes out, leaving the bathroom in darkness. Within seconds, the shower jets turn to icicles.

No! Her hair is still soapy. Gritting her teeth, Penny rinses off as quickly as she can in the icy water, goose pimples rising on her skin. Aaargh! She leaps out, gasping.

Damn. That's her phone.

She grabs for a towel, dragging it about her haphazardly as she runs the length of the apartment for her phone.

Satchel.

On the hook.

The ring tone is about to end…

She plunges her hand into the side pocket, rummaging for the device. "Yes?" she says, breathless.

"Pandora. Where are you?" Her mother's voice is strident. "We expected the three of you half an hour ago. Your father's beside himself with worry."

"Mum. Hi. We had to tidy up at Mārama's before we could leave. Talk about a mess: it was like cleaning up *The Rena* oil-spill. There were cornflakes all over the floor. Dinner plates. The entire contents of the cutlery drawer. And then there was the Tupperware: it took me a while to match the containers to their lids—"

"So you're all still at Mārama's?" Mum interrupts.

"No, no, we left there forty minutes ago."

"Well, where on earth are you?"

Normally Mum only has to check the fleet GPS updates to know exactly where they are. Penny and Matiu often joke that whereas everyone else has Big Brother watching them, they have Big Mother. That's the downside of having free access to a fleet vehicle owned by your parents, and the reason Matiu is forever turning off the tracking feature. But the Solaris they'd stolen from the *Yongyang* hasn't been fitted with a GPS yet, leaving Mum guessing where they are. It must be driving her nuts.

"I'm at home," Penny says. "Having a shower." Although, right now, it's her foyer getting the shower, cold water dribbling off her hair and pooling in a slick on the tiled floor.

"At home? But you were supposed to come straight here."

"Mum, I've been up since sparrow's fart, working a case. I needed a shower."

"There's no need to swear, Pandora. Yes, I know about events at the wharf. They're saying on the radio there was some sort of gas explosion and people were killed. Dad said you'd be there. Anyway, what with the explosion, and then the earthquake, your father is pacing the living room like a caged animal. I've never seen him so anxious."

That *is* unlike Dad. He's usually unflappable. You don't build a billion-dollar business without some nerve. But then again, the quake's epicentre was close to Rangitoto Island, so Mum and Dad must've really felt the jolt up on the waterfront in St Heliers.

"Tell Dad not to worry. We're all fine, although it took Matiu a bit to calm Whaea Mārama. Did you phone the care agency about Mrs Hamon? I still can't believe she would just up sticks and run like that—"

Dad's voice rumbles in the background.

"Pandora. Just come home," Mum pleads.

The door buzzes, startling her.

"Hang on, Mum. That'll be Matiu at the door. Let me…" She punches the lock.

The door swings open.

"Craig!"

What's *he* doing here? Penny attempts to adjust the towel, which seems to have shrunk since she got out of the shower. Unlike her, Craig Tong isn't the sort to be caught out in the wardrobe department. As always, his tailoring is impeccable: Penny's never seen him with so much as a crease in his vintage Armani suit.

His tailing skills—not so much.

The Transport Minister's Adjunct steps inside and closes the door, throwing his suit jacket over a chair and gesturing to Penny to continue her conversation.

In Penny's ear, Mum is fizzier than powdered sherbet. "Craig's there?" she coos. Penny imagines her waggling her eyebrows. "I'll let you go then, sweetheart. No rush at all. I'm sure Dad'll be fine now that he knows Craig's there with you. Byeee."

Ugh. If she didn't risk losing the towel, Penny would throw up her hands. Honestly. Mum has this crazy idea that Penny and Craig are going to provide her with a bevy of little grandbabies. As if! All they've had is a couple of dinner dates.

"Mum, really, it's not what you think. He's just—"

She may as well save her breath because Mum has hung up.

"Pandora," Craig starts.

Penny whirls. "It's Penny!" she blurts. "What's going on, Craig? Why are you here? And why were you following Matiu and me earlier?"

Craig opens his mouth to protest, but Penny raises her hand. "Don't bother to deny it. I know it was you. I recognised your car."

Tilting his head to one side, Craig gives her a goofy grin. "You recognised my car."

The towel is slipping. Penny clutches it to her chest. "Cut it out, Craig. Come on, out with it. What's this about?"

Craig picks a piece of imaginary lint off his sleeve. "I know about the gang massacre on the wharf," he says. "At the Ministry we get an alert anytime there's an emergency at a major transport hub. I probably got the call before you did."

"So?" Penny replies, cold water dripping down her neck and onto her shoulders. *Surely, he didn't come to gloat about who got up earlier this morning.*

He smiles. "I was worried about you. I came to check that you were safe."

Penny draws her shoulders back. "I'm perfectly safe as you can see. In fact, I've been safe all morning. Why wouldn't I be? Given that the Armed Offenders Squad and half of Auckland's finest have been watching my every move. And then, when I left the wharves, I was perfectly safe again because I was with *my brother.*"

Craig nods, the way you do when a child is talking and you're only pretending to listen. "I heard Hanson's old gang were involved."

Penny frowns. So this is about Matiu. The same old story. Matiu went down for working with the gangs, *ergo* he must still be working with the gangs and any suspicious death, nefarious cult activity, or unexplained massacre must be all his fault. Penny has no idea when Matiu has the time to do all the crime people want to blame him for.

Marching forward, she thrusts her index finger at Craig's perfectly groomed chin, to hell with being polite. "Matiu had absolutely nothing to do with the massacre at the wharf!"

"Pandora, please, you have to listen—"

"It's Penny! And I don't have to anything. This is my apartment and I want you out of it, now!"

Craig runs a hand through slicked back hair. "Where is Matiu, anyway?"

"I believe you know the way out."

"Inspector Tanner threw you off the case, didn't he?"

"Don't forget your jacket."

"Think about it. Why would the police remove you from the case? You don't really believe it's because the Yee family name was on the ship manifest? No one can be that naïve..."

What? Penny's mouth drops. What exactly is he implying? That the police have deemed her guilty by association? She staggers backwards in shock...and slips on the puddle on the tiles. Instinctively, her arms bolt outwards to break her fall.

The towel!

She's falling...

In a single stride, Craig sweeps forward, gathering Penny up in his arms, and in that moment, the door flies open.

CHAPTER 9

- Matiu -

It's totally not what he was expecting to see when he opens the door, not something he thinks he *ever* wanted to see, but in the same moment of sheer humiliating disgust he feels a flare of wrongness, fired by filial concern. Penny, half-naked, wrapped up in the arms of none other than slimy old Craig Tong. Matiu absorbs it in a flash, even as he's stepping forward; the way Penny is pushing back, gripping her towel, how gravity seems to be playing a nasty game and Tong is just in the right place at the right time to make the most of the opportunity and put his big bear-paws all over his sister. It's the only explanation that holds any water, because the alternative... Well, that's just not Penny.

Tong looks up in time to see Matiu bearing down on him and turns his back in classic ruck-and-maul style, releasing Penny to gravity as Matiu piles into him and drives him across the kitchen floor. Tong tries to push back but his lawyer shoes slide on the tiles; even so, he manages to hook an arm under Matiu's knee and yank. They tumble, arms and legs flailing, into the back of Penny's couch.

"Woah! Settle down!" Tong yells, but Matiu is faster, and not really listening anyway. He rises to crouch over the man who thought he might lay a hand on his sister, and draws back an arm to deliver what will be one of the most satisfying right hooks of his life.

"Matiu, no!"

But the fist is flying, and it comes as a shock when Tong's arm snakes out, lightning-fast, and brushes the blow aside. Off-balance, Matiu isn't ready for the follow-through, as Tong seems to coil up from the floor, grabbing Matiu's left arm and twisting it behind his back, rolling up and over and pinning him to the floor with his knee.

"Matiu," Tong says calmly, barely panting, "I think you think you saw something happening that wasn't happening. Can we all take a minute to breathe?"

Matiu strains against Tong, but he's a big lad, and strong, with more chicken dinners under his belt than Matiu. Face pressed to the floor, Matiu can see Penny now, edging around the kitchen, behind the couch. "Get your hands off me," he growls, but doesn't bother following it up with a threat. Tong might not've ever been in a street fight, but he's been on the rugby field and he knows how to put a player down so he stays down. Accidentally of course, Ref.

"Matiu, it's not what it looks like," Penny says, the towel clutched tightly around her. "I slipped, that's all. Craig was trying to stop me falling over."

Tong eases his grip and Matiu worms out from under him, coming back to his feet in the same smooth motion that Craig draws himself up in. They face each other,

Tong with that irritating little half-grin on his face, palms open, Matiu's fingers rolling in and out of fists. But he holds back, grudgingly, wincing at the ache in his shoulder. Tong was fast. Faster than any head-boy-turned-politico had any right to be. A sliver of doubt splinters Matiu's simmering rage. What had Tong been doing for those couple of years after they left school, when he went down to Wellington, before coming back with his flash job in the Transport Ministry? Or is Matiu just getting slow? "What are you even doing here?" he hisses, opting for the path which seems less likely to end with his face back on the floor.

"Your mum asked me to drop by and check the apartment was secure. Had no idea anyone would be here."

"Um, if you boys can promise me you aren't going to kill each other, I'll just go and get dressed," Penny says, and makes a line for the bedroom door, pushing it closed firmly behind her.

"Bullshit." Matiu fixes him with a gravelly look, then eases his shoulders and moves to the door, pushing it closed until it latches firmly. He goes to the kitchen bench, losing himself in the comfortable routine of making coffee. He needs more caffeine, and something to do with his hands. His arm is aching where Tong had it twisted up behind him, but his pride hurts more. "Why aren't you racing up to City Hall or wherever to help manage the post-disaster clean-up? Shit man, you're in Transport, and the roads are insane out there! You've got better things to be doing than running errands for my mum." The coffee machine hisses. Matiu watches the black liquid pour into the cup. Glances at Tong. "I'd offer you one, but I know you've got other things to be getting away to, so I won't hold you up."

Tong regards Matiu with that same smile, like a dead lizard baking on a rock. "Some things are more important than others. Anyway, I was on my way past, so it was no big deal to swing by. Turns out Penny was here but the door wasn't secure, so it was lucky I arrived or who knows who might have broken in." He drifts to the lounge and pushes aside the blinds, revealing the hazy expanse of the city spread out below.

Matiu taps sugar into his mug. "And it was just convenient that she happened to be wearing nothing but a towel, and you were there to grope her when she fell over?"

Tong stiffens but doesn't bite. "Everyone's got secrets, Matiu. Maybe your sister even has some secrets from you?"

"Pretty sure none of them involve getting naked with you, bro." He moves over to stand beside Tong at the window. "Your fantasies aren't hers." He sips his coffee. Tong spares him a glance. "Might be less awkward if you're not still here when she gets out of the bedroom, eh. She's probably listening at the door, waiting for you to bugger off."

Tong nods a little nod, but diligently ignores the suggestion. They stand in silence for a moment, the only sounds the muffled shufflings of Penny in the bedroom getting dressed, and Matiu slurping his coffee in the most annoying fashion he can manage.

"You've got some moves on you," Matiu says at last, acknowledging the efficiency which Tong put him down with. "What part of white-collar school teaches you to fight like that?"

Tong shrugs. "I did some self-defence, learned a bit from my brother, you know. Nothing serious."

"Right." Matiu nods. It's a bullshit answer, but it's the only one he's going to get. "You should go."

Tong's jaw is set, but he eases out a sigh, and claps Matiu on the back. Coffee spills on his fingers, the tiles. "Be good, get home to your family," Tong says, and strides for the door. Matiu waits until the door clicks shut before dashing to the sink and running cold water over his scalded digits. Then, wrapping a wet tea-towel around the burn, he moves to the door and twists the deadlock. Even if all the power fails that, at least, should keep anyone else from just waltzing in on his sister.

Penny emerges from the bedroom, looking fresh and yet dishevelled, like the shower washed away the grime without making a dent in her exhaustion. But she's clean, and wearing substantially more than a towel. "Is he gone?"

Matiu nods, knocking back the dregs of his coffee. "Yip, I showed him the door."

"From the floor?" She manages a giggle. An actual giggle. What the fuck?

"Hey, I had that situation under control."

"He kicked your petootie, little brother. I've never seen him move so fast."

Matiu glowers at her. "Don't get any dumb ideas. He's a smarmy little prick and if I didn't like him before I like him even less now."

"I know what it is," Penny says, as she moves to fix herself a coffee. "It's because that was classic cop self-defence. Bring back some memories, did it?"

Matiu walks back to the window. She's right, and that's what stings. One move from Tong, and Matiu was ready to receive handcuffs. You can learn that shit in a self-defence class, for sure. But to actually pull it off against someone who knows how to brawl, who learned it in the gangs, on the street? That's not tick-the-box training. That's reflex. Instinct. A reaction born of hard graft and repetition. "We need to go."

"I know; Mum will be beside herself."

"We're not going home."

Penny gives him a withering look. "Why on earth not?"

"Erica needs our help. Charlotte's gone AWOL. Again."

She walks across the kitchen, combing her hair, and sits at the table with her steaming mug. "There's just been an earthquake, cell towers are down. We need to let things settle before we all start panicking about who's not answering their phones."

"Erica says Charlotte got a text from the Touching the Sun crowd. To meet at an abandoned community hall. Penny, if Kerr has something else planned, then it's started."

Penny takes a deep breath. Like him, she's looking at the staggering high-rises, the patchwork of green spaces and rooves, the flash of water, the undulating ripples of Auckland's skyline. Every hill a sleeping giant.

"You're not going to drive us to Mum's, are you? Even if I insist? You'll just get in and drive wherever the hell you like and I'll argue and you'll ignore me because if I could drive myself places I would. Right?"

Matiu nods. "Pretty much."

Penny sighs, heavier this time. "You do realise that makes you some sort of sociopath, don't you?"

He shrugs. "I left Mārama in the car with Cerb, so we better go."

Cerberus bounds across the carpark, stretching his long legs and shaking out his fur. The community centre has an eerie feel, like a house too long abandoned and suddenly waking to disquiet spirits in its joists. A few cars are parked haphazardly across the asphalt, as well as several bikes either resting neatly in the rack or dumped at random where their riders abandoned them. Heat ripples across the tarmac.

"But there's no-one here," Matiu says, peering through the glass. He tries the door handle again. It doesn't budge. There's nothing to suggest anyone has been inside for years.

"Well, are any of these Charlotte's car?" Penny asks. "You've been to her place, haven't you?"

Matiu turns to the carpark, frowning. "Don't think so, pretty sure she catches the bus like most people. I only went inside her house, checked out her bedroom. Didn't go snooping through her garage, that'd be pretty rude." Cerberus has run back to the Solaris, parked just inside the driveway, where Mārama is leaning against the door. She leans down to rub him behind the ears, then he races off again, chasing imaginary sticks.

"Well, there's no-one here. So whatever Erica was concerned about, she can relax, right? Now, can we get out of this heat and back to Mum's? She'll be sick with worry." Penny pulls her phone from her pocket and checks it. "Hey, there's better signal here than we had before. I'll try calling her, let her know where we are."

Matiu crosses to the first car, a decrepit old station wagon which has seen better days. He peers in the window, then tries the handle. The door opens. A small cascade of rubbish spills out, mostly paper wrappers and cardboard cups. The stink of sour wheatgrass washes over him, and he recoils.

Working through the lot, Matiu discovers that every car has been left unlocked. Nor are any of the bikes chained up. Penny comes back over to him, slipping her phone away. "I've put her off a bit longer, told her we were trying to get some emergency supplies, but of course she insists she has plenty and we should just get home. So come on, you've seen what you need to see."

Matiu turns to her, shaking his head slowly. "I should've been the detective, you know. How is it you're the one working for the cops and you miss the clues?"

Penny huffs. "Well, I was on the phone. What did you find?"

Matiu opens the nearest door, closes it. Turns to the car beside it, opens and closes the door.

Penny's brow furrows. "No-one locked their cars?"

Matiu points to the bicycles laid out in front of the building. "Or those."

"So, whoever came here didn't care about making their stuff secure, and they're not here anymore..."

"So they all left together, with no intention of coming back. Ever."

Penny's cheeks go pale. "Can I smell wheatgrass?"

Her phone rings.

CHAPTER 10

- Pandora -

"Tanner here."

Penny inhales. He'd be calling to tell her that her parents had been cleared of any misgivings, that their name on the manifest had no bearing on her involvement, and that Mather, bent under the work and peeved at having to put up with Cordell, had insisted she be reinstated. She takes a moment to revel in smug satisfaction, breathing out slowly before replying, "Yes?"

"Yee. Whereabouts are you?" Tanner rumbles. "I'm going to need you here."

"I think there's been a mistake," Penny says, as sweet and light as pavlova. "Are you sure you want me? Perhaps you meant to call Dr Mather? I'm not currently contracted to the police—something about my parents, and my *brother*, being under suspicion."

"This is something else. Another case."

Penny hesitates. As much as she'd enjoy making the detective grovel, she can't afford to burn bridges. There's her mortgage, Beaker's salary, and the loan from her parents to consider.

"Do you want the job or not?" Tanner says, impatiently. "Because I think you have some relevant expertise."

Relevant expertise? Intrigued, Penny's mind races through the possibilities. Tanner's head of homicide, so whatever this new case is, it has to involve a suspicious death or presumed murder. Something she's seen before. Another bog body? Unlikely. That first incidence was exceptional. A once-in-a-lifetime thing. You'd have a better chance of winning the Powerball jackpot than uncovering a second preserved specimen in New Zealand's tropical humidity. Maybe a locked room situation? It's not as if those are everyday occurrences, either. She runs through the other cases she's worked on for the police and shivers. A victim missing the back of his head. An innocent man brutally tortured in a chop shop. Three people murdered in the bowels of the museum. A doctor immolated in a fire, but not before he'd put out his own eyes...

Tanner interprets her silence as consent. "Where are you?" he asks. "How soon can you get to Māngere?"

"I'm in Sandringham, the other side of the Manukau Harbour, but Matiu…um…my driver is with me, so depending on the traffic, I could be in Māngere in twenty minutes."

"I'll see you at Māngere Community Hall in fifteen," Tanner says. "And you better call your offsider to tag along. I reckon you're going to need some help." He hangs up.

“Who was that?” Matiu asks. “From the way your face shrivelled up my money’s on Cordell.”

Penny gives her pony tail a tug. “Not Cordell. Tanner.”

“Surely that’s good, then? Mather’s whining got you back on the case.”

“Nope. Tanner wants me for something else altogether. Something which *fits my expertise.*”

“What’s that supposed to mean?” Matiu says, trying yet another car door and finding it open, too. He ducks his head and rifles through the glove box, still desperate for some clue to the abandoned vehicles.

“I don’t know,” Penny replies. “He wants me and Beaker to meet him over at the Māngere Community Hall.”

Matiu stands up. “Another hall? What are the odds of that?”

Penny’s eyes widen.

Matiu reads the answer on her face. “Yeah, I don’t like it either.”

Suddenly, it is imperative that they get to Māngere. Penny turns on her heel, calling, “Whaea Mārama!”

“Cerberus, come here, boy!” Matiu shouts.

They run back to the Solaris.

Taking the South Western Motorway is out of the question. One look at the on-ramp tells them all they need to know: the route is bumper to bumper with traffic. Little wonder. Forced out of workplaces and schools by the quake, half the city’s population are making their way back to the suburbs, advised to stay home until they’re given the all clear. Meanwhile, the other half, those who have the necessary authority to *give* the all-clear—engineers, electricians, linesmen, and emergency service personnel—are on their way in. The result is like two opposing scrum packs coming together. It doesn’t help that traffic lights are out in places, possibly due to the power outages, or the result of quake damage.

His brow creased in concentration, Matiu carves a route through the back roads, cutting corners, accelerating away from bends, skipping into gaps before they close, even undertaking a bus on the inside lane.

In the back seat, Mārama giggles like a girl, as if they’re on some kind of dodgem ride.

“Matiu,” Penny warns.

“What?” Matiu says, his tone all innocence. “Tanner did say to get there in fifteen minutes, did he not?” Checking the side mirror, he ducks into a clearway—*outside of the designated hours!*

Penny squeaks. “He didn’t give us *carte blanche* to break the law!”

“You say potato, I say potāto,” Matiu quips.

Honestly, he’s so infuriating.

“What’s up with Beaker?” he asks.

"I woke him up. He's says he's getting dressed now. I told him to be outside on the street in five and that a Yee fleet car would pick him up. With a bit of luck, he should get to Māngere not long after us."

"Who did Carlie allocate the job to?" Matiu switches his eyes to the rear vision mirror, then back to the road. The action is deliberate—an unspoken question about Mārama. They both know a crime scene is no place for her.

"I asked Carlie to send Whaea Amy," Penny says.

Matiu nods.

Whaea Amy isn't their real aunt, but she's been with the Yee family business for years, ever since Matiu and Penny were children, so of course they call her aunty. Capable and fun, she was often assigned to do the school pick up. Penny remembers she'd always enquire about how their day had gone, although never directly. She wouldn't say, "How was your day, Pandora?" or "Hello Matiu, what did you get up to today?" like other grown-ups. Instead, she'd ask, "Did anyone pick their nose at school today?" or "Whose teacher has the wackiest laugh?" or "Hit me with your ten best excuses for not doing your homework." She'd always managed to draw them out, even Matiu who'd been quiet and brooding as a child, and while they were giggling and snorting at her outrageous questions, the drive would fly by. But Whaea Amy hadn't just driven Penny and Matiu places: her warm nature and quiet acceptance meant Mum and Dad had called on her to accompany Mārama on errands and appointments too, especially in those early days before Mārama's mind had slipped into another, less vivid, realm. Which means that not only can Matiu and Penny trust Amy to take their aunt back to Mum and Dad's, but Whaea Mārama will be happy enough to go with her.

"We got lucky," Penny goes on. "Carlie said Whaea Amy had just dropped off a fare at the airport. She's probably with Beaker now."

Nodding a second time, Matiu pulls the Solaris off the roundabout into Coronation Road. Penny sucks in her breath. It's déjà vu. Just as they'd seen in Sandringham, the streets around the community hall are lined with vehicles.

Penny and Matiu exchange uneasy glances.

There's nowhere to park, the grass verges crammed with cars, so Matiu slows, looking both ways, searching for a spot.

To Penny's left, Mount Māngere pokes its grassy knobbed shoulders above the modest suburban streets. Penny knows the domain well, occasionally walking the track to the top, sometimes bringing Cerberus for a romp on the terraces. There's plenty for him to explore: the double-cratered hillock is humped and hollowed, scattered with lava bombs thrown out during the mountain's last epic eruption 70,000 years ago. Still evidence of the original pa site, too. Penny can only imagine what it must have been like to live up there in those days. Like living alongside the gods. The views will have changed over time—from lush bushlands to today's vibrant cityscape—but breath-taking, nonetheless. You can see forever up there:

across the city to Rangitoto Island in one direction, and over Puketutu Island to the Manukau Heads on the other. It's a special place, the kind where you can reach out and touch the heavens with your fingertips...

All at once, Cerberus howls. Startled, Penny glances back. The dog has dropped into the footwell and is frantically trying to squeeze his gangly doggy bulk into the small space. Hackles raised, he bares his teeth and growls, the sound so desolate that Penny's marrow turns to jelly.

What's up with him?

Twisting within the confines of her safety belt, Penny's reaching a hand back to ruffle his ears and reassure him when she catches sight of her aunt. Penny's heart seizes. If Cerberus is spooked, Mārama can only be petrified. She's the living embodiment of the hollowed-eyed figure in that Munch painting.

Gripping the fabric of her dress in white-knuckled terror, Mārama's mouth quivers in a soundless scream.

Penny whips her eyes back to the front and grasps Matiu by the arm. "Maṭiu! Something's wrong with Mārama…" She trails off. Matiu's expression is the mirror image of her aunt's. What's wrong with them all?

"Pen…" Matiu's moan is full of agony, and he's panting, as if he's in pain. His eyes have a faraway look, of longing, or despair.

Oh cripes. They're going to hit a car. Penny grabs the wheel, swerving the Solaris away from the kerb and back into the middle of the road. This is ridiculous. They have to get off the road or Matiu's going to get them all killed. She slaps her brother on the arm, willing him to snap out it.

"Matiu, can you hear me? I need you to turn right. Go back a few streets. Find a space so we can stop."

He blinks.

"Matiu. Turn right now."

"OK," he croaks.

Thank goodness.

He almost misses the junction, turning them sharply into Hastie Ave.

Nothing. Still nowhere to park. The streets are chock-full of cars and Penny would bet her right arm that every one of them is unlocked and abandoned.

Mārama groans.

"Matiu," Penny urges. "Go left into Crawford. Left here. Turn!"

Finally, she spies a space up ahead. Fortunately, Matiu seems to have recovered, at least partially, because he manoeuvres the Solaris up onto the verge without being told.

He puts the car in park, then throws opens the door and rolls out onto the grass.

Penny too is out of the car, rounding the back of the vehicle, to check on Mārama. The door open, Penny leans inside to comfort their aunt. Meanwhile, Cerberus is attempting to change footwells, his muzzle resting on Mārama's legs.

"Matiu? You okay?" Penny says, while Mārama clings to her like a wet swimsuit. "What's going on?" Her aunt mumbles something incoherent into Penny's shoulder. Penny feels her tremble.

On his hands and knees now, Matiu shakes his head. "Dunno," he gasps. "Bit of food poisoning, I guess. Feeling better now."

"But Mārama's got it, too. And it hit her at exactly the same time."

Using the Solaris for support, Matiu staggers to his feet. "Milk must have been off."

Penny frowns. Such a violent reaction from just a teaspoon of milk? And to hit that fast? Penny's doubtful. Matiu doesn't meet her eye, instead gazing back down the road towards the mountain.

"Well, I'm pretty sure Cerberus didn't have a cup of tea at Mārama's," she says.

Matiu brushes the grass off his knees, the colour slowly returning to his face. "You know how dogs are, Pen. They have a sixth sense for these things."

It's true. Studies have shown that dogs can integrate visual and oratory cues to differentiate human emotion, and Cerberus has always been sensitive. He must have picked up on Mārama's distress, recognising her malaise even before Penny did. Look how he's clambering over her now trying to comfort her—the big softie. Penny gives the Lab a scratch behind his ears.

A Yee fleet car pulls close to the kerb beside them. The doors open and Whaea Amy and Beaker pile out.

CHAPTER 11

- Matiu -

The glare of sunshine on the white paint of the Solaris drives back the darkness, this well of black which was drawing him down. The sound of voices muffles the lingering, echoing scream that had come from nowhere, yet somewhere familiar, somewhere close, somewhere impossibly *here*.

But that's all it was, a reflection; an echo. A glimpse of something darker. Something they missed. The old volcano has borne brooding witness to many a horror in its long lifetime, and today its very bones have cried out with the pain of whatever new atrocity has taken place under her watchful eye.

Taking a deep breath, Matiu pulls himself together, fingers drumming a rhythm on the bonnet. He turns as Mārama wraps him in a hug, her thin arms brittle as firewood as she draws him close, and then she is gone, and the sun hammers down and the scream still echoes, distant, in his head. Calling. Like somewhere a window has cracked open and from the darkness beyond comes a wind, cold and sour and haunted by the voices of the ghosts who want to step through. It may not be wide enough for them yet, but they will howl and rage and scrape their fingers along the glass until it shatters.

A patrol car pulls up alongside them, and Penny is talking to someone, and they're bundling into the car, Penny up front and Beaker in the back. Matiu gets in the Solaris, Cerberus bounding in behind and, like he's falling into a dream, the car is driving. Turning up the sloping, winding road which he knows will take them to the carpark and the ranger track, up the wide, angry shoulders of a volcano which, like her many close relatives, merely slumbers here on the fringes of the human world. This place which is the domain of Rūaumoko, just one step between the shifting heat of the earth's crust and the screaming dark of the underworld.

It's all coming together, and it's all falling apart.

Matiu shakes his head clear. This is no time to freeze up. Shit just got real. He needs to be on his game. He rolls his window down and lets the hot, fetid wind rush over him. Tastes the anticipation. Rolls it on his tongue, and grins a grin which just might be a little bit mad.

- Pandora -

Tanner is MIA. Turns out, Māngere Community Hall is just the police staging post and the crime, and Tanner, are somewhere on the domain.

"He's up on the mountain," says the officer at the domain entrance. The poor man looks as pasty as Matiu. His eyes are smudged with dark rings and his fringe is plastered to his forehead, while at the back his hair is sticking up on end, as if it's been crushed under a baseball cap for hours. He waves vaguely towards the track that snakes up past the children's playground equipment.

"How will we find him?" Beaker asks.

"You can't miss him. He's a bear of a guy. Size of a small truck and a horn to match."

"I meant, how will we find him on the domain? It's a big area."

"He'll be somewhere near the top. There are a couple of uniformed officers hovering on the tracks, keeping the public away from the crime scene. They'll be able to direct you. Hey!" he shouts as a car pulls in. "You can't park there, mate. That space is reserved for the pathologist." He hurries away.

Shouldering their gear, Penny and Beaker head up the track, while Matiu trails with Cerberus.

"What's up with Matiu?" Beaker asks.

"Food poisoning," Penny says.

"Ah."

"And Charlotte is missing again."

Beaker stops dead a moment. "The woman with the baby? The one Sandi Kerr was trying to sacrifice a few months back?"

Penny nods. "The same."

"Shit a brick!" Beaker says, his cussing startling a couple of sheep near the fence and causing them to scatter. He skips a little to catch up to Penny. "Is she still mixed up in that weird cult, then?"

Penny holds the gate while he steps through. "I don't know. Possibly. Her sister says she got a message asking her to go to Sandringham Community Hall, but when Matiu and I got there, all we found was a slew of abandoned cars. If Charlotte was there, we didn't see her. We didn't see anyone."

Arching an eyebrow, Beaker runs a hand through his mop of ginger hair, the gesture making him look even more like the iconic muppet character he's named for. "That's spooky," he says.

They're quiet for a bit, saving their breath for a steep flight of wooden stairs.

When they reach the top, Penny says, "I'm hoping it's nothing. More likely, she's been caught out by the quake. Probably stuck somewhere in traffic with the baby and an uncharged phone. Maybe the house got shaken up and she didn't feel safe, so she left in a hurry forgetting her device. Her place is pretty old. I think Matiu said it was built in the eighties. If it was anything like Mārama's… You should've seen her kitchen, Beak: it was a total train wreck, stuff everywhere. Anyway, the point is, there could be a heap of reasons why Charlotte isn't answering her phone."

"Hmm," Beaker murmurs dubiously.

Penny isn't convinced, either. Matiu said Charlotte had received a text from someone inside the Touching the Sun crowd. It's possible that one of the cult's lieutenants also works for the city Civil Defence Department, but hardly probable. Too much of a coincidence. Plus, if Charlotte had received a call from the cult, then there is a good chance she took up that call, in spite of what she went through in the rooftop garden of the Sedge restaurant. Cults are clever like that—enlisting, and then brainwashing their members so they respond without question, like a bunch of brain-dead zombies. There'd been a flurry of research on the subject after the rise in extreme cults in the early 2020s. One study by a UK researcher, herself an escaped cult member, showed how cults appeal to people with especially strong ideals. Passionate people with a commitment to creating a better way of life. Only, the cult will take that passion and commitment and harness it to their own ends. Erica's sister Charlotte had quickly become enamoured with the happy and wholesome philosophy of Touching the Sun, which came complete with daily servings of microgreens, wheatgrass and spirulina juice. The problem was, the healthy lifestyle they were touting was just window-dressing. The pretext. Because on the way to the body cleanse, the Touching the Sun cult had also cleansed her mind.

Penny sighs. Poor Charlotte. She'd had no way of knowing. Desperate for a baby, she'd thought Kerr and her cronies were helping her improve her chances of conceiving. Instead, they isolated her from the outside world, from her family and friends, from other members with whom she might find solidarity, and even her own rational thoughts.

They erased her rational thought.

Penny still finds it horrifying that a person can become so disenfranchised, so dissociated and alone, that actions and behaviours which other people consider preposterous would feel normal to them. But then, she'd seen it for herself on the roof of the Sedge when Charlotte and her baby had nearly lost their lives. So if the Touching the Sun cult had called her, Penny is sure that despite her efforts at rehabilitation, Charlotte would have been tempted to respond.

She shudders.

And if Charlotte did go to Sandringham, where is she now?

The gradient, and Beaker's huffing, increase exponentially as they approach the summit. Sweat dribbles down the middle of Penny's back. The climb isn't particularly tough, but without breakfast and in this heat, even Penny is feeling it. About twenty metres from the top, an officer blocks the trail.

"I'm afraid this portion of the park is closed to the public," she says. "Unexpected hazards resulting from the quake."

Unexpected hazards. Penny almost snorts.

"We're from Yee Scientific," Beaker replies. "Here to see Detective Inspector Tanner. We're a bit late."

"Yeah, well, we're all a bit late getting here today, aren't we?" the woman says softly.

"I'm sorry?"

"Nothing. He's just over the ridge."

Penny turns to check on Matiu, who is dawdling fifty metres back. She gestures to the officer to let her know that Matiu is with them, and they carry on. There's not far to go, but the blazing mid-morning sun makes the last steps seem interminable and even the breeze blowing in off the harbour is too hot to offer relief.

"Are we there yet?" Beaker moans.

Penny grins. His face is almost as red as his hair. "Just a bit further." Stepping over the lip of the crater, she gazes down at the scooped-out core, and the sweat freezes on her back. Her breath freezes too, her chest wall constricting around her lungs.

"Oh my God," Beaker whispers beside her.

Penny sinks to her knees on the grass, breathing in rapid, shallow breaths. She hugs her arms about her. What's happening to the world? Two massacres in one day. How is it even possible? All these people: there has to be at least a hundred of them.

Now she knows what the officer had meant about everyone arriving too late. And why so many cars had been abandoned outside the community centres. Why hadn't the police been told? Surely, someone must have known this was about to happen. Penny's shock turns to anger. They knew and yet they *chose* not to say anything. The smallest clue would have been enough, the merest soupçon to raise the alarm. Why hadn't they phoned it in, so the police could do their job? A text, a tweet, a hashtag, hell even ten measly characters could have avoided all this…this…*waste*.

Except it isn't exactly the same as this morning. For one, the bodies don't appear to be mutilated. There was no sudden biofueled explosion to fling butchered dismembered limbs across a blistered tarmac. No, this was quietly done, in silence, without fanfare or fireballs. Penny can tell because seen here, from above, the bodies form a pattern laid out on the slopes in neatly concentric whorls, increasingly tighter as they descend to the centre at the base of the hollow.

Penny is certain they laid themselves out this way. They did it voluntarily. She doesn't need to look to know they all have the same motif tattooed on the inside of a wrist. Concentric whorls like a stylised koru, with a slash across the meridian: the emblem of the Touching the Sun cult.

An eerie ululation echoes over the domain and Penny looks up as Matiu and Cerberus come over the brow of the hill.

CHAPTER 12

- Matiu -

The fern is a plant of special significance to the people of Aotearoa. Represented by the koru, a curling inward spiral, it is a humble inhabitant of the bush, with dark fronds that turn in on themselves and only occasionally uncurl when the sun hits them through the shade of the trees they hide beneath. Over the centuries, it has come to represent the country's sense of nationhood, an iconic swirl gracing the jerseys of national sports teams, government departments and the tail fins of the now defunct state airline. It symbolises pride, unity; humility and endurance. Survival.

Matiu had never realised how much the symbol means to him as a New Zealander, as Māori, until he stands on the lip of the crater, looking down into the maw of Mount Māngere, and sees that symbol laid out below him in flesh and bone, a corruption. A spiral of death descending into the grassy centre of the dormant volcano's cone. Side by side, arms linked at the elbows, dozens of corpses staring blindly at the scorching sky. The koru means life, renewal. Rebirth. Not death. Not *this*.

Beside each body, a dirty plastic bottle, spilling dregs of a thin green liquid. Uniformed police mill about the scene, bagging the empty bottles, photographing the victims' faces, taking cold, dead fingerprints. A drone flits back and forth overhead, the lens on its underslung camera glinting in the sun as it captures a record of the mass suicide.

Cerberus whines and strains against his leash as Matiu wanders along the perimeter tape. A ritualistic killing, the Touching the Sun wheatgrass juice, the bizarre symbology. It's got Kerr written all over it. But she's upped her game, or morphed it into something new. Not a single victim in a secret place, but a crowd out in the open, at a place where the line between this world and the realms of Rūaumoko and Hine-nui-te-pō grow thin.

There's a roar building in the back of his head, a rushing white noise like an approaching waterfall, its current drawing him closer to the edge, and the plummet into oblivion. He fights back the urge to let it draw him in. He needs to focus now, and focus hard. The fingers of his left hand drum against his leg, thrum, thrum, thrum, a rhythmic counterpoint to the thunder of the beyond. A quiet challenge. The roar recedes, but only slightly. Just enough to choke back the scream rising in his throat, a desperate howl he had barely heard even though it's coming from his own lungs. He stifles the cry, withering under the odd stares drifting his way.

At the very centre of the spiral, in what must have been the throat of the volcano several thousand years ago, there's a gap. Matiu can practically see Sandi Kerr there, standing over her lambs, the shepherd holding the sacrificial knife. Asking them—no, *telling* them—to give their lives for whatever it is the madwoman seeks. A gate to another world, or the open jaws of a being as dark and vast and hungry as the night itself.

But Kerr is not there. Her body does not lie sprawled among the victims. This fate is not a price she herself was willing to pay. Cerberus tears against his grip, eager to run, though whether the dog wants to be away from here, or if he's sensed something he needs to harry down, Matiu doesn't know. Penny is somewhere, hopefully turning this tragedy into a chance to learn more about their nemesis. She'll do that, with her tape and test tubes and lines of numbers. But this is where it happened. Cerberus knows it, can feel it just like Matiu can. Whatever Kerr has done here, she left traces that no amount of forensic sampling or number-crunching is going to reveal.

He's tempted to let the dog loose, but that'll just land him in the crap with Penny and probably Tanner. Besides, he has a more pressing issue, and he scans the dead faces as he circles the crater, ducking under the tape in the hope that no-one calls him out. Each body he passes is a tiny relief as he searches for Charlotte's face among the victims. Cerberus leads the way down the spiral of death, nose to the grass, as Matiu looks from face to face, seeing only strangers. The cops, absorbed in their macabre work, have lost interest in Matiu, so out of place in his leather jacket and shades in the blistering heat, following his dog down the curl of the koru towards its beginning. Or possibly its end.

Cerberus is yanking harder on the leash now, a low growl in his throat, and Matiu hurries to keep up. Still no Charlotte. The descent is dizzying and the roar builds once again in the back of his head, an insistent pressure, a stinging pain.

"Hey, you need to get back behind the tape!"

Rumbled. Matiu flashes the cop a grin. "I'm with forensics. Special Dog Unit. Check with the chief."

He carries on, as radios crackle and footsteps thump behind him. The cop's striding towards him, stepping over bodies, not following the curve of the death-koru, reaching out for him. Matiu hops forward, leaping a corpse to land in the centre of the spiral.

Cerberus howls. The sky turns red.

Matiu drops to his knees, both hands flat on the ground, and the scream from beyond rips through him.

He looks up at the sky that twists and coils, arcs with lightning rendered in jagged curves, the sharp ends wrapping round on themselves leaving after-images tugging against the back of his eyes like fishhooks. Glancing left and right, he sees no police. No bodies. Just the crater, a shell of ash and rock, scored by a single shape: the koru, blistering the earth in a curl of embers. Like the world has turned inward; like time has fractured and spat him out in this broken shard of existence which should not be.

Cerberus jinks this way and that, barking, eager for something Matiu can't see, thick white spittle hanging from his jowls.

Heat draws his eye down, to the dirt beneath his feet which smokes and crackles with hot ash. He's standing in a fire, in hot mud, the earth giving way and opening beneath him, something moving in that unseen place below where the spiral twists down, like a net, drawing madness up from the depths. Beneath his palms a pulse, dragged up from under the skin, the scales of something vast, amorphous. Something that breathes the sky itself.

In the hazy mists of legend, Māui hooked this fish from the sea, set his feet against the ocean bed and cast out with his nets and his hooks to draw the great monster from the deep. He beat the fish with his patu, bludgeoned it until it was still, carved out the lakes and rivers and gorges and hacked up the mountains and hills, set it to dry under the southern sun so that people might walk upon it and call it home, *whenua*. But there is a kind of life within this fish yet, the leviathan they call the North Island, Te Ika a Māui. A half-life, half-death, it smoulders just below the skin, these dusty scales that separate man from monster, living from dead.

There is a power in death. The dead call to the dead.

That must be Kerr's plan. Burial grounds are *tapu*, their dark bond with the realms of the dead tied up in the *waiata tangi* which are sung for the spirits to carry them safely to the underworld. With no waiata to bind these lost spirits, where will they go? What might they *break*? The space between here and there? Just a crack, enough to let something push through?

The earth beneath him ripples. Where it splits, it bleeds, hisses, screams...

Matiu hits the ground suddenly, dirt in his nose and an arm driven up behind his back. His own world rushes back, the other gone in a painful rush, and even over the roar which might be blood coursing through the veins of some sleeping giant, he can hear Cerberus, the yelps of the cop as he unhands Matiu and turns to pry the dog away.

"Matiu!"

He rolls over, staggering to his feet as Penny rushes to him, hands on her hips. "Hey, sis."

"How many times do I have to tell you about staying behind the crime scene tape? Cerberus, cut that out!"

Then Clark is there, and another uniform, and Penny is staring daggers at Matiu. He needs to tell her about the crack in the world, about the unsettled ghosts, but she won't listen to that. Best not leave her in the lurch, either. He can make this work for both of them. "Sorry, Pen," he mumbles, "it's just, I thought I saw her. Thought I saw Charlotte."

Penny's features soften briefly, then harden again. "Where?"

He gestures vaguely away from him. "Over there, ish, you know..."

"Matiu..."

"You think you know one of the victims, Mr Yee?"

Matiu shifts his gaze to Clark. Yip, a good cop on the hunt can't resist a tasty bit of bait, can he? "*Potential* victim. Girl we know, girl *you* know, actually, from the rooftop? Had the baby? She got a message to go to Sandringham Community Centre, same deal as you found at Māngere. Got a message from a guy goes by name of Axel Weis. You should look him up, might help you get to the bottom of this."

Clark scribbles on his tablet and gives Matiu a nod. "Thanks, that might help. Harris, leave these two to carry on their work, will you?"

Penny watches Matiu very firmly as the cops grudgingly drift away, and Clark traipses off, cellphone to his ear. "Did you really think you saw Charlotte?"

He shrugs. "Something bad happened here."

Her eyes widen. "Well duh. Anyone can see that."

He shakes his head, starts walking back up the spiral, away from that terrifying nadir where reality splinters and falls into the void. "No, worse than just this. It's... I don't think it worked. Kerr, whatever she's trying to do, she failed. See, she's..." He stops walking, turns to Penny, glances at the hazy murk of the horizon beyond, the smudge of the harbour. "Every time, she gets closer. The museum, the baby. That was what, ancient Egyptian, then something out of Eastern Europe? Now she's figured out it has to be true to the land. Her magic has to work with this place, these spirits."

"There *is* no magic. This is a suicide cult, plain and simple, and we need to stop it from killing anyone else, all right?"

Matiu nods. "Charlotte's still out there somewhere. So's Kerr. We need to find them."

"Yes," Penny says, taking his hand and heading back up the hill. "Yes, we do. And you are going to watch from just on the *other side* of that crime scene tape. OK?"

CHAPTER 13

- Pandora -

Penny glances skyward. Close to midday. All at once, she feels as old as Methuselah, rather than a spritely thirty-five. She sits back on her haunches. "No obvious trauma anywhere," she says from behind her breathing mask.

Slightly higher up on the hillside, and also sitting on his haunches, Beaker doesn't look up, too busy examining the body of a young man in his twenties. "I'm not seeing anything either," he says, lifting the sleeve of the victim and checking the man's forearm for injections or patches. "Although an injection site would be easy to miss. I think the simplest explanation is the most likely."

"They *drank* the Kool-Aid," Penny says.

Beaker drops the man's sleeve and nods. "Far easier to get people to drink something than suffer an injection."

Penny stands up, the white hazard suit rustling. As soon as she and Beaker had seen the similarity to the iconic Jonestown tragedy, they'd demanded Tanner's people stop what they were doing immediately and kit up in chemical-biological hazard suits complete with OSH-certified self-contained breathing masks.

Tanner hadn't been impressed. "What's wrong with our normal coveralls? Surely, they're sufficient?"

"Nope, not going to cut it. Whatever these people ingested, it was lethal."

"And the masks?"

"If this massacre was styled on the 1978 Jonestown event, then it's possible the victims ingested Potassium Cyanide."

"When it's wet, the crystals emit hydrogen cyanide in small droplets," Beaker added.

"One gust of wind and your people could die," Penny said.

Tanner rolled his eyes. "Come on. You're being overdramatic. If the poison was windborne, wouldn't we be dead already?"

To be perfectly honest, if they were dealing with Potassium Cyanide, they were bloody lucky no one *had* dropped dead, herself included, given that she'd dashed after Matiu when he'd bolted down the hill to scour the site for Charlotte.

She shrugged. "Maybe the only reason we're not is because the air inside the crater is stagnant, captured by the sides of the cone."

"I reckon it's the only good thing about this lack of breeze," Beaker griped, wiping the back of his neck with his palm to make his point.

It was too much for Tanner, who threw up his hands. "This is all I need," he thundered. "Mountains of bodies turn up all over Auckland, and meanwhile these earthquakes are shaking us to buggery, the power is failing, it's as hot as hell, and the press are clamouring all over us for a scoop."

"The press can wait," Penny said. "So can the dead for that matter. It's the living we need to consider. Just now I saw one of your officers unscrew one of the bottles and take a whiff." She rounded on Tanner, her face level with his chest pockets, and put her hands on her hips. "The guy's a shoo-in for this year's Darwin Award for stupidity. He took off the lid and sucked in a gulp. Just like that. Insisted he wasn't going to drink it, only sniff it. What do you teach your people, anyway? Don't they know that fumes can be toxic, or at the very least noxious?"

Tanner's face had puckered with concern. "Oh fuck," he'd croaked. "Who was it? Is he going to be OK?"

Penny clucked her tongue. "Ramsey. Lucky for him, he doesn't seem any the worse for wear."

"You should probably have Clark send him to the hospital to be on the safe side," Beaker had chipped in.

Tanner hadn't said anything, not to them, but as he'd turned on his heel and stalked off, he'd roared blue-murder at anyone within cooee. "Clark, send someone with Ramsey to Greenlane Hospital. And make it quick. Seems the idiot may have breathed in some poison. Jones, we're going to need haz suits—the expensive ones—and I need them here yesterday. See to it. Wineera! Get your guys to pull the cordon back to the top of the crater: the doc says the poison could be airborne… Did you bring in a local elder in yet? We need to get this site blessed, so the consults can start work. They'll need suiting up, too. I'm damned if we're going to lose anyone else..."

Her stomach rumbling, and her limbs heavy with fatigue, Penny moves to the next corpse in the line. "I agree, poison by ingestion seems the most likely scenario. You know I asked Ramsey what the stuff in the bottles smelled like."

This time, Beaker looks up, his masked face staring at her like a startled clone trooper.

"It was for science," she says.

"And?" he asks.

"He said it was like lemon pepper BBQ seasoning. Know any poisons that smell like that?"

Beaker shakes his head. "No, but the almond smell of Potassium Cyanide could have been masked by the carrier solution. We can't rule it out yet."

He's always such a stickler for rigour.

There's a muffled shout from below them, deep in the gullet of the volcano, the voice breathless and cracking, "Over here! This one's alive!" an officer calls.

Airborne droplets be damned. They run: Penny, Beaker, Tanner, and a half-dozen police and support crew charge down the mountainside with their hearts in their mouths. Suits crackle, knees creak, and boots thunder. They tear into the crater, leaping over the sleep-dead corpses, their arms outstretched and their gloved fingers snatching uselessly at clumps of grass to slow their descent. They could be children running downhill for lollies thrown by a clown. Someone alive in all this destruction? It is too amazing not to witness with your own eyes. It's a miracle. A gift from the gods.

Whoever it is, please let them make it, please let them make it. The mantra pounds in Penny's head, keeps pace with the cadence of her feet. *Please...*

Then suddenly, instinctively, they all slow and pull up, hovering close at hand while at the same time trying not to crowd the officer who'd called out.

Tanner breaks the spell, pushing to the front of the crowd. Dressed in the white hazard suit he looks like a yeti from Datlov Pass. "What have you got?" he booms.

The officer stumbles to his feet, a small child in his arms. "It's a kid. A baby."

Penny's heart flips. Squirming in the officer's grasp is a boy of around two, with curly brown hair and chubby wringed wrists. It isn't Charlotte's baby, but it's clear from the way the child is straining to wriggle free of the officer's grasp, that his mother is the mound slumped next to the officer's feet. "Mummy!"

Clark—ever the quick-thinker—rushes in and places a mask over the child's nose and mouth before he draws breath a second time.

The child kicks and roars. A good sign.

"All these people with masks over their faces," Matiu mumbles at Penny's shoulder. "Poor little shit must be terrified. Probably thinks we're all aliens or something."

He's right. They're traumatising the poor child. "Let's get him to the top of the hill," she says. "Maybe a cuddle with Cerberus will calm him."

They troop en masse up the hill, carrying him beyond the cordon.

The boy, Carlos H., can tell them nothing, of course. He's far too young. Were it not for the label sewn into the back of his t-shirt, they wouldn't even know his name. At Jonestown, they'd dosed the children first, figuring their parents wouldn't resist once their babies were dead. How then, had this boy survived? Perhaps he'd fussed and refused to drink the concoction? If so, he was the only one. There was no sign of anyone changing their minds at the last moment, no evidence of last-minute escapees, no gaps in the spiral pattern.

"Little tike was asleep," says the officer who found him. "Guess his mother couldn't bear to kill him."

"She's abandoned him to Oranga Tamariki," Matiu says morosely. "Not much difference."

He has a point. New Zealand's track record for looking after its youth isn't hot.

"They do their best," Clark says.

Matiu looks away. Carlos takes advantage of Matiu's inattention to yank on Cerberus' ear. Cerberus, to his credit, doesn't flinch.

Penny and Beaker have a drink, then they suit up again and go back to work. One thing is true, discovering the boy has given the entire investigative team renewed vigour. By the time the social worker arrives to accompany him to the hospital, Carlos and Cerberus are firm friends, and Penny and Beaker have done all they can in the field and are packing up to leave.

CHAPTER 14

- Matiu -

Matiu lurks in the shade of a puriri tree, watches the kid laughing and scratching Cerberus behind the ears, running and jumping and tossing a stick they found beside the road. Boy and dog, dog and boy. Carlos is having so much fun with the ambulance and the dog he hasn't even figured out his mum's dead. She won't be taking him home or dishing him up cheesy pasta with little sausages and cherry tomatoes for dinner tonight. What was going through her head when she trekked up this hill, kid in tow, her and all the others? Did they know they wouldn't be coming back down? Fucked-up world. That's all he can think.

Sandi Kerr's got a lot to answer for.

But she's not alone. Matiu slips his phone out, presses the earbud into his ear, ignores all the missed calls from Dad and swipes up a number. While it rings, Cerberus thunders past, jowls flapping as he hunts that pesky stick. Carlos has an arm on him for a wee tike, Matiu'll give him that.

"Bro."

"Scour. What's the word?"

"Word is you never call me unless you want something, and last time we talked I had to fall off the face of the earth to save my own arse. Got a fucken nerve, bro."

"Gotta keep you on your toes. You got systems, you gotta keep them fresh, make sure they work. Think of it as a bit of live testing. I did you a favour. How'd your toys hold up?"

"Coulda lost a lot of shiz that night, Yee."

"But you didn't. Put the shits up you, that's a good thing. Makes it all feel worth it, helps you find room to improve. Right? I've got your back, brother."

There's a silence on the line. Matiu can almost see Scour sucking his lips against his teeth. "What gives with you?"

Matiu smiles. "Someone I need to find. Preferably before the cops do."

"Shit, man. Never easy, is it? Never, 'Bro, what was the BBQ ribs recipe from that classic Rodriguez Grindhouse double feature?'"

"Never make a phone call if you can Google it. Shit I need right now I can't Google up."

Cerberus rushes past, stick in mouth. Carlos shouts and whoops. Boy and dog, like a bright little sliver of sanity has cracked through the clouds of nightmare that cloak the city, clouds only Matiu can see.

"Your mystery man got a name?"

"Axel Weis."

"Got any more to go on?"

"Fucked up little cult called Touching the Sun. Organic veggies and a side of suicide in one happy bundle."

"Seriously, you need a hobby. And it's beef brisket, 12 pounds smoked for 12 hours at 250, in case you're wondering."

"What is?"

"*I don't use no goddamn foil.*"

"Do less drugs, bro. You're losing me."

"There's a whole world of culture out there just passing you by, Matiu Yee. Get a Cineflix account and stay home sometimes, hashtag grindhouse. Blow your mind wide open."

"Hello? Hello? I can't hear you; you're going into a tunnel!" Matiu makes crackling noises and swipes the call off. The earbud goes dead, and he reaches up to pull it out.

Blow your mind...

A chill rolls over him, as if the sun has turned suddenly cold, as the words echo through his head, but not in Scour's voice.

...wide open...

Like a shadow, coming and going beneath racing clouds, Matiu senses the form behind him, in the dark places beneath the tree he leans against, wavering. There and not there.

...right out the back of your little skull...

Matiu whirls, knowing he won't be there, the ghost who haunted him once and haunts him still, a flicker behind his eyes, a voice in his head he thought he'd banished.

Makere.

He bites his tongue, hard. Tastes blood. He won't yell, won't call the cops down on him again. His fingers grip the bark of the tree, so hard it hurts. No sign of a dark figure lurking beneath the branches, whispering in his ear. His vicious alter-ego, trapped for so long on the other side, has split the veil and now walks in both worlds, just as Matiu does.

Makere, who threatened him once with trading places, sucking him into the desolation of the underworld to repay him for living this touched life beneath the sun. Makere, who Matiu had dared to hope was gone. Gone, but never forgotten. Changed, not defeated. Reminding Matiu he's still here. That he can still reach out and touch him.

A hot wind rolls off the city, driving away the cold, and the sun pounds down. Matiu turns again, and again, but there is no Makere to be seen. He slips his jacket off his shoulders, slides down to the grass with the tree at his back.

Watches a dog chase a stick, and a boy laugh. Drums his fingers on his legs and chokes back the urge to scream.

- Pandora -

Inside the cordon, in the decontamination area, Penny rolls the haz suit down the length of her body and steps out of the fabric.

Not far away, Matiu and Cerberus are waiting for her under a tree in the shade. Penny gives them a wave.

"Dr Yee?" The mask muffles Clark's voice. He shifts it back on his head, revealing a crease on his forehead where the breathing apparatus has pinched his skin. His hairline is damp with sweat. "If you're all set, we'd like to move the bodies to the cool store now," he says.

"Cool store. Which cool store? You're not taking them to Puketutu Island?" Penny asks. It's one thing to store the corpses from the wharf in Kerr's former premises, but storing those poor Touching the Sun disciples there, even temporarily, when there is every chance Kerr is responsible for their murders? It's hard to stomach.

Even Clark can see the irony. "Unfortunately, we don't have much choice. With the morgue full, there is nowhere else. Better that these people are moved to Kerr's cool store, rather than be left to simmer where they are now. The bottom of that volcano is as hot as a wok."

"All the same, it doesn't feel right." Penny removes the protective booties and adds them to the pile for disposal.

"There's no way Kerr has access to the site if that's what you're worried about. Not since the police ministry seized the island," Clark adds. "We've removed all the group's records, changed the security codes, and Tanner has uniformed officers guarding the perimeter, at the gate…they're all over the place. Believe me, even if she wanted to, Sandi Kerr will never get to these poor people ever again."

Penny can't help but be sceptical. The woman has managed to evade the police at every turn. "What happens in a civil defence emergency?" she asks. "A city the size of Auckland has to have other contingencies?"

"We're not quite at that point, Dr Yee," Clark replies, but Penny has to wonder. So many dead and all of them as good as murdered. Still, where the city elects to store its deceased citizens is not her call, and she and Beaker have all the photos and samples they need for now. She nods her agreement, albeit reluctantly.

"Hang on, what about Cordell? Surely, he'll want to have a say about—" It's too late. Clark has his mask back on and is scurrying over the lip of the crater.

Penny gets cleaned up, then steps over the crime scene tape and trudges across to Matiu, a heavy sample bag slung over each shoulder.

Seeing her approach, Cerberus stretches the leash to the limit, bounding over to crowd her legs. He's so frantic to get close to her he almost knocks her over.

Penny buries her hands into the fur around his ears. "Hello, my good boy. Did you have fun with Carlos? Did you? Was that fun, then?" she says in the silly voice she saves only for him. The Lab nuzzles her thigh, encouraging her to keep scratching. A little of her tension drops away. There's nothing quite so joyful as cuddling a dog—a 'bundle of longing' as Pulitzer poet Mary Oliver called it—and even though she and Matiu only adopted Cerberus a few months ago, Penny couldn't imagine her life without him. "Any news on Charlotte and the baby?" she asks, her fingers still massaging under the dog's chin.

Like an old man, Matiu wince-creaks to his feet and brushes off his jeans. "Erica called to say she's heard from her. She's on a bus."

"Well, that *is* good news," Penny says cheerfully. Still scratching Cerberus, she tilts her chin towards the lip of the crater. "Under the circumstances."

Matiu's eyes cloud over and he clenches his palms. "Penny," he says through gritted teeth, "this business…"

"I know, I know." She leans her upper arm against the puriri, taking comfort in the solidity of its trunk. "Two mass murder events and a major earthquake before lunch. Let's hope the gods can hold fire for an hour or two because I don't know how much more I can take today. And I've been hanging out to go to the loo for ages."

Matiu's face softens and he grins. Reaching out, he lifts the sample bags off her shoulders, leaving her with only her satchel. "Gimme the bags, then. Here, you take Cerberus. Is Beaker coming?"

Free of the extra weight, Penny rolls her shoulder, working out a kink. "He wanted to go straight back to the lab, but I told him to go home and have a nap first. I don't want him carrying out benchwork when he's overtired—it's far too dangerous. He said he'll catch a lift in one of the vans."

"I wouldn't want to be seen dead in one of those vans."

"He'll be in the cab…oh. That was a joke."

Matiu gives her a punch on the arm. "Just checking you were awake. Come on, let's get you home." Hitching up the sample bags, he turns and sets off down the hill.

Penny grasps the trunk of the puriri. "Matiu, I can't. I don't have time to go home. I have to make a start on these samples."

Not bothering to look back, Matiu waves a hand in the air. "No benchwork when you're tired. Far too dangerous, Pen."

"Matiu, you don't—" Penny's phone vibrates in the satchel at her hip.

Hundreds of phones had gone off while they'd been working in the crater: desperate family members trying to get hold of the victims. They'd called and called and called until Penny was sure she'd heard every ringtone imaginable: Marimba, Xylophone, Star Wars, Crazy Frog, Pick up Your Phone by Mr T. Those unanswered ringers were achingly desolate. Her heart had gone out to the people on the other end of the line, people who were probably still unaware they would never speak to their loved ones again.

Rather than add another ringtone to the requiem, Penny had turned hers off. Now she scrambles to check her messages.

It's Mum. Fifteen missed calls—sixteen including this one—Mum's last two text messages filling the screen in full caps of neon yellow on a sky-blue background, no less.

—PANDORA, WE DO NOT APPRECIATE BEING IGNORED. CALL HOME IMMEDIATELY.

—PANDORA, YOUR FATHER AND I ARE STILL TRYING TO CONTACT YOU. WHERE ARE YOU BOTH? ARE YOU STILL AT MĀNGERE?

Puffing the air from her cheeks, Penny switches the device off, gathers up Cerberus, and hurries down the hill after Matiu. One thing is sure: right now nothing could be more dangerous than facing Mum and Dad.

Opening the rear door, Penny grabs one of the bags from the back seat and throws it over her shoulder. She could leave them in the car—these Cool-Spec specimen bags are designed to refrigerate biological samples for up to 24 hours—but ever since that misplaced bog body incident, Penny prefers to keep her samples close at hand.

"Why did you have to park so far away, anyway?" Penny asks while wrangling Cerberus out of the vehicle. "There was a space right out front. I saw it when we went past." For some weird reason, Matiu has elected to park the Solaris in a back alley a street back from Mum and Dad's.

"Pen, come on," Matiu says, lifting the remaining sampling bags off the back seat. He waits for the door to close automatically. "You know why. We *stole* this car from a crime scene. We can hardly park it on the street outside the house. You want me to get my probation revoked?"

Penny's eyes go wide, and she can't help panting: breath after breath. "*Stole* it," she sputters. She can feel herself slipping into hypocapnia. If she doesn't watch out, her blood pH will rise, and she'll go into respiratory alkalosis. She slows her breathing in an attempt to control the concentration of dissolved $C0_2$. "Matiu, what the hell?" she yelps. "You told me this was Dad's car!"

"Shhh. Pen. You might want to keep your voice down. If Mrs Vaughn at number 35 hears you, she'll have it broadcast via *DishIt* even before we even get inside the house."

Pursing her lips, Penny looks about furtively. The alley provides back yard access to a line of exclusive single-posh-family mansions, all bordered with stucco fences as high as the city regulations permit so the plebeians can't see how the other half lives and get ideas. With the exception of a few city-compulsory recycling bins, and some battered e-bikes used by non-live-in domestic staff, the alley is empty. No one at any upstairs windows that she can see. Still, you can't be too careful.

Penny lowers her voice to a hiss. "You told me it was a Yee fleet vehicle, one of a consignment. I distracted Officer Clark while you drove it off the ship! Oh my god, that means I'm complicit, doesn't it? I helped you to deceive the police. If Tanner finds out, I'll never get another contract with the department again..." Her fingers tingle.

Matiu shrugs. "That's OK. I don't remember there being any labs in prison. It only encourages the meth dealers, ya know?"

Penny's head is spinning now. Meth dealers? Prison. The penny drops. "I could go to prison! Matiu, I can't go to prison. I have a business to run. I have to pay Beaker. I still have to—" She's hyperventilating again. Fighting back nausea, she leans against Mrs Vaughn's back fence and puts her hands on her knees.

Matiu slips the sample bag off her shoulder. "Pen, calm down. I'm kidding, OK? It's definitely Dad's car. We didn't steal it. We were just making sure it didn't get impounded for a couple of years while Tanner's minions sort through the fiasco on the wharf."

Hyperventilating...

Breathing into her cupped hands, Penny looks over her fingers and glowers at her brother. It takes her a few moments to recover. Meanwhile, Cerberus takes advantage of the delay in the alley to lift his leg against one of the rubbish bins.

When she's got her breath back, Penny pushes away from the fence and cuffs Matiu on the arm. "Why even joke about something like that?" she says.

He pauses, his brow creased and his fingers fiddling with the latch on the Cool-Spec bag. "I don't know. Just thinking out loud, I guess. I'm worried about Dad."

"What are you on about? He had his medical last week. Mum said it was fine. No sign of diabetes or anything."

"I don't mean his health. I think he's in trouble. Like he might have inadvertently got himself involved in something shady. I mean, he asked me to steal the car." His hands full juggling the bags and also Cerberus' wandering leash, Matiu has dropped his leather jacket.

Penny bends to pick up it up. Shaking the dust off the leather, she drapes the jacket over her arm. "We've just been through all this. You said it's his car. You said we didn't steal it."

"It is, and we didn't. But there's something off about the whole thing."

Penny rolls her eyes. "Not this again. I know you have these premonitions and, sure, sometimes they turn out to be true, but this is *Dad* you're talking about."

"You think I don't know that? It's just there are things that don't add up."

"What things?"

Matiu's gaze follows Cerberus as the dog sniffs the tyre of one of the bikes. "I'm certain Dad knew we were at the wharf this morning, before we even arrived."

Penny cocks her head. "So? He was probably listening to the news online and put two and two together."

"At 2am?"

"Mum snores. Maybe he couldn't sleep."

"And then there's the way they've been phoning us all morning, wanting to know where we are. Dad *and* Mum. How many times did you say Mum called you?"

Penny sighs. "Sixteen missed calls..."

"And Dad's called me six times. That's twenty-two missed calls between them. Not to mention the times we actually picked up."

"The fleet cars have GPS tracking, so they've gotten used to knowing where we are. Plus, there was a major earthquake, Matiu. Of course, they were worried about us. Any parents would be. They were worried about Whaea Mārama, too. There's absolutely nothing shady about those phone calls. I'd be more worried if they *hadn't* called."

"But why have me remove the Solaris at all? Why the big hurry to get it off the *Yongyang*?"

"Maybe they've promised it to a big client."

"A prototype?"

Penny folds her arms. "I don't know, Matiu. Mum and Dad don't tell us everything. Maybe they've decided to retire and they want to upgrade the fleet and sell the company as a going concern."

Matiu shunts the Cool-Spec bag higher on his shoulder. "It still doesn't explain why they're in such a hurry to get their hands on the prototype, or why Dad insisted that I get you to use your influence with the police to do it."

Penny's stomach lurches. *He what?* Frowning, she stammers, "He.... because..." She clamps her mouth shut. She has no answer. Sure, Mum and Dad can be a pain. They're the quintessential helicopter parents: opinionated, overbearing, and always sticking their noses where they're not wanted, but there is no way they would ever put Penny and Matiu at risk, not willingly. Matiu's right: something's off.

"How serious do you think—" she begins, but Matiu cocks an eyebrow indicating Mrs Vaughn at one of the upstairs windows.

All charm and cheese, he gives the busybody a neighbourly wave. "Not now, sis," he says quietly. "Let's just play it cool and see how things play out, OK? We can talk about it later."

- Matiu -

As he walks away, leaving Penny pale and shaking in the alley behind him, Matiu surreptitiously fishes his phone from his pocket and checks the screen. It's a juggle, between sample bags and a heaving great golden Labrador, but he manages it. While he was waiting for Penny and Beaker to finish up, he had a chance to explore the Solaris some more, and tapped into the reversing camera and the dash camera, both of which feed into the integrated security system which has its own GPS tracking and network connection, which just needs to be integrated into the despatch command UI for Carlie to be able to track the car at all times. He'll put that off as long as he can. Meanwhile, he's synched the system up and he can keep an eye on both where the car is and what's going on around it from the comfort of his own pocket.

People might have killed for the sake of laying their hands on this car, so while Matiu's nervous about just leaving it parked on a swanky suburban street in plain sight, he's even more nervous about who might be watching their parents' apartment block, waiting for the car to rock up, ready to put a bullet through whoever steps out of it. Of course, he can't voice these fears to Penny. She's already on edge, and exhausted. Plus, she has to deal with their parents, very soon. That'll be harrowing enough, without adding a carjacking into the mix.

Not to mention he's going to have to answer to his father when they get upstairs. He was insistent they deliver the Solaris to the depot, and Matiu simply hasn't. Dad will be livid, at the disobedience, yes, but also for whatever reason it is that this damned car is giving him a stress ulcer. An ugly knot twists in his belly. This might not be the usual family dinner, where everything slides off Teflon Matty and burns Penny instead. Dad's hot as a firecracker right now, whatever's going on. But one thing Matiu knows for sure: whoever wants the Solaris knew to try and jack it off a freaking international cargo ship, and went in with enough hardware to start a civil war to achieve that. Not just one gang, but two. They're going to guess that the first place it's likely to go is either to the Yee transport yard or one of their personal residences. Despite the piles of charred corpses the Solaris has already generated, once the perps regroup, there'll be more. Matiu needs to stay one unpredictable step ahead of them the whole time. He needs to keep the car off any network except his own personal tether to his phone, because as soon as it touches a hub, anyone will be able to hack its location.

He waits for Penny at the corner, letting her catch up before they turn onto another neatly-appointed street where the buildings loom larger, multi-level apartment dwellings with elegant yet robust entranceways that could double as embassy security points in a crisis. As they walk, he scans the vehicles parked along the road, looking for watching faces, suspicious characters. Nothing jumps out at him, but he's not really sure what he's looking for. Kingi, maybe? A car hums down the street, windows tinted, giving nothing away.

"Let's just get inside, eh. I'm starving. Reckon we can crack into Mum and Dad's earthquake rations?"

Penny glances over her shoulder, watching the car go past. "I'm not sure today's little rumble really qualifies as enough of an emergency to break open the vault. But there might be some leftovers we can scavenge."

Matiu slows his walk, waits until the car rounds the bend before hurrying down to the apartment entrance and holding the gate open for Penny, scooting her through and pulling the gate shut before the car comes back. Better safe than sorry, on days like this.

CHAPTER 15

- Pandora -

Alerted by the apartment's AI system, Bituin is hovering on the landing when the lift opens, her slim fingers fluttering on the ties of her apron. "Penny…Matiu, thank goodness you've arrived," she gushes. She bustles forward, grabbing Cerberus' lead from Matiu. "Better let me have the dog. I'll find a spot for him in the shade on the veranda. You know how your parents are about pets in the house—"

She's talking too fast.

"Bituin, are you okay?" Matiu asks.

The housekeeper shakes her head. "It's your parents. I've never seen Mr and Mrs Yee so worried. Ever since breakfast, your dad's been patrolling back and forth like a beefeater at the Tower. I wouldn't be surprised if he's worn a track in the carpet."

Stepping around Cerberus, Penny leans in and gives Bituin a quick peck on the cheek. "Well, there was no need to worry. As you can see, we're both fine. Anyway, if Dad's been pacing, it'll give Mum an excuse to get the carpet-layers in, won't it?" She chuckles. "Although, when did Mum ever need an excuse?"

But Bituin doesn't return Penny's smile. "You don't understand." She twists the leash around her wrist. "Nine years I've worked for your parents, and they've never been this upset. Never. Not even when your aunt went missing."

"Didn't Amy explain that we were fine when she brought Whaea Mārama back?"

Lowering her eyes, Bituin stares at the marble entrance tiles.

"Bituin, what happened?" Matiu asks.

"Mr Yee shouted at her." Bituin almost chokes on the words. "He said she should've insisted you all come back together. He threatened to *fire* her."

"That's just bluster," Penny says. "Whaea Amy is like family. Dad would never fire her. Mum wouldn't let him, for a start."

The housekeeper looks up, her dark eyes shiny. "I don't know," she whispers. "Nothing has been right today. *Mrs Yee isn't wearing any makeup.*"

Penny's heart lurches. She looks at Matiu in horror. Their mother without makeup? "I think we'd better hurry," she says.

Bituin scrubs at her face with the back of her hand. "I'll see to the dog and then bring through some tea." She scuttles away, Cerberus trailing after her, his claws scritch-scritching on the marble.

"What'll I do with the sample bags?" Matiu asks.

"Maybe just leave them here, near the door."

"Allows for a quick getaway. Good thinking, Watson," Matiu quips grimly. He stacks the bags near the entrance and Penny lays his leather jacket on top of the pile.

"Let's do it, then," she says. She doesn't move.

Matiu doesn't move either.

"Come on."

"Age before beauty, Pen." He does a stupid swishy bow then sweeps his hand to the right, inviting her to lead the way.

Penny shivers. So even Matiu is rattled, and he's run with Hanson's gang, watched a mate immolated in an attack intended for him, battled a berserker on the roof of a skyscraper...

Oh for goodness sake. They're their parents. What could possibly happen?

Turning on her heel, Penny strides down the hall and throws open the double doors.

Dad is standing at the drinks table. He swivels, a glass in his hand, the liquid sloshing precariously. Penny swallows as his eyes widen and he lifts his chin, looking for all the world like a bull elephant about to stampede. Even his ears are flapping with rage. "Where the hell have you two been?" he roars.

"Working, Dad," says Matiu, strolling past Penny with his usual infuriating air of nonchalance. *Wasn't he the one who just insisted that she go first?*

"I was working a case," Penny stammers.

"Two cases, actually," Matiu says. "I've been driving her. I reckon we've covered half the city." He gives Dad a pointed look. "But of course you'll see that when you check the car's *gas consumption*."

Dad's jaw twitches. "You didn't reply to our messages. I called. Texted. Your mother called, too. We asked you both to come home."

"Yip, couldn't be helped," Matiu says. "Penny's been suited up like the Michelin man, and it's a bit hard to get your hands in your pockets for the phone."

"I'm assuming *you* weren't wearing a suit."

Penny shivers. Dad's voice is too even, too measured, too *contained*.

Matiu lifts the bottle off the drinks table and makes a show of checking the label. "Not initially, no, but I had a few things on my mind. Like securing a prototype, hiding it from the authorities, oh, and avoiding my probation officer, since both those things could land me back in prison...that sort of thing." He replaces the bottle.

Dad's eyes flash and his face colours. "Where have you stashed the Solaris? You were supposed to take it to the depot. I've got people waiting there to process it. You better not have stopped off to show it to any of your former associates. That car is—"

"Gee, Dad," Matiu says softly. "Here I was thinking you were worried about us."

"What? No!" Firing a look that is pure venom at Dad, Mum flies across the room and drags Penny and Matiu into a hug. "*Of course,* we were worried about you! Your father didn't mean that, Matiu. You have to understand that the stress has been unbearable. We've been beside ourselves all morning, haven't we, Hing? And then there was the earthquake, and we had no idea where you were and if you were safe…"

Ducking under her arm, Matiu slides out of Mum's grasp readily enough, but Penny's arms are stuck at her sides and, having already lost one of her captives, Mum doubles down, crushing Penny in a bear hug. She may not be wearing any makeup, but she's positively drenched in Lorde perfume. Penny's in dire risk of death by patchouli inhalation. She holds her breath while Mum rabbits on…

"Then when you didn't come back with Mārama, and Amy told us Pandora had been called away on another case, we were worried again. You're our *babies*. We can't bear to think of you in danger. That's why I wish you'd give up that lab job, Pandora. Everything's been worse since you've worked there."

"I don't work there, Mum, I own the business."

Matiu drops into one of Dad's Care-Less chairs and plonks his feet up on the footrest. "How is her working there worse, exactly?" he says.

Mum's voice rises. "Because she's working for the police, isn't she?"

"Kiri…" Dad sets his glass down. Some of the contents slop on the table.

"It's because what she's doing is so dangerous," Mum witters on. "Craig knows. He was telling us all about it."

Still trapped in Mum's embrace, Penny's spine does the Spidey-thing. Craig? What would an aide for the Transport Minister know about her job with the police? "What was that about Craig, Mum?"

"Yes, what did Craigie have to say, Mum?" The sweetness of Matiu's voice barely hides the challenge in his tone.

Penny glances at Dad and bites her lip. *Full bull elephant.*

Suddenly releasing Penny, Mum steps back and smooths her skirt. "Nothing. The same as everyone else," she says. Penny isn't fooled. She knows that look; it's the same look Mum gives Dad when she doesn't want him to know about a handbag she's just purchased, or a new pair of shoes, or that imported Iranian rug that turned up in the hallway. 'This? You remember this, darling. I bought it *ages* ago.'

Yep, they're definitely hiding something.

"Why don't you tell us what everyone's saying?" Matiu leans over, lifts a gooseberry from the fruit bowl and pops it in his mouth. "Penny and I haven't had time to follow the news." Like a fresh scab that's started to itch, Matiu can't leave it alone. *Let's just play it cool and see how things play out, he said.*

Mum's eyes flick to Dad. She gives a girly shrug. "Just that a whole pile of people died."

"On the wharves." Matiu's mouth is full of gooseberry.

"Yes, on the wharves. Where else?" She sits down, deflated, and clasps her hands in her lap.

"The police spokesman—" says Dad, taking up the baton.

"Noah Cordell," Penny says.

"Yes, him. He made a point of telling the press that he'd been *authorised* to say there'd been a gas explosion which had resulted in an unspecified number of deaths. But the man fiddled with his tie and his manner was all wink-wink-say-no-more, so anyone watching knew it wasn't just a gas explosion. Some of the other media outlets are speculating that the gangs were involved."

"Oh, they're involved." Matiu drops his feet to the floor with a clunk. "I recognised a few faces from Hanson's mob."

"Matiu!" Penny exclaims. "You can't say that. We're not supposed to give out details of an ongoing investigation to members of the public. It's in my contract."

"It's not ongoing. Not for you. Tanner threw you off the case."

"It doesn't matter anyway, because your father and I aren't members of the public," Mum says taking Penny's hand. "We're your family, which means we have a right to know what's going on. Isn't that right, Hing?"

"Family has a right to know what's going on," Matiu says. He gets to his feet. "Funny you should say that because Penny and I could say the same thing."

Oh no...

Matiu and Dad square off. Matiu clenches his fists. Dad steps forward.

All at once there's a rustling outside the door.

Thank goodness! "That'll be Bituin with the tea," Penny chirps. She turns, shaking off Mum's hand, but before she can take a step, the doors fly open and for the second time today she's confronted with Craig Tong.

The only consolation is, at least this time she's wearing all her clothes.

- Matiu -

"I bloody knew it!" Matiu spins away from Dad, crossing the space towards Tong in a few easy strides, fuelled by indignation. "You've been tailing us! What the hell, Tong?!"

Craig holds up both hands, as easily a display of innocence as a rugby fend. "Woah, buddy. Take a breath, shall we?"

Penny's suddenly outstretched arm catches Matiu in the chest, the lightness of her touch enough to halt his charge. "Matiu, just calm down."

"You followed us from the docks this morning, you were at Penny's apartment, you just cruised by on the street outside and now here you are, busy Mister Department of Transport guy with nothing better to do on the day of a major civil disaster than keep tabs on people like us. What gives, Tong? Spill it!"

"Matiu!" Mum's shriek is nothing compared to the rushing in his ears, the thunder of blood and rage and the old Matiu wanting to leap forth, unleash hell on this guy who seems to keep showing up where he's least wanted at the most inconvenient moments. But Tong has had Matiu laid out on the floor once already today so, even fuelled by all the boiling fury beneath his skin, he hauls back.

"Why are you following us?!"

"*MATIU!*" Their father's roar might've rattled the crystals on the shelf, or it may have been an aftershock. Either way, Matiu draws a long, shuddering breath, bites his tongue, and holds Craig Tong in his angry glare. "Craig is doing as I asked him, because he knows how to follow instructions, unlike *some people* in this house."

The temperature in the room drops by several degrees. In the silence that follows, Craig takes a step forward, allowing Bituin to pass him with the tea tray and place it down on the table. She then retreats, closing the door behind her and leaving Craig standing there, fiddling with the buttons on his sleeves like some action movie hero.

Mum goes to the table and starts pouring tea, the cups chattering on the saucers as the teapot trembles in her grip. "Craig has been such a wonderful support in these difficult times," she prattles. "Things are very dangerous out there and Craig has been kind enough to—"

"He's not kind enough to *anything*," Matiu interjects, backing up now, half-turning so he can see both Dad and Craig at the same time, like the pair of them are hunting wolves and he the injured deer, the scent of blood in their noses. "There's something wrong about this whole thing, the attack at the docks, the car, all of it. You two know something, and don't try to shut me down, because Dad's been on my back about that bloody car all day and Craig should have far more important things to be doing right now than checking up on us."

"Now wait—" Tong tries, but Matiu ploughs on.

"How long have you been stalking us, Tong? And all this bullshit, taking my sister out to dinner, making all those dreamy eyes at her?" Penny turns, her cheeks suddenly pale, her mouth falling open like the hinge in her jaw has failed. "How long are you going to keep pretending like maybe you and her have some sort of romance going on, when you're just using her to stay close to whatever the hell it is Dad's got going on? You think I can't connect the dots? Shit's been going south ever since we had those Chinese suits come in off that ship, way back last year. I drove them in from the airport to meet with Dad and the Ministry, and now boom, another ship out of China and the gangs are all over it, and here you are, with your boardroom suit and your Jason Bourne moves, turning up conveniently every time little Matiu needs to be put in his place."

He expects Tong to protest, to try to placate him with that smooth, creamy grin of his, the locker room camaraderie, but his face is shifting, becoming grim.

"Whatever crazy ideas you might've got in your head, Matiu, I really do like your sister." The smile flashes, silver like a fish in a lake, catching the sunlight and all for Penny, then vanishes. "But you'd be better off putting your misplaced suspicions up on a shelf out of reach of children. You'll just get yourself into trouble you can't get out of."

Matiu stalks toward him, fingers flexing. "Sometimes that's just what I do, Tong. Sometimes I get into trouble that's more than I can handle, but I sure as hell don't run away from it."

"Enough!"

Small yet compelling, the voice stops him in his tracks. All eyes turn to face the hall doorway, the spectre hanging there in the sunlit dust, wraith-thin and frail as dry paper. "Enough," Mārama croaks again, clutching the doorframe, her fingers skeletal against the ivory paint. Her eyes pierce him like two hot knives, stabbing him with their accusations of disappointment.

The fight drains from Matiu and he spins away, rushing to her side.

"No fighting," she murmurs, wrapping an arm around his waist and leaning into him as he holds her. "There's enough fighting out there. We don't need it in here too."

He hadn't realised how little there was left of her until this moment, her bones like twigs beneath old flax. A husk still clinging to life, refusing to die, because there are things that must be done. "We're not fighting, we're...discussing."

"Be a good boy, son. Fetch me a cup of tea."

Gently, Matiu helps her across the room and sits her in Dad's big recliner, rocks the footrest up, drapes a blanket over her legs. Awkward quiet layers the room. Matiu can feel Dad's eyes on his back, senses his seething, yet what's worse is that he knows Tong isn't looking at him. He's looking at Penny. And she's looking back at *him*. He wants to scream.

"Sugar?" Mum offers, her voice brittle and her hands shaking as she pours a fresh cup for Mārama.

"Just milk," Matiu corrects, and turns to take the cup from her.

Mārama's eyes are half-lidded, the effort of the past moments having robbed her of her strength. Matiu sets the cup down on the little table beside the chair and rubs the back of her hand. She whispers something, too faint for Matiu to hear. He leans in. "What's that?"

"He's close," she mutters. "So close."

"Who?"

"Don't let him in. He'll knock, he'll hammer against the earth. He will come with the rising tide. This is the moment. Save your fight, Matiu. Save it for when it matters."

"Mārama—?" But she's gone again, drifted off to the haunted places beyond.

Matiu sits for a long moment, Mārama's fingers like the drying branches of a desiccated bush in his hand.

"Well," Mum says at last, "since we're all here, shall we have some lunch? Craig, would you like to join us?"

Matiu strokes those fingers, so like his own and yet so unlike. So much a part of him and yet so distant. So thin, like the essence of her has been sapped away to that other place, slowly eating her body just like it has eaten her mind. But not her heart. Her heart remains firmly here. He can feel it beneath her skin, thready but solid when it comes. Determined. He could stay here all day, turn his back on it all, and just let his pulse keep rhythm with hers. Knowing that these times must be growing short. She won't be with them for much longer, not as long as the place beyond keeps calling to her. Keeps feeding on her.

"Matiu? You hungry?"

Penny's hand on his shoulder. He should go. He just doesn't want to, in case this is his last chance to have these moments with her. Every time he walks away from her, it might be for the last time.

CHAPTER 16

- Pandora -

Lunch! Penny hasn't got time for lunch. She should really head straight to the lab and get to work on the samples stowed in the Cool-Spec bags in her parents' hallway. With the huge job of identifying the bodies still to be completed, relatives of the dead at Māngere won't have been informed of the tragedy yet, but as soon as they are, their natural response will be to ask questions. Grief-stricken and incredulous, they'll want to learn everything they can about their loved ones' last moments.

—What was in the Kool-Aid they'd ingested?

—What effects would they have noticed?

—How long did it take?

—Did they suffer?

Using practical, methodical, *painstaking* scientific analysis, Penny and Beaker should be able to provide families with those answers. They can isolate the poison, its concentration, perhaps even its source. They can extrapolate from the agent's data safety sheets and online medical databases to point to the likely effect of the poison and assure them of the rapidity of their passing. Yee Scientific will be able to provide those answers at least. Determining why a legion of men and women took their own lives is another story, the human psyche a never-ending enigma and mob behaviour just as elusive. Why, for example, would a group of people—men and women with families and friends and lovers, with *children*—willingly descend into the cone of a volcano, lay themselves down in a koru shape, and carry out the most immutable of acts? Why *that* volcano? Why that shape, which is so imbued with meaning? Didn't they realise that the koru is a symbol of life, not death? And if they were hurting so much inside that they couldn't bear to go on, why didn't they say something? Why not reach out and let someone know? Why go to this extreme?

Why?

Penny shivers. Even with the most advanced technologies available, science might never be able to answer those questions, the truth like a starry spinifex seed tumbling along a windswept beach, the feckless gusts lifting it just out of reach, answers that little Carlos, wondering why his mother chose to leave him, could chase for a lifetime.

Mum's voice interrupts Penny's train of thought. "Pandora, why don't you take Craig into the dining room and keep him entertained while Dad and I help Bituin rustle up lunch."

It's a rhetorical question, phrased as a command. Penny wants to protest, since her analyses might provide the only solace for the victims' families, but one glance at Matiu and Mārama and she relents. They're huddled together, Matiu with his hand over Mārama's, comforting her as he did after the earthquake. Her brother and his birth mother need each other right now. An hour's delay isn't going to change the outcome for the victims. Besides, she needs to eat something if she hopes to stay on her feet much longer.

Penny looks again at Matiu, then murmurs, "This way, Craig." Still carrying her tea, she shows him through the double doors into the dining room. "Beatrice, please open the curtains," she says.

"My pleasure," the smart system replies and the voluminous taffeta curtains, closed to keep out the heat, pull back to reveal the expansive view across the harbour to the city. In the CBD, the Sky Tower spire cuts into the faint swirls that still streak the skyline, the southern lights so fierce they have persisted into the daylight hours.

Craig leans in, whispering in her ear, "It's just lunch, right, or should I be making a getaway now?"

Matiu had talked of a getaway only twenty minutes ago.

Penny takes a sip of her tea. "Craig Tong, surely you're not afraid of a ham sandwich?" she quips.

Craig places his hand on the window frame and stares across the harbour, his expression sober. "I'm fine with a sandwich. Hell, she can even put ham on it if she likes, but if your mother brings out crispy skin suckling pig, no matter how good it looks, I'm out of here."

Penny giggles at the mention of the Chinese wedding banquet dish. "Oh, so you don't believe in marriage?" she says teasingly.

He turns to her, brown eyes startling against the blue. "I'm all for marriage," he says softly and, in her hand, Penny's teacup rattles on its saucer. "It's mothers who scare the crap out of me!"

A wave of emotion floods her and Penny isn't sure if she's disappointed or relieved. It's a joke. Reference to a conversation they shared a couple of months ago. They'd been at The Sedge restaurant, an *avant garde* eatery on the city waterfront. After a couple of wines, Craig had told Penny about his mother, a woman the same height as a domestic broom and weighing little more than cushion stuffing. Newly bereaved, Mrs Tong had eschewed moving into the Titirangi townhouse of Craig's brother and his family, electing instead to live with Craig. Now, the diminutive Chinese woman was severely cramping Craig's style, killing him with kindness and stinking up his posh inner-city bachelor pad with her favourite Chinese delicacies. Some of which required long periods fermenting in dark places.

Penny giggles. "I doubt even Mum could rustle up a roast pig in ten minutes, but you never know, my dad might have some 100-year-old duck eggs stashed in the laundry cupboard."

Craig wrinkles his nose as if he's just got a whiff of those sulphurous century eggs. He rolls his eyes. "Pen, please, don't get me started."

Deliberately, Penny places her empty teacup on the sideboard. "Why were you following us this morning, Craig?"

Craig puts his own cup down and stuffs his hands in his pockets. "It's a long story," he says. "I'm not sure you'll believe it."

Penny folds her arms across her chest and says nothing.

"Okay. Here goes." He straightens his tie, pushing the knot up against his Adam's apple before releasing it again. "Last year, your parents entered into a joint venture with the Chinese to fund some ground-breaking research, something which could drastically change New Zealand's future." He pauses. Coughs. "I don't think even your dad realised just how important that relationship would turn out to be. He was just trying to keep his business humming along, you know? Reinvesting profits to create a new business opportunity. It's good practice if you want to stay current. Anyway, my boss—"

"The Transport Minister," Penny states.

His hands stray to his tie again. "Um…right. The Minister. Yes. Well, given the importance of the Yee family fleet to New Zealand's transport infrastructure, and in light of the sensitive nature of the research, the um…Minister wanted to make sure your parents didn't find themselves in a situation where they were… um…inadvertently influenced by a foreign power. So, they assigned me to monitor the transaction, inserting me into the negotiations through a role established for me at the Transport Ministry and also asking me to develop a more intimate relationship with members of your family—"

Penny holds her palms up, urging him to stop. "Hang on, hang on…"

"Penny, I know this sounds—"

"Wait. You're trying to tell me you're a government spook, and you've been wooing me in order to get closer to my parents?"

"You have to understand; we were worried that Matiu—"

Her eyes water. "You're a *spy*."

Craig twiddles a bevelled cufflink. "Penny, I'm so sorry. I wanted to tell you—"

"The tail this morning; that was just routine spy stuff?"

He stares at the floor. "Yes."

Penny can't help it. She bursts out laughing. "Honestly, Craig," she sputters though a fit of the giggles, her sides already beginning to cramp. "That was terrible. If you're going to have a hope in hell of making it as a politician, you're going to have to learn to lie better than that!"

"Stand clear of the doors," Beatrice announces.

Wearing a frilled Amber Peebles skirt, Mum sweeps into the room preceded by a fresh spritz of Lorde perfume. Unlike earlier, her makeup is perfectly applied.

"How are my lovebirds getting on?" she says, sending Penny into a new fit of laughter.

Red-faced, Craig steps away from Penny to the window. "We're fine, thank you, Kiri."

Penny doesn't answer. She is incapable of speaking. Ten minutes later, she's still trying to get herself under control when Bituin enters with the sandwiches.

- Matiu -

Matiu steps away from the recliner, the room grown quiet around him. Mārama has drifted away again, drawn down by the exhaustion of the day, the heat, of wrestling her own demons in a body grown ever weaker. He looks around for Dad, expecting him to be there, waiting in the shadows for a chance to strike without all the women in his life coming between them. But Dad is in the kitchen, getting lunch for his guests, because that's what they are, Penny and Matiu. Guests. Strangers under their parents' roof.

Never mind that the city is reeling from a major earthquake and two massacres. Or that the thin line between this world and the one beyond grows thinner by the minute. Lunch is still lunch, and the protocols must be observed. Napkins, and the right size forks. As if any of it actually *matters*.

His thigh buzzes. He checks the message.

NO REAL AXEL WEIS. BEST RESULT IS ALEX WISE. CHECK IT.

Matiu drifts over to the couch and slumps down, tapping into the zip link Scour has sent. A visual fills the little screen, optimised for neural link outputs, designed to fill the air in front of the viewer if their hardware supports it. Matiu never bought into neural buffs, always had enough going on in his head without needing any more getting in there. So he scrolls around the data report, old school style. Scour's search has summarised all the key results in a sort of webbed starburst of words. In this case, rather than a single central point there are two central nodes, linked by a wavering line; a query added in by Scour to compare the results. Axel Weis with Alex Wise.

Axel Weis is an author, but clearly a pseudonym, because the only results that can be found are to a handful of self-published works covering a range of topics from organic chemistry to self-sufficiency to mythic lore and the spiritual nature of the unseen. But aside from the books and the obligatory social media presence, nothing real.

Alex Wise, on the other hand, is a scientist, Auckland-based but with work stretching as far afield as the South Island and even, on rare occasions, into parts of South-East Asia. Privately funded R&D trips that caught the attention of the scientific community and made the journals. Extravagant. The two personalities would appear to be unrelated, and Matiu is about to swipe the whole search away as a waste of time before he reads an article title that turns his blood cold.

AUCKLAND MEDICAL TEAM BREAKS NEW NANOTECH LIMITS

He taps into the link, scans it. Most of the report is beyond him, but about halfway down, another name jumps out at him, and the blood that was already cold goes icy.

Buchanan.

One of Sandi Kerr's collaborators and victims, a medical researcher who Matiu found in a burning building, his eyes plucked from his skull. Buchanan was using nanotech to combat cancer cells. Wise and Buchanan were working in nanotech together. It's not hard to make the connection from Wise to Kerr, and if Axel Weis really is the laziest author-anagram-pseudonym ever, and Wise is using that persona as a cover for his Touching the Sun activities, then...

Charlotte is still in danger. She was on a bus, Erica said, last they talked, a brief word before Erica's battery died. What sort of bus? There were mini-buses parked at the bottom of Mt Māngere, empty. Matiu sits terribly still for a moment, his fingers cold, his stomach a yawning pit. *He'll hammer against the earth,* Mārama had said.

The deaths on Māngere are not the end of it. Kerr wasn't there, Wise wasn't there, and the earth was not torn asunder by the thing from beyond, the thing Matiu has fought against toe-to-toe in the darkness and driven back once before. They haven't succeeded yet. The sacrifice has never been enough. Even all those bodies were too few to tear down the wall between this world and the next.

The vision hits him hard, pinning him to the couch and knocking the air from his lungs. Miles of gentle rolling peaks and hillsides, a landscape rippling beneath a fiery sky, the ocean a roaring tide on all sides. The hilltops vomit smoke into the clouds, and the soft skin of the earth tears open, reducing the cityscape to pulver. Chaos swirls around a point, the sky above twisting into the shape of a koru as the clouds condense, pregnant with choking ash, but Matiu can't tell where. The city is a burning wreck, adrift in a raging sea, caught in the grip of a cyclone.

And from that point, reaching up to the twisted sky, they come. Sinuous and shining black, they writhe from the shattered earth, pulsing and lashing, and they drag something with them, some leviathan mass, its hungry shriek of triumph the howl of the storm, the torment of this broken world.

Matiu soars over the rubble of a city cast down, his mind's eye drawn inexorably toward the chaos at its centre, the stake in its heart. Below him, bodies by the thousand, stampeded by the wounded and the terrified, the raw power of panic and blind horror. The Sky Tower looms closer, like a needle puncturing the sky, but that is not the centre. The harbour bridge heaves and roils, shedding metal from its hide like a chained beast straining to break free, but that is not the eye of the storm. A peak rises behind the waste of the city centre, behind the splintered skeletons of burning skyscrapers, and from its maw the fire rises, embracing the behemoth that has split the veil between worlds, the thing Matiu has faced, dreamed, dreaded.

He races on, weaponless and without a plan, seeing only the creature in all its dark splendour swelling to blacken the sky, and something else. Something clinging to the tentacles that weave and lash. A figure. Small, too far away to make out a face, but Matiu knows who it is, knows it like the blood in his veins.

He cannot fight this. Mārama was right, they should've run. The tide rolls in, time runs out. Everything falls. All he has are his hands, these strange, glowing hands...

He looks down. His palms are open, and spread between them is a ball of light, too bright to gaze upon, a miniature sun whorled around with coiling patterns. Its heat burns him. Surely, it will burn the beast as well.

The nightmare rushes in. He raises an arm, filling the darkness with light. The face of the figure that rides the monster, his face, cracks a demonic grin...

Matiu gasps, sits up.

The room is dark, quiet but for the hushed breath of the aircon. Mārama's eyes are open, staring into his. Seeing what he saw. The curse of the blood that binds them.

Sucking down breaths, he stumbles to the window, pushes the curtain aside. Auckland, hazy and sprawling. It's the same hot summer day. The sky is not on fire. The world is not rent asunder.

"Not yet," Mārama whispers, as if reading his mind.

But he knows where it will happen. And he knows who will ride the beast when it comes.

CHAPTER 17

- Pandora -

"Pandora, a little decorum in front of our guest, please! What on earth did you say to her, Craig? I haven't seen my girl this giggly since her teens."

Hhhheeee...

Craig moves the flower arrangement from the table so Bituin can set down the platter, and smiles weakly. "Um…I'm really not sure." Carefully sliding the vase of protea stems onto the sideboard, he turns to Mum. "Something about ham sandwiches maybe."

"You don't like ham?" Mum's eyes get that wild look and she goes into full camp-mother mode. "Do you prefer chicken? Or perhaps a slice of roast pork? Bituin, is there still some roast pork in the fridge?"

"No, no, please, there's no need. Ham is fine. I like ham," Craig says quickly.

Roast pork! Ppppffffft...

Mum glances at Penny, who is desperately trying to suppress a guffaw, and her face brightens. "Aaah." She waggles her index finger in front of her face. "You two don't fool me for a minute, you know. Not one minute. You think I can't see what's going on here? I'm not so old that I can't remember how it feels to be young and in love."

At the word 'love,' Mum lays a hand on Craig's cheek and Penny has to admire him for facing his fears, because the man barely flinches.

Penny snatches at the paisley armrest of Mum's Queen Anne wingback. She can't breathe. *Make her stop. Please!* Penny implores Craig with her eyes.

"Mrs Yee…Kiri…I really don't think your daughter—"

"That's the thing about sweethearts, isn't it?" Mum barrels on. "You start out playing it cool, acting aloof and pretending that you don't give a damn, but you can't keep secrets from your family: we all know it's a subterfuge, a ruse to cover the truth."

Nooo! It's too late. All this talk of secrets and subterfuge has triggered her limbic system, tickling the amygdala and the hippocampus in her brain, which then activate the motor region, and Penny's off again, awash with dopamine and endorphins and doubled over in spasms of uncontrolled laughter. By the time Matiu joins them for lunch, Penny feels like she's done a twenty-minute ab work-out and planked for another five, but she's managed, at least, to wrestle her laughter back to the occasional muffled snort.

"Where's Mārama?" Mum asks. "And your father? He can't be still on the phone?"

"Haven't seen Dad, but Mārama's tired, Mum. I took her back to the guest room to lie down."

Mum clucks in disapproval. "It's this morning's earthquake, and that awful woman abandoning her in the thick of it. It's got her all unsettled."

"Yes, that'll be it," Matiu says. As usual, Mum doesn't catch the sarcasm.

Camp-mother persona again: "I'd better go and check on her. Bituin, would you mind making up a tray and taking it through to the guest room, please? Lunch for two. I'll have mine with Mārama. See if I can coax her to eat something."

Suddenly chastened, Penny's laughter evaporates. Poor Mum. It isn't easy for any of them to see how insubstantial Mārama has become. How anxious and birdlike. Each unsettling life event driving her deeper into the fog of her psychosis. She's like one of those old-fashioned Post-It notes: even the smallest knock and her lucidity peels away. Matiu doesn't see it that way, of course. Tethered to one another for all time, Matiu sees only beauty and poetry in Mārama's singularity. Perhaps he sees a certain strength there too, because Mārama is nothing if not resilient. The thing is, if Mārama were to let go completely, if she stops struggling and lets the tide take her where it will, Penny fears Matiu might sink with her.

"Craig, I hope you'll excuse me," Mum says. "Family calls."

"Of course," Craig says, taking her hand in farewell. Hopeless at lying, he isn't lacking any of a politician's oily charm.

"Beatrice, doors please," Mum says. Craig relinquishes her hand and Mum leaves the room with a swish of her Amber Peebles' skirt. Since every action requires an equal and opposite reaction, Dad enters from the other end of the room before the doors are fully closed.

"Where's your mother?" he asks.

"Not joining us," Penny says.

"Gone to look in on Mārama," Matiu adds.

Penny imagines a flicker of annoyance on Dad's face, then it's gone, replaced with his usual all-business demeanour. "Well, let's eat then, shall we?" he says. "Please, take a seat, Craig."

Matiu and Penny sit in their usual seats opposite Dad and Craig. In Mum's absence, Penny lifts the platter and offers it first to their guest and then to her male relatives. She knows she shouldn't, that you should always push back against centuries of gender and cultural conditioning, but she's been up since before 3am, hasn't eaten since yesterday, and simply doesn't have the energy right now. Sometimes you have to pick your battles.

"So how about you give us a sit rep, Craig," Dad asks, brushing a stray crumb off his sleeve onto his napkin.

Caught unawares, Craig covers the lower half of his face, swallowing his mouthful before replying. "Sir?"

"The earthquake. The traffic congestion," Dad prompts.

It amazes Penny that there are *any* cars on the roads these days. A couple of decades ago, the census results showed there was a car for every person in the country. That was before rising fuel costs, import taxes, tight family budgets, and climate consciousness stepped in and the numbers of vehicles on the road declined sharply. But in an earthquake the last thing people are thinking about is climate change.

"Oh. Right," Craig replies. "Unless there's another big quake, Transport don't expect the disruption on the main arterials to last much more than a few hours. There might be a knock-on effect later today at around five. Mostly, people have gotten used to the earthquake swarms, but a big one like this morning gives everyone the jitters. For a while there, it was crazy. People cramming the streets trying to get home. I was out on Favona Road near Māngere earlier and got a peek at the traffic on the South Western Motorway. Eight lanes, all at a standstill. It was like looking at queues for Disneyland, and in *this* heat. I imagine there were some hot tempers out there."

Penny nearly drops her sandwich. Favona Road is near Māngere. She glances at her brother. Had Matiu noticed?

Matiu pours himself a glass of water from a carafe on the table. "Favona Road."

Yup, he noticed.

"That's a long way from the Ministry offices, isn't it?" Matiu goes on. "What were you doing over there?"

Reaching for another sandwich, Craig throws him a crooked smile. "Avoiding those congested motorways."

Matiu stands up. Slowly, he sets his napkin on the table and rubs his palms together. "Why don't you just come clean and tell us why the hell you were following us this morning?"

"I wasn't following you—"

Matiu slaps his hand on the table. "Bullshit."

"Matiu!" Dad pushes his chair back, the table still between them. "That's enough. Craig has already explained why you saw him this morning. There was nothing sinister about it. He was worried about Pandora, that's all."

Matiu sneers. "Oh he was worried about her, was he?"

In stark contrast to Mum, Dad's sarcasm antenna works just fine. "Yes. He was." Dad walks around the table and stands in front of Matiu. Not in his personal space but almost. A boardroom power play. "Just so you're aware, I wouldn't have known about the events on the wharf if Craig hadn't phoned to tell me. He could have ignored it, but knowing the police had engaged Pandora, he took it upon himself to call me."

Matiu doesn't back down. "I'm not buying it."

"Why is it so hard for you to believe that Craig has strong feelings for your sister?"

Matiu's jaw ripples.

Penny's teeth ache. Do they have to argue about her when she's right here? But it's the fact they're arguing and not the content that concerns her most. Without the intervention of Mārama's fragility and Mum's trusty pot of tea, they're likely to kill each other. Those two have always been like fire and water: Matiu's hot-headedness pitted against Dad's icy resolve. Not for the first time, Penny wonders if Matiu inherited his fiery temperament from his birth father? There was no way of knowing. Mārama, destroyed by the relationship, had never revealed his identity and Mum has never really had any interest in finding out; in the early years because Matiu's birth father might have turned up to lay claim to the baby, putting paid to the whāngai-adoption of the little boy Mum so desperately wanted, and now because questions about Matiu's paternity might push Mārama off the ledge and into the abyss of insanity.

Matiu cackles. "You know, I'm not sure who's more stupid: you or her. People like Tong don't date girls like Penny. Can't you see he's *playing* with her? Buttering her up with his posh suit and last-minute reservations at The Sedge. What I want to know, is why?"

Penny can't breathe. It's as if she's stuck on a crowded train. *People like Tong don't date girls like her.*

Dad rounds the table. "Now look…"

Her chest tightens. *People like Tong don't date girls like her.* If that's true, why had Craig been following them? When Penny had demanded an explanation, he fed her that cock-and-bull story about being a spy and she'd been too busy laughing to ask for the real reason.

Suddenly, Craig pings the side of his water glass with a knife, the sound signalling the end of the round. "Matiu, Hing, please. If I could explain."

The Yee men turn, their eyes flashing: hot and cold.

"Go on," Dad says carefully.

"You're both right."

Penny frowns. *What?*

"Obviously I called Hing as soon as I learned that Penny had been called out to the incident on the wharf. I was worried about her safety."

Matiu rolls his eyes. "I suppose you're going to tell us that you rushed down to the wharf to check on her."

Craig takes Penny's hand, looking at her when he replies, "Yes."

Matiu scoffs.

"But that's not the only reason I went."

Penny pulls her hand back.

"I don't have to tell you that the Yees own the largest private transport network in the country," Craig continues. "For that reason alone the fleet is listed in the country's national security plan as an essential emergency resource. Naturally, when I received the notification from the Ministry this morning, I went to the wharf to get the lay of the land. Then, when Hing said his new research prototype was on the ship at the centre of the tragedy and that Matiu had secured it, I followed you to make sure you weren't followed."

Matiu raises his eyebrows. “You followed us to make sure we weren’t followed. Security of the nation’s transport network. Seriously, is anyone buying this crap?”

“Matiu, I saw you both leave in the prototype. What if someone else had seen you? Whispers high up were already talking about gang war. I couldn’t take the risk.”

Matiu stares at him, the kiri tuhi on his face darkening with menace. “What if they didn’t see us but followed you?”

“They didn’t. Trust me.”

“That’s just it. *I don’t.*”

“Maybe we should give him the benefit of the doubt,” Penny says. “I have a hunch he’s telling the truth. He’s not very good at lying.”

“Every gang member in the city might be after us and we should put our trust in your hunches?” Matiu pats her gently on the shoulder. Penny knows Matiu loves her, yet even so, a thousand years of patriarchy is conveyed in that tiny gesture.

She grasps her brother by the wrist. “Sometimes you have hunches,” she whispers.

- Matiu -

Penny’s grip is cold, ice to Matiu’s burning skin. Her touch, so gentle yet somehow so firm, holds him there. It’s the hand of the big sister who comforted him all those times he was tormented by the voice in his head, the ghost at his shoulder. As Dad and Craig Tong loom before him like a pair of hunting dragons, flames licking along their lips, the firm grip of her calm reason holds back the madness.

“Sometimes you have hunches.”

He’s not sure if she means him especially, his visions of terrible things that might be, or just people in general, herself included, but her point is clear enough. “You’re a scientist,” he grumbles. “You’re meant to work with evidence, not feelings.”

“It all starts with feelings, though. First there’s the feeling that you want to know the truth, then you get a feeling for what the truth might be. Then you go looking for that truth. If we’d never wondered what all the bright lights in the sky might really be, we might’ve never built telescopes and discovered that the stars are suns just like ours, with worlds all their own. If we’d never grieved for those who died of sickness and disease, we might never have searched for cures, learned medicine. It all starts with feelings. That’s where my evidence is, Matiu.” She taps her chest with her other hand. “It starts in here.”

It’s a bluff, it has to be. She’s defusing Dad and Tong, putting herself on the line to talk Matiu back from something he’d otherwise regret. He hopes she doesn’t end up regretting it more than he would’ve regretted laying into Tong. Laying into Dad. “I should take you back to the lab. You’ve got heaps to get done.”

“I can drive her,” Tong offers cheerily, as if all the tension of the past minutes has just drained away like the last of the coffee from the pot. “You’re going to deliver the Solaris to the depot, remember?”

“What a good idea,” Dad agrees. “The sooner that car is locked up safely, the happier we’ll all be.”

"Fine," Matiu growls, something about the exchange rankling in the back of his mind, though he can't quite figure out what. "I'll drop the damn car off." With a huff, he buries himself in opening up a ham sandwich and adding lots of mayonnaise and pepper. His hand hovers over the bowl of salad leaves, microgreens by the looks of it, and then snatches up the sandwich and stomps towards the front door, feeling all those eyes on his back. He doesn't say goodbye.

CHAPTER 18

- Matiu -

On the street, the heat continues to thump down, rolling across the city in waves. Matiu chews his sandwich, sweet and salty, occupying his hands and his thoughts so he won't dwell on whatever the hell is going on that he just can't work out.

The Solaris is right where he left it. Aside from its unfamiliar, alien lines, it's not a spectacular vehicle. Not likely to draw the eye of anyone in this neighbourhood at least. In fact, it almost looks like the sort of car an enthusiast might build in their own workshop, moulding panels out of fibreglass and rendering components from nylon or spun steel on a 3D printer. Only when you do that, you tend to finish the job by making the whole thing unique. This car is so white and bland it just blends in unless you're looking for it. Yet it's the finish that makes it so strange. The way the light hits the paint, it seems to shimmer and shift, like there's some invisible prismatic layer hitting the back of the eye, outside the visible spectrum, that he just can't see. What is up with that?

The doors unlock as he steps close and he climbs in, preparing himself to be hit by stifling heat. The car's interior is cool. Weirder and weirder. As the dash lights up, the battery display presents at 100%.

The pieces finally snap together. The strangeness of the surface, the battery readings, the cool interior. The whole car is photovoltaic, a heat sink soaking up solar rays and feeding the batteries. Matiu turns to peer closely at the window. A lattice of fine silvery lines, practically invisible, runs through the glass. Even the windows are part of the grid. It's a self-charging electric car. Like the impossibility of perpetual motion, the self-charging electric has been the holy grail of the eco-transport industry for decades, knocked back year after year by the oil moguls. Someone had done it, and it probably shouldn't have been a surprise it'd be the Chinese. There'd be a catch, of course. Long drives by moonlight were out, for a start. And if you weren't paying to put fuel and oil in the car, you'd be paying to replace batteries as they wore out. There'd be some economics attached to it somewhere that kept some rich fat bastards afloat, but that was a conversation for another time.

He taps the motor to life and pulls out onto the street. The Solaris runs with barely a hum, the whisper of new tyres on hot tarmac. It'd certainly make a difference to the company balance sheets, not having to pay for fuel and servicing on a whole fleet of these. But looking after an electric is a whole different game than maintaining a combustion engine. He'd love to take this by someone who knows a bit more, but even Matiu can see the folly of that. Somehow, probably through the Chinese connection to the gangs, people know about this car and will want to get their hands on it. Memories of Screech flicker by, his body parts in bloody pools on the concrete floor, the chop shop boiling into flames. Scour, burned by Matiu Yee and not wanting to get involved.

Yee, too dangerous to be around. It was one thing being part of the gang, working the seedy underside of the city. That had been a game. This business of being a responsible part of a private corporation is downright deadly.

He dials Erica. The call goes straight to messaging. Damn it all. He's free for the moment, no Penny, no dog, no despatch bugging him. Funny, there was a time he avoided her calls. Now it bothers him that she doesn't answer his. He could take this opportunity to go looking for Charlotte. He even has an idea where to start. But defying Dad over delivering the Solaris might be a really bad idea. Doing the opposite of what Dad wanted has always been something of a habit for him, prodded as he was by Makere's whisperings. Without the constant drip of venom in his ear, it's been easier to think, to make clearer decisions. But old habits die hard.

Heat shimmers across the roads, sunlight flaring off windscreens. He pulls up at a red light, contemplating his options:

Go searching for Charlotte in the chaotic aftermath of the earthquake;

Take the Solaris to one of his other disreputable acquaintances to check out how it ticks;

Hunt down Makere, whatever form he's assumed in this mortal world, and send him back to where he came from.

So many choices. None of them good.

He dials Carlie at despatch.

"Hey, Matiu. We've been expecting you."

"Yeah well, you know. Family Lunch and Other Disasters is the name of my next punk band. Some days go like that."

"Ooh, were you in a band? I didn't know. Would I have heard you on the radio?"

"No, Carlie, it's just..."

"Because I try to listen to all the kiwi bands I can, support local artists and all that."

"Carlie... Oh dear. Trollscat. I was in a band called Trollscat. Look it up. Hard to find though, might take you a while. We were a bit shit." The light turns green and he pulls away from the intersection, moving into the haphazard traffic. "I'm heading your way, got a new car that Dad wants stored securely. You won't recognise it in any of the usual ways, so I'll call you when I'm coming down the access road."

Won't recognise it. Yet Craig Tong knew what it was called. Craig Tong, who hadn't so much as seen the damned car, knew it was called the Solaris. How did he even know that?

"OK, Matiu. Now, what did you say, Trolls and Cats? Googling that now. Byeee!"

The line goes dead. Matiu shakes his head, settles into the drive, thinking about how much Craig Tong seems to know that he shouldn't. The battery dips to 99% and holds steady. The city slides by in a gritty haze. He'll get the car to the depot, hand it over, pick up a Commodore, and go looking for Charlotte. Whatever Tong is up to, that'll have to wait. He could pick Erica up, since work will almost be done by then, if she went back to work at all.

Idiot. He dials her desk number. The phone rings and rings, then goes to the answer service. "Hello, this is the phone of Erica Langley, Corrections Department Probation Services, please leave a message."

Matiu contemplates swiping the call off but relents. It's been hard enough to reach her without abandoning his options. "Erica, it's Matiu. If you need me, just call. I'm around." It's lame, but the only thing he hates more than talking to the voices in his head is talking to machines. He hangs up and drives on.

It feels strange to be doing as he's told. He never knew how strange it would feel until today, this strangest of days. The streets are still awash with the dazed and confused, the city heaving from its unsettled breakfast rumble. There's a sense from those Matiu passes of disconnection, of breakdown. Earthquakes are a thing that happen somewhere else, not Auckland. In any case, it's not as bad as it could be. Matiu's been keeping an eye on the news feeds to see if the massacre on Māngere has been reported yet—somehow the cops have managed to keep that under wraps—and although there's widespread minor building and infrastructure damage, no deaths have been reported, or even serious injuries. Civil Defence centres have been operating but aren't even expected to be open more than a night or two as the utilities get the gas and power and water back on. Auckland might not be used to earthquakes, but this is New Zealand. The city is still built in anticipation of a big one.

The background morphs from housing to retail to motorway to retail to industry to housing, then back to retail and industry as Matiu gets a few blocks from the New Lynn depot. He taps his screen to call Carlie back on the main despatch number.

The phone rings, rings, cuts to messaging.

Matiu frowns. Despatch's whole job is to answer the phone. In fact, he can't think of a time he's ever called despatch and not had an answer. This is literally the first time he's even heard the message recording. *Yee Transport thanks you for your call. Unfortunately all our operators are busy right now, please leave a message and your query will be placed in our priority response queue.* Today is, admittedly, a strange day, but there's no reason for at least one of the despatchers not to have answered the phone. He tries again. The ring tone is eerie as it echoes through the Solaris' speakers. It goes to messaging again. *Yee Transport thanks you—*

Matiu swipes off as a light shifts red in front of him. Pulling up at the intersection, he checks all his mirrors, suddenly sweating, and scrolls for Carlie's cell phone. Dials.

It rings once, twice. Then the ring tone ends and there's a scraping, a scrabbling on the other end. Breathing and the unmistakeable rub of awkward hands on the phone mic. A harsh whisper. "Matiu?"

"Carlie? What the hell? Why is no-one answering the phone?"

"Matiu, there are people here. Someone opened the gate and they came in; they've got guns! They're... I'm under my desk, just like lockdown procedure. The control room's locked but they're out there, in the depot. I don't know who they are, but I called the police and then the line went dead and I don't know what else to do!"

The light shifts green, and Matiu lurches away from the intersection. The Solaris responds with a surprising turn of speed, and he dials it back before the car careens into a truck coming the other way. Collision alerts flare on the dash, then Matiu is accelerating down the road, weaving around a car, a bus. "Carlie, are the cameras still up?"

"I think so. What are you going to do, Matiu?"

Matiu taps the screen in the dash, bringing up the network settings. There's a booster on the depot roof that broadcasts a block out from the yard entrance. If he can get the Solaris to hook onto the signal, he might be able to back-door into the camera feeds and get a clue about who the hell is going Rainbow Six on his friends. Tricky, while also dodging traffic. Sometimes being a lone wolf really sucks. Can't even get Scour to patch in because the Solaris isn't on any net to be found.

He rounds a corner, sees the depot gate up ahead. A black van is parked across it at an angle, lurched up across the footpath. Matiu slams on the brakes, slewing to a stop in the middle of the road. There are also several motorbikes on the footpath, and a handful of figures hanging around the gate who appear to be carrying something like assault rifles. The Solaris has found the network but without the encrypted passcode he'll never get on. He's blind.

One of the gun-slinging gangsters points, says something to someone nearby.

Matiu's stomach sinks. It's OK, this is what he wanted. Get them away from the depot, away from Carlie and the others. He'll be the bait. It's him, or the car at least, they want.

The Solaris pings. It's on the network. What the fuck? So the car comes with its very own in-built hacking assistant. Handy and terrifying all at once. Matiu tries not to take his eyes off the gangsters, like a lure hanging in a river waiting for the fish to strike, as he taps the screen, bumping through the network map to find the CCTV feed.

Images tile across the screen, relaying the extent of the infiltration. Motorbikes everywhere, gangsters in leather and bandanas. Many faces he knows, Hanson's old crowd. Who are now run by...

Simon Kingi appears from around the end of the van. Shadows loop and curl around him. He fixes Matiu with a look, the chill eyes of a dead man. The last time Matiu saw Kingi, they'd just fallen from a skyscraper and should've both been smashed to bloody meat on the road. Yet here they are, looking at each other across a space impossibly wide, and deadly narrow.

Then the world is in motion. Men are running, jumping on their bikes, kicking them to life and roaring down the road. Matiu hits reverse, peels backwards, spinning the wheel, and then slams into drive and floors the pedal. Like a rabbit fleeing a pack of hounds, Matiu speeds away from the depot, away from the gangsters on his tail. Away from the sight of Simon Kingi, with the tentacles spooling from his back, twisting in the sunlight. Tries not to see what he saw in that moment, the way the tentacles curled up and around.

The way they took on the shape of the koru.

CHAPTER 19

- Pandora -

Penny ducks her head into the guest room to say her goodbyes to Mum and Mārama. The room is dim, the curtains drawn. The lunch tray lies untouched on the dresser.

"Mum?"

There's a muffled snore and Penny's heart softens. Their backs to the door, Mum and Mārama are spooning on the narrow bed, Mum's well-fleshed arm draped over her sister's kindling limbs. Even in the half-light, the gentle rise and fall of their shoulders tells Penny all she needs to know. They're out to it, the poor things. Wrung out by the day's events. It's bad enough at the best of times: Mārama struggling to maintain her foothold on reality, and Mum trampled beneath guilt and love, but today has been especially taxing.

Careful not to rouse them from their dreams, Penny closes the door softly, then retrieves Cerberus from his exile on the rear balcony.

When she returns to the vestibule, Craig is shouldering the sample bags.

Bituin turns the strap where it is twisted near his neck, laying it flat against his skin, the gesture startling Penny with its familiarity.

"Ready to go?" Craig asks. Did he notice the intimacy of Bituin's gesture? He gives no indication. "Is this everything?"

Penny nods. She gives Bituin a peck on the cheek. "Where did Dad disappear to? I should let him know we're heading out."

"He's in his office. Said he had work to catch up on."

"Okay. Probably best not to bother him, then."

Bituin raises a weak smile. "Is Mrs Yee okay?"

Cerberus surges between them, breaking Penny's hold on the housekeeper's arm. "Mum and Mārama are asleep."

Pursing her lips, Bituin says nothing. She wipes her hands on the tea towel at her waist.

"Try not to worry," Penny says.

"Beatrice, let us through," Craig commands the smart system, and the elevator doors slide open.

Stepping outside is like lifting the lid on the rice cooker.

"Where's your car?" Penny gasps, the humidity squeezing the air from her lungs.

"Two streets over." Even Craig's cool façade is melting in the heat.

"I hope you've turned the aircon on."

"Never turned it off."

The conversation stops as they hurry on, desperate to get out of the heat, the atmosphere like a weighted blanket on their shoulders. Tendrils of hair escape from Penny's ponytail and stick to her nape. Even Cerberus is drooping, with his tongue hanging out and his tail slumped.

Why on earth did Craig park so far away? And how can he still be wearing a tie and jacket?

They're nearing the alley where Matiu parked the Solaris. Penny glances down the lane. The Solaris is gone, only the e-bikes and the rubbish bins remaining. An ice-cream wrapper skates along the asphalt, lifted by breezes too hot to offer relief.

There's a distant clunk as Craig's government-issue Mercedes recognises the key in his pocket. Park lights flicker up ahead. Thank goodness because Penny is positively dying. She almost expires covering the final fifty metres. Throwing open the rear door for Cerberus, she piles into the passenger seat, punching the button for the seat cooler and leaning back to savour the cold seeping into her spine.

Aaaah.

The boot closes and Craig appears, minus the sample bags and his jacket and tie. He slides into the car in a waft of cologne, his muscled arms straining the white fabric of his shirt.

"Hot enough for you?" he says, rolling up the heat deflector and slipping it into the footwell behind him.

Penny squints against the sudden glare that pounds the windscreen. "I think it's getting worse."

"Yep. Looks like we're in for another Indian summer."

It's an understatement, since every summer for the past fifteen years has been hotter than the last, average temperatures in the city bordering on thirty degrees, highs nearing forty, the relentless heat broken only by the violent night-time thunderstorms, the thunder-god Tāwhirimātea, with his anger-management issues, as frustrated as everyone else at it being too hot to sleep.

Penny sighs. "An apocalypse, more like."

Craig grins. "Let's hope not." He puts the car into gear and slides into the street, turning left and left again, before taking the arterial towards Penny's laboratory.

"Thanks for driving me," Penny says, feeling human now the cooler is doing its work, her core temperature returning to a homeostatic range.

They approach the motorway and the traffic thickens and slows, like protein molecules congealing at their isoelectric point.

"No worries. Happy to help."

"Hmm. Dad seemed very keen to have Matiu deliver the car to the depot."

"It's an important project," Craig says.

More important than the wellbeing of his children?

"Penny—" Craig begins, and her pulse skips a beat.

Now. Craig's going to tell her now: the real reason he was following her and Matiu this morning, the reason he turned up at her flat, and why he'd appeared again at her parents' house. The reason she's in his car right now.

He likes me.

But Matiu's earlier accusation has run rough-shod over her ego, trampling it underfoot like a discarded entry ticket when the game has been played. *People like Tong don't date girls like Penny.*

Penny frowns. Why the hell not? What's wrong with her? Why shouldn't Craig date her? She and Craig have things in common: a passion to make it in their chosen professions, overbearing parents who can't help interfering, siblings who can do no wrong, a love of fine cuisine… Sure, Penny's not as focussed on her appearance as Craig is, and yes he has some annoying misogynistic ideas about the kinds of clients she should work for, but since heaps of men share the same misguided paternalistic ideas despite nearly two centuries of women's suffrage, she can hardly hold it against him. As men go, Craig Tong isn't the worst.

People like Tong don't date girls like Penny.

Damn Matiu for putting this earworm in her head. Now it's burrowing inside her skull, eating away at her self-esteem. Why does Penny care what Matiu thinks? Why does she care what *anyone* thinks? She's worthy of being loved. She is! And by someone who wants her for herself, and not just for what she can do for them—like Cordell.

Suddenly, a thought smacks her between the eyeballs, white and hot, like a migraine.

What does Tong want?

"Why don't you drive?"

"I'm sorry, what?"

"Oh, you know, I was just wondering, that's all. This isn't the first time you've needed a lift. It's no bother, really, I'm happy to do it, but it's weird, isn't it? Your parents own this epic transport empire: the largest private fleet in the southern hemisphere, and yet you don't drive."

Penny rubs at the webbing between her thumb and forefinger in an attempt to ease away the mounting headache.

"I'm just saying, it's ironic, that's all."

They reach the on-ramp and slow to a stop.

"An enigma," he adds.

The lights are out and the motorists on the freeway, already irascible and impatient, are loath to move over for the newcomers. Penny's own irritation rises. They could have avoided the motorway by opting for a different route. Why hadn't Craig done that? Now she's stuck in the car with him, the traffic's crawling, and there's at least half a kilometre until the next off-ramp.

She twists in her seat, leaning across the console to give Cerberus a pat. "You okay, Cerb?"

Used to working with politicians, Craig isn't fooled by her diversionary tactics. "Penny, come on. It's not like you're not smart enough. I'll bet you can recite the entire periodic table, all twenty elements. I suppose you can list all their characteristics, too."

"124," Penny interrupts.

"124 characteristics?"

"No, there are 124 elements on the periodic table. Two new elements were discovered after the successful reanimation of the Mars Rover project a few years back, and then there's Quhhar, an element described by Marie-Joseph Quhhar and her French team last year, which brings us to a total of 124."

They roll forward a couple of centimetres until they are neck and neck with a standard white utility van. The serial killer in the driver's seat flashes her a smile.

"See?" Craig goes on, "If you know there are 124 elements on the periodic table, then I reckon you could study up and pass the written driver's test."

Penny flicks a piece of fluff off her shirt. "Maybe it's because my not driving guarantees Matiu a job."

Craig cackles. "Good try, sister, but I'm not buying it. Your dad's fleet has never been in higher demand; one more client, even a high-priority client like his baby girl, isn't the reason."

"Well, maybe it's because when he's driving me, Mum and Dad know he's not getting into any trouble. He *is* still on probation." She shivers, the seat cooler suddenly too cold.

Craig slicks his hair back. "Yeah, I'll admit that's more plausible, but it's still not the whole story, is it? The fleet cars are all connected to the network. Carlie, your girl in despatch, has them tracked to the nearest millimetre, which means at any given moment Hing Yee can tell you the whereabouts of every vehicle in the fleet, who the driver is, what direction they're travelling, their average speed, the fuel left in the tank, even the seat adjustment. Hell, he could probably tell you how many calories the driver has consumed and the last time they reapplied their deodorant. So, if your brother is driving one of the Yee family fleet cars, I'm pretty sure your parents know exactly what he's up to, whether he's driving you or not."

"Except when he turns off the GPS."

Or when he's driving a Solaris prototype.

"He does that? Turns off the tracking? Goes against your father's regs?" Craig clucks his tongue. "Then he has more balls than I gave him credit for."

Penny turns away, looking out the window to hide her smile.

The driver of a standard white van, thinking the smile is for him, waggles his eyebrows salaciously.

Penny snaps her eyes back to the front as a space opens in the lane to their right. Craig checks the rearview mirror before crossing into the gap.

"So?"

"So what?"

"What's the real reason you don't drive?"

Penny breathes deeply. "I can't."

"Because your eyesight isn't good enough?"

"Because I killed someone."

To his credit Craig doesn't ask again. Instead, they travel in silence to the next offramp, where he turns off, driving two blocks to a nearby park. He pulls into the carpark, taking one of the three spaces shaded by the desiccated canopy of a single plane tree.

He doesn't speak then either, just stares out over the football field and fiddles with the last button on his shirt while he waits for her to start her story. What did she expect? She can hardly drop a sentence like "I killed someone" without offering some kind of explanation.

On the side of the field, someone has left behind a single rugby boot, although she can't imagine how because in neon orange it's hard to miss. Penny stares at it until her eyes blur.

Finally, she says, "I used to drive. Had my first lesson at fifteen before I had even sat the written test."

Craig looks at her. Tilts his head.

"Not on the street," Penny clarifies. "Whaea Amy had me driving around the depot parking lot when it was quiet. I got my learners, then my restricted, then I did an advanced drivers' course to expedite my full licence. By the time I finished school, I'd also completed the two transport service licences, and, because I was hanging around the depot so much, Frank, who was our yard manager at the time, put me through forklift training." She trails off as a seagull flies in, perching on the edge of a nearby rubbish bin for a moment before flying away again.

Craig doesn't comment. In the back seat, Cerberus yawns.

"I was twenty-two: home from university for the summer and working for Yee's, trying to get some cash together to cover a few extras during term time. I should have known something was going to happen because it'd been weird all day. The weather, I mean. The sky was that yellow-grey, like a Claude Monet sunrise, and there was a bit of drizzle and because it was after a dry spell, the roads were slick with summer ice, you know?"

She pauses, her eyes on the playing fields, but her mind tracing back to the grey of the sky and that glint of gold.

"I was the only one in the car—one of the fleet cars. I was coming back from a job and there was a truck coming the other way. The driver hit some grease, skidded across the centre line. He was coming right at me, so I swerved. The truck grazed the front corner of my car, pushed me back and sideways off the road." She grips the door handle. "I didn't see the cyclist. Just didn't see him. Afterwards, they said they picked up pieces of bike fifty metres away." Her breath is shallow. Years ago and still she can hardly breathe. "Somehow, he landed on the windscreen. The bike went out from under him and he flew. His forehead struck the glass, there was this look of shock and then…his face collapsed. He was ten. His name was Luke. I think his eyes were blue."

Her own eyes well up and in the distance the neon shoe pixelates.

Craig leans over and wraps her hands in his. "Pen, it wasn't your fault."

"It's what the police said, but if I hadn't swerved—"

He squeezes her hands. "It wasn't your fault."

"You think I haven't told myself that?" Her voice falters. "It doesn't make any difference. Whenever I get behind the wheel, all I see is Luke's face."

"It was years ago," he says softly.

"Not for me."

"You could try again."

She wipes her eyes with the inside of her elbow. "No," she says. "I can't."

For a long while Craig doesn't push it, content just to sit with her, the pair of them looking out over the empty park.

Until Cerberus farts.

Craig groans. He winds down the window and pumps up the aircon. "Really?"

"Sorry," Penny says, laughing. "I should have told you he has a tendency to do that."

"That's not all you should've told me," Craig says as he reverses the car and pulls out of the carpark. "Who knew you could drive a forklift?"

CHAPTER 20

- Matiu -

Matiu brakes hard and swings the Solaris left, cutting inside a bus as horns blare and the bikes in pursuit whip by, rubber burning as they skid about after him. He jinks the car right, slotting into the space between the bus and the parked cars ahead, and floors it. This time he *can* see the battery meter falling. He's got no chance of losing the half-dozen motorbikes in this traffic, and he can't outrun them on the open road, either. Just once, he wishes there was a cop car somewhere nearby. A bit of red and blue strobe right now wouldn't go amiss to discourage his pursuers.

The New Lynn train station is a confusion of people hanging around, cluttering up the footpath. If this was an action flick, there'd be a convenient level crossing up ahead and a mile-long freight train that he'd cross the tracks half-a-second ahead of, leaving the gangsters in a cloud of rubber dust on the other side. But this is Auckland, and the railway lines don't conveniently crisscross the city. Not with conveniently large freight trains, anyway. And with power out across the region, he can't even hope for a poxy electric passenger train to skim through, buying him precious seconds.

The idea hits him almost like a freight train itself. Weaving past the shopping centre, he makes a break for Great North Road, speeding like a mad thing between the scattering of traffic while the motorbikes howl in his wake. He handbrakes the left turn into Fruitvale Road and accelerates towards the level crossing where the railway lines intersect the street. The bikes are at his boot now, and he sees something glinting in the mirror, a flicker of spinning metal. A chain? A flail? A grapple?

The level crossing races up. He brakes hard, screeching tyres thumping onto the channels where the tracks cut under the tarseal, swings the wheel right and hurtles the car off the road and onto the railway lines. The wheels thunder on the sleeper edges, throwing stones out to either side, and the motorbikes pause as they come around to watch him go. They're all road bikes, not dirtbikes. The Solaris isn't intended for use off-road either, but Matiu is willing to take that risk to make his getaway. The gangsters aren't quite so ready to break their precious Harleys by daring the railway sleepers. Or maybe they just think he's crazy, driving headlong onto a railway line where he could get wiped out any second by an oncoming train. Either way, they dwindle, and the car shudders in protest as every joint rattles and shakes.

Matiu stops short of patting himself on the back for his clever escape. The next level crossing is at Glen Eden, and it won't take Kingi's boys long to work that out. They'll be there waiting for him. But maybe his luck will hold.

The tracks veer left and then right, and on the left there's a service road. Matiu gives the Solaris some extra speed and then yanks the wheel over, careening up and over the rails and slewing across the gravel in a cloud of dust. Gonna need a wheel alignment after this, for sure. Slowing, he limps the car towards the locked gates. He's still trapped, still a sitting duck.

The Solaris pings, advising him that it has accessed the local rail authority network and what would he like to do?

Matiu grins. "Open the gate." The gate swings open with a low whine of electric servos. This is too easy. He understands why everyone wants this car.

Pulling out onto Rua Road, he takes the first left into a residential street and slips into a driveway of a house that looks empty. He winds down the window, listens for the roar of distant Harleys, and breathes. He sits for a long moment. With any luck, they'll have abandoned the depot, left Carlie and the rest of them alone.

His phone rings. Unknown Caller. It might be Erica. He swipes to answer on speakerphone.

"Yo."

A low static hiss, wordless.

"Hello? Who's this?"

The hiss rises and falls, like breathing. Like the rush and retreat of waves on shingle. *Hisss..shhhh...hisss...shhh...hisss...shhhh...*

Bad connection. Matiu reaches down to swipe the call off when he hears, below the static hush a low rumble, a whisper, a voice.

...Matiu...

Someone trying to reach him, to talk to him. He waves the phone around, as if he can get a better signal somewhere at the far end of his arm, but with all the outages today he'll be lucky to get a clear connection even if he could squeeze a couple more bars out of nothing. "Who dis?" he says again, the hiss pulsing in his ears.

...hisss...shhhh... son...

Matiu drops the phone in the passenger seat. It lies face-down on the leather, quietly sucking in its impossible breaths. He wants to grab the phone, end the call, switch it off, pull out the battery. Yet something tells him even that wouldn't end the hiss, the pulse, the voice.

That voice, so familiar yet different. Like Makere, like himself. But older. No, not just older. *Ancient*. Burning with bitterness and rage. That breathing sound, the laboured hiss of the wounded, pushing themselves up off the floor, spitting blood from their mouths ready to take another swing.

Outside, the sun is falling through the afternoon clouds, casting Māui's ropes in long, bright lines from earth to sky, those ropes Māui and his brothers cast across Ra, the sun, to slow his race across the heavens. And they hauled him down, and they beat him until he promised to obey. Those ropes are pulling Ra down, the day is dying, and as it does, time is running out.

Matiu's phone rings.

It's sitting in the console, not lying on the seat. Like the past moments are a blur, a glitch in the timestream. But the voice still resonates behind that pulsating hum.

...son...

Unknown Caller. He answers anyway.

"Matiu?" It's Erica.

"Hey you." Breath rushes back in, filling a void inside him he hadn't realised was full of nothing. "What up? You doing any work yet? I thought your battery died."

"I bought an external battery pack, you moron," says Erica. "But listen. Charlotte wasn't on the bus. I've been down at Britomart all freaking afternoon, watching the buses come in, ducking every time there's been an aftershock, sweating my ovaries out, and she's not turned up."

"Can't say I know the bus system that well, but there's nowhere else she could've got off? Maybe with all the traffic disruptions they've diverted the buses? Albany, maybe?"

"The signage all says delays, but no cancellations or diversions. She should be here by now."

She was on a bus. It doesn't take a detective to figure out it isn't a public transport bus. Charlotte's riding off into the sunset, on a Touching the Sun holiday package to hell. Not even to hell and back, just to hell. A one-way ticket.

"I'll come find you."

"What are you thinking, Matiu?"

"I might have an idea where she is."

"This is about the cult again, isn't it?"

"See you in a bit."

He ends the call, breathes hard, as somewhere, through buildings and down the empty spaces between haunted streets, the grumble of motorcycles echoes their frustration. He pulls back into the street and drives away from the sound.

The tide is rushing in. Time is running out.

And the voice in the waves said his name, called him *son...*

- Pandora -

Opening the rear door of the Mercedes, Penny releases the hound from hell into the gloom of the basement carpark. "Let's go, Cerberus," she says. "I think we've well and truly outstayed our welcome this time."

"Stop apologising, Pen." Craig pops the boot and removes the sample bags. "Honestly. You can't help it if your friend is a real dog."

Penny rolls her eyes. "I can't believe you said that."

"I—" The ground trembles underfoot.

Penny thrusts out a hand, stabilising herself against a concrete pillar while the quake rattles on…and on. Damn, it's persistent. Still going… Dust shakes from the concrete slabs above them. Cerberus growls from deep in his chest.

Bracing her feet, Penny slides her hand down the pillar and crouches, one arm over the dog to comfort him. "Shhh."

Before she knows it, Craig has crossed the gap from the car. He places his hand on the pillar, shielding Penny and Cerberus with the width of his back. The tremors continue. Penny's heart thumps along with the rocking.

Would it ever stop?

"Is this the big one?" she whispers.

"No," Craig says. "Aftershock. We just have to wait it out." Something in the way he says it instils her with confidence.

"OK." Trying not to think about being buried alive under the giant slabs of concrete overhead, she loops her arms around Cerberus' neck and hugs him to her. "How long has it been? A minute?" she asks her knees.

"Not that long," Craig says.

"Enough to cause a tidal wave?"

Sprawled clumsily over 1200 square kilometres, the central city occupies an isthmus between the Pacific Ocean and the Tasman Sea. More than a million people live in that tightly packed strip of land. A tsunami would be catastrophic.

"Not going to happen," Craig assures her. "See? They're slowing."

Penny closes her eyes and concentrates on the vibrations rippling through the pillar and into her hand. They do feel like they're tapering off.

Eventually, the tremors hiccup to a stop.

Craig waits a few seconds before straightening up. He exhales, a long slow breath. "There you go. Just a bit of dirt moving back into place."

Penny isn't sure she'd call the Pacific Subduction Plate a bit of dirt, but she's too relieved to be back on solid ground to argue. She accepts his proffered hand and gets to her feet.

"Right, let's get these specimens of yours up to the lab."

A phone bleeps. It isn't Penny's ringtone.

Swinging the sample bags out of the way, Craig digs in his pocket. "Tong here." His eyes widen and he nods. "I know where. I'll avoid the motorway. Be right there." He hangs up. "Penny—"

She's so wracked with shame she can barely meet his eyes. With all that's happened today, she hasn't spared even a second to ask about his family. "Your mum?"

"No, no, she's fine. Mum's been staying over at my brother's. This is work. An emergency. I'm so sorry. I don't like to leave you on your own, not straight after—"

"Now who's apologising?" she says. "I'm fine. If someone's in trouble, then you should go. Here, give me those bags." Slipping Cerberus' lead over her wrist, she drags the bags off his shoulder, staggering a little at the sudden weight.

"Thanks, Pen." He turns and runs to the car, shouting over his shoulder, "Call you later. And don't use the elevator!"

Penny waits for the clank of the garage doors on the floor above her before dialling her own mother. May as well do it now and save Mum recording another sixteen messages on Penny's phone. Weirdly, there's no answer, so Penny leaves a text. That done, she tugs on Cerberus' lead, letting him know they're on the move.

They head past the lift and the crudely written and badly spelled *'awaiting city enginers'* sign, to the stairs. Penny notes that the lights are still on, so the power outages over this side of town must have been minimal, or at least short enough for the little generator the body corporate had installed to keep pace with the power requirements of the building's tenants.

Keen to get out of the shaky basement, the dog strains on the lead, practically dragging Penny up the stairs, although, what with the heat and weight of the bags almost cranking her arm off, she's secretly pleased for the extra help. Even so, by the time she reaches the top of the stairs, she's breathing hard.

She punches the keypad and lets them in, then sets the bags on the floor while she rolls the ache out of her arm. Cool air-conditioned freshness soothes her skin. The fridge hums a welcome.

Suddenly, Cerberus' hackles rise, the bristles bunching at the back of his neck. He definitely senses something. Another earthquake? Penny doesn't take any chances: She yanks on the lead, shoving a lab stool out of the way in her haste to pull the dog under the nearest workbench. Breathless, she waits for the shaking to start, already regretting that Craig had to leave. Minutes tick by, but there's nothing.

Cerberus continues to growl. Out in the open, the fridge whines in alarm.

It *must* be an earthquake. A big one. The tension is killing her.

Long minutes pass.

Penny's ears perk up. Hang on. Is that someone in the office? She pokes her head out from under the bench. "Who's there?"

Her mind bubbles with possibilities. Had someone broken in? Who would have an interest in her lab? Um…only the members of *two* opposing gangs. They'd be wanting to obliterate any data collected from the wharf. Or maybe it would be a cult member, looking to destroy the data from Mount Māngere? *Or maybe one of Matiu's takeout boxes has been in there so long that it's got up and walked away.*

Penny shakes her head. Even a takeout taniwha is unlikely. As William of Occam might say, "Numquam ponenda est pluralitas sine necessitate." Don't look for a complicated solution, when a simple one is easier to test. A simple way to find out who could be in the office, is to climb out and look.

Clutching Cerberus by the collar, Penny clambers out from under the bench. "Hello?" she calls. "Is someone there?" She steps forward.

The fridge shudders and falls silent.

"I said, 'who's there?'"

Matiu appears in the corridor. Only it's not Matiu. He has the same voice, the same dark hair and darker eyes. Like Matiu, he sports a *kiri tuhi* tattoo on his face, only in this case, the message in those strokes is unmistakably violent.

Makere.

It isn't her first encounter with the man her brother calls his imaginary friend. The first time, Penny had been in a lift, catching a glimpse of him in the angle where two mirrors met, and then, later, they met again in a dream. But the last time she'd seen him, he'd been falling from a high-rise, an electrical storm fizzing all about him.

It was a fall he shouldn't have survived…

Get a grip, Penny. You're a scientist. You don't believe in ghosts. Matiu had fallen from a rooftop and he had survived, so why not Makere?

Penny holds Cerberus in check, breathes deeply, and scans the man's face. On closer inspection, it seems Makere hasn't come away unscathed from that last encounter after all. There's a lumpy purple-red gash where Cerberus' incisors pierced the soft flesh of his throat, and a flap of scar tissue puckers at the edge of his eye, its size a perfect match to the prong of a garden fork. Her own handiwork.

"Penny," he says, in that mocking way of his. "At last." He moves towards her.

Cerberus isn't having a bar of it. He lunges at Makere, straining at the leash, his teeth gnashing.

"Such a warm welcome."

Even with Cerberus filling the space between them, Penny struggles to keep her voice from trembling. "How did you get in?"

"All the questions you want to ask me, and you ask that one? You're not a tiny bit curious who I am?"

"I know who you are. Mārama told me."

Makere nods. "Ah, Mārama. My father spoke of her with fondness once. So strong and beautiful. But nothing endures, does it? Even her vow to hold her tongue. But of course, if you know who I am, then you'll know how I got in."

Penny's mind races. How had he got in? The keypad entry? No, even if Matiu and Makere were twins, their thumbprints wouldn't be identical. Studies show that conditions in the womb have an impact on the final fingerprint-makaurangi.

Makere's grin is slow and languid. He leans his elbows on the bench and cups his chin in his hands. "I love watching you; the adorable way your eyebrows come together when you're thinking. Did you know I can see the science in your head? Blue-green, like the inside of a paua shell."

"Why are you here, Makere? What do you want?"

He straightens. "My father sent me. He wants to meet his son."

"Why? Are you not good enough?"

His eyes flash, but he doesn't bite. Instead, he edges closer, keeping just out of reach of Cerberus' snapping jaws. "It's been a long time," he whispers. "Our father's getting old. He wants to take down the walls between us, for us to be a family again. Is that so hard to believe?"

Penny snorts. "Such noble intent. If that's how he feels, where the hell was he when Matiu was growing up?"

"It's never too late to try again."

Penny steps sideways. "Well, I rather think that'll be up to Matiu."

Makere sucks air over his teeth. "Why so hard, Penny? You could encourage him, be the one to reunite us." He takes another step around her. They are two duellists, circling one another, parrying barbs.

"I could, but I won't."

Makere's grin hardens. "Mārama's defiance hasn't served her well."

Suddenly grasping a graduated cylinder from a shelf, he smashes it against the bench. The glass splinters, slivers flying. A stray shard stabs Cerberus in the snout. The poor baby yelps and shies away.

But now Penny's trusty guardian is out of the way.

Makere leaps for her, his steely fingers closing on her arm. Before she has time to think, he's wrapped an arm about her neck, the smashed cylinder aimed at her throat, grazing her skin. A runnel of blood rolls down her neck, its metallic odour sharp in her nostrils.

She stops struggling. When it came to contests of strength, Matiu always won. But just occasionally, if she used her wits, Penny could beat him…

"Kill me," Penny goads, "and your father can forget about playing happy families with Matiu."

Makere's voice is icy on her neck. "There are other ways…"

Penny seizes his wrist. She pulls it tight to her chest, yanking down and away, taking the broken cylinder out of contention. Then she twists under his arm and kicks out hard, hitting the back of his knee and sending him sprawling in the shattered glass.

She has to go now, before he recovers. She turns, following the sound of Cerberus' barking, but Makere is too fast and is already rising. He charges. Reaches for her. Penny ducks, sliding out of his grasp. For an instant they're both scrambling on the floor. In seconds, he'll have her. She won't get the better of him a second time.

At the other end of laboratory, the door clicks open. "Penny. You there?"

Penny gasps. Beaker! What is he doing here? She told him to stay home.

Makere growls under his breath. He rolls to his feet and wipes blood off the back of his hand. "Later, little sister," he says as he slips into the shadows at the far end of the bench.

"Beaker! Look out! There's—"

"Penny?"

She looks up. Lanky as a lancewood, Beaker peers over the bench, his face shiny from his climb up the stairs. "What's up?"

"Did you see anyone on the landing?"

Her lab technician runs a hand through his crop of red hair. "I saw the city engineers on the first floor. Post-earthquake checks of the elevator. Talk about a waste of resources. What about the buildings they inspected this morning? They're only going to have to go back and—"

"No one else?" Penny interrupts. "You didn't see…Matiu?"

Beaker shakes his head. "No. What's going on?"

Shaking with shock, Penny puts her hand on the bench and hauls herself up. She gestures at the shattered glass. "Nothing. A broken graduated cylinder. It must have been left on the bench and got knocked off in that last aftershock."

"Shit. Sorry, Pen. That might have been me."

"Actually, I think I was the one who left it out."

His brows crease. Beaker points at her neck. "You've got some blood on you."

"Really?" Feigning ignorance, Penny raises her hand covering the spot where Makere nicked her with the cylinder. "It'll be Cerberus' blood," she lies. "When I saw he was cut, I tried to lift him off the glass."

Beaker laughed. "You tried to lift Cerberus? Duh! That dog weighs as much as you do."

"I didn't say it was smart. Would you mind taking him into the office, while I clean this glass up?"

"On it. Let's go, Cerberus. Follow Uncle Beaker."

When the pair have left, Cerberus padding a trail of bloody smudges across the floor tiles, Penny pulls a pair of gloves from a container on the bench, and, getting down on her hands and knees, she sifts through the shards on the floor.

There has to be one...

Come on...

At last, she finds it. Penny lifts the petal-shaped shard to the light to examine the dark smear which holds the answers she needs. Then she drops the glass shard in a specimen jar, crosses the lab, and hides it behind the reagents in the cool store.

CHAPTER 21

- Matiu -

The city is confused. This stretch of road abandoned, ghost-town style, over here every car in Auckland trying to cram into the same space. Smoky home-blend biodiesels, whining old electrics on their last legs, vans and flatdecks and motorbikes, all of them wanting to get in Matiu's way. Finally, he finds a spot to park the Solaris, down an alley on broken yellow No Parking lines next to a dumpster, but he won't be there long. Just long enough to get to Britomart and find Erica.

The smell of the nearby docks hits him as he rounds the corner onto Queen Street. Was it only this morning he was down this way, five hundred metres up the road, looking at the carnage of the shootout? Or was that yesterday? Last week? Another life? And just across the street, the skyscraper where not so long ago he'd fought Simon Kingi beneath an angry sky, an alien place from which he'd fallen...

The memory washes through him like ice water, and he hurries on.

The city is rotten. Fermenting with memories, none of them making any sense. Matiu wonders how much of what he remembers is real, how much of it fractured dreams. He doubts he'll ever know for certain. Penny is constantly questioning his grip on reality. Considering what he's seen today, he's starting to wonder if *the world itself* is losing its grip on reality.

Britomart is definitely a bedlam all its own. Whole sections of Queen Street have been coned off to isolate masonry which has tumbled from the historic waterfront buildings, causing a logjam of buses in the narrow corridor that's left between workers clearing debris. Add to that the milling masses either waiting for buses or loitering around because the trains are out of action, and it's like there's a parade in town. A parade of hot, scared, frustrated people. A tinderbox. A powderkeg. There's no ticker tape, but there could be a riot. Matiu puts his head down and pushes through the crowd, looking for Erica. Dials her number, gets the cell service overloaded message. Too many people, lost and afraid. Too many questions.

Weaving through stationary buses hissing sweet electric ozone, he crosses the street and heads for higher ground, the stairs to the transport operations centre, beneath which the trains sit silent as they wait for the power to come back on. At the top, he turns to survey Queen Street. Directly behind the clusterfuck of jammed buses and trucks, the HSBC and PWC towers loom, fingers stabbing down from the sky and reminding him that Kerr, and Kingi, are still on the loose. A hot wind blows off the harbour, ruffling his hair. He stands above the masses, rimmed in falling sunlight as the day dies, his eyes drawn away from the search at hand and back to that night, the storm, the skyscraper roof, the fall. Did he really live through that night? Or is this just some sort of hell without a name?

"You took your time."

Erica grabs his hand, spins him out of the oblivion he'd been spiralling into, and tugs him into a hug. Blindsided, he returns the embrace awkwardly. Her nearness still strikes him as strange, yet compelling, even if the closest they've ever been was that one, unexpected kiss while they hid from Kerr's unknown henchmen. He's not just her client now. He's...something more. Something he's not sure he's comfortable putting words around.

"This is purely a professional thing, you understand," she says, holding him tight. "Research shows that physical contact in the wake of traumatic events can help ease mental and emotional fatigue."

"So, I'm just like your, what, hug-buddy? No strings attached?"

"Something like that."

She draws away, looks him in the eye. He can't help but notice how her lips are parted, just a little, glistening in the afternoon light. He looks away.

"You said you thought you might know where Charlotte is."

He glances south, visualising the place through the walls and roofs that block his view. "I think so. I..." He was going to say he saw it in a dream, but that'll sound crazy. Maybe crazier than normal. "I've got some good intelligence—"

She punches his arm. "You? Intelligence? Whatever."

"Bully." He winces.

"That didn't hurt."

"It hurt me on the inside."

"Oi. Focus. Charlotte."

Matiu hooks his arm through the crook of her elbow and strides for the stairs, easing her along with him. "Let's go for a ride."

"Less cryptic chivalric bullshit and more details, Mister," she protests, but joins him in tackling a path through the crowd. She doesn't pull her arm free of his.

"Not here," he grumbles, and they push and weave across the road and away, until they reach the Solaris. Not towed, not clamped. Still got all its wheels. "Here's to the breakdown of civilisation and the collapse of bureaucracy," Matiu says, as Erica eyes the car.

"This isn't your usual ride, is it?"

"Oi, focus," he mimics. "Charlotte?"

Giving him an eyeball that couldn't be much hairier, Erica slips her arm free and slides into the passenger side. Dropping into the driver's seat, Matiu relaxes a fraction. Tension ripples through him, and he rolls his neck. Glad to be out of the eyes of the twin towers staring down at him, back with a wheel in his hands. Backing out of the alley, he heads away from the crowd.

"Have you seen anything about Mount Māngere on the feeds?"

Erica bites her lip. "Yes." Even with everything else giving up around them, you could trust social media to spread the juicy stuff. "She's not there, is she?"

Matiu shakes his head. "I…we were up there. I looked. She's not there."

Erica's stare is pale, hollow. "But you thought she might be? Are they really all...?"

"Dead?" He nods. "Every last one. Apart from the kid. There was this kid, Carlos, he was all good. You know, not all good, because he lost his mum and..." Matiu trails off. The rest of the thought bites too deep.

"You think it's Kerr, don't you?"

"Got her piss all over it. Reeks of it."

Fractured sunlight splinters Erica's features, promising the fall of night. From the corner of his eye, Matiu can respect the grim set of her jaw. Like hell will Erica let Sandi Kerr lay so much as a finger on her sister again. This night will be long, and dark, and terrible. "So where are they now?"

"The first lot of victims abandoned their cars at the Māngere Community Centre, then took themselves off up Mt Māngere. Still no sign of anyone at Sandringham, or around there. Closest volcanic cone to Sandringham is Mt Albert. Since the first attempt was a failure, she'll be trying again, but we might be able to stop it, if we get there in time."

"A failure? Wait, what? There's a lot to unpack here. What's up with the volcanic cones? And how is a hundred people committing open-air suicide a failure, other than a failure of humanity as a whole for letting it happen?"

Matiu sucks his lips against his teeth. Grinds. It's not the place he saw in the dream, but dreams can't be trusted. Mt Albert makes the most sense, another sleeping cone, posing for thousands of years as a pretty little hill with lots of hidden dells and bush. Beneath their feet, so many sleeping volcanoes. "The thin places," he says, throat thick. "Where the worlds scrape against each other."

"Not making any sense here, Matiu."

He doesn't expect her to buy it. The peak from his dreams, watching over the city as it burns, is there, calling to him. But he can't be distracted. Kerr is fucked in the head for sure, but she's not *that* mad. Too public. Mt Albert has to be the logical choice for a second try.

"The suicides, they're not suicides. Well, they are, but they're a murder of sorts. A killing. A mass sacrifice. An offering."

Erica is quiet for a moment, but she's been here. She was on the roof that night, she knows what Kerr is capable of. How deep her insanity runs. What a madwoman might believe. "To what?" she asks quietly.

Matiu shakes his head. Crazy people Erica will understand. Monsters, less so. "Let's just find her, eh?"

- Pandora -

"Pen, you done?" Beaker pokes his head around the office door, a plastic lunch box clutched limply in one hand.

"Just about," Penny says as she brushes the last splinters of glass into the pan.

"Good. Because I've got no idea what's got into Cerberus. He's going completely apeshit in here. I can't get him to stand still long enough to look at his nose. Not even after I offered him a sandwich."

"OK, I'm coming." Making a mental note to order a couple more graduated cylinders, Penny tips the glass into the recycling, hangs the brush and shovel on a hook behind the door, then stoops to mop up the little trail of bloody nose smudges. When the laboratory floor is clean, she heads to the office.

Cerberus bounds into her arms.

"Ooof," Penny says, fending him off so he doesn't suffocate her. She pushes him gently back to his haunches and gives him a reassuring hug.

"See? I told you he had the jitters," Beaker says, placing his lunch box on the sink and handing her the first aid box instead. "Something's put the wind up him. He's clingier than wet togs straight off the beach."

Maybe so, but his doggie instincts are spot on, Penny thinks. There's definitely no love lost between Cerberus and Makere. Not after their last encounter.

She crouches to take a quick look at the dog's nose. Good. The bleeding has stopped. The laceration isn't particularly big, but where the glass has caught the flesh on an angle, the wound is deepish.

"Can you really blame him?" she says to Beaker as she opens the first aid kit and takes out a tube of antibiotic cream. "Don't forget Cerberus has been with us most of the day. He's smelled the same things we have. Witnessed the horrors we did. You think he doesn't know?" Penny dabs antibiotic cream on Cerberus' snout, keeping the application thin since the dog is just as likely to lick it off.

Cerberus baulks, so Beaker crouches beside Penny, one hand on Cerberus' collar and the other petting the dog's coat to keep him still. "Yeah. It's not like you can erase those images either. As soon as the police dropped me home, I took a shower then tried to catch some sleep, but it was a waste of time. I kept seeing flashbacks of those poor people, their faces…"

Penny nods. It's classic PTSD. She's seen those flashbacks. She should probably keep an eye on Cerberus' behaviour, since clinginess is a key symptom of PTSD in dogs.

"Carlos," Beaker goes on. "He has no idea. His mother…you know, when the story gets out..." His voice cracks. Absently, he tweaks the dog's ear. "I mean, I'm not sure we can even imagine what that kid's life is going to be like."

Penny stops her dabbing and looks at her colleague. Immediately, the dog's tongue snakes out, tasting the ointment. Penny scratches the floppy dog-ear closest to her.

"I shouldn't have come back," Beaker says. "You sent me home to sleep and by rights I should still be there not back here thinking about doing benchwork after the day we've already had, and the hours we've put in. There's a chance we could make mistakes."

"Today a graduated cylinder, tomorrow…"

"It's not funny, Pen."

"I know. I'm sorry."

"Look, to hell with health and safety, and fuck the overtime hours, OK? I just need to work. *I need to do something.*"

"OK." Normally a stickler for safety regulations, Penny's eager to get stuck into the analyses, too. It's the only way they know to exorcise their demons. "I won't tell the safety inspectors if you don't. We'll just have to make sure we keep an eye on each other," she says. Giving Cerberus a last pat, she puts the ointment back in the canvas bag and gets to her feet.

But the task is so daunting, there are so many analyses to undertake, Penny hardly knows where to start.

How about you start with getting your lab coat on?

She walks to the bank of hooks at the front of the lab and takes down her lab coat, slipping her arms into the sleeves and turning down the collar.

"I suggest we take a dual approach," Beaker says, obviously thinking the exact same thing as she is. He buttons up his own lab coat and clips on his radiation badge. "What say I get started on verifying the identities of the bodies, and you work on determining what the toxin was?"

"Sounds good," says Penny, and the fridge hums in agreement. She lifts the first sample bag from the pile on the floor and checks the label. Without looking at Beaker, she says, "What do you think about starting with the scene residue in the bottles, rather than the biological samples? I know it's more customary to begin the other way around—"

"No, testing the residue makes sense in this case," Beaker interrupts. "Given what we saw at the scene, there's a high possibility the poison was delivered in the cordial the victims drank. And if this is Kerr's handiwork, then we should probably look for cyanide and ergot alkaloids first, since she's known to use those compounds."

"Good point. I'll start with a qualitative benchtop test for cyanide on the contents of the cordial. At least that way, we'll know what we're dealing with."

"Or not," he says.

"Or not," she replies.

"It's definitely the quickest way for us to eliminate cyanide though, since we'll need to store some heparinised samples at 4°C before we can check the bloods."

Beaker's right: delays in sampling and storing the samples from the Mt Māngere scene means the bloods will need more preparation. Penny snaps on a pair of gloves. "And for the ergotamine-lysergic acid, what do you think? Simple HPLC-FLD?" she says, although the acronym is as much of a mouthful as saying high-performance liquid chromatography with fluorescent detection.

Beaker nods. "Yes. That should work for qualitative and quantitative analysis of all the main ergot alkaloids. Maybe try a mix of acetonitrile with ammonium carbonate as your buffer. Gave us pretty good results when we were testing the Touching the Sun hippy juice."

Penny smiles. "Let's get to it then."

Cerberus, mistaking her comment for a command, goes to his bed near the door and curls up on the quilted cushion, his wounded nose resting on his paws. Maybe he finds the normality of them getting on with their work comforting, because the hound closes his eyes.

"Pen?"

Penny glances over to where her lab technician is unpacking one of the sample bags. "Yes, Beak?"

"Use the fume hood," he says in his best chemistry professor-speak.

Penny grins. Already she's feeling better. It's good to have a plan, and something concrete and productive to do. Practical hands-on activities are a great way to ground yourself after a trauma, anchoring your mind in the present by engaging the senses: touch, sight...

"Mind if I put on some tunes?" Beaker asks.

"Be my guest," Penny says. Music is another great way to distract the consciousness. Away from Makere and his threats.

Beaker points the remote at the lab's archaic sound system and, with a flick of his wrist, brings up a playlist of local bands. Penny recognises the first bars of ApocalypseMetronome's latest single.

Humming to the music, she goes to the reagent store and searches the containers on the shelves. She's going to need an aqueous sodium hydroxide solution, ferrous sulphate at 10g/L, and hydrochloric acid...

Just half an hour later, a lack of blue colour in the test solution rules out cyanide.

- Matiu -

The sky is fading towards night as they pull into the deserted carpark and look around. There should be cars, or vans, but there's nothing. No evidence at all that a number of people arrived here and abandoned their vehicles, and their lives. "They're not here," Matiu says. "Maybe the quakes rattled them."

She punches him in the arm. "We've come all this way, let's at least take a walk around."

Shrugging, Matiu gets out of the Solaris, locks it as Erica steps out and shuts the door. If Kerr hasn't led her sheep here then he knows where they'll be, or at least he thinks he does. He and Erica might be wasting their time, but if it'll put Erica's mind at ease, he'll walk.

"Ōwairaka. Lot of history to this place," he says as they cross the unlit carpark and enter the old roadway, now a walking path only since the Council barred the maunga to vehicles back in the late twenty-teens. "Some iwi called it Te Ahi-kā-a-Rakataura, the long burning fire of Rakataura. Which is funny because it's sort of proof that early Māori knew the mount was a volcano, but European geologists reckon they don't know when it was last active. Course, legend says Rakataura crossed the ocean from Hawaiki riding a taniwha, so maybe it was a dragon, and this is where it went to sleep." He's rambling, dredging up half-remembered stories Mārama used to kōrero over their walks around Maungakiekie, but it's better than letting Erica's razor-edged tension cut into him like a silent knife. "Another story says someone murdered his son, so maybe it's a metaphor for his grief, or his anger, or something. You think someone could do that? Wake a sleeping volcano with just their pain?"

The look Erica shoots him is lost in the darkness, but he feels it anyway. Withering, but not quite scorching. "You told me you weren't doing drugs anymore."

Matiu shrugs. "Time and a place, right?"

"What else?"

"What do you mean?"

"You said there's a lot of history. That's all just...legend. Speculation."

Matiu frowns. "Just because it sounds unlikely doesn't mean it didn't happen."

"Geology doesn't lie."

"It might." His frown deepens. Did Erica just sound a little bit like Penny there? A thought flashes suddenly bright in his memory. "Actually, now you mention geology, there's the story of Ruarangi, who led his people from the pā on the maunga to the sea through a lava tunnel when they were under attack from another iwi."

Erica stops. "So, there might be a tunnel? Another access, somewhere hidden? Kerr and her lot, they might've parked there and walked through?" Desperate hope colours her words.

Matiu shakes his head. "I doubt it. Most of the peak of the mountain was stripped back by pākehā quarry operations in the nineteenth and twentieth centuries. If there were any tunnels, they're long since dug out or covered over. But get this: the park's locally known as Ōwairaka, after Wairaka, who was a chick from Tahiti way the hell back around the dawn of time, and she was shit-hot on a surfboard, and that pissed off her hubby—she probably shredded the waves better than him, you know?—so what does she do? She ditches his lame arse back in Tahiti, comes to Aotearoa taking all the coolest cats from the island with her, and she and her old man form their own iwi right here, on this mountain. But for real, she was a surfer before surfing was even invented, I shit you not. Google it."

Erica nods. "I'd heard that story. Never told quite like that, though."

The trees thin, revealing an open field. Not a body, living or otherwise, to be seen.

"Is this the rugby pitch?"

"Nah, see down the end?" Pale shapes stand silent in the dusking evening light. "I'd say this is the world-famous-in-their-own-lunchtime Ōwairaka Archery Club. Don't you listen to their podcast? It's pretty sharp." There's a suave unruffled Matiu in here somewhere, he's certain. But for some reason the only one he can find to operate his tongue right now is the mildly befuddled and not terribly funny one that gets nervous around girls he likes. That guy is *so* annoying.

"OK, we're wasting time." She turns to him. "Tell me you've—"

Erica's jaw drops as her eyes slide past him, to the sky above.

Matiu twists his neck to follow her gaze.

Colours creep across the darkening belly of Ranginui, pale sweeping sheets of pounamu and blood. “Tahu-nui-a-rangi,” Matiu breathes. The appearance of the aurora australis has become more regular of late, yet the sight still fills him with awe and dread alike.

“They’re so beautiful,” Erica whispers, as the lights drift across the night like the wings of some vast ethereal beast.

“Yeah,” Matiu starts, “but—”

He catches himself as Erica wraps an arm around his, pulling him closer, staring in rapt wonderment at the ghostly display in the sky, the long-lost fires of ancient Polynesian sailors who made it as far as the southern ice only to become trapped there forever, their bonfires painting the night. *But*, he wants to say, *there’s a whole lot of science that Penny forced me to listen to about this, shit that suggests the planet’s guts are up and shifting around and it can only be bad, and every time we see it it’s stronger and brighter and it might as well be the fucking Necronomicon opening up in the sky to drop Ragnarok right on top of us and everyone else’s apocalypses at the same time.*

But Erica’s clinging to him, like she’s one of those ancient canoes that bore his ancestors here so long ago and he’s the anchor stone, buried deep in the sand, keeping her from being swept out into the dark, raging madness of the sea, the sky so deadly and seductive with shimmering lights. “Yeah,” he murmurs. “Yeah, it’s nice.” She turns to him again, those lips parting just slightly, hints of green and red starfire slipping along the wetness that glimmers like the aurora. He can taste her breath, so close to his, as he leans closer...

His phone rings.

Damn it! Whatever the hell it is, it can wait! Some moments are just too good to go to waste for the sake of a phone call.

He fumbles the phone from his pocket, swipes the call to messaging, and looks back at Erica. But the moment is lost.

“Come on,” she says, all business once again. “Let’s get back to the car. On the way you can tell me exactly where you think we’re going to find my sister, before it’s too late.” She spins on her heel and strides back down the path.

Matiu grinds his teeth and lurches after her.

The whistle of air and a soft thunk are all the warning he gets. As the arrow wobbles wildly in the trunk of the tree it just hit, missing Matiu’s ear by a matter of inches, he grabs Erica’s hand and runs.

“Matiu—”

“Head down, move!”

“Who is it?”

Matiu weaves a little, even though they’re already in the trees again and down the other side of the rise. “Kerr might not be here, but someone is. She knew we’d be coming looking for her here, so she sent someone to wait for us.”

"And what, kill us?"

"No, just a little long-distance acupuncture. It's like phone sex but with more actual penetration."

"I wish I had your class; I really do."

Then they only have breath for running, and the hope they reach the car before whoever has the bow and arrow gets close enough to take another shot.

CHAPTER 22

- Pandora -

At the bench, Penny straightens up. Her neck is killing her. Arching her back, she tips her head first to the left, and then to the right. Ouch. That hurts. Her trapezius muscles feel like rock. Sitting too long in one attitude as Austen would say. She massages her neck with her fingertips. Well, with her latest assay set up, this would be a good time to take a break.

Taking off her lab coat and laying it across the lab-stool, she gives Beaker a wave, makes a drinking gesture, then heads to the office to put the coffee on.

As she passes, Cerberus lifts his head and then gets up and pads after her.

By the time Beaker joins them in the office, Penny has applied another smear of antibiotic to Cerberus' nose, and poured two cups of steaming coffee.

"Here you go," she says. Her fingers hooked through the handle, she's preparing to pass Beaker the cup when the ground rumbles. Penny freezes mid-pass. The surface of Beaker's coffee quivers in the cup. "Not again," she says.

Thankfully, this one doesn't last long. She hands the cup to Beaker.

"Better drink it quickly before the next one comes, eh?" Beaker says, taking a slurp. He sets the cup on the counter and lifts the lid of his lunchbox, pulling out a sandwich.

He offers her the box. "These aftershocks are a pain, aren't they? I ruined a whole tray of samples in that big one about a half an hour back. Had to start over. Like we haven't got enough to do. You probably heard me swear."

Penny snorts. "Tell me about it. I only just managed to stop a reagent bottle from sliding off the bench." She helps herself to half a sandwich from the top of the stack. It's a Kiwi classic: Marmite and cheese. "Thanks." She takes a bite, savouring the salty flavour.

"I guessed as much when I saw you climb up on your lab-stool and push the glassware to the back of the shelf," Beaker says.

"Well, I can't afford to lose any more stuff. I haven't finished paying for all this wondrousness yet." She waves her sandwich in the air, pointing in the direction of the laboratory.

Wide-eyed, Cerberus wags his tail and looks longingly at her sandwich.

"It's all insured, though, right?" Beaker says.

"Of course. It was a condition of the loan."

And my dad for that matter.

"But," she says, "being insured can be a fat lot of use if a disaster is widespread. Did you know that after the 2011 Christchurch sequence, residents made more than 650,000 insurance claims?"

Still munching, Beaker takes a second sandwich out of the box. "2011 was a long time ago, boss. I was still in primary school." He mumbles through his mouthful, "I remember we had a coin trail for the victims…"

Beaker reaches out, offering her the lunchbox once again.

Still on her first sandwich, Penny refuses with a shake of her head. "I read somewhere that there were people in Christchurch still waiting for their cases to be resolved more than a decade later. A decade! And that wasn't just the private insurance cases, either. Even the Earthquake Commission took forever. A lot of those folk gave up and left town. Abandoned their homes."

"So I take it from this doomy-gloomy conversation that you think we're heading for the big one?"

"I don't know, Beak, but the signs aren't great, are they? Take a look around: we've got earthquake swarms, this god-awful heat, power outages, and the southern lights giving us a light and sound show every night for a week. This far north, too. It's unheard of."

"I thought the government had been making pretty good progress since they introduced the Climate Restoration Act. Pulling out all the stops to clean things up."

Penny shrugs. "Maybe it's just too little, too late."

Although, now Beaker has mentioned it, environmental changes could have had something to do with the massacres. They create a kind of climate tension in people. There's evidence for it going back as far as Egypt's Ptolemaic period when studies were still recorded on papyrus scrolls: a volcanic eruption, or a prolonged drought or climate event, would inevitably result in unrest among citizens. Sometimes, the people would revolt. Or a civil war might break out. Maybe that's what this is. Maybe Dad's Solaris wasn't the *cause* of the brutality of this morning's attack, but rather a *symptom* of that malaise. Perhaps the same was true for the Māngere deaths, with despair as the motivator...

Penny and Beaker say nothing for a moment, both of them chewing their sandwiches and staring out the window across the hazy rooftops to the horizon. After a while, Cerberus nuzzles Penny's hand. He lifts his big liquid eyes to hers.

Oh, go on then.

Relenting, she opens her hand and lets him snaffle up what's left of her sandwich crust. When it's gone, he licks any remaining antibiotics off his nose. Penny sighs.

Clicking the lid back on his empty lunchbox, Beaker picks up his coffee cup again. "So how are you getting on?" he asks.

"I'm still a bit shaky. Pleased to be working, though. Takes my mind off it…" She catches his look of bemusement. "Oh, you mean how am I getting on with the analyses." Hiding her embarrassment, she brushes some imaginary crumbs off her hands. "Fine."

"Any idea what the poison was?" Beaker says.

"It's weird, but my qualitative tests don't show the presence of either cyanide or ergot alkaloids. In fact, so far I haven't found evidence of anything lethal in the cordial."

"What? Nothing?"

"Just a mild soporific."

Beaker tops up his coffee from the pot and, turning, he leans back, one elbow on the counter. "Well, that makes sense," he says. "If you're going to harm a bunch of people, best to make sure they're compromised first. That way, they're less likely to fight back."

Penny has to agree with his reasoning there. It's a strategy that's worked for rapists and predators for millennia. Even mosquitoes use it. But it's the *complexity* that bothers her here. She says as much to Beaker. "If you can convince a person to drink the cordial, then wouldn't you just spike the cordial with your poison of choice? Why go to twice the effort and find some *other* means to deliver the lethal dose?"

"That's easy," Beaker says. "They were worried that they'd get caught."

Cerberus gives Penny another nudge, no doubt looking to scavenge more food. She turns away from him. "OK, let's say you're right," she says. "If it wasn't in the cordial, how exactly was it delivered? We didn't see any puncture wounds, no ligatures, broken necks…"

"Inhalation?" Beaker suggests. "The air in the crater was pretty still. Maybe whoever incited them to do this put on a gas mask, released something into the air, then took off."

Pushing aside Cerberus' lead, Penny sits on the sofa and takes a sip of her coffee while she ponders this idea. The dog rests his damaged nose on her knee. At last, she says, "Surely, if it were gas, some of the victims would have tried to crawl away. Think about it: a lot of suicide survivors say they regret their decision just seconds later. In a group of that many, you'd think *one* of them would have had doubts."

Beaker pauses, then nods. "You're right. Statistically-speaking, someone should have broken ranks, and yet no one did. That koru shape was just too perfect."

"Which means they'll have been killed by lethal injection, delivered in an unlikely spot, like between the toes. We must have missed the puncture wounds, that's all," Penny says. "We'll have to wait and see what Mather finds when he does the autopsies."

Beaker stands up. "Unless it was delivered by adhesive," he says, excitedly. "Adhesives would be easy enough to peel off after the deed was done."

"Good thinking, Beak. Adhesives are a definite possibility." Penny drains the last of the coffee, then, pushing Cerberus off her, she gets up. "I'll send Mather a text with a heads-up to check for evidence of adhesives."

"And injection sites. We may as well be thorough," Beaker says. "And tomorrow, we can start checking the bloods for poisons. Just as soon as I've finished getting the samples ready for analysis." Yawning, he tips the dregs of his coffee in the sink and puts the cup on the drainer. "I better get back to it then."

Crossing the office, Penny rinses her own cup and puts it alongside his. "And I'll join you just as soon as I've taken Cerberus downstairs for a bit of a run-around. Maybe I'll see if I can get Mather on the phone while I'm out there."

"Sure thing." Beaker flips his lunchbox in the air and, nearly failing to catch it, stumbles into Penny's shoulder. That's when she notices just how bruised and bloodshot his eyes are.

"Beak, you're exhausted. It's nearly five. The bloods can wait til tomorrow."

He yawns again. "Yeah, come to think of it, I am starting to feel like a zombie. I'll head out in a half hour. I've got a couple of things I want to finish up first."

"How were you planning on getting home?"

"Uber."

"No, you won't. I'll call and find out where Matiu is. He can't be far away. I'm sure he won't mind running you home."

"OK, thanks. That sounds great."

She picks up Cerberus' lead from the edge of the sofa. On cue, the retriever scuttles over, his doggie paws sliding on the shiny surface. Penny clips the lead to his collar.

"Back in ten," she says. Already, Cerberus is dragging her to the door.

In the lobby, Penny pushes her face to the mirrored glass and looks up and down the street. The only occupant, a worried-looking woman in her fifties, hurries into an apartment building a few doors down, leaving the street deserted. Penny shivers. So empty. The usual crowd of unruly intermediate school kids who loiter by the dumpsters have stayed away today, kept home by the earthquakes. For all the times Penny's asked why they had to choose to hang out here after school, and didn't they have homes to go to; she wishes they were here now. She presses her forehead closer to the glass for the widest angle and scans the road again. Is Makere waiting for her?

There's nothing. Still, Penny hesitates.

Cerberus tugs at the lead, keen to get outside. *Stupid.* She should have thought to ask the dog. Penny checks his body language: his tail is wagging, and his stance is loose. There's nothing to suggest he's agitated. Nothing to indicate Makere is out there.

Penny cracks open the door a fraction. Looks out.

Still empty.

She pushes it open and steps outside, Cerberus rushing through the gap beside her. He yanks on the lead, gently urging her forward, heading left towards the greenspace with its small dog park.

"OK, OK, I'm coming. Hold your horses, will ya?" Still nervous, Penny hurries along behind him, past the fence with the word BASTARD emblazoned in silver spray paint, her eyes checking the side streets for Matiu's creepy doppelgänger.

By the time they reach the dog park, her back is damp with sweat, all the accumulated heat of the day radiating up from the footpath. There's only one other person at the park: a man in a blue hoodie. He leans over the fence, his elbows propped up on the metal crossbar, while he waits for an overactive Jack Russell to stop careering about and do its business. Penny hasn't seen the pair before, but then plenty of people will have been displaced by this morning's earthquake. She gives the man a quick nod of acknowledgement before opening the gate and letting Cerberus off the lead.

While Cerberus dashes off to introduce himself to the Jack Russell, Penny sits on a nearby bench in the shade and takes out her cell phone.

Twelve new messages from Mum. Penny sighs inwardly. She'll have been trying to reply to the call Penny made to her hours ago from the garage.

Better put her out of her misery.

Penny punches reply and waits for Mum to pick up. Busy tone. She frowns. Could they be calling one another at the same time? It wouldn't be the first time. She waits a bit longer then hangs up. She'll try again in a minute.

In the meantime, she texts Matiu: Where r u?

She watches the screen for the bouncing dots to appear, but there's no response. Typical bloody Matiu. Delivering the Solaris to the depot shouldn't have taken more than an hour, even with the traffic delays. So where the hell is he? Penny smiles. He'll be checking on Erica and Charlotte, making sure they're both okay. Mum's right: phoning is one thing, but there's nothing like actually laying eyes on your loved ones after a trauma. And Erica and her sister mean a lot to Matiu. Penny recalls the wash of emotion on his face when he'd realised Charlotte wasn't among the dead at Māngere. Well, anyone would have been relieved, but this was something more. For all his tough-guy demeanour, Erica had gotten under Matiu's skin. She's important to him and Penny's not sure he even knows it.

Cerberus' low-pitched bark carries across the dog park, the Jack Russell responding with a stream of yaps. Penny looks up. The pair are running along the fence-line side by side. Just normal doggie socialising. The man in the hoodie seems unperturbed.

She dials Mather, but the call goes to answer phone. Penny hopes that means he's gone home to get some sleep. Although, with two massacres to process, the poor man might never sleep again. She leaves a message, updating him about the poisons she'd managed to eliminate, the presence of the soporific, and Beaker's adhesive theory. Then she tries Clark.

He picks up on only the second ring. "Clark here."

"Officer Clark. This is Penny Yee."

"Oh. Hello, Dr Yee. What can I do for you?"

"Just touching base really. I was wondering about Carlos."

"Dr Yee, you know I can't reveal..." He pauses. "Social services say they've located a great-aunt. They're making arrangements to place the boy in her custody."

"That's fantastic. I'm so pleased." Penny's surprised at the tears that well in her eyes.

"Yes. Finally, some bright news in all this mess. Social services say it might take a few days: there's a mountain of paperwork to get through."

"Of course. Still, it's great news." She wicks the tears away with her knuckle. "Thank you for letting me know."

"Was there anything else, Dr Yee? Only, I'm a bit busy—"

"No, no, you go ahead. I'm sorry to have bothered you. We'll talk again when you're free. Thanks again for letting me in on the good news."

Clark has already hung up.

Still no answer from Mum, so she checks her social media for information about the massacres. Finding the official report, she fast-forwards past Cordell's Windsor knot and smooth-as-silk delivery, heading straight for the comments. There's a lot of speculation: doomsayers claiming it's the end of the world, or perhaps some kind of copycat attack like the Rainbow Warrior terrorism of the 1980s. One man, calling himself UF Otherworld, claimed an alien spaceship had touched down on the wharf. Otherworld reckoned the southern lights were proof of their approach, that the government had known about it all along and was now conspiring to cover it up. Some people had come closer to the truth, suggesting there'd been a gang rumble, but those comments were long on speculation and short on specifics. For the moment, there is no mention of the Māngere mass suicide. Penny swipes back to her contacts.

This time when she calls home, Mum picks up. "Pandora! Is Matiu with you?"

Why does she always ask about him first?

"No, Mum. I haven't seen him since he left to drop off the Solaris."

"He's not with you? But I've been trying to get him on the phone for hours now."

"Did you try the depot?"

"Yes, of course, I called the depot," Mum says, sounding irritated. "They don't know where he is either. No one's seen him since the attack. And because he hadn't delivered the vehicle yet, Carlie can't track him."

Penny leaps up from the bench, sweat trickling down her back. "Wait Mum, back up. What's this about an attack?"

"I told you. Some people attacked the depot just as Matiu was arriving."

"What sort of attack?"

"What do you mean, what sort of attack? With guns, Pandora. What other sort of attack is there?"

With guns? But New Zealand doesn't have a gun culture. People don't just wander about Auckland city brandishing guns. Firearms are strictly reserved for the military, the police, the armed offenders' squad, transport authorities, and security details on government farms…

On the line, Mum is getting hysterical, her voice so shrill that Penny can't make sense of what she's saying.

"Mum, slow down. Can you sit down somewhere? Is Bituin with you? Are you sitting down?"

It takes a few moments, but finally Mum mumbles, yes.

"Right. Do you know if Matiu's okay?"

"I think so. He drove off. Dad's down there now organising the fleet to go out searching. He said the CCTV cameras at the depot show Matiu leaving."

"Was anyone else hurt?"

"No one else, although naturally everyone's in shock. They had *guns*: rifles or something. Pandora, why hasn't Matiu called to let us know he's all right? I felt sure he'd be with you. Do you think they've got him?"

"Who? The police?"

"No! Not the police. Simon Kingi and his gang."

"Simon Kingi!" Penny exclaims.

The man in the blue hoodie looks up.

Penny's lungs squeeze. Her heart pounding, she steps away and lowers her voice. "Mum, what the hell is going on?"

Mum sighs. "It was all recorded on the CCTV footage," she says, her voice suddenly weary. "Simon Kingi and his men ambushed the depot."

Penny's mouth drops open. This can't be right. Simon Kingi is dead.

In her head, Makere's voice whispers: *the evidence says otherwise.*

"No. Kingi's dead," Penny says aloud, as if saying it out loud will make it true. "I saw him fall."

Matiu fell, too.

"He's dead," Penny insists.

And yet his body was never found.

Penny's fingers tighten around the phone. Her diaphragm contracts. She can hardly breathe. Behind her, Cerberus barks.

Makere! Is he here?

The phone still pressed to her ear, she twirls, nerves zinging.

It's nothing. Just her jumping at shadows. The man in the blue hoodie has collected his dog and is heading off down the street, the little Jack Russell darting off in all directions, ignoring his owner's calls to come back.

"I know it seems incredible, but Craig saw the footage," Mum says in Penny's ear, bringing her back to the present and pushing all thoughts of Makere out of her head. "He identified Kingi."

Penny closes her eyes. There are so many things she doesn't understand. Clearly, Craig had left her and gone to the attack at the depot. Why didn't he tell her, since it concerned her? The attack occurred at the site of her parents' business. Her brother had been on the scene. Why keep her in the dark? And what business did an adjunct to the Transport Minister have at the scene of an armed attack, anyway?

And how would Craig have known Simon Kingi well enough to identify him?

Her head swimming with unanswered questions, Penny concentrates on what she does know, counting the facts off on her fingers.

No one had been harmed in the attack.

Matiu was alive last time anyone saw him.

This isn't his first car chase.

He's still driving the Solaris prototype, supposedly the fanciest piece of automotive machinery the country has ever seen.

He's in love, even if he doesn't know it, so it's likely he doesn't have a death-wish.

Plus, Penny hadn't noted any random explosions while she'd been browsing social media, so that had to be a positive sign.

"Mum, try not to panic," she says, trying to be as upbeat as possible. "If I know Matiu, he'll be lying low until the heat is off. Remember, he used to be part of Kingi's gang, had his finger in all their affairs, so if anyone knows how to steer clear of them, it's Matiu."

"That's what your father said," Mum says quietly.

"See? Everything is going to be fine. Although, if Matiu is trying to stay out of sight, it might pay to get Dad to call the fleet back."

"But the fleet aren't looking for Matiu. They're looking for Mārama. That's what I've been trying to tell you: Mārama's gone missing."

She flings open the gate. "Cerberus! Come."

The dog must catch the urgency in her tone because he abandons the steaming pile of dog turd he's been investigating and comes straight away.

"Good boy." With trembling fingers Penny clips on his collar and ushers him through the gate. Then they're off and running, back to the laboratory.

The street is empty. Penny's footsteps echo off the buildings. Penny cringes at the sound. The heat is unbearable. She's almost expiring. Still, she doesn't let up. Mārama's missing, Kingi's back, and Makere's hovering in the wings…

Barely slowing, she jabs at the phone to call Matiu again.

Pick up!

The phone picks up.

"Matiu!"

But there's a whirr as the phone clicks and Matiu's voice answers, "Hi! This is Matiu. Unfortunately, we are experiencing some technical difficulties right now and won't be able to take your call—"

Penny hangs up and keeps running. Nearly there. Two more blocks. Sweat drips in her eyes. She wipes it away and hurries on, crossing the intersection…until she spies the dumpsters.

Penny stops dead.

It's the man from the dog park. In the blue hoodie.

Mum's words come back to her: "I felt sure Matiu would be with you." Wouldn't her brother's old cronies think the same thing? They might have sent someone to watch her. This man perhaps. She leaps into the alley, dragging Cerberus with her. Peeks out, her heart in her throat.

"Bella," the man calls. "Come on."

Her knees trembling, Penny waits. Is it a ruse?

"Bella."

The Jack Russell darts out from behind the dumpster and runs right past his owner. "Oh for goodness sake." The man breaks into a jog, heading off in the other direction after the errant terrier.

Penny doesn't take any chances. She and Cerberus sprint across the road, Penny reaching out to slap her hand on the keypad.

Inside.

Slam the door.

They fly up the stairs, two at a time.

CHAPTER 23

- Matiu -

There are four of them around the Solaris. Matiu sees the circle of motorbikes before he sees the gangsters and manages to skid into the shadows of the trees, hauling Erica with him, before they're seen. Two of the figures are intent on breaking into the car, while two keep watch. In the gloom the men look hunched, the darkness looping around them, caressing them. Pressing himself against a tree trunk, Matiu breathes hard, placing a finger to Erica's lips and pointing to the gangsters. Behind them, someone with a bow and arrows and a damned fine aim, no doubt closing in on them right now. Ahead, a brawl Matiu can't hope to win, even with Erica there to kick some butt. Not if these guys are Kingi's, not if they've been painted by the same brush that turned Hanson and Kingi into monsters. He's got enough nemeses already, sure doesn't need a whole taua of them dogging his every step.

Still, Matiu can't just hide here in the trees and hope they'll all go away. Either they'll steal the car, leaving Erica and Matiu stranded here, or the archer will catch up, and for all Matiu knows that guy might be wearing IR goggles, so hiding in the shadows won't help them at all.

Matiu drops to his belly, pulling Erica down with him. He tugs his phone from his pocket and taps into the settings, searching for networks and devices.

"What are you doing?" Erica hisses, pulling her jacket around her.

"Improvising," Matiu replies, locating the strongest local wi-fi signals. At least three houses adjacent to the carpark have domestic networks the owners probably think are pretty secure. Ha ha. Matiu tags all three and runs Scour's custom cracker, confirming access to two of the three in seconds. The third successfully rejects his attack. Making a note to tell Scour his shit needs updating, Matiu drops into the first network, swiping up the security system, arming it and flooding it with activations, then moves onto the next house.

Sirens and blue strobes leap from the houses, and on instinct, the gangsters around the car drop their marks and dash for their motorbikes. In a roar of engines and a shriek of rubber, they scarper. It won't fool them for long, especially if Kingi really wants this car, but with any luck they'll be halfway up the road before they realise the lights and sirens aren't cops but residential alarms. It's a dead-end street, so this situation is a long way from over. They'll be meeting those guys again on the way out of here.

"C'mon!" Matiu breaks cover and runs for the Solaris, Erica close behind. Their footfalls hammer on the asphalt, Matiu fumbling for the keytag which he'd zipped carefully into an inside pocket so he wouldn't lose it. Should've kept it in easy reach, should've known he'd end up needing to make a quick getaway. Should've parked the other way around, ready to race out of here. Should've...

The sound is worse than a gunshot, a soft severing of air, feather-light and deadly, and the pain a muted, otherworldy thing. A white spiral, clean and precise, perfectly formed, almost artful. He's been punched plenty of times, even taken a bullet once. Those are pains you know about, a ragged assault on the senses, big and honest and obvious. This is something altogether new, the experience as pure and unexpected as the dark rills of blood that spatter the Solaris' white door, even as he stumbles, his shoulder a pulsing fire, his muscles screaming as they pull and wrench around the shaft driven through him.

"Matiu!"

Got to keep moving. Arrows, fast as a rifle. Loose, new arrow, notch, draw, aim, loose. Rinse and repeat. But his body just wants to move down, towards the road, shock racing in to fill the void that his ability to think has vacated. The door snaps open in front of him and he's being hauled, tossed bodily into the back seat. Pain is his new, overwhelming reality. The world spins in the light that flares from the car's ceiling, and Matiu doesn't remember the white leather of the back seats being smeared with red.

Another door opens and slams shut. "How the hell do you start this thing?" Erica's shouting now, shouting at the car, and the Solaris obligingly turns on.

Matiu shakes his head, pushes back the pain, and tries to sit up. The arrow skewering him scrapes on the seats. "I can drive," he mutters, which is ridiculous and he knows it, but Erica is way ahead of him. Slapping the gearstick, she hits the accelerator and spins the wheel, reversing into the roadway before dropping into gear and speeding away from Ōwairaka.

Matiu slumps forward, clinging to the back of the passenger seat, watching in a daze as his blood runs down the arrow shaft to pool in the footwell. "Someone in the club," he wheezes. "Kerr had a Touching the Sun acolyte in the archery club. This was bait. A decoy. To catch us."

"No shit," Erica growls, "but I think we've got a bigger problem."

Matiu looks up blearily. Racing down the street towards them are four headlights.

"Soldiers," he reasons. "Everyone has soldiers. This is war. Those we sacrifice, those we send out to fight."

The four motorcycles sweep past and spin around in the rear-view mirror, the roars of their engines unnaturally loud in the night.

He's been shot with an arrow. He's never been shot with an arrow before. Not exactly something he'd planned to tick off his bucket list. He should probably get to a hospital, but if he does, they'll make him stay, want to stitch him up and ask a whole lot of inconvenient questions, and then he'll never find Charlotte. If he needs stitching up, he'd prefer to do it himself. He's seen this shit in the movies, it can't be that hard, can it? Gripping the passenger seat with one hand, he grasps the shaft where it protrudes from his trapezius, slick with warm blood. Twists.

The pain is impossible, a wave of fire and blackness sweeping through him, making him choke. He barely swallows the urge to vomit.

"Brace yourself!" Erica warns, and the car suddenly brakes, lurching sideways. There's a tortured scream of metal and a howl of pain, quickly lost as the Solaris accelerates again.

Swirling patterns of light and dark spiral through Matiu's vision and he bites back a sob. Turns out snapping an arrow off when it's driven from one side of your body to the other isn't as easy as it looks in the movies. Instead, he gets a grip on the shaft and yanks hard, pulling it through his already tortured flesh. The pain is still intense, but less so. This won't knock him out, and once he's pulled it right through, pulled the damn thing right out of his body, he'll be able to think again...

The Solaris swerves hard to the right. Lights flash in the window and there's a squeal and a resounding smash as something heavy whirls past the windows. Erica jerks the wheel over, braking hard, and then the car tears away again, leaving a trail of broken metal and limbs in its wake.

Part of Matiu wishes he could be seeing this, because damn it would make a fine action sequence. Another part of him wonders where the hell this Erica came from, this desk jockey who's in her element roughing it at high speed with killer bikers, a crooked grin on her face as she leaves the gangsters in pieces behind her.

Almost out, the arrow refuses to come all the way, despite Matiu's best efforts.

"The fletching's caught on your leather jacket, so you won't get it any further," Erica says, sparing him a quick glance. "Fat lot of use that thing did you, eh? Good effort, though. Hold on just a minute longer, all right?"

Matiu droops. Stares at his blood on the floor, on his hands. The arrow with its scarlet tip.

Someone had shot him with a goddamned arrow. And his armour wasn't worth a damn. If he's a soldier, then this does not bode well.

"Hold still. This is gonna hurt."

Matiu grunts, holds the headrests tight as Erica grips the exposed arrow shaft in both hands and strains to snap it in half. The carbon flexes but doesn't break.

"Fuck," she mutters. "This is professional deer-hunting ammunition."

"Oh deer me," Matiu quips, grimacing.

"Let's hold off on the dad jokes at least until we've managed to stop the bleeding, shall we?"

The car's first aid kit is scattered on the passenger seat. Erica had ripped away Matiu's shirt to tape a couple of flimsy gauze pads around the arrow. The pads and tape alike had quickly become saturated with blood and hang heavy on his skin. The little scissors had no chance of cutting through his leather jacket, so blood still leaks down his back, warm and sticky. His head is fuzzy. The idea of an ambulance keeps trying to creep in, making more and more sense. But this is not a time for sensible ideas.

His phone buzzes in his pocket. "Hi," Matiu says to the blood on the floor. "This is Matiu. Unfortunately we are experiencing some technical difficulties right now and won't be able to take your call." The phone keeps ringing. "Please leave your name, number, and bank account details, and we'll despatch a cockroach disposal team to your location within the next twelve to eighteen weeks. Beeeep." The phone stops. How very obedient.

"Stay with me, and don't quit your day job for a career as a stand-up comic," Erica says, having emptied out the glovebox and found nothing that might aid in the removal of an arrow from human flesh. "There's a servo around the corner, they might have an emergency toolkit. Stay right here, I'll be back in a minute."

Then she's gone, and the door is closed and the light is dimming, and Matiu breathes hard. Feels the dark closing in, the shimmering greens and reds that paint the sky crawling over the windscreen. He has no idea where they're parked, his world contracting down to the burning pain in his shoulder, the pool of blood at his feet.

He doesn't hear the door open or close, but he knows when he's there. Makere. Just a thin shadow, reclining in the back seat. Matiu smells smoke, hears the crinkle of cigarette paper burning. Wants to turn and confront his lifelong foe, but his head is too heavy. The walls around him are too black, and all there is right now is Matiu, and Makere, and their pain. The one thing they've always shared.

"Tonight's the night, bro," Makere says. "Look at Ranginui. Feel Papatūānuku. Listen to Rūaumoko. This is all about the ending of what was, and the birth of something new."

Matiu concentrates on not passing out. Makere can't know these things, can't see the future. He's a figment, a smudge of Matiu's own fragile psyche smeared across his waking madness. Makere isn't here, he can't be here, he's never been here. All he is, all he knows, are Matiu's deepest fears. He's the imaginary friend who always hated him, the fear Matiu hid behind, his fear of being left alone. Left behind.

"Just stop talking," Matiu says, breathing through the pain. "Nothing you can say can hurt me, bro. You're not even here. You don't fucking exist."

"Not here, eh? Can't hurt you?"

The arrow twists, bright agony. Matiu screams.

"You've had this flesh so long and look how you've wasted it. Abused it. Damaged it. You don't deserve to be the one walking around in this stolen skin. You had your chance, you fucked it right up, bro."

"You drove me to it! You were in my ear, all the time! You're the reason!"

"Keep blaming me, it won't make any difference to Hine-nui-te-pō when she comes for you."

Matiu sucks a hard, hot breath. "You got anything useful to say? Or did you just come to gloat over something that's never gonna happen?"

“You want to know?” Makere leans in, the smoke from his breath clouding around Matiu’s head. “You want to know I’m more than just a voice in your head? You want me to tell you something that can’t possibly be hiding in your subconscious? Something to prove to you that I’m as real as you are? If I tell you something, and it’s true, then will you believe?”

“What could you possibly tell me that I want to know?”

Makere sniggers. “I know where she is.”

“Who?”

“Sandi Kerr. Charlotte Langley. Mārama. Take your pick.”

Matiu’s breath catches. “You don’t know.”

“They’re where they’ve all been promised. They’ve found Eden at last.”

“Eden?”

The door snaps open, light flooding the back seat.

“Eden?” Matiu says again, trying to twist around. No Makere. Like he was never there. Like he never *was*.

“What?” Erica says, brandishing what looks like boltcutters. “What about Eden?” She sniffs. “Have you been smoking in here?”

“Eden,” Matiu repeats, then the dark swirls in and takes him down with it.

CHAPTER 24

- Pandora -

Penny and Cerberus break into the laboratory at a run. "You took your time," Beaker says. He's hanging up his lab coat.

Penny doesn't reply. Spinning, she turns and slams the door behind her. Only then, does she stop to bend over, put her hands on her knees, and breathe in hard.

"Pen, what's wrong?" Beaker says, abandoning the coat hook to approach her.

Everything's wrong! Penny stares at his shoes while she sucks in another breath. And another. And another. It isn't the stairs that have her breathless: Yee Scientific is only on the second floor.

Beaker scratches Cerberus' jaw while he waits for her to catch her breath.

At last, Penny stands up. "I just spoke to Mum. Simon Kingi and his biker gang mates turned up at the depot. They were *armed*." The words crackle on the air like burning undergrowth.

Beaker's face drops. "Hang on. Simon Kingi. Isn't he—"

"Dead?" Penny replies. "Apparently not."

Beaker brings his hands to his face. "Oh shit, Pen. What happened?"

"Nothing," Penny says, and her shoulders slump. "Well, nothing happened at the depot. Who knows what happened after that? Mum says Matiu drove off and drew Kingi's men away. It was the last anyone's seen of either of them."

"So Kingi was after Matiu?"

"He must've been!" she wails. "Why else would he come to the depot? My parents do not do business with gangsters!"

"I didn't mean—" Beaker begins. "Shit," he says again. "There's no chance that Matiu's got himself tangled up with that lot again?"

Scowling, Penny puts her hands on her hips. "No! Of course not. Kingi tried to kill Matiu. He tied our aunt to a lightning rod. In the middle of a storm! There's no way Matiu would have anything to do with him. Wouldn't touch him with a ten-foot bargepole."

"OK. Sorry. Just checking. What are we going to do?"

Penny feels her chin tremble, the tough-girl resilience from her phone call with Mum rapidly crumbling. She throws up her hands helplessly. "What *can* we do, Beak? Hope Matiu got away. Wait for the police to turn up Kingi." Penny paces back and forth in front of the laboratory door.

"It'll be fine," Beaker says, his tone jovial. "If the police are on to it, then I'm sure they'll find him."

Shaking her head, Penny glances away. She knows he means well, but the platitude irks her. How can he be so confident? The police didn't find any trace of

Kingi before, not even after *months* of looking. What makes him think they'll have any more hope of finding him now? Or *ever*? Worse, as the new leader of Hanson's gang, Kingi probably has access to bolt-holes all over the city. There's no end of places he might be holed up: in an unused basement somewhere, the back office of a warehouse, or an isolated farmhouse. What if his cronies have caught up with Matiu? They could've taken Matiu to one of those secluded bolt-holes by now. They might have strapped Matiu to a chair, padded the walls to dampen any sound, laid plastic sheeting on the floor…Kingi would have all the time in the world to exact his revenge. The way he had with Matiu's friend Screech. She stops pacing and shudders. Tears prick at her eyes.

"Penny." Wrestling with his awkwardness, Beaker steps over and reaches out a hand, tentatively resting it on her shoulder. "Come on, Pen. Try not to worry." He gives her shoulder a comforting squeeze. "If there's one thing I know about your brother, it's that he's pretty good at getting himself out of a scrape."

Penny responds with a weak grin. "That's true. He could wiggle out of most things. I recall him being pretty good at getting out of the dishes."

Beaker's face flushes with relief. He drops his hand and steps away. "You know, I was going to head out, but I think I'll stay on a bit longer. Maybe make us a cup of tea…"

If only a cup of tea would fix this.

"No Beak, really, there's no reason for you to stay on. Oh—" Penny slaps her palm to her forehead. "I was going to get Matiu to take you home, wasn't I? I'll call the depot now…" She trails off. Bites her lip. "I forgot. It might be a long wait. My dad has half the fleet out looking for my Aunt Mārama."

"Your aunt? Was she at the depot?"

"No, she was at Mum and Dad's. She must have slipped out while Mum and Dad were dealing with what was going on at work."

"I'm sure she hasn't gotten far."

But a sudden realisation sends blood thrumming to Penny's temples. What if Mārama had heard her parents talking about the attack? What if she'd decided to go looking for Matiu? What if someone—someone other than Matiu—were to find her?

The panic must be etched on Penny's face, because Beaker raises both hands as if to hold back her fears. "She probably just got it in her head to walk home. Didn't you tell me at Māngere that the earthquake had unsettled her?"

With dread pooling in the pit of her stomach, Cerberus chooses that moment to pad over and sit on her foot, and there is something so ordinary, so unflappably casual, about the dog's action, that Penny can't help but smile. "You're probably right," she says. Maybe she's panicking about nothing, after all. There's no reason to think Mārama heard anything. It's not the first time she's given Mum the slip.

"I'm sure your dad's people will find her."

"Yeah." Penny bends to rub the dog's ears. Cerberus looks up at her with his big doggie eyes and his beat-up nose… All at once, Penny realises there *is* something she can do. But to do that, she'll have to get Beaker out of the way first.

Beaker moves towards the coat hook. "Well, if I'm going to stick around a bit, I may as well prep some more samples." Taking down his lab coat, he thrusts his hand into the armhole to turn the sleeve the right way around.

Penny marches over and snatches the lab coat from his hands. "No you won't," she tells him. On her tiptoes, she pops it back on the hook. "You're going to call an Uber and you're going to go home. The samples will still be there tomorrow."

He tilts his head to one side. "You're sure? You seemed pretty upset just a minute ago."

"Beaker, if you don't go home, I'm going to mark this up on your performance review."

"Oooh," he says, grinning. "Bringing out the big guns, eh? OK. I'm going." He gets out his phone, makes a text, then slips his phone back into his pocket. "Fifteen minutes, depending on how long the guy takes to get through the traffic." He moves towards the sink. "Maybe I'll clean some glassware while I'm waiting…"

Penny raises an eyebrow. "Beaker."

"On second thoughts, I think I'll wait in the lobby." He pats his phone through his pants' pocket. "Should be enough time to get in a chapter of my book."

For a moment, Penny worries about gangsters hovering on the street outside, but she quickly dismisses any misgivings about Beaker's safety. Since the former tenant—a tertiary provider—vacated the building due to a lack of bums-on-seats, heaps of small businesses have rented premises in the former classrooms. Sure, Penny got the laboratories, but there's a dental surgery in one of the back rooms, and a small law firm on the third floor. For a while, she'd suspected there had been a brothel operating on the top floor. The thing is, people come in and out all the time. Even if someone were watching the building, they'd have no reason to think Beaker is known to either Matiu or Penny. To them, he'd be just some random waiting for a ride.

Beaker opens the door. Turns. "See you tomorrow, then."

"Not if I see you first," Penny says, and she shoos him out the door.

The minute he's gone, and the door is shut firmly behind him, Penny checks her phone. Still no reply from Matiu and, surprisingly, nothing from Mum either. She thinks about calling Craig to pump him for details about what happened at the depot, but her pride won't let her, and she's already rung Clark, so she can hardly call him again.

She sniffs. *Well, I'm sure as hell not calling Cordell.* Until she gets an update, she's stuck here at the lab. Penny looks across to the bench where she'd been working on the cordial residue earlier.

Beaker isn't here…

She clucks her tongue.

It wouldn't take long.

Her mind made up, she puts on her lab coat and strides across the lab to the cold store. Once inside, she pushes aside the reagent bottles until she finds the specimen jar with the sliver of shattered cylinder. She lifts the petal-shaped shard from the jar and holds it to the light, examining the blackened smear.

I think it's about time we find out if Makere really is Matiu's brother.

With a quick glance over her shoulder at the door, Penny snaps on a pair of gloves, scrapes a speck of blood off the glass with a blade, and places it in a cuvette. Adds DDT, proteinase, primer, polymerase. She discards the pipette tip, spins the sample in the centrifuge, then slides the cuvette into the benchtop DNA-sequencer. Then she drops the lid and presses start. The Breadmaker™ hums as it warms up.

With nothing left to do, Penny drops the shard back in the specimen jar, and replaces it in its hidey-hole at the back of the cool store.

When she returns, Cerberus is circling the bench, a low growl rumbling in his throat.

"Shhh, boy. Let's just see, OK?"

The hound ignores her, keeping up his patrol around the Breadmaker™.

Penny lets him pace. It'll be over soon enough. She leans back against the bench to wait for the Breadmaker™ to do its magic. Talk about aptly named. Without this machine, she and Beaker would be monitoring algal blooms for the council, that is, if they were still in business at all. Penny watches as the crystal display tells her what stage the assay is at. Still in incubation right now, but eventually it will pass to elution, and then the annealing and digestion phases…

Cerberus' bark makes her jump.

"Stop that, Cerb. I'm jittery enough as it is."

The refrigerator murmurs something, like an ornery teenager mumbling under his breath. "And I don't need your tuppence worth either," Penny says.

The thing is, whatever she tells herself, she does feel bad. Fingerprinting Makere's DNA feels like a betrayal of Mārama. All these years, her aunt has never revealed who Matiu's father is. She'd never mentioned Makere either, not until Penny asked her just a few months ago. But that hadn't stopped Makere haunting Matiu throughout their childhood. Why though? If they were brothers and had been separated from one another, that was hardly Matiu's fault.

Cerberus growls again.

"No. I'm not taking it out. We need this. We need some answers."

The dog continues its pacing.

The machine clicks through its cycle.

Suddenly, Cerberus lift his head and howls. Penny's hair stands on end. In the same instant, the machine's stop-alert shrieks. The troubleshooting light blinks RED, RED, RED.

No! Not this again.

But it is happening again. Smoke is pouring from under the Breadmaker's™ lid, bringing with it the putrid grey-green stench of decay. The smoke alarm wails. Penny's heart pounds with the din. The machine's temperature shoots up.

Cerberus' hackles are raised, too. The dog leaps at the machine, his eyes white with rage or terror. He falls back, teeth slashing at air. Like hell's hound, he is wild, drooling, ferocious. And he's not about to give up. Snarling, Cerberus leaps again, flinging himself at the Breadmaker™. Curved white teeth graze the side of the machine, leaving behind strings of saliva and deep gouges in the casing.

She doesn't even attempt to get to the machine. She tried that once before and Cerberus wouldn't let her near it. There's no point in trying. She risks losing an arm. Or, in his frenzied state, Cerberus might decide to rip out her throat. But he could also kill himself at this rate. She needs to stop the machine.

While the dog leaps again, this time scrambling onto the benchtop, Penny takes two steps to the wall and yanks the cord out of the socket. In the same movement, she pushes the Fire Alarm to off and sends a 'false call' notification to the fire service.

Instantly, the noise halts. The blinking lights cease. Automatic ventilators start up, sucking curls of smoke into the grills.

Heaving a breath, Penny leans against the wall.

Cerberus drops to the ground, whining softly.

"Bloody hell, Cerberus," she whispers.

She steps towards the machine. It's still hot from whatever corruption provoked the trauma. Using her lab coat pocket to protect her fingertips, she flips up the lid. A waft of pungent gas hits her in the face, making her eyes water. When the fumes have dissipated, sucked away by the ventilators, she peers inside. Her heart staggers.

She doesn't want to believe it.

The cuvette is still intact, a blackened kernel like a puckered walnut in the trough. The machine is disconnected, so there's no digital read-out, but the paper print-out is coated in Bisphenol A, which is heat resistant. Using her lab pocket glove, Penny unclips the casing and unwinds the feed. She looks at the read-out and her eyes blur.

Cerberus barks and Penny almost jumps out of her skin. She looks up to see him sprinting across the laboratory.

Someone's coming!

Penny pivots, crumpling the read-out and slipping it into her back pocket, as the laboratory doors fly open and Erica and Beaker plunge into the room, Matiu slung between them in a fireman's carry.

After that nothing else matters because all Penny can see is the blood.

CHAPTER 25

- Matiu -

Thoughts are a maddening whirl, sharp-edged like the sea below, the clouds above. Matiu stumbles to the edge of the cliff, sinks to his knees. This place at the brink of all things, a place he's been before. The precipice, where he watched Mārama stand tall to do battle with a taniwha, the monster that lies beneath all his darkest dreams. He can feel pieces of himself chipping away, shards splintering from his knees, his palms, his heart. The pain is a blanket, scorching his brittle limbs. He coughs, and blood showers the grass like tiny wet rubies.

We're all made of glass. We might last forever, if only we didn't break.

The angry sun is rising. Loops of fire coil away from his edges to burn the sky and the churning sea. *Ra.* Bitter, bloody Ra, reined to the earth by the trickster Māui and his brothers. Beaten into submission, forced to crawl, not run, across Ranginui's vast emptiness. Enslaved to humanity, those wretches who should be bound to scrape and dig in the earth yet who walk and run beneath his gaze while he, the sun that scours all things, must limp from dawn to dusk. Biding his time, waiting until the moment is ripe before having his revenge against all Māui's children.

Time is a spiral, swallowing us inch by inch, down into her eternally hungry throat, so full of glistening teeth. So choked with all that's left of those who've gone before. We're all her victims, eventually.

This time, there's no monster broaching the waves. No Mārama, swinging her taiaha, the battle-staff of her ancestors. There is only the sun, only Ra, carving his path across the horizon, straining at his ropes. One vast, raging eye, glaring down at Matiu.

It blinks.

"This should bring him round," says the sun, or maybe not the sun, some other voice, familiar, unwelcome, slick as an oily sea. "It's a mix of coagulant, painkiller, and stimulant, with a side of mental sedative. Breakfast of champions."

Matiu breathes hard, head spinning. There's a new pain, this one in his arm, tiny yet ablaze, a hot match driven into his skin. His chest shudders.

"What?" Shocked outrage. That must be Penny. "We need to let him rest, not wake him up. Where did you even get that stuff?"

The horizon is falling down, and Tane Mahuta bends his knees and presses his hands and his broad shoulders against the expanse of his father Ranginui's eternity, plants his feet hard into the soft, life-giving soils of his mother Papatūānuku. He flexes his massive legs, thrusting up with his mighty arms. Where the love of mother and father had once held all their children crushed in their dark embrace, now the great kauri tree presses up and up, and into that place there comes light and wind. While their parents wail with the pain of separation—for their own son is driving them apart—their children are free to run and yell and war together.

Simpler times. Not this rushing light burning his eyes, the rasp of air against his throat, the reminder that his body is a shell, a vessel that can be drained. Broken. Like glass. Just the disagreements of gods, the myths of creation. How much easier it all must have been back then, when the world was young.

"Matiu, bro, can you hear me? Matiu?"

Craig Tong. Of all the people to bring light to his darkness, why did it have to be Craig Tong?

"Craig, leave him be." Penny. Reliable, dependable Penny. The light. The breath of fresh air, the wind in his hair. "He's lost a lot of blood. He needs to sleep."

"Penny, this can't wait."

"The hell it can't!"

A slamming door, maybe. Then blissful quiet, and the sound of breathing. His breathing? He's not sure. There's something warm in his hand, it's...another hand. His pulse threads up a notch, and for a moment he's back there, on the clifftop, looking out across the sea into the blazing sun, and the sun is not the sun but a man, a warrior carved from head to toe with burning moko, striding across the waves towards him, and his face is Matiu's. The cliff gives way and he topples forward into the void, towards the roaring sea below.

- Pandora -

Practically shoving Craig out of the office, Penny pulls the door closed on Matiu and Erica, and steps into the laboratory.

Beaker and Cerberus, waiting like a pair of expectant fathers, get to their feet. "Is Matiu going to be all right?" Beaker asks. "There was a lot of blood."

"I think so," Penny says. "Once we got him cleaned up, the wounds weren't too bad, although he's in a lot of pain. We've given him some pain relief." Folding her arms across her chest, she shoots a glare at Craig. "He just needs to *rest*, that's all."

Beaker picks up a surgical glove, stretching the Nitrile fingers in and out like an accordion. "Yeah, but Pen, wouldn't he be more comfortable at the hospital?"

"I *tried* to get him to go. Erica tried, too." Penny's shoulders slump. "Matiu refuses to give in."

"Ah, yes," Beaker says. He lifts his eyes to the ceiling. "I should have known. That famous Yee determination."

"He's stubborn, all right," Penny agrees, only belatedly realising that she is also a Yee and that Beaker's statement probably includes her.

"Penny," Craig's voice is solemn, "If your brother's awake, don't you think we should at least ask him some questions? It could give the authorities a head start on finding whoever did this."

Penny whirls to face him. "What do you mean, whoever did this? We *know* who did this. Simon Kingi and his henchmen did it. Matiu drew them away from the depot, and they chased after him on motorcycles and attacked him. If the police want to hunt down Kingi and his brutes, then they need to get off their tushes and do their jobs! They have it all recorded on CCTV. You identified Kingi yourself—*a man who is supposed to be dead!*" She puts her hands on her hips. "And that's another thing, Craig Tong. Why didn't you tell me there was something going on at the depot? You just upped and left. You knew my family was in danger and yet you didn't say a word."

Craig takes a step back, his face a rictus of confusion.

Penny doesn't let up. She stalks across the lab towards him. Damn the man. He needs to stand up and accept his part in this mess. How could he not tell her? He let her carry on as if nothing was happening, and while she might have played it down for Beaker, the truth is Matiu is lying in the next room looking like a giant has prodded him with a pickle fork. She could have lost her brother. If that arrow had grazed just a fraction to the left, Matiu would likely be dead. And if Erica hadn't been with him, if his probation officer girlfriend hadn't tacked him together and driven him here, Matiu could be bleeding out, alone and in pain on some dingy Auckland side street—

Penny lets out a sob.

Craig takes two steps forward and gathers her up in his arms. "I'm sorry. You're right. I should have told you," he says, his breath in her hair.

"I should have *been* there, Craig. I might've been able to stop it," she murmurs into his chest. She's grateful that he doesn't refute it. What could she have done that Erica hadn't?

While she's standing there in his arms, savouring the way his shirt smells faintly of oranges, her cell rings. "I'd better…" She steps away from Craig, wipes her eyes with her sleeve, and takes the device from her pocket. "Hello?"

"Dr Yee. It's Officer Clark."

Penny's heart kickflips. She slaps her hand over the microphone. What should she do? How much do the police know? What if they want to talk to Matiu? They always think he's guilty of something. What should she say? "It's Clark," she whispers.

Craig and Beaker shuffle closer. Craig nods at her to continue. "Find out what he wants."

Penny lifts the phone to her ear. "Yes?"

Craig and Beaker lean in as Clark speaks, "I'm sorry to bother you, Dr Yee—I know it's been a very long day—but I wondered if you would mind coming out to Puketutu Island?"

"Come to the island? What? Right now?"

"Well, yes."

"Can't it wait until tomorrow?"

"You'd think so, but Dr Cordell says not. He believes he has uncovered something of significance in the um…Māngere case."

"The Māngere case. Cordell? What does he think he's doing? He has no right. Officer Clark, please tell that peacock not to touch my cadavers. They're nothing to do with him. That is *my* contract. Tanner gave it to *me*."

"Yes, I know, I did try to explain that to Dr Cordell, but he can be very insistent."

"Maybe if you get Tanner on the phone—"

"Detective Inspective Tanner's not available right now."

"And Mather?"

"Still here, although to be fair the man is half dead on his feet with exhaustion."

"Then can't you—"

"No, I thought of that, too," the officer interrupts, and the fatigue in his voice reminds her that Mather isn't the only one who's been up since 3am. "Unfortunately, Cordell won't be satisfied telling his news to Mather and asking him to pass it on. He insists you ought to be here for his announcement."

An announcement? What is this: a school assembly?

"I'd really like to get this sorted if I could," Clark goes on. "I still have one house call to make before I clock off, and I promised Mrs Clark I'd be home before midnight."

"Officer Clark, would you hold the line a moment, please?"

Penny puts her hand over the mic a second time. "What do I do?" she whispers.

"We should go," Beaker says. "You know what Cordell's like. If we don't go, he'll muscle in on the contract."

Penny glances towards the office. "I can't leave Matiu."

"Why not? Erica's with him," Beaker says. "They'll be safe enough in the building. No one will even know they're here if we lock the doors and put the nightlights on."

"That's true," Penny says thoughtfully. "And as long as Erica's here, I guess Matiu isn't going anywhere."

Beaker cups his chin, pretending to give the question some thought. "Arguing with your probation officer? Hmmm. Probably not recommended."

Penny looks at Craig. "Unfortunately, I don't drive…" She trails off pointedly, giving him a chance to intervene and offer them a ride to Puketutu Island.

What will it be, Craig? Me or your precious prototype?

Craig hesitates.

She should have known. People like Tong don't date girls like her.

"Well, I guess that answers that question," Penny says briskly. "Beaker, if you don't mind driving, we'll take *Matiu's fleet car*, since he won't be using it."

She takes her hand off the mic. "Officer Clark, are you still there? Beaker and I will be there in twenty. In the meantime, please do whatever you can to keep Cordell's mitts off my case." She swipes the phone off.

"Penny…"

Ignoring Craig, Penny addresses Beaker. "Let me just look in on Matiu first,

OK? I'll tell Erica what's happening, check she's okay minding Cerberus, and then we'll go. Do you want to grab a sampling kit?"

"Penny, please—" Craig says.

Penny turns her back on him.

"Um, sure," Beaker says, and he scuttles off, clearly detecting the ambient awkwardness at around 999,999 parts per million.

"Penny." Craig takes her by the arm, turning her towards him. "Please, let me drive you."

"Don't you mean, let me drive you *in the prototype?*" Her voice is as brittle as glass. "It wouldn't do to have anything happen to the precious car."

Craig shakes his head. "No, I mean, I'll take you in the ministry vehicle. We'll leave the Solaris where it is, downstairs in the parking garage."

Penny twists her arm out of his grip. "Why?"

"Because Kingi's boys could still be out scouring the streets for Matiu."

"Ha!" Penny scoffs. "I knew it. You don't want to risk the prototype. It's safer off the streets, hidden in the basement, isn't it?"

Beaker returns, his jacket on, and the sampling kit slung over his shoulder. He takes one look and turns on his heel. "Oops, I think I forgot something," he mumbles, and he ducks away.

One hand on her hip, Penny taps her foot. "Well?"

Craig rubs at a spot on the back of his wrist with his thumb. "It's true the technology is safer in the garage…"

Penny snorts. If only she had a gavel, she'd bang it on the benches. Whirling, she marches for the office. She's about to yank open the door, when, over her head, Craig reaches out a hand and holds it shut.

"…but that's not why we're leaving the car where it is," he says.

"Open the door, Craig."

But Craig doesn't move. Instead, he lowers his head to whisper in her ear. When he does, his breath is soft on her cheek, "Because if Kingi's men find it, the last thing I want is for them to find you."

- Matiu -

He's not sure how long he's been out when he wakes, gasping, from a dream of sinking. He jerks upright, clutching his head, reminded immediately of the pain as his shoulder flares once more.

"Easy, Tiger." Erica's voice, calm. "You've had a busy night." She presses him back down into a pillow.

"It's not over," Matiu mutters, his throat raw. "He's coming."

"Don't worry about Tong. Penny took him with her to Puketutu Island. Something about Cordell. They'll be gone a little while; you need to get some rest."

"Not Tong," he murmurs, "Not him."

Matiu takes in his surroundings. The room is dim, a single desk lamp in a corner throwing enough light to see by. Penny's office just off the lab, and he's laid out on the couch. He takes a moment to take stock of his physical state, running a hand across his chest under the blanket. His shirt is gone, replaced with gauze pads and medical tape and compression bandages. The pain is less than he'd expect, and his heart is pounding, probably on account of whatever Tong stuck in his veins. Still, this is going to hurt like a bastard in the morning. His left arm aches and he swats at it, finds a tube sticking into the soft skin in the crook of his elbow.

"Quit squirming," Erica says. "You're not the only one with needles in you."

Turning his head, Matiu twists to see Erica, pulled up in the office chair beside him. There's a dark shape between them, some reappropriated lab equipment with a plastic bag hanging from it, tubes running in and out, red with fluid. "You're...?"

"Think yourself lucky that your sister keeps records of things like her brother's blood type, and that we happen to be a match."

"Right," Matiu says. "OK."

"I think the words you're looking for are: 'Thank you, Erica Langley, for saving my life back there, and for giving me your blood, so I don't die even more.'"

He nods. "That too." There's a pause. "How can I die more?"

"It's a turn of phrase. Don't be pedantic."

"A turn of phrase you just made up."

"Glad to see you're feeling better. Don't think this means I'm not still angry at you."

"Angry at me?" He forces a laugh. It hurts. "What for?"

"How about getting yourself shot with an arrow, for starters? I expected better of you."

"Sorry. The battery ran out on my force-field."

"Don't be a smart-arse."

Matiu wants to respond, but it's too much effort. *Thinking* is too much effort. Still, time is slipping by. How long has he been out? Putting aside the cocktail of both good and bad luck that have brought him to this moment, and the knife's edge of fate which could have so easily tipped him the other way, he had a mission. There were people he had to find.

Sandi Kerr. Charlotte Langley. And had Makere said Mārama? But Mārama's safe at home with Mum and Dad, isn't she? "Erica? Mārama?"

He waits for her assurance, but it doesn't come, just a tight-lipped silence in a room grown suddenly colder. He sits up again. "Where is she?"

Erica grips his hand tighter. "They're not sure. CCTV footage from the front of the building shows her walking away with a woman, looks like someone she knew. You don't need to be worried, they're just not sure where they went."

"A woman?"

She shrugs. "Older woman, by the looks. Here, your mum sent a screenshot."

Erica holds up her phone, tapping open a message Penny had forwarded her, the screen suddenly bright in the dark room.

The image is blurry, the camera probably jostled out of focus by the day's shakes. But there's no missing that hideous leather patchwork handbag. "Mrs Hamon," he breathes. "She's her caregiver. Was, anyway." Matiu sinks back, both the pain and a sense of relief drawing him down. Mrs Hamon is all right. He can just imagine Mārama sending off a secret text, sneaking out past Mum, meeting her friend down the bottom, them getting on a bus together and going...

Where?

Mrs Hamon has no family, her kids moved to the South Island for the cooler weather years ago, and her husband is long gone, dead of a brain tumour some ten years earlier. Matiu had heard all her stories in the couple of months she'd been looking after Mārama, when he'd drop in for tea and a biscuit with his birth mother. Came from the agency, she said, but Matiu had never checked out *what* agency, exactly. Figured it was all legit, paid for by Mum, or healthcare funding or whatever. Just lovely doddery old Mrs Hamon, her family all gone, and her home baking, wheatgrass cookies with tangy spirulina icing. Always tasted weird to Matiu, but he ate them anyway, to be polite. Mrs Hamon, who was up and out the door as soon as the quakes hit even though, in her own words, Mārama was like the only family she really had. Almost like she'd got a message, a call to be somewhere, somewhere more important than looking after the only family she had, the person she was employed to care for, major disasters notwithstanding.

He jerks up like a shot, feels bandages or maybe skin tearing with the motion. "Mrs Hamon," he gasps. "She's with Mrs Hamon."

Erica's look tells him that even if she doesn't know what weird chasm Matiu has just leaped in order to reach whatever it is that's rattled him, she trusts it'll be on the mark. "So, that's OK isn't it? Mrs Hamon's her caregiver."

"No. Yes and no." He fumbles with the needle in his arm, where Erica's blood slides into his body, one heartbeat at a time. "She's a plant, for Touching the Sun. They sent her there, to get her close to me. But Mārama knows, it's why she always made me eat the biscuits, wanted me to work it out."

"So if Mārama knows Mrs Hamon's Touching the Sun, why would she leave a safe place with your mum and dad to go with her? It's clear she wasn't kidnapped this time."

Matiu swings his feet to the floor, clarity coming with a dose of terror. Cerberus leaps to his feet, stretching out his long legs. "Because she won't run away from this fight. She's walking into it. And she wants me to follow her."

Erica is silent a moment. "Where are they, Matiu? You know, don't you?"

He nods. "Eden."

She leans in. "The garden? Some weird mythical other place?"

Matiu shakes his head. "No. The prison."

CHAPTER 26

- Pandora -

Twenty-five minutes later, Penny, Craig, and Beaker cross the causeway to Puketutu Island. On one side of the road, they're flanked by the wastewater reservoir and the southernmost reaches of Manukau Harbour, and on the other by Māngere's tidal flats. Ordinarily, you wouldn't see much at this hour of the evening, but with the green-gold streaks of the southern lights lighting up the sky, the island's volcanic cones—one original and one made of reconstituted biosolids—are silhouetted against the skyline. As panoramas go, it's really quite beautiful. Hard to believe that half the island recently housed the headquarters of a psychotic cult leader, and that the other half is made of poo.

Craig follows the road curving to the south and heads through the pines. Penny imagines the conifers' aromatic tang, which is infinitely better than imagining the stench of a mountain of poo. Of course, she can smell neither, since Craig has the windows up and the air conditioning cranked up to full.

"We're here," Beaker says as they pull up to the Kelliher Mission, the Spanish-inspired former residence which is still standing after more than a century.

They're greeted by police wielding assault weapons. A small group, but they're wearing more protection than a satellite crew about to be launched into orbit. So not just any security detail: these guys are prepared for company.

Craig rolls down the window. "Excuse me."

When the officer ducks his head, the australis glow picks up the shine on his forehead and the white of his name badge: Wester.

"Private property," Wester says without preamble. "You need to turn around, Sir."

Lifting his phone from the dash, Craig shows the man his ID screen. "Craig Tong. Transport. I'm to get the science consults to a Dr Cordell. Any idea where we might find him?"

Behind Wester, one of his colleagues snorts. "Just follow the fucking hot air," she mutters.

Wester ignores her. "He's over that way, Sir," he says, indicating the direction with the barrel of his gun. "Follow the road around to the warehouse. You'll find the laboratory and the cool stores alongside."

Craig gives him a wave of acknowledgement and they move off.

It isn't hard to find. They follow the road past overgrown gardens and hip-height lawns to a corrugated iron warehouse with double roller doors and beyond that a line of attached outbuildings. Clark is waiting for them outside the furthermost building, perhaps alerted by the officers. As they pull up, he grabs the handrail, steadying himself as another aftershock hits. Penny and Beaker wait for the shaking to subside before quitting the car and joining him on the porch.

"Thank you for coming, Dr Yee, Mr Beaker."

"I'm not sure if you've met Craig Tong," Penny says. "He's—"

"From the Transport Ministry. A colleague of your father's. Yes, I believe we've met," Clark says.

Craig shakes the officer's hand. "Apologies for the intrusion, Officer Clark. Dr Yee needed a ride," he says.

"Oh," Penny says. "I forgot. This is police business. Craig, I'm afraid you won't be able to come in."

Craig lifts his hands in a classic don't-shoot position. "No worries at all. I'm happy to wait outside in the car."

But Clark ushers Craig in with them. "Come on in, Tong," he says. "You may as well. I can't imagine Cordell has anything sensible to say."

Inside, the laboratory is over-bright. Not a bad setup, if a bit old-fashioned. There's a large laboratory area, with some smaller offices coming off it, and the chiller doors at the far end making it accessible from the warehouse and also from the lab.

"Yee," Mather says, as they approach. "Sorry to drag you out. I told Cordell that whatever he had to tell us, it could wait until morning, but he's convinced that—"

Mather's words are drowned out by a shout from the other end of the room. "Pandora!"

Penny cringes.

"You're here. Terrific." Cordell bustles over. He's wearing a lab coat embroidered with the Touching the Sun logo. Visible at the neckline, his Windsor knot from this morning hasn't budged a millimetre. "Believe me, you'll be pleased you came. Pity Tanner couldn't be here too, but Officer Clark says he's unreachable at the moment. What's the world coming to, eh? When the Detective Inspector elects to go home early on the darkest day in our history."

"I said that he was unavailable, not that he'd gone home!" says Clark.

Penny sighs. "What's this about, Noah?"

Cordell beams. "I've only solved your case for you, Pandora. And without a fully operational laboratory to conduct the analyses. Imagine what I could have achieved if I'd had access to my own facilities and its state-of-the-art equipment."

And if you were the assigned scientific contractor.

"That's great, Noah," Penny says. "Naturally, we're grateful for your support, but—"

"Have you even started the analyses yet?"

Beaker pushes forward. "Hey! There are a lot of samples. They all had to be properly prepared first," he says.

"Yes, but you'll have done some preliminary tests, right?" Cordell urges.

"We've conducted some initial tests on the cordial in the bottles," Penny concedes.

"And you found nothing. No evidence of poison. Am I right?"

Penny frowns. "What's this about, Noah?"

Cordell beams. "No poison. Or at least nothing lethal. Am I right?"

"Just a mild soporific," Beaker says, looking puzzled.

"Back up a bit," Clark says. "How do you know all this, Cordell? Did you find a witness? Someone who knows what happened up there on the mountain? If you've obtained new evidence about the case, you should have brought it directly to the police."

Cordell waves a hand in front of his face, dismissively, as if he were brushing away a fly. "It's fine, Clark," he says, heavy emphasis on the fine. "Tanner gave me clearance, remember? An overseer of sorts. I had the officers brief me when they brought the bodies in from Māngere."

Penny's hackles rise. What the hell? Tanner did *not* appoint him overseer. Mather arches a brow. Beaker shakes his head. Even Craig looks surprised.

"Now hang on," Clark says. "I'm pretty sure Tanner didn't mean for you to run around the city playing detective."

"Of course not." Cordell grins. "And nor did I need to."

Mather heaves a sigh. "Cordell, if you could just get to your announcement please, I'd like to call it a day."

Cordell giggles. "Over here. Come and look. I've got it all set up."

He leads them to the microscope. It's a basic model, the kind you'd find in a high school science department. "Take a look." Cordell can barely contain his excitement.

Penny steps up to the apparatus and looks down the scope. She stumbles back, her mouth agape. *Oh!*

Beaker and Mather take a look, then Clark and finally Craig.

"What am I looking at?" Craig asks while still peering at the slide. "These little tubes?"

"Nanobots!" Beaker breathes.

Mather nods. "Not what I expected to see either."

Penny's mind is racing. Nanobots are an expensive technology. Delivering a poison using the microscopic techno-warriors is certainly possible—if the bots are programmed to pass through the gut—but why complicate things, when the Touching the Sun acolytes were prepared to drink the cordial? It doesn't add up.

His brow crinkles; Beaker appears to have come to the same conclusion. "You're postulating that the poison was delivered by nanobot? What, after being injected into the bloodstream? But we didn't find any injection sites."

Mather rubs a hand over his five o'clock stubble. "Injection sites don't always reveal themselves in the field, Beaker. They can be tiny. I'd be more likely to pick those up in autopsy. Although, injecting the bots makes sense, if the killers wanted to achieve a delayed response. All they'd need to do is programme in a time delay."

"Maybe whoever orchestrated the massacre triggered them using some kind of timer?" Clark suggests.

"Allowing enough time for the victims to congregate at the site and arrange themselves in a koru shape," Beaker says.

"Cult members might have done those things, anyway," Clark replies. "They're already indoctrinated to do as they're instructed."

Cordell giggles again.

"Shit," Craig says, shaking his head. "Let me get this straight: you're saying these tiny tube-bots are like little packets of C4 circulating in the blood? Someone somewhere takes their finger off the switch, and kaboom?"

Beaker chuckles. "Well, that's a bit simplistic, but yes."

Craig gives a low whistle. "Microscopic weapons of mass destruction."

"Yes," Clark says quietly. "So it seems."

"Wait," Penny says. She steps back for another quick look down the scope. "These aren't blood cells on the slide. They look like…like…tongue cells."

"Hooray!" Cordell bursts out as if she were the birthday girl at a surprise party.

Mather nudges Penny out of the way and takes a second look. "Damn. I saw the bots and didn't pay any attention to the tissue sample."

Beaker shrugs. "I did the same."

Cordell chuckles. "The plot thickens!" He folds his arms across his chest.

"For crying out loud, Cordell," Mather says, his face flushed. "You clearly know more, so why not tell just us? None of us are in the mood for your silly guessing games."

"Yes, please, if you could just get to the point, Dr Cordell," Clark adds. "This is a serious matter. Multiple lives have been lost."

They all turn to Cordell, and Penny realises it was what her former mentor had wanted all along: their full attention.

Adjusting his tie, Cordell puffs out his chest. "I'll explain."

Mather rolls his eyes. Happily, Cordell doesn't notice.

"Given that Dr Mather had his hands full with the victims of the wharf incident, I selected one of the Māngere victims at random and had it wheeled into the lab to examine it. I wasn't looking to undermine Pandora's work, you understand, but, having worked with her for some years, I'm aware she can be a little slow."

"Thorough," Beaker interjects. Penny smiles at his loyalty.

"Yes. Perhaps thorough is a better word. It's a trait I cultivate in all my protégés, and one of the reasons I hoped to uncover some means of streamlining the work."

"Cordell," Clark warns.

Cordell sniffs. "Anyway, with the gurney positioned here next to the work bench, I turned away to set up a simple assay…" Moving like a 1960s Captain Scarlet puppet, Cordell mimes his actions. "…and when I looked back the victim's tongue had blown up like a balloon. Swelled maybe four or five times its current size."

"Jeepers," Beaker says. "Those poor people."

"They suffocated," Mather whispers. "Choked on their own tongues."

Penny shivers.

Cordell clears his throat. "Yes, yes. Those were my exact conclusions. So reacting quickly, I sampled the tongue tissue and discovered the nanobots, effectively blowing the lid on the entire case, and no doubt saving hours of unnecessary analyses. It was as well I did because the response was short-lived, the tongue deflating in a matter of minutes."

"What happened to reanimate the nanobots in the first place?" Mather asks. "Did you do something?"

"Nothing whatsoever. In fact, I wheeled two additional cadavers out of the chiller in case there was something local which had prompted the reanimation, but there was no change."

"Which makes your discovery the result of a confounding variable," Mather says.

"A random factor," Beaker adds.

"Dumb luck," says Craig.

His face flushing pink, Cordell adjusts his tie. It's all Penny can do to hide her smile.

CHAPTER 27

- Matiu -

The Solaris is parked in the basement. It looks like one of Penny's crime scenes, with blood all over the white panels, the back seat, and smeared across the concrete floor. *His* blood, Matiu realises, his head hazy. Between the blood loss and whatever arcane shit Craig Tong injected into him up in the lab, he feels light as air, bright as a flame.

There's pain, but it's a strange ghost of a thing draped over him, trying to be noticed. Matiu has a lifetime of experience at tuning out the ghosts that try to get his attention, and this is no different. He may regret it later, when body and mind suture back together, but the events of the past couple of days have convinced him that if he doesn't act now, if he doesn't follow this thread down into the black hole where it's leading him, there may not be a later. Not for him, not for anyone.

"So let me get this straight," Erica says, wrangling Cerberus on his lead and carrying on a conversation Matiu had lost track of. "You had a vision of Mount Eden erupting and destroying the city, and your ghostly twin brother also came to you and said that we'd find Kerr at Mount Eden." She tugs open the back door, regards the drying blood with disgust. She's pale, even in the dark. Matiu wonders how much of her blood she's given him to replace the cups of it he spilled in the car. "So now we're going to rush over there, hoping to find Charlotte and Mārama and stop Sandi Kerr, even though we're both at the wrong end of the recovery cycle, and the whole thing feels like just another trap, like Mount Albert was." She opens the boot, searching for a tarp, a blanket.

"Pretty much," Matiu nods, dropping into the passenger seat. "Because it's the best lead we've got, and if we don't go and it was the right thing to do, then we risk losing them both." The dash lights up. Battery power is sitting around 72 percent. It's the lowest Matiu has seen it.

"Without police backup or anything." Finding nothing useful in the boot, Erica takes her thin jacket off and spreads it on the back seat, then gestures for Cerberus to jump in. "You'll be getting my drycleaning bill, you know."

"Blood on the outside, dog on the inside? I don't think even drycleaning can save that," Matiu chortles. "As for the police, let's just say I've found the police to be less than helpful in most of my dealings with them in the past, and they'd probably look at me a certain way if I was to mention monsters."

She gives him an alarmed look as she slides into the driver's seat. "Who said anything about monsters? Anyway, if we do find them there? Then what are we going to do?" Erica heads for the exit.

Matiu grins. She's arguing, but she's still driving. She knows it's a dumb idea, but she's along for the ride anyway. She needs what's at the end of this road as much as he does. "Not sure. We wing it, I guess."

"Oh excellent," Erica growls, pulling onto the street. "Because that's worked so well for us so far. You've got ten minutes to make a plan, all right?"

Matiu's grin widens. He knows he should be terrified of what's to come, consumed by the knowledge that Mārama is in the hands of the enemy and the tide she warned him about is rushing in, but he can't wipe his dumb grin away. Erica said *us*.

- Pandora -

All at once, there's a loud rumbling and the sky flashes. Streaks of red light up the concrete walls. Penny jumps as the thunder booms. Another storm. That came up quickly. Then she catches the look on Craig's face, the oblique glance he throws at Clark, and her blood freezes. Wait! There was no delay between the thermal expansion of the plasma in the lightning channel and resultant shock wave…

"Get down!" Craig screams.

The next thing she knows, Penny is sprawled on the floor, shoved under a bench by Clark. Overhead, the storm crackles and booms. Only, it's not a storm. Those are gunshots. Lots of them. The air is hammered with noise. One of the upper windows shatters and a bullet strikes the opposite wall, spraying bits of concrete into the room. Facing her, his hands over his head, Cordell tucks his body into the foetal position.

"Shots fired at the Kelliher Mission House on Puketutu Island," Clark says into his radio mic, and Penny marvels at his cool. "Multiple active shooters. Request Armed Offenders backup."

This makes no sense. Who would be shooting at them? Beside her, Cordell whimpers. "Are you hit?" Penny whispers. Cordell replies with a shake of his head. "Mather?" She casts around for the pathologist.

"Over here. I'm fine," he calls from under another desk.

"Beaker?"

"I'm okay," he calls. "But a bit of glass hit me. Took out a chunk of flesh."

"Serious?"

"It's bleeding. Might need a couple of stitches."

"Hold tight. Keep some pressure on it. I'll come over and take a look," she says. "Wait!" She twists her head. "Where's Craig?" Her pulse jumps.

Pulling a gun from a shoulder holster, Clark peeps over the bench. Frowns. "He went out there."

"He went out there?!" Gasping, Penny struggles to a crouch. "What the hell?"

"I'm going, too. Tong has his people out there. I have to help them."

His people? What people? Transport staff?

"Don't be a twat, Clark," Mather says. "Wait for your backup to arrive. You go out there and you'll only get yourself killed." On his feet now, Mather glances over the bench, ducking his head again when a new burst of gunfire erupts outside. "Shit!"

Trembling with disbelief, Penny reaches out to touch Clark on the sleeve. "Toeva. Please. Don't go."

Clark gives her a smile. "Dr Yee, I'm a policeman. It's my job."

"It's your job to stay here and protect us," Cordell says, now on his hands and knees beneath the bench. "Not to go chasing after idiots, with a death wish!"

"You'll be fine. Keep away from the windows. Maybe see if you can do something for Beaker. I'll take the side door. Mather, please lock it after I leave." Keeping low, Clark moves to the door, opens it a crack to check the coast is clear, before turning back to them. "All of you, stay down and don't come out until you get word from Tong or me," he says.

"You better come back in one piece," Mather says. "I really don't wanna see your naked arse on one of my gurneys."

Clark grins. "I'd rather you didn't either."

As the door clicks shut behind him, Penny remembers Clark's birthday. Probably not the party he had in mind. The silence lasts just minutes before gunfire erupts again. Men shout back and forth amid intermittent gunfire. Mather creeps to the window.

"See anything?" Penny asks. She glances at Beaker. Lying on the floor just metres away, his hand clasped around his arm, blood seeping through his fingers.

At the window, Mather blows out slowly. "Three bodies on the ground. Two dead, one injured. Poor bastard is trying to drag himself into the alley between the buildings."

"Craig?" Penny calls as she scrambles between the benches to Beaker.

"No, your boyfriend's still alive," Mather says, not looking back.

Relieved, Penny lifts Beaker's fingers to peek at the wound, causing fresh blood to ooze through his shirt. Damn. She closes her hand over the gash.

"But he and the police guys are pinned down at the far corner," Mather goes on. "Fuck. Clark can't do anything from where he is. He needs to move. If he fires on the bad dudes, he risks hitting Tong's group." Outside, more rounds are fired. Mather hurls himself to the floor as a shower of bullets hit the building.

With more glass raining about them, Penny casts around for something to wrap Beaker's arm. She can't see a first aid kit, and she has nothing useful on her, no scarf or even a long-sleeved shirt.

"What's happening now?" Cordell shouts.

Brushing bits of glass off his lab coat, Mather checks again. "Clark's gone!" He presses his face to the glass. "Shit, I can't see him. Wait! There he is. Pulling the injured guy to safety. Guy's got a gang jacket—one of theirs. Bloody hell, that takes guts."

"What do you mean?" Cordell says. "Gang members are hardly going to shoot at someone helping one of their own."

"Geez, Cordell!" Beaker says.

He's not wrong. For a Rutherford Medal winner, Cordell can be so dense. How she ever hooked up with the man, heaven only knows.

"You're assuming the shooters are willing to leave survivors," Mather says wryly.

To his credit, Cordell pales.

"Hang on. What's this?" Mather gives a low whistle.

"What? What does that whistle mean?" Cordell demands. "What's going on?"

"A bunch more have arrived."

"Another gang?" Penny blurts, while attempting to lift Beaker's legs onto the upturned stool.

"Just late to the party, I think."

"How many?" Penny is still struggling with Beaker's legs.

"These guys must have approached from the other side of the island."

"What guys?" Finally, Beaker's legs are above his head.

"Hid their vehicles in the trees."

Beaker tightens his fingers around his arm. "Just go, Penny. I'm fine, here."

"You sure?"

"Go!"

Penny stretches out a leg and clambers over the glass, squeezing into the gap between the wall and the window.

"Pandora, do you think that's wise? You really ought to come back to this side of the room," Cordell says. "Clark said we should stay out of sight."

Ignoring Cordell, she sucks in a breath and squints through the grubby pane. It's hard to tell exactly what's happening with everyone hunkered behind cover—police cars, a van, buildings, a fence—but Mather's right, those are gang members. And stationed all around the courtyard, they have Craig and the police surrounded. "We have to do something," she says.

"No, we don't," Cordell insists. "You heard Clark. We need to let the police deal with it. He's already called it in. The cavalry will be here any moment."

"Tong might not have that long," Mather says.

"Well, what can we do?" Cordell groans. "We're all scientists here, not soldiers!"

Mather looks at up Penny, a smile spreading on his face. "This is a lab," he says.

Penny grins back. "And what self-respecting lab doesn't have alcohol?"

"There'll be a reagent store somewhere," Beaker calls.

Already, Mather is tearing off his lab coat. "We're going to need some fabric strips," he says. "You wanna look for the solvent?"

"On it." Penny crouch-runs to the cupboard, flings open the door. Wrong cupboard. This one's full of Erlenmeyer flasks.

"Not that one! It's the cupboard on your right," Cordell says.

Penny yanks it open and start pushing bottle after bottle, checking the labels. Dimethyl sulfoxide. Acetonitrile…

"Hurry!" Mather calls. "Any alcohol will do!"

Yes, yes…ethanol, methanol, isopropanol! Four full bottles. Penny grabs them in a bear hug and runs across the lab to Mather, using her tummy to push the bottles onto the bench. Before she's even stepped back, he's opened one, pouring the alcohol onto the fabric strips, ready to stuff them into the bottles.

Under the bench, hovering near their knees, Cordell pipes up. "You should add dishwashing liquid, Mather. The fire will adhere better, and it'll create a smoke screen."

Penny pauses. It's not a bad idea.

But Mather cranes his neck and checks the courtyard. "No time. This will have to do."

"A light! We need a light!" Penny squeaks.

"In my pocket," Mather says. Penny picks up the remains of his shredded lab coat and fumbles with the fabric until she locates the plastic lighter. Mather thrusts out his hand, but instead of handing it over, Penny tightens her grip.

"Wait!" she says. "These bottles aren't going to be much use if they fall short. You can throw farther than me. What say I light them, and you throw them?" She hands him a pair of heat resistant gloves and some safety goggles.

"Right," he says. "Good thinking." He slips the safety gear on and between the two of them, they carry their homemade weapons to the front door and set them on the floor. Mather opens the door a crack, then takes off the safety goggles. "Can't see a bloody thing," he grumbles.

"Think you can you reach them from here?" Penny asks.

"Maybe. I'd prefer not to create more bodies, if I can help it. You might not have noticed, but I already have a bit of a backlog."

Penny nods.

"Let's do it, then, shall we?" Mather says.

"Be bloody careful!' Beaker calls.

Holding the bomb away from her body, Penny flicks her thumb and touches the flame to the fabric. The rudimentary wick whooshes alight. Penny hands the flaming bottle to Mather, who opens the door, and, his torso still protected by the timber, leans back, and flings the firebomb across the courtyard.

Penny counts off three seconds before lighting the second bottle. When Mather ducks back inside, she hands him the next sputtering cocktail, and he throws again. A third time. Flick, whoosh, swap, throw. Neither of them says a word.

On the other side of the door, men and women scream. More shots crack. Penny can only imagine the waterfall of fire raining on the gang members. Those clad in leather and wool would be reasonably well protected, but synthetic stockings would melt into skin, burning off lashes and hair and lips…

When the last cocktail has been launched, Mather slams the door and pulls Penny to the floor as a volley of bullets hits the timber above them. They scramble backwards into the room and duck under the bench.

"Are you okay?" Mather asks.

Penny nods. "Did it work?"

"Not exactly. We should have used the detergent. Only one man's clothes caught fire. It was enough, though: while his mates were smothering the flames, Tong and his guys moved into the warehouse."

Penny exhales heavily. "Thank heavens."

"Thank heavens!" Cordell squawks. "What are you talking about? Now they'll be after us. The gangs. We all saw what they're capable of this morning on the wharf. We should hide in the chiller."

"Great idea, Cordell. You go first," Beaker says.

Mather scrambles to the window and risks a peek. "Yeah, I don't think we're the ones they're after…"

Crouched low, Penny joins him. Her heart sinks. There have to be twenty gang members crowding around the battered roller doors of the warehouse. One of them kicks at the door, the metal clanging. Far off in the distance, sirens wail. Penny almost weeps with relief. Surely, they'll leave now.

Except they don't. Someone appears with a crowbar. Another man has a hammer. The others line up, their rifles raised, ready to light up just as soon as the door is lifted.

No, no, no. Penny turns. She needs to create a distraction. Enough time to allow the police to arrive. But what? Molotov cocktails are out. The cupboard is bare: no more alcohol. She scans the room desperate for something to great a diversion. Microscope. Gurney. Burners. There! Since the mission house was never plumbed for gas, the lab's Bunsen burners are fuelled by gas cylinders. It's better than nothing. Stooping to pick up a shard of glass, Penny runs to the nearest cylinder and slices through the flexi-hose connecting it to the burner. Then she swivels the pallet jack and hurries for the door, one hand steering the pallet, and the other fumbling with the valve on the cylinder.

Damn it. It's like a bloody jam jar: too stiff to turn.

Grabbing the pallet, Mather muscles her out of the way. "I can do that. You get the hose," he shouts.

Penny collects up the dangling pipe and runs alongside the pallet truck, glass crunching underfoot, while she scrabbles in her pocket for the lighter. "Noah, open the door!"

"Pandora, you can't really intend to—"

"Open the goddamn door, Noah!" Mather roars.

Finally, Cordell leaps into action, banging his head on the bench and knocking over a lab stool in his haste to get there. He punches the door open and, like a pair of crazed berserkers, Mather and Penny bounce down the stairs, off the porch, and into the courtyard.

In the moment, Cordell's comment about idiots with a death wish flashes through Penny's mind. The gangsters turn, but it's clear they're not expecting a welcoming committee. At least, not one as badly thought out as this. Behind woollen balaclavas and camo bandanas, their eyes widen. It's all the time Penny needs: she raises the hose, pointing the pressurised flow in the direction of the gangsters. Then she flicks open the lighter and ignites the gas.

Flames burst forth. A raging torrent of heat. Charging forward, with Mather at her flank, and the hosepipe breathing fire like a dragon's nostril, Penny spews the fiery arc around the courtyard. The flames spurt in a blazing river of orange and blue. Overhead, the southern lights glow green and gold, the evening alive with light and noise.

Penny can't see beyond the wall of flame, but she hears the cries and the slap of feet. The crowbar clattering to the asphalt. Sirens getting louder. Long minutes pass. Penny doesn't stop. She paints the courtyard with fire. Eventually, beyond the sizzling veil, the roller door rumbles. Someone shouts. "Dr Yee. Mather! They're gone."

Her heart in her throat, Penny drops the hose. Behind her, the valve grinds as Mather turns off the gas. First Clark, then Craig, stride out of the warehouse into the courtyard.

Suddenly, Craig breaks into a run, heading for her, for Mather, a gun in his hand.

"No Craig, you don't understand. I—"

He tackles her, the gun exploding near her ear. She lands heavily on her shoulder, the smell of oil and flame in her nostrils, her breath stolen from her lungs. Time suspends while she lies there, crumpled on the asphalt, the world oddly silent, as off to her right, someone, not Mather, tumbles sideways from the gap between the buildings.

Penny blinks, her eyes fixed on the small red dot oozing at the centre of his forehead.

CHAPTER 28

- Matiu -

"Well, slap my arse and call me Charlie," Matiu says, scrolling down the tablet screen. "Look at that." He waves the device Erica's way as she changes lanes. Images of the historic black stone walls of Auckland's oldest prison, once a British Army stockade and looking like something out of a Welcome to Sunny Mordor postcard, compete with pretty blocks of text for her attention.

"Umm, driving here, Sherlock."

Matiu relents. "So about ten years ago, after decades of contention, they isolated the old prison from the modern one and turned it into a research library with residency programmes and accommodation, focusing on the region, allowing researchers from outside Auckland, or outside New Zealand, to carry out academic study of local interest. It falls under the Historic Places Trust, but it's administered by a private company called the Eden Fellowship Limited. And guess who's on the Board of Directors?"

"Sandi Kerr?"

"No such luck. But Alex Wise is."

"Who happens to be Axel Weis, who sent Charlotte that message."

"The same. Most likely the guy you met on that rooftop, the high priest."

"So she's been using the cover of the research institute to investigate things like what's stored in the museum basement, and might've even had public grant money to fund it. I don't suppose you ever thought to check the Companies Register to see what other entities Kerr's name might be attached to?"

Matiu gives her an arch look "Entities?"

"Corporate entities, companies. Businesses. Societies. You have actually *done* some research, haven't you?"

Matiu looks out at the night-shrouded buildings rolling by, bathed in orange streetlight and the spidering threads of the aurora australis.

"Oh for fuck's sake, Matiu. Don't tell me you've just been waiting for her to turn up again? To kidnap some other poor girl, to murder someone else?" Erica throws her hands up, then quickly grabs the wheel again. "I thought you would've at least checked out all publicly available sources if you were seriously trying to track this woman down!"

"Hey, we passed everything we knew on to the cops, and in any case, we practically solved their cases for them. So if they're still neck-deep in new cases and can't follow up on old ones, you can't hold me over the coals for that."

She huffs. "Never mind. Let's assume the prison isn't another misdirect, while also assuming they're going to be expecting us. What's the plan?"

Beyond the window, Maungawhau, Mount Eden itself, dominates the dark horizon, shimmering green and red under the southern lights, like the shoulder-blades of a sleeping giant twisted uncomfortably in its millennia-long slumber. Matiu's silence stretches out across the strange glowing night, over the hiss of rubber on tarmac. "We can't plan for this. We don't even know what *this* is."

"Aargh!" Erica hits the brakes so hard the car slews around.

Matiu grabs at the doorframe, pain searing up his side, and he scans the street beyond the window, looking for the cause of Erica's alarm.

"You!" she howls, thumping the wheel. "You're so, so...you do this thing, where you make me think you've got it all together, you've got everything sorted, but it's all a sham! Here I am, trusting you to save my sister, and you don't know the first thing about what we're heading into, or how we're going to deal with it. You've actively discouraged me from involving the police, because fucking monsters! You wave those fingers and cast your little spell and I just follow you along, into whatever disaster is coming next. You got yourself shot with an arrow, and I had to run down men on motorbikes to get us to safety, and yet here I fucking am, still with you, still riding into this...fucking hell!"

Matiu opens his mouth to formulate at the very least an inarticulate rebuttal, but he can't, because Erica has crushed her lips to his, her hands on his face, her breath hot and sour, tasting of heartsick desperation. It lasts a long moment, and then another, and one more, before she breaks away, breathing hard, scowling at him.

"Just tell me one thing," she says, her voice hoarse in the semi-darkness of streetlights and starfire. "Tell me that when we find these fuckers, we're going to end them, for good this time. No letting them get away to run off and hide, no coming back from the dead. We end this, tonight. Once and for all."

"Even if it kills us?" Matiu cocks an eyebrow.

She leans in, brushes a lip against his ear. "Even if it kills us."

He swallows hard. Wants to touch her so badly it hurts.

A horn blares. Cerberus whines softly, big dark eyes looking up at them from the back seat. Erica returns to the wheel and sets the car in motion again. Staring fiercely out into the night, her eyes shine. They drive in silence for a while, the roads eerily quiet.

Then, "Matiu?" she says at last.

"Erica?"

"Actually, don't let it kill us."

"Right."

"I got a bit carried away in the moment."

"Understood."

"Good."

Erica rounds a bend and pulls to the side of the road. From here, they can see the brooding grey walls of the modern correctional facility a couple of blocks down.

"Don't get too close," Matiu says. "The whole perimeter's covered in cell-jamming towers that block out any sort of wireless in the vicinity."

"And you know this because?"

"Let's just call it inside information." Matiu grits his teeth, shutting out the memories of his time inside those walls, those long dark days with no-one for company but Makere. Makere in his ear, Makere in his dreams, Makere creeping around behind his eyes.

Railway lines run along one side of the prison facility, with the motorway behind, and in its shadow, like a relic of a lost world, the crenelated stone towers of Old Mount Eden Prison. "If you're just inside the shadow of that jamming tech," Matiu goes on, "and you've got the inside of the building shielded from that convenient taxpayer-funded umbrella, then no-one can get near your network unless they go in by cable. And why bother? It's a lame old research institute now, or a museum or a library or whatever. Who else knows it's really a home for miscreants and criminals, if this really is Kerr's new home base?"

"Well, lover, if we're going to walk this dog, we should do it now."

"Full of surprises, aren't you?" Matiu says to her back as she exits the car and lets Cerberus out. Slowed by the pain in his side, Matiu opens the door and steps onto the footpath, falling into a sort of limping shuffle beside Erica as she sets off down the road towards the prison. Just two urbanites out taking their dog for a leisurely stroll through the industrial wastes of the prison district in the middle of the night. *Nothing to see here, Officer.*

"You know," Erica says, glancing at the sky and the painted lights that walk across the dark, "it feels like they're really here now, like, right over top of us."

The thought fills Matiu with a chill dread he can neither place nor name. "Penny says they've got something to do with the magnetic core of the planet moving around."

"Did she also say that it's nothing to worry about? Because Penny would know, right?"

"She said you can throw your old compasses away, if that's any reassurance."

"But she didn't say not to worry."

"No. No, she did not."

The old prison building sits dark, carved in the shadows thrown by the modern facility and the motorway behind it. Matiu notes the aging dome cameras mounted at strategic points on the walls. More like a decrepit antique than a villain's lair. No lights burn in its windows. The rail lines sit silent and cold. If something sinister is going on behind those walls, they're keeping it awful quiet.

"I think I'm getting one of your funny feelings," Erica says, straining to keep Cerberus from tearing off down the footpath. He's been cooped up a while.

"What's yours say?" Matiu asks, though he thinks he knows.

"It's like we've arrived just a bit too late."

"Yeah," he agrees. "Like we've missed the bus."

Matiu slips his phone from his pocket, dials Scour's number and drops it back in his pocket, tapping his earbud on. On the next street corner is a network hub cabinet. Hopefully, he can rely on the slovenly security standards of Auckland's civil IT engineers to help him out in this darkest of hours.

The phone buzzes several times before picking up. "What the fuck, Yee? You got any idea what time it is?"

"I thought you'd be up for your morning run by now. Day's wasting."

"It's... Fuck. Yee, it's 11.20. Sane people know that it's not polite to make phone calls after 8pm."

"The only thing more overrated than polite people are sane people. I need a favour."

"You need more than a favour; you need a kick up the fucking arse."

"Can you ping my phone and hook into the nearest fibre hub? Then I need to locate a specific network port and bypass the firewalls. Looking for a workstation or a server with a CCTV rig. I'll make it worth double your usual fee."

"Double my after-hours call-out fee, you mean."

"See, I always picked you as the entrepreneur. Never know when opportunity might come knocking."

"Give me a minute."

Matiu's earbud hums. The prison is now behind them, the motorway flyover looming ahead. Cerberus pauses at the network cabinet with its layers of graffiti and relieves himself noisily.

Erica gives Matiu a quizzical look as they pause, mouthing the question, *Who are you talking to?*

Matiu mouths back, *Better you don't know.* Erica's glare could nail him to the wall. They resume their walk, under the motorway, away from the prison. Cerberus jitters back and forth, like he's hunting the shadows for rabbits, or demons.

"Nodes are up, bro. What you trying to hit?" Scour asks. There's a pause. "Holy crap, you're at Mt Eden? You *trying* to get yourself back in there? I never knew you were that homesick for your old cell."

"Consider this my interest in historic places. I need the old prison, it's a research library now."

"Well, that should be easy enough to crack."

"Don't count on it."

"Dude, I can see it, but it's got some serious hardcore protection in place. It's not off-the-shelf. You sure it's just a library?"

"If it was, my life would be far less interesting."

"Hopefully there's enough juice in the tank to crack this sucker, but I gotta warn you, anything this solid might have backlash measures in place."

"Serious? I thought only defence installs had that shit."

"That's what I mean. This isn't far off military grade. Whatever they're researching in there, they don't want anyone seeing it. Chances are they'll want to burn anyone who tries."

Matiu forces a laugh, but his guts are churning. "Let's just knock the bastard off, eh?"

"It's your funeral, bro."

"You forget, man. *Au naturale*. No neurals. What are they gonna hit?"

"Luddite."

Matiu pulls his phone from his pocket, the screen a confused mash of high-speed code. Then he's looking at the front end of Touching the Sun's main server. It even has the weird eye symbol as its wallpaper, now staring up at him from his phone's screen. Creepy.

A cold sweat breaks out on Matiu's brow. He doesn't have long. He taps into the VMS, accesses the CCTV playback, whizzing back through the minutes, scanning over corridors and rooms and parking lots, all completely abandoned.

Until one hour ago on the time stamp, when a mass exodus took place. There are four buses, streetside, pulling away from the curb. Matiu pauses, Erica crowding in close to watch on his phone as a horde of people exit the prison through the old front entrance, cross the empty railway lines, and cram onto the buses. Young people, old folk, as diverse a mixture of colours and faces as any Saturday morning at St Luke's Shopping Centre. "There," says Matiu, pausing the image. Mārama, Mrs Hamon, and Charlotte, huddled together but a distinct part of the group. Along with hundreds more, all swarming aboard the buses like kids on their way to a field trip with the promise of ice cream and an early home time.

"Where are they going?" Erica asks.

Matiu considers getting Scour to set up a trace through the traffic cameras, following the convoy of unmarked buses through Auckland's nightscape, but he already knows, deep in his gut, where they'll end up. "Maungawhau," he says. "They're going up the mount. Something's coming, and Kerr knows it." Behind the buses, a silver Ford Falcon. "That's her," Matiu says, glimpsing the blond tresses through the windscreen as the car passes, leaving the street abandoned. Then there's a high-pitched shriek in his ear, and he tugs the earbud out as if it's on fire, tossing it away. He's still shaking his head when his phone suddenly grows hot, and smoke starts to pour from around the screen. "Shit!" Matiu drops the phone as it bursts into flame on the concrete.

"What the hell?" Erica jumps out of the way of the tiny fireball.

Matiu rubs his ear, where the high frequency scream is still ringing in his skull. "Backlash tech. We just got double-whammied, an aural spike and a kill-switch attack. Kill-switch tricks the phone into thinking it needs a lot more power for a few seconds, surges the draw on the battery, the lithium combusts and it's all over."

"So, what were you saying about neurals?"

Matiu grimaces. "Backlash tech'll do the same thing to a neural implant if that's how you're connected, fry it. Inside your head. Not pretty. Can't pull it out and throw it away like an earbud."

Cerberus is leaping about, barking at the smoking, sputtering pool of melted plastic and burnt metal that used to be Matiu's phone. Erica kneels by the dog and rubs his ears to soothe him. "So, we dodged a bullet. But we saw what we needed to see. Now, if I was a boatload of buses headed for the best photo opportunity in town, where would I go?"

"Puhi Huia Road. There's a bus park."

"And you know *this* because?"

"Hey, I can't help it if tourists are careless with their valuables."

"Who is this monster I've fallen for?" They turn and hurry back towards the Solaris, the cold black walls of the old prison watching them all the way.

"Just call me your favourite client."

"Most high-maintenance is more like it."

"How many of your clients would agree to both dog-walking in the middle of the night and repeatedly rescuing your missing sister from psychotic loonburgers?"

"It would be a short list, for sure. But don't let that go to your head."

Clambering back into the Solaris, Matiu settles in, feeling strangely naked, disconnected without a phone. Erica peels out onto the road, hauling the car around and heading south. The southern lights spread their glow over Maungawhau like the wings of hunting taniwha.

CHAPTER 29

- Pandora -

Craig helps Penny to her feet. "Are you hurt?"

"Craig. That man. He, he—"

... has a tiny red hole in his head, like a laser pointer! Her knees buckle but, his hand gripping hers, Craig keeps her on her feet. "He was going to shoot you, Pen. I couldn't let that happen. I had to take him out."

Penny's head is fuzzy. "Why would he shoot me?"

"Probably because you were mowing down his mates with a flame thrower," Mather says, from behind her.

"It's entirely my fault, Dr Yee," Clark says, hurrying over. "I thought the man was unconscious, so instead of cuffing him, I left him in the recovery position. I should've been more vigilant. Thank goodness Tong's reflexes are as sharp as they are. A split-second later and we might have lost you."

"Tong!" Detective Inspector Tanner sweeps onto the scene like a king into court. When he reaches dead centre, he turns in a slow circle, his hands on his hips. "Bloody hell, man," he bellows. "What the fuck happened here?"

"Gang attack," Craig replies.

"I made a flamethrower," Penny murmurs.

"Didn't we already do this today?" Tanner says. "Remind me never to collaborate with the SIS if this is the mess you're going to make."

It's like Penny has water in her ears. Did Tanner just mention the SIS? With her knees finally under control, Penny tunes in to the conversation.

"It's a different group, Sir," Clark says. "The attack at the depot was Hanson's old crowd, being led by Kingi."

"Clark's right," says Craig. He crouches beside one of the fallen men and nods towards his jacket. "This isn't the same gang. These are Han triad members, judging from their patches. I counted around twenty of them during the standoff. I should've anticipated something like this. Assigned a bigger detail."

Clark clucks his tongue. "To be fair, troops are thin on the ground at the moment."

"No shortage of cadavers, though," Mather says, gazing pointedly at the bodies.

"Yup. It's been one hell of a day," Tanner says.

Getting to his feet, Craig shakes his head. "We're lucky more lives weren't lost. As it was, the Han had us pinned down, only taking off through the trees when Penny here opened fire with her crazy benchtop weaponry. Wester and a couple of my men went after them. I don't suppose your lot intercepted any escapees on the way in?"

"Negative."

"Blast. Let's hope Wester can rustle up a straggler. We could do with the intel."

"You're convinced this is about the prototype?" Tanner asks.

Penny whips her head up.

"Have you got a better explanation for the gang rumble at the wharf this morning? We suspect the leak came from inside the Chinese research unit who constructed the Solaris. Hing Yee was able to procure a staff list. I've got my people working on it."

"Okay, that's enough!" Penny stamps her foot. She rounds on Craig, her hands on her hips. "What's going on? What's my father got to do with this? And who exactly are *your* people?!"

Craig takes a step back. Clark colours and Tanner takes a sudden interest in his shoes. Mather checks the valve on the gas cylinder.

Tanner also has a death wish today, because he's the first to speak. "Right, well, I think I'll leave this evening's paperwork to your boys, Tong. Mather, I'm assuming you can handle the bodies?"

Mather nods. "Sure thing. We can squeeze a couple more in the chiller. Although—" He checks his watch then pulls a face. "…they're going to have to go on *tomorrow's* schedule."

"Penny, let me—" But Craig doesn't get a chance to finish, the whump of chopper rotors drowning out his words as a violent wind blows across the courtyard.

"Dammit," Tanner curses. "Press helicopter. How the hell did they get here so soon?"

"I'm going to guess they followed the sirens," Craig shouts.

The din above them making it impossible to talk, they all watch as the chopper hovers over the trees, then drops out of sight. Given the dopplering of the sound, Penny guesses it's about to land on the lawn of the mission house.

"They're going to want a statement," Craig says when the noise has died down.

"Police training exercise," replies Tanner, barely missing a beat.

"Been scheduled for months," Clark lies.

A shout comes from behind them, and Penny swings about to see Cordell and Beaker emerge from the laboratory, Beaker leaning heavily on Cordell's shoulder. Pale and dishevelled, the pair blink in disbelief as they gaze around the courtyard, taking in the devastation. "A little help, please," Cordell says.

Penny feels a pang of guilt: in all the excitement she'd forgotten about Beaker. The poor man. His sleeve and hands are soaked with blood, and the wound on his arm has been crudely bandaged with white fabric—a Molotov cocktail wick from Mather's shredded lab coat. Plus, she'd left Beaker alone with Cordell. She should probably give him hazard pay for that alone.

"Cordell!" barks Tanner. "Just the man. It seems the press have arrived…" Tanner strides off to brief him.

"Penny," Craig begins.

"Not now, Craig." Penny brushes him off as she hurries across the courtyard to Beaker. Since Cordell has left with Tanner, her technician is sitting on the asphalt, his back to the porch, his injured arm cradled against his chest.

"Penny," Craig says again. "Please. About before. I wanted to—"

"If you want to do something, we're going to need a first aid kit."

"First Aid here," Craig shouts.

As if by magic, one of the Kevlar-clad squaddies jogs over with a green canvas bag, which Craig hands to Penny.

"Thank you," she says curtly, opening the bag, the graze of the zip equally curt. Taking stock of its contents, she removes a pair of surgical scissors. Then, softening, she says, "Let's take a look at this arm, Beak. Try not to move, okay?"

"Penny," Craig pleads. "I tried to tell you. You didn't believe me."

"Not right now please, Craig," Penny says. Turning her back on him, she hacks away at the fabric at Beaker's sleeve.

Craig grunts. "You're being ridiculous."

Even Beaker lifts his eyebrows at that.

Penny snorts. He thinks *she's* being ridiculous. "If you don't mind, Craig, I need to see to *my people.*"

The scissors' blade touches skin, and Beaker shivers. Penny peels back the sodden sleeve and slices away the blood-soaked scrap of lab coat. Thankfully, the bleeding has stopped, but the wound is deep and probably painful.

Beaker peers at the ragged gash. A mistake. He wavers, teetering sideways.

Leaping to catch him, Craig turns him about and lowers his head to the ground. "Watch yourself there, Beaker. Looks like you've lost a bit of blood."

"Yeah," Beaker whispers.

Penny places a gauze dressing impregnated with antibacterial honey over the wound and tapes it down firmly. "I think he's going to need some stitches," she says.

"I'll take him," Clark says, appearing at her shoulder. "It'll be quicker than getting an ambulance out here."

"What about the press helicopter?" Penny says.

"I don't recommend it," Craig says. "They'll want their pound of flesh—most likely they'll pump Beaker for information about what happened here."

"They're hardly going to stick him with sodium pentothal," Penny snaps. "No, wait. You secret agents probably have more effective substances now, don't you?"

"Um. I don't mind waiting," says Beaker, lifting a hand weakly.

"It's no bother at all," Clark replies, crouching to give Beaker a reassuring pat on the knee. "I promised to stop in at hospital social services on my way home, anyway."

Taking a silver emergency blanket from the first aid kit, Penny shakes it out and tucks it around Beaker's shoulders. "I'll go with you," she says. She gets to her feet.

"Actually, it'd really help if you and Mather could stay on here a few minutes," Craig says, taking the first aid kit from her and handing it off to Clark. "So we can clear up what happened here."

"I promise to take good care of him," Clark says, tucking the first aid kit under his arm.

Beaker smiles. "Try not to worry, boss."

Penny purses her lips. She's run out of excuses.

Two of Craig's team have been helping Mather lift the bodies onto gurneys. Craig signals them over. "Help get Mr Deaker into Officer Clark's car, will you? And be careful about it. He's lost a bit of blood."

Penny put her hands on her hips. "Just so you know, Beaker, if you're planning on using this as a pretext for a day off work, I'll need a doctor's note."

Mather grins. "They give you any problems, give me a call; I'll sign that note for you," he says, leaning in and clasping Beaker's hand as he's carried past.

- Matiu -

True to Matiu's prediction, there are four empty buses parked in a line at the top of Puhi Huia Road. Erica pulls over on the dark side of the narrow street, away from the security floods, and puts the Solaris in park. Sandi Kerr's silver Ford Falcon is nowhere to be seen.

"They've gone up the mount," Matiu says, opening his door and stepping out into the sultry night. He aches from head to foot, and he's never felt so weak.

"You know that we can drive up there, right?"

"Not exactly the stealthy approach though, is it?" He lets Cerberus out, who immediately goes into a crouch, hackles raised, and starts growling. "I know, boy," he says, crouching to ruffle his ears. "Something's up there."

Erica comes around to join them. "That *something* is a horde of people walking towards a mass suicide, if today's events are anything to go by," she says. "We need to stop it from happening again."

Matiu stands, looping Cerberus' lead around his palm. The dog strains forward, pulling on his arm, causing Matiu to yelp in pain and quickly hand the leash off to Erica.

"It's more than that. Kingi and Makere are tied up in this somehow."

"Makere?" Erica says. "Who's that?"

Matiu flinches, like she just tried to hit. He stumbles on. "Makere's...he's...another guy, from the gang, sort of high up. Whatever Kerr's doing, Makere's been trying to prevent us from stopping her, usually by throwing Kingi and his boys at us. He wants her to succeed because it's good for him. And I don't think she has any idea."

Erica tugs Cerberus in to heel. "I'd like to say you're overthinking this, but it makes a weird sort of sense. Kerr is playing with shit she doesn't understand, isn't she?"

Matiu nods to himself. Makere is a power Kerr doesn't understand. But Makere understands what she's tapping into. "He knows that she doesn't know what he knows, and that he knows what she doesn't know. You know?"

"I have no idea what you just said. And do *you* know?"

Matiu grits his teeth. "Not enough." He kneels by the back seat and runs his fingers along the upholstery.

"What are you doing?" Erica asks.

"Bit of theft prevention." His fingers find a loop of webbing and he gives it a yank, wincing. The back seat comes loose and he hauls it up, expecting to see the car's battery array beneath.

The space is empty. No batteries here. "Damn," he mutters, letting the seat fall back. He checks in the boot, finding only the spare tyre. "Oh shit."

"What?"

Dumbfounded, Matiu walks around the car, pops the bonnet and opens the small cover that conceals the two small battery cells he had previously assumed were auxiliary power. "Grab me that toolkit out of the boot, will you?"

Erica brings it to him. "You care to share?"

Matiu shakes his head slowly as he selects a screwdriver and begins disconnecting one of the two cells. "These are the only batteries in the car. These are it."

A red warning light starts blinking as Matiu removes the first terminal. He ignores it and pulls the battery free. It's heavier than a lead acid, surprisingly dense for its size. Slipping it into one pocket and the screwdriver into another, he ducks his head inside the car and checks the dash. Even with the ignition off, a red battery warning light is now illuminated on the dash. "Solaris, start," he says. The car doesn't respond.

Dropping the toolkit on the front seat, Matiu looks at Erica. It all makes sense. "This is why everyone wants this car. It's a whole evolution in battery technology."

As he closes the door, Erica tries the button for the central locking. Nothing happens. "Great work, Sherlock, but now we can't even lock the damn car. Some security system that is."

Matiu shrugs, dropping the bonnet. "Doesn't really matter, does it? No-one can steal it now." Grinning, he sets off up the road toward the pedestrian track that ascends the mount. Cerberus strains to follow, and Erica hurries to catch up.

"So, any thoughts on a plan yet?" she huffs.

"Save the day, get the girl, and ride off into the sunset."

"The sun's already set, and you don't have a horse."

"Let's not get caught up in the details, all right? And you didn't say anything about the girl."

"Don't get presumptuous. It doesn't suit you."

- Pandora -

Penny watches as Clark pulls out, the police car skirting the patch of grass where Cordell is conducting a television interview, the area lit up like a concert. Tanner was right to enlist Cordell: he's far more at ease looking down the lens of a camera. Maybe he should consider a new career as a TV personality and leave the way clear for Yee Scientific to become the foremost contract science laboratory in the city. She snorts. *Chance would be a fine thing!* Well, no one can say her current contracts aren't interesting: she and Beaker are no longer monitoring algal blooms. She closes her hands over the handle of the pallet jack. Although days like this one, she could do without.

She scans the courtyard for Craig, so she can give him a statement and get out of here, but he's busy with *his people*, whoever they are. Standing beside the roller doors, Wester is briefing him on something. The pair of them point at the trees, then back towards the mission house. Craig barks commands. There's more pointing. Now, a couple more of Craig's ninjas join them. Penny sighs. Looks like whatever he's doing is going to take a while. Mather has disappeared too: no doubt looking for chiller space to squeeze in the victims of this latest shoot-out.

She shrugs. May as well make herself useful inside. Sending a quick text to Matiu's phone to let Erica know she's going to be a bit longer, Penny heads back into the lab. She pauses on the doorstep and clucks her tongue. It's like a bar fight in a western saloon—all shattered windows, upturned stools, broken glass and shredded fabric, even a trail of dark blood splotches. *Beaker's blood.* Penny sits down on a nearby stool. Takes a few deep breaths. In the middle of the fracas, flooded with adrenalin and distracted by what was going on outside, things in the lab hadn't seemed so bad, but now, looking at the devastation…how Craig, and then Clark, had the nerve to step outside into the melee, heaven only knows? Training, she guesses. Maybe there's a secret academy. A Hogwarts for spies…

Puffing the air from her cheeks, Penny jumps off the stool. She snaps on some gloves, searches the drawers for a fresh lab coat. The logo doesn't impress her—Touching the Sun—but, made of sturdy cotton, it offers a protective layer, so it'll have to do. Then she sets about sweeping up the glass with a broom she finds stashed with some other cleaning gear near a clean-up sink. There are glass shards everywhere. On the benches. The floor. Her satchel. She lifts it and gives it a shake. When she's swept up as much as she can, she sets the stools upright, returns the Bunsen burner and the safety goggles to their places, dumps what's left of Mather's lab coat in the bin, mops the floor, and wipes down the benches with decontaminant.

She's returning the Decon to its shelf when she spies the open reagent cupboard. Whoops. She made a bit of a mess when she was rifling through the contents earlier. She should probably give it a quick tidy. Secretly, Penny loves these kinds of jobs and, honestly, this cupboard could really do with some help. Some ninny has only gone and organised the reagents into alphabetical order! She shakes her head. That's so dangerous. Even a high school chemistry technician knows better than this. Lifting the bottles and flasks out of the cabinet, Penny sets about segregating them into compatible chemical families.

Hmm. Let's just separate the inorganic from organic compounds for starters, shall we? No, no, no, we definitely do not want oxidisers and reducers clumped together on the same shelf. And aluminium and bromide do NOT go together either...

Standing on a stool, Penny shifts the containers about, grouping the $I_{\#1}$ metals and hydrides, then the $I_{\#2}$ acetates...on to $O_{\#2}$ alcohol and amines... There's not much in the way of alcohols: she's cleaned those out making the Molotov cocktails. Mather is going to need to order some more.

Hang on. What's in this bottle? It's not labelled. Penny lifts it to the light. The solution is as black as petroleum. Potassium permanganate? No, not purple enough and there's already a bottle of permanganate. How much permanganate does a lab need, anyway? It's possible it's a food grade chemical. It's dark, so it could be vinegar. Or maybe Cola. All at once, Penny has one of those Eureka moments. *Ink.*

The door slams behind her, and Penny almost falls off the stool.

She turns. It's Mather, pushing the pallet jack and cylinder, and he's got Craig Tong in tow. "Dr Yee!" Mather exclaims, lifting his arms as if he were an evangelist preacher. "I just *love* what you've done with the place."

Grinning, Penny slips the black liquid back on the shelf and closes the door. "No problems," she calls across the lab. She steps down from the stool. "It's the least I could do. Besides, I noticed you had some new clients to sign in." She pauses, horrified at herself. "Sorry, that was crass."

Mather waves his hand in a dismissive gesture. "In my line of work, an appreciation of black humour is a part of the job description." He looks around the lab. "I don't suppose you found the cylinder store? Now that we're not using it as a flame thrower, we should really put this away." He pats the cylinder.

"Maybe that back room?" Penny says, pointing. "Only, it's locked. I tried to open it earlier, so I could mop under the door."

"Here, let me try," Craig says.

Penny rolls her eyes. "I suppose you're going to tell us you have one of those universal key-swipe cards that you see on the movies—" she begins, then stops, her mouth dropping open, when Craig holds one up.

He waves it in front of the door. There's a click as it swings open.

He steps through first. "Just more laboratory space. Looks like they were using it to store some old equipment. There's a cylinder cage in the corner."

Penny moves aside to let Mather through with the pallet jack, then follows him in. Mather opens the cage and twists the cylinder onto a stand, chaining it safely in place. Penny takes a look around. It's just a storage room as Craig said. On the benchtops are a half a dozen light microscopes with poorly-fitted dustcovers, an old centrifuge, and a liquid chromatograph. On one side of the laboratory, pushed up against a wall, is a large apparatus, about the size of a small car, which has been covered with a tarpaulin.

"I wonder what the elephant in the room is?" she says.

"I don't know. Maybe an old server?" Craig suggests.

"Let's look, shall we?" Mather slides off the cover.

Penny gasps. "Oh wow." She can't believe it. This could be the answer. And if it is, it's going to save her *so* much time.

"Blimmin' Cordell!" Mather says. "I thought he said he was thorough. Not bloody thorough enough, was he? He should have wheeled those other cadavers farther into the room."

"I agree, it would have helped," Penny says. Right now she's too jubilant to be bothered with what Cordell should or shouldn't have done. "The important thing is, we now have a pretty good candidate for what triggered the nanobots to inflate."

"What?" Craig asks looking from Penny to Mather. "What did Cordell do now? What am I missing? What even is this thing? An iron lung?"

"It's an old permanent state MRI machine," Penny says, the discovery allowing her to put aside her annoyance.

Mather pokes at the dials. "Ancient, more like," he says.

Craig frowns. "And that's relevant because..."

"It operates by magnetic resonance."

Craig arches a brow.

"We think the nanobots in our massacre victims were triggered by a change in the magnetic field."

CHAPTER 30

- Pandora -

Penny and Craig help Mather replace the tarpaulin over the MRI scanner.

Linking his hands and stretching his arms, Mather yawns. "If it's all the same to you two, I reckon I'm going to mosey on home," the pathologist says.

Frowning, Penny turns to Craig. "I thought you wanted us to hang around for a debrief."

Craig coughs and straightens his tie. "Dr Mather's already answered my questions."

Mather flicks the lights off. "Got them all correct, too," he quips as they follow him out into the courtyard. Outside, only the ninjas remain; Tanner, Cordell, and the camera crews long gone. A truck-trailer has just pulled out, Craig's bullet-riddled vehicle on the back. Someone is nailing plywood over the laboratory's empty window frames.

"Hey, good work today, Yee," Mather says, lingering in the courtyard.

"You too." Penny hitches her satchel up on her shoulder.

"Seriously, that flamethrower was the most fun with chemistry I've had in ages. And on one of the darkest days of my career."

"One of the darkest days in our history," Penny agrees.

Mather sighs deeply. "Well, as the saying goes, there was never a night or a problem that could defeat sunrise or hope, right? Talk to you both tomorrow." He leaves them under the soft-focus light of the aurora australis.

Neither Craig nor Penny speak, both waiting for Craig's ninja to finish boarding up the laboratory. Finally, the man stuffs the last couple of nails in his pocket, flips the hammer, and heads off. Penny can still hear him whistling as he rounds the end of the warehouse.

She wraps her arms about her shoulders. "Why don't you just ask me what you need to know, so I can go home?"

"I'll drive you. We can talk on the way back to the lab."

She shakes her head. "Don't bother. I'll get my dad to send a car."

"Penny, please. Let me drive you."

Penny shrugs. "Whatever." She's being churlish, she knows, but Craig *misled* her. He deliberately withheld information from her. Things that concerned her. About Mum and Dad. And Matiu. About *her.*

Still, she needs to get back to the lab and check on Matiu. If she goes with Craig, she can answer his questions and, at the same time, he can answer hers. He *definitely* owes her some answers.

She lets him lead her to a nondescript sedan. Not the one they came in, since that one has more holes than a regular sock drawer. This one has been parked at the rear of the warehouse and out of the line of fire. Craig opens the door for her, and minutes later they're on the road, driving through the pines and the knee-high weeds, slowing only briefly for the roadblock at the entrance of the Kelliher Mission House. Wester gives Tong a quick salute as they pass. It's not until they've traversed the tidal flats that Craig speaks. "I'm really sorry, Penny." His jaw ripples. "Really. I should have told you sooner."

Too right, you should have.

"Just answer me this. When you took me for that dinner at the Sedge, was that real?" She watches him for his reaction.

Craig takes his eyes off the road, meeting hers. "It was real."

"But it was also for work, for *whoever* it is you work for. Intelligence Services."

Craig doesn't deny it. "That doesn't make my feelings any less real."

Penny bites her lip. So Craig's feelings are real. *What* feelings? *How* does he feel? Does it even matter? Feelings are tenuous ungraspable things. Feckless, fleeting…

"What's your connection to my parents?" she demands.

"We're friends."

"Craig."

"Okay. The truth is, I spent eight years in intelligence learning all manner of things from cyber security, to arms and combat training, and a myriad of survival techniques. Believe me, I've faced all kinds of lethal situations, and yet nothing, *nothing*, scares me more than your mother with a ham sandwich."

Penny hides her smile behind her hand. At least, he's not lying. "And losing the prototype. You don't want to lose that, either."

Craig pulls off the road and into a drive-in burger place. He orders them burgers and a couple of Cokes. Then he pulls the car up to the delivery window to wait for their order. "The prototype." He sighs. "Your father—Hing—commissioned the research. The investment was intended to keep the Yee fleet ahead of the competitors. The government chipped in with a grant. Turns out the research company was a front…that's not important. Anyway, the results, when we got them, were spectacular: rechargeable solar batteries no bigger than a ladies' handbag. Naturally, the government was interested. Because our families were friends, because of our shared Chinese heritage, the SIS had me work with your father to develop the technology and get it into the country."

Is he telling the truth? Mum loves Craig, positively adores him, turning into chocolate whenever he's in the room, and Dad likes him well enough, but a collaboration? She sucks in a breath, realisation dawning: Craig calls Dad Hing. Hing! That means Dad *respects* Craig—he must do, or he would never have let Craig call him by his first name.

A girl in a bright pink uniform passes a paper bag through the gap. "Two Kiwi beef with cheese with medium fries and Cokes."

"Thank you." Craig passes the bag to Penny and pulls back into the traffic.

The smell of grease is divine. Penny helps herself to a couple of fries. "What have the gangs got to do with it?" she asks.

"The same as everyone."

"All this carnage for a battery?"

Pulling into a layby, Craig turns off the engine. He removes the lid from his Coke, takes a drink, then says, "Look around you, Pen: the aurora australis, the earthquakes, this never-ending heatwave. You're a scientist. You have to know that the signs point to a reversal of poles. Someday, maybe sooner than we think, magnetic north is going to switch from one end of the globe to the other. When that happens, there's a good chance the national power grid will go down. Maybe not straight away. Maybe in patches. But in that case, it's pretty clear whoever has access to power will *hold the power*. It's why the Solaris is so important. And why the gangs are desperate to get their hands on it."

Penny passes him a burger. "Dad didn't want Matiu to have it. He suspected Matiu was still running with the gangs."

Craig removes the beetroot from his burger, laying it on the paper wrapping. "Actually, that was me."

Penny takes a bite of her burger and waits for him to go on.

"Let's face it, Matiu took the fall for Hanson. He went to *prison*. That suggests a certain amount of loyalty."

Penny puts the burger down. "Now look—"

"But Penny, as soon as I saw that arrow buried in your brother's side, I knew I'd made the wrong call. In fact, I realised that Matiu's inside knowledge of the gang made him our very best chance of keeping the prototype safe. I decided to leave it with him. I trust him to keep it safe."

"You put my baby brother at risk!"

"For the country."

"Craig, he could have died!"

Craig slams his hand on the dashboard. "Well, it was him or you!"

Penny gasps. She stares out the window, the passing traffic lights pixelating through her tears. Craig leans over and takes her hand in his, his fingers still cold from holding the cup. "I made a mistake," he breathes. "I'm sorry."

"Well. Thank you for saving my life," she whispers.

"Thank you for saving mine."

- Matiu -

Cerberus growls low in his throat. The trees press in around them, crawling with shadows the colours of the overhead aurora. Somehow, the night seems darker here. As if the lights above are sucking away what little brightness remains in the world below.

"It's coming up on midnight," Erica says. "We should hurry."

"I don't think midnight's her cue," Matiu says. "This isn't witchcraft. Not in the traditional sense, anyway."

"Still, they've got an hour on us. They could all be drinking the Kool-Aid right now."

Matiu huffs. Truth is, whatever Tong dosed him up with is wearing off, and half his body feels like it's on fire with every movement. "It wasn't Kool-Aid, it was wheatgrass juice."

"Who wasn't going to get caught up in the details?"

It's only a few hundred metres from the carpark up to the summit but tonight, injured and weighed down by the presence of the southern lights feathering the sky, to Matiu it feels like a marathon.

The sound of several throaty engines drifts up from the road below, drawing closer. Matiu glances back down the path. He'd recognise the thunder of a Harley from any distance. "That's Hanson's boys. Kingi's boys now, I guess. We'd better get off the path."

Erica turns to look and Cerberus whips about, tense as a spring ready to uncoil in a flurry of tooth and nail. "Can't we outrun them?"

Matiu snorts. "You might be able to. Me, I can barely jog. And we know they're not going to interfere with Kerr. They're coming for us."

Luckily, Matiu and Erica are still in the belt of bush that cloaks the mount's lower flanks. Matiu ducks off the asphalt path and slips between the trees, moving carefully. If he thought it was dark out there, it's even darker in here.

Erica follows, drawing a reluctant Cerberus with her. Twigs and leaves crunch underfoot as they press deeper into the cover of the trees, moving steadily uphill. Searching for handholds amongst the branches and stumps, Matiu stifles small grunts of pain.

In the distance, they hear a car door slamming. Angry shouts.

"Damn," Matiu grumbles. "If we'd thought about it we would've rigged the car to blow up."

"Think of the paperwork that would've made for me," Erica hisses, then they both drop low and fall silent as boots thump up the path. Cerberus pulls at the leash, a low growl swelling in his throat.

On the path a dozen figures pass, obscured by trees. Something about the bikers' broken silhouettes suggests they're not entirely human in shape anymore, but it could just be the strange light. One stops, right where Matiu and Erica stepped off the path into the bush. Turns to gaze into the shadows concealing them.

Simon Kingi.

Matiu hunkers lower, his skin crawling at the sight of the lazy tentacles writhing on Kingi's back. Erica won't see them. She'll see arms of flax waving in the breeze, even though there is no breeze. But Cerberus sees. His growl rumbles louder, threatening to burst into a bark, to give them away. Matiu clamps a hand around his muzzle.

"Why don't you let the dog speak," croons a soft, deadly voice at his shoulder. "He makes more sense than you most the time."

Matiu twists around, but Makere isn't there, whispering in his ear. He's standing on the hillside, cloaked in an impossible red light, both arms wrapped around Erica, one hand clamped hard over her mouth. With a swift twist, Makere snaps her neck. Her head lolls to the side, her eyes black pits where they used to shine. She didn't even have time to cry out. Makere lets the body fall, laughing.

Matiu surges to his feet, rage propelling him up the hillside, vision narrowing to a tunnel at the end of which is nothing but Makere, the other half of him, the brother who was never meant to be. Matiu staggers forward, fists swinging, but Makere is faster, hands striking out and grappling his wrists, holding him there. His touch is all kinds of cold, the chill of dead things burrowing into Matiu's skin. Matiu tries to kick out but his feet are tangled in branches, limbs. Erica's limbs. Where the hell is Cerberus?

An inarticulate roar bubbles up in his throat as he lashes out, driving his head towards Makere, but the killer has the advantage of being on the uphill slope and Matiu's head slams harmlessly into Makere's chest.

"The sooner you give this up, the better," Makere says, in that deceptively smooth tone. "You can't win, anyway."

Matiu jerks and throws himself sideways, trying to dislodge Makere's footing, but his foe is implacable. He can feel bandages tearing free and fresh blood flowing warm down his side. "Sure as shit...won't go down...without a fight!"

"You remember Māui?" Makere says, unperturbed by Matiu's flailing. "How he threw out his ropes and brought down the sun? Beat Ra to a submissive pulp, made him *obey*?"

Matiu grunts and strains, a puppet in the grip of a demon.

"You think Māui cared about obedience, about following the rules, rules like gods lording over men? You think Māui cared when he beat the sun from the sky or stole fire from Mahuika? We make our own rules." Makere chuckles. "Even the sun must answer for its crimes, eh? And the sons, brother. Do the sons pay for the sins of the father? Or do we inherit them?"

"Grrhhng," Matiu growls, unable to break free.

"Your father, Matiu. What rules did he break? And who's going to pay the price? What will it be paid in? Blood, perhaps?"

"Don't know," Matiu hisses through clenched teeth, through his pain, "who my father is."

Makere shrugs, and with another easy flick of his shoulders sends Matiu tumbling into the dry leaves. Pain wracks him, driving him to the ground. "You should know by now, bro. Should've worked it out, you and all your playing detective. The clues are everywhere. Hell, even Mārama's been trying to tell you, but carefully, because he's listening, always listening. Why do you think he took away her power to put thoughts and words together? He can't have anyone reveal his nasty little secrets. Secrets like you, like me. But you, I need you. Kerr needs you, not that she knows it. You're the last piece of the puzzle, Matiu Yee, hiding there behind that false name, like you're not your father's son."

"Not a false name!" Matiu manages, rolling onto his knees, struggling against the agony of his wounds to find his feet, to stand up and confront his shadow, his enemy, himself. "I am a Yee, and to hell with the father who never had the balls to own up to it!"

He manages two steps before his knees fold and he collapses, gripping a tree so he doesn't end up back on the ground.

"Truth is, I reckon you *have* worked it out, you just don't want to believe it. And that's fine. Makes what I have to do that much easier. Ignorance is bliss, bro. Peace out." With a gesture, Makere fades back into the darkness, the bloody glow that shrouded him drifting away like mist.

"The fuck...!" Matiu curses, lunging at the place where Makere was, where Erica's body lies twisted and still, where the shadows lay deepest because of the secrets they hide, the secrets Matiu rails against, the secrets he knows deep inside but refuses to accept. Because for all that he walks with one foot on the other side, there are things too insanely fucked-up for even him to contemplate as reality. He falls, his strength failing, reaching for Erica's lifeless shape, still warm, still warm...

"Matiu?" A hissing in his ear.

He gasps, blinks.

"You right?" Erica asks. She's beside him, flattened against the tree trunk, Cerberus gripped tight to her chest, her hand wrapped around his muzzle. "Thought I lost you there for a sec. Hell of a time to take a nap and start sleeptalking."

"But, you..." Matiu whispers, then shuts up. Another of Makere's nasty tricks. But why? If only he could work out the long game. If only he knew what the trap was he was walking into.

"Kingi's gone, and we need to move. You with me?"

Matiu nods, rises to a crouch. The pain is bearable again. Makere is gone, for the moment. And his father? *Their* father? Where's he in all of this? Only one person knows, and she's up this hill, lying down in the glow of the burning night sky to die for Sandi Kerr.

Not on my watch.

"Let's go."

- Pandora -

Back at the laboratory, Penny knows before she's even touched the keypad that something's wrong. "Craig," she whispers, but already he's drawn a gun from a shoulder holster inside his jacket. He puts a finger to his lips and nudges her to one side, so she's out from the door frame. *Out of the line of fire.*

It's all Penny can do not to squeak. Craig has a gun! Intellectually, she knows he's a spy, but getting her head around the fact is a whole other thing.

Craig nods at her.

Safely pressed against the wall, Penny trembles as she touches her thumb to the pad, unlocking the door.

Craig kicks it open with a heavy thud. His gun raised, he charges in. Penny peeks into the lab. The lights are on, and everything's in its place, and yet it's all wrong. Where is Cerberus, leaping up to slobber all over her? Where's Erica, her face pinched with worry for Matiu? And Matiu? Where's Matiu?

Craig is running from room to room, throwing open doors and whipping into spaces like he's a movie detective. No one in the lab, or the office. The bathroom is clear, too. There's just the cool store left. Craig gestures for her to stand back. Soundlessly, he approaches the door. Penny's pulse gallops. Her lungs scream. She's in danger of hyperventilating. *Please don't let them have been murdered and their mutilated bodies dragged into the cooler.*

His face set, Craig raises his gun. He moves closer. Flicks the latch. Thump. Open. "Clear." He lowers his gun and steps back. "There's no one here."

Her shoulders dropping, Penny lets out a breath. "I don't understand. Where are they?"

"Let me check the building. Lock the door behind me," he demands. "Don't open it unless you identify either Matiu or me. I'll be right back."

"Be—"

The door swings shut, and Penny is left alone, the hazy green-gold lights of the aurora australis slicing through the laboratory windows. It's eerie; like steam rising from the Pōhutu Geyser at night. Minutes pass. Penny waits, sick with worry. She should never have left in the first place. She should've known Kingi wouldn't give up. The man had wanted to mess up Matiu so badly that he'd returned from the dead. He was hardly going to abandon his crusade after one botched attempt.

Frowning, Penny looks around. The laboratory is exactly as she left it. That makes no sense. Even injured, it isn't like Matiu to go down without a fight.

In the silence, the fridge hums and tsks, and Penny shudders, blood freezing in her veins. "You're right," she murmurs. "Kingi only had to threaten to harm Erica or Cerberus, and Matiu would have followed along like a baby."

There's a tap at the door. "It's me, Craig."

Her legs heavy, she trudges to the door.

He bounds into the room and slides the gun into his holster. "The Solaris is gone," Craig says.

Penny isn't surprised. "You didn't really think Kingi was going to leave it? Whoever controls the power, *has the power*, you said." Her lip quivers.

"This doesn't mean the gang has Matiu."

"Where is he then?"

"Pen, come on. Your brother's not stupid. If he had an inkling Kingi and his men were on to him, if he thought they were on their way here, he would've taken the Solaris and got the hell out."

"But Craig, he's injured," Penny wails, "and you pumped him full of drugs."

For a moment, Craig rests his hand on her cheek. "That was hours ago. Let's just see what we can find. Maybe they left a note. We won't panic until we know for sure, okay?"

She bites her lip, and nods.

"Right, while I look to see if they left anything behind in the office, why don't you check your phone in case he called you?"

Her phone! Of course. She should have checked it before instead of standing here covered in goose bumps like a Christmas chicken. Penny takes the device out of her satchel and scrolls through the messages. Mum. Mum. Mum…nothing. Matiu hasn't called her. Worse, her text to him two hours ago hasn't been delivered.

CHAPTER 31

- Matiu -

The sound of a revving chainsaw right beside them sends Matiu scrambling for cover. "What the hell is that?" he hisses, throwing himself painfully against a nikau trunk.

"That's my ring tone, you got a problem with it, you got a problem with me." Erica fishes the phone from her pocket. "It's your sister." She swipes to answer, the growl of the chainsaw suddenly, mercifully muted. "Hey, Penny."

Matiu spreads his hands in confusion, gesturing in such a way that he hopes will convey to Erica both just how disturbed it is that her ringtone is a motherfucking chainsaw, and also his deeper consternation that she and Penny have traded cell numbers.

"Yeah, he's with me, here you go." Flat-lipped, Erica hands the phone to Matiu.

"Hey, Sis."

"Don't you 'Hey, Sis' me! Where the hell are you? You're meant to be on the couch at the lab, recovering from an arrow through the chest! Not off gallivanting around the city with your girlfriend doing...whatever it is you're doing." Her voice cracks. "What *are* you doing?"

"A little trick I call saving the world. You know the tune, hum it with me."

"Matiu, this is no time for jokes. Do you have any idea what I've been through in the last couple of hours? I've been shot at, I've..."

"Wait, what?" Matiu stiffens, all his witty repartee draining away. "Shot at you? Who shot at you? I thought you were with the cops?"

"I am, I... I was. The Han triad, they attacked the cold store facility on the island. Maybe they thought that's where you'd stashed the Solaris, I don't know. But...people died, Matiu. People were trying to kill me, and instead, I watched them die."

Matiu sinks onto a fallen ponga trunk. The fibrous bark is like a pig's bristles under his legs. Erica is watching him in alarm. "Penny, just chill, all right." He can hear the thin thread of her composure down the line, pulled taut to the point of breaking. "It's over now, right? You're safe? The cops did their job and kept you out of the line of fire? What about Tong? He's some sort of ninja, isn't he? Bet he just karate-chopped them all into the middle of next week."

Penny is silent for a long moment, too long. "I might've killed some of them, Matiu. Hurt them, at least. It's... I don't know how it happened, but we were going to die and we had to do something, and..."

"Penny, ssshhh, just chill, OK. Penny?" Suddenly, the distance between them seems too vast, from this mountain of madness to the island of the insane. Further than a brother and sister should ever be, a darkness as thick and wet as nightmare separating them. Smothering the light. For the first time in his life, he wants her to be there, not so she can hide him from the world, but so he can hide her. Her reality, the thing her every thought and action hinges on, has been shaken. She needs him, right now, and he can't be there. He can't do anything. Except lead her into more danger.

"Where are you, Matiu?"

"Maungawhau. Kerr's here. She's led a bunch more people up here to die. That's why we're here, we have to stop them."

"For crying out loud, Matiu, it's not your job. Call the police, let them deal with it. You...you need to get away from there, get home. Let Tanner and Clark know, they'll get someone in to break it up. I... I need to know you're safe."

Matiu swallows a hard knot in his throat. "Mārama's with them. So's Charlotte."

Penny is quiet for so long Matiu thinks the line might've gone dead. He pulls the phone away from his ear to check the battery hasn't run out. "We know what causes the deaths," she continues at last. "It might be possible to stop it." Her voice is thin, but steely.

"I'm not sure we're going to be able to stop this, Penny." The honesty burns, and he has to look away from Erica's wide-eyed glare. "This is everything Mārama's been warning me about. This is the moment when the curtains open and the monsters run free."

"Matiu..." Penny sounds like she's at the bottom of a well, the connection between them growing frail, hollow. "I need you to do something for me."

Matiu nods. "Do what?"

He can sense her struggle down the line. She's strung out across this abyss of the unknown, fighting everything she's been taught to trust, while trying so hard to believe even a little in her brother's cursed vision. Because when he said monsters, she didn't tell him to grow up. "I need you to hold them off. For as long as you can. I need time, to get to where you are. We can save these people, but only together. Can you do that for me, Matiu? Can you hold back the monsters?"

Matiu's eyes sting. He never thought it would hurt so much to hear his sister say she believes him. To accept that his reality just might be able to exist alongside hers. "Fuck, yeah," he says, but it's a broken sound. And Penny doesn't hear it, because the signal has died, and all that comes back to him down the line is that awful, nightmare-riddled blackness, haunted by the empty spaces in between.

– Pandora –

Numb, Penny disconnects the call.

Matiu. Monsters. Kerr. There has to be a way to stop this madness. There must be. I just have to...I have to... She inhales deeply, but her chest tightens, as if she's swimming through mattress stuffing and quaffing great mouthfuls of cotton wadding each time she takes a breath. It's too white, too thick. Suffocating. And there's something she isn't quite grasping, something flitting about in her subconscious like a fantail. Penny's certain she'd know what it is, what she has to do, if only she could just breathe.

In the laboratory, when she can't put her finger on an answer, she goes back to the beginning and lists the facts. Penny screws up her eyes and concentrates on what she knows. She knows this isn't about the Solaris. Not really. This isn't just about a battery, or wheatgrass, and it isn't about supremacy of the gangs. This isn't even about Kerr, although the high priestess of darkness and her cohort have their part to play.

"This is everything Mārama's been warning me about," Matiu had said. He'd crumbled after that. "Monsters," came his whisper, the word barely spoken, like a tissue swirled away on a breeze, and in that moment every hair on Penny's head had stood on end. Well, the aurora australis can dance its merry dance all over the whitewashed walls of the laboratory, even that shimmering opalescence won't hold back the darkness. If Matiu's hunch is right, then very soon, the world will be cloaked in shadow, and unspeakable things will prowl beneath the darkened folds. "Monsters." Matiu's seen them, and there have been times when even she's glimpsed… Penny can't explain it, heaven only knows it goes against everything she believes in, defies every law, every principle, but she *believes* Matiu when he says, when he *whispers,* that the day of evil has arrived. She might roll her eyes and scoff at his hinky feelings, yet her brother has never been wrong, as much as Penny wishes it were otherwise.

"So?" Craig demands. "Where are they? Is Matiu okay?"

Penny blinks. "They…they're…" she chokes.

"At the hospital?"

Penny shakes her head. "No, not the hospital." She gasps, breathing at last. "They're somewhere…they're...at Maungawhau. I—"

"Maunga. Maunga," Craig says, seizing on the word. "That's Māori for mountain, right? Which mountain? Penny, do you know how many mountains there are in Auckland? The entire city is made up of mountains. It's a bloody ring of volcanoes, for God's sake!"

"Fifty-three."

"What?"

"There are fifty-three monogenetic volcanoes in Auckland," she blurts, knowing immediately that it's not the factoid she needs, that the answer is still somewhere in her head, infuriatingly out of reach.

Impatient for the translation, Craig lifts his phone, speaking authoritatively, like the government attaché Penny had always understood him to be. "Siri-9. Which mountain is Maungawhau?"

Before the virtual assistant can get a word in edgewise, both their phones blare, the *da duh da, da* notes of Penny's *Imperial March* narrowly beating out Craig's theme tune from *Mission Impossible.*

"Tong speaking." Craig puts the phone to his ear and steps away.

"Hello?" Penny says.

"Dr Yee? Clark here."

Penny's ribs tighten. She reaches out to steady herself against the bench. *Oh god, no. Not Matiu. Not yet. Please. I need more time. I haven't...*

"I know it's late." The officer's voice is oddly upbeat for this kind of news. "But I knew you wouldn't mind since I have an update on Beaker."

Beaker?

"That gash on his arm was deeper than we all thought—turns out he needed eleven stitches—but he came through with flying colours and the doctors dosed him up on painkillers and antibiotics, so he should be good to go tomorrow. To work, I mean. No medical certificate necessary. I've got a uniform running him home now."

Matiu isn't dead. Penny can't believe it. There's still time. Her legs feel like jelly.

Over by the window, Craig raises his voice. "How many? Jesus. Not again. You've got to be kidding me!"

"Oh and another thing…" Clark says.

Penny's heart stills.

"That appointment I mentioned? I dropped in to see little Carlos at Social Services. Now before you worry, he's doing just fine, but the paediatricians have diagnosed a mild case of chicken pox, so for safety's sake, they're keeping him overnight for observation before delivering him to his grandmother tomorrow as planned. Anyway, he wasn't asleep, so I stayed a moment to read the boy a story—*Hairy Maclary from Donaldson's Dairy*—and he asked about the doggie. He meant your Cerberus, of course. I had a little chuckle over that. After all the bad news we've had today, I thought you'd like to hear—"

"Wait. Chicken pox. You said he has chicken pox."

"Yes, that's right."

Somewhere, in Penny's head, a soap bubble pops.

"Clark! Does Carlos have a Touching the Sun tattoo?"

"I don't think…"

"Clark. Please. It's important. Do you remember Carlos having a tattoo?"

There's a pause.

"No, he didn't, Dr Yee. I know because I was holding the book in one hand and Carlos was holding the other side. It was a large book, wide, and he was using both hands, so both of his wrists were visible. He didn't have a tattoo."

"Where are you now? At the hospital?"

"Yes. Wouldn't you know it? I missed my birthday dinner—"

"Don't go yet. Stay there until I've called you back."

"But I told my wife... Are you sure this can't wait until tomorrow?"

"Toeva! Whatever you do, *don't* leave!" Penny presses the phone off, then runs to her satchel, pulling out the microscope slide she'd salvaged from the lab at Puketutu Island—the tongue sample with the nanobots that Cordell made.

"I've gotta go," Craig says, leaving his spot by the window and marching towards her. "Satellite images show busloads of people converging on Mount Eden. Tanner suspects another massacre's about to go down and, right now, the police department is a bloody shit show—woefully short-staffed with half of them running around the city chasing down gangs and the other half mopping up today's earthquakes. I'll call you as soon as I can."

Penny whirls. "Wait! I'm coming with you." She dashes to a microscope and flips off the dustcover, thrusting the slide under the stage clips.

"Pen, you can't. This is police business."

"You're not the police." She clicks a screenshot of the slide on the microscope and sends it to her phone, before striding back to the bench to stuff the device in her satchel.

"I'm...that's just splitting hairs. Tanner called me in. I have to go."

"Siri-9," Penny interrupts, speaking to Craig's phone. "What's Māori for Mount Eden?"

"I'm not arguing with you on this."

"The Māori name for Mount Eden is Maungawhau," Siri-9 announces.

"You see?" She slips the satchel over her shoulder. "Matiu's at Maungawhau."

Craig sighs deeply. "If your brother's there, I'll find him for you, I swear."

"You have to take me!"

Craig strides for the door, jaw set. "Not happening."

"I might...I know how to stop the killings," she blurts.

He spins. "What?"

"But I can't do anything from here," she says, yanking the Breadmaker™ cord from its socket and wrapping it around the appliance. "You have to take me with you."

"Penny—" he begins.

She puts her shoulder to the apparatus and shunts it off the bench. "Take that, too." Craig leaps, catching the Breadmaker™ before it topples. He staggers backwards under its unexpected weight. "Put that in the car," Penny orders. "And be *careful* with it. I just need to check something. I'll be right down."

Not waiting for his reply, she dashes to the cool store, takes the specimen jar from its hidey hole, and slips the shard into her pocket. Then she runs into the office and rifles through the file basket next to her computer. *It has to be here somewhere. Nope. It should be with my notes for the Fletcher case, I'm sure I made a hard copy...no, not that one. Here!* She grabs the article—"Nanobots in Medicine: Modern Approaches to an Old Technology" by Dr P. David Buchanan—and, the elevator still out of service, she flies down the stairs.

Craig has slowed to adjust his grip on the DNA analyser when Penny overtakes him on the second floor. "Don't they require a fitness test at the Secret Service?" she shouts back over her shoulder.

Flushing pinkly, Craig picks up the pace. "Has anyone ever told you how much you're like your mother?"

In the car, the Breadmaker™ safely installed on the back seat, Penny turns on the interior light and flips through the article.

"So, tell me how we're going to stop this," Craig says as he pulls into the street.

"Shhh," Penny says. "Give me a sec. I'm working on it. So far, it's just a theory."

"Great! A theory!" Craig scoffs. He takes a left.

Penny folds the article and rests it on her lap. "I can't help it. It's the best I can do. I'm sorry if I don't have time to carry out the analyses, to check all possible parameters, and give you a best-case scenario. It's the middle of the night, the police are short-staffed, and hundreds, possibly thousands of crazed zombie people are zoning in on Mount Eden, *where they plan to off themselves*, no doubt after first placing themselves in a convenient koru pattern." She breaks off, realising she was shouting. "I'm working on it," she says again.

His lips pursed, Craig accelerates into the traffic on the arterial and says nothing. The Mount Wellington streetlights streak by in an elongated blur.

Penny takes up the article, scanning it for the section she read when she and Matiu had been working the Darius Fletcher case, the first time they came across Kerr and her diabolical penchant for human sacrifices. *There.* Biting her lip, she reads the text once, then re-reads it. She grapples with her satchel for the photo of the slide, examines it carefully, then snatches up her phone. She punches in the number.

"Hello?"

"Clark! Are you still at the hospital?"

"Yes, I'm still here. But I can't stay. Detective Inspector Tanner needs me to—"

"…Go to Mount Eden. Yes, I know. Before you leave, I need you to raid the hospital stores for containers of *varicella zoster* vaccine." She checks the article, running her finger down the page. "Look for a product called N-GenZostavax. As much as you can get your hands on. Enough for hundreds of people. Then meet me at the base of Mount Eden." She peers at the GPS on the dash. Where would Matiu have parked? She shakes her head. It doesn't matter. He's somewhere up there on the mountain. "Hillside Road," she tells Clark. "We'll meet you at the end of the cul de sac. And hurry!"

"Dr Yee, I can't just remove hospital medications without the proper authority…"

"Toeva. I need those meds. If not, Kerr's going to murder more people. Hundreds of people. Families. Children. Kids like Carlos. You think today's been bad—it's not over yet, and it's only going to get worse. If we don't get off our arses and do something now, from this day forward, your birthday's going to be remembered as the worst day in New Zealand history. The worst! Get Mather out of bed it you have to. Tell him the bots have been hiding in the dorsal horn ganglia." She shuts the phone off.

The car screeches into a corner, the wheels slewing on the rubber-concrete hybrid, before regaining equilibrium. Four hundred metres on, Craig turns to her. "Okay, let's hear this theory. What are these dangly horn things?" he demands.

She sighs. "The varicella virus presents in two forms: chicken pox, the all-over red currant rash you see in children; and shingles, a really painful localised blister, which usually occurs under the ribs. People who've had chicken pox are still able to contract shingles because the virus lies dormant in the dorsal roots of the nerves."

The indicator ticks slowly as they turn into the next street. Craig frowns. "Sorry, I'm just not seeing the significance."

Penny blows out long and hard, then takes a deep breath. Rolling up the article, she waves it in his direction. "Before his death, Kerr and her Touching the Sun cult were working with a medical researcher. You might know of him. He was in all the glossy magazines, bit of a highflier. This researcher, Buchanan, was trialling a protocol using programmable nanobots to destroy inoperable cancers. His poor patients, all terminal, were clutching at anything which might serve to prolong their lives. Posing as a counsellor, Kerr was able to tap into his patient list, and those unfortunates became the first human victims of Kerr's sacrifices. Matiu and I, we…" An image of Buchanan's lifeless body flashes in her head: his skull caved in, the dripping empty eye sockets, flames licking at his feet. She closes her eyes and opens them again, blinking away the vision and continuing with her story. "Back then, Kerr was content to kill individuals, but as you can see, lately she's moved into the big-time, and that's despite being on the police's most-wanted list. Nowadays, she gathers her victims from the cult itself, her scientists at Puketutu Island taking advantage of Buchanan's bio-carbon nanobot research to introduce programmable nanobots into cult members by way of their tattoos—and all under the guise of horticultural research."

"You know all this how?"

"I don't know. Not for sure. It's just a guess. But I did find a bottle of ink in the reagent store at Puketutu." Listening to herself, Penny knows it sounds lame.

Craig shakes his head. "Please tell me you found bots in the ink."

Penny rolls the paper between her fingers. "I didn't look. But it's unlikely."

"In the victims' blood, then? You must have looked there."

"Of course we did. Beaker looked, and Mather did, too. They didn't find them because the inactive forms aren't in the blood; they're hidden in the dorsal root ganglia."

"Like the shingles virus."

"*Exactly* like that." She taps the rolled-up article with her index finger. "In fact, Buchanan spliced the *zoster* virus onto his nanobots, pre-programming them to travel to specific sites in the body and carry out their designated function—in this case, hypervascularity of the tongue, causing suffocation. They might also be acting on centres in the victims' brains, causing them to make pilgrimages to certain venues…"

Craig slaps the steering wheel with his palm. "Okay, I think I get it. So, let me just get this straight: since we know that the bots are triggered by a magnetic source, like the permanent state MRI machine at Puketutu, all we have to do is get to Mount Eden, find the source, and Kerr's murderous little plot will fail!"

"Hmm," Penny says. "I suspect Māngere has a natural magnetic source buried under the mountain—a lodestone of magnetite rock, most likely."

Craig's face falls. "Fuck. That's that then, isn't it? If the same applies to Mount Eden, there's no way in hell we can get a digger in to excavate the site in time. And even if we could, how are we going to move a rock that big?"

Penny puts her hand on his shoulder. "We can't. It doesn't matter. I don't think that's the trigger anyway. Not this time."

"You're not making any sense. If she's not using a magnetic source, then how is she going to do it?"

"You said it yourself, Craig. Look at what's been happening to us lately: this dreadful heat, the algal blooms, earthquake swarms, power outages, the southern lights shining for days and days."

"Reversal of the magnetic poles?"

Penny nods. "I think when the magnetic field drops below a certain point, Kerr will get the reaction she wants…"

Craig clenches his teeth. "For fuck's sake. What is wrong with that woman, anyway? She has to be some kind of monster, to want to murder all those people. And to what end? Why? That's what I want to know. Why?"

Penny shivers. *To let the monsters in...*

All at once, the buildings around them tremble, and the ground cracks, opening like a zipper before them. "Look out!" Craig screams. He swerves violently.

The car spins through the air.

CHAPTER 32

- Matiu -

The summit of Maungawhau is a strange, undulating loop under the silver sheen of the moon and the coruscating red and green of the aurora, punctured by a black hole in the middle which stares up at the sky like a blind eye; the crater, a gentle grassy bowl, an innocuous reminder that this city is built on the bones of ancient violence, a promise of destruction which never goes away, just slumbers.

From their vantage point in the trees northeast of the lookout, hunkered against the trunks, Matiu and Erica can see the curve of the crater's southern lip, which rises above the northern rim by several metres. What they see there is enough to chill them both to the core. The bodies are laid out, arms linked, from the crater lip and descending, following the contour of the hollow down, out of sight. There's movement among them, and even from here the song they're singing drifts on the night. Some tuneless folk chant, the words muffled and obscure. Not English or Māori, something older, primeval, dredged up from whatever dark place Kerr found her other spells. A summons, perhaps, to the mouths and teeth that lurk behind the veil. The willing victims are lying there, probably spiralling down in the same koru shape as the previous victims, staring up into the shifting southern lights, as if waiting for those fingers of green and red to reach down from the sky and pick them up, carry them away. To lift them into the sky, to touch the moon.

To touch the sun. Just as their prophetess has promised.

Matiu would rush over there and start hauling people out if not for the pain that defines his every movement and the bikers who are patrolling the walking path around the crater like sentries. They all sport a weapon of some kind, be it shotgun or cricket bat or crowbar. They're spread thin with a lot of ground to cover, so while there'll be some gaps in their vigilance, it won't be enough to allow him the time to disrupt whatever Kerr is doing down in that crater before they get in and break him in half.

Beyond the crater rim, the lights of Auckland spread out around the mount like a glowing lake peppered with a million tiny candles. And past the city, the black of the sea. The rising tide.

One of the bikers, wreathed in shadows the colour of fresh blood, stands on the lookout and turns a slow arc, scanning the bush and the paths leading up from the carpark. A rifle is slung loosely in his hands, and his hair hangs in greasy dreadlocks down his back. In the shifting overhead glow, they seem to crawl across his shoulders with a life of their own.

"All right," whispers Matiu, hoping that if he talks the solution will present itself, "we need a distraction. Something to get these guys to run in the opposite direction, just long enough for one of us to get into the pit."

"The pit?"

"The crater, whatever." Matiu can't help but think of it as a pit, a descent into Autōia. "Once we're down there, we get to Kerr and take her out. Simple."

"Hate to rain on your parade, Rambo, but we don't even know if Kerr is here, since she's pretty good at not putting herself in harm's way, and also, neither of us is likely to be able to take anyone out. You're the walking wounded and I'm not exactly the Black Widow."

"Neither of us, no. But Cerberus knows who he's looking for." Cerberus growls, low and angry. Matiu ruffles his ears.

Erica is quiet for a moment. "OK, maybe that has some merit. How do we distract them, then?"

"Well," Matiu considers. "It'll need to be something big. We saw Kerr's car leaving the old prison, but it wasn't down with the buses, so chances are she drove up the access road and parked in the upper carpark, at the south end by the summit marker. If I sneak around there, get to the car, break the fuel lines and set it on fire, that should get them all running, right?"

"There's so much wrong with that plan, I don't even know where to begin."

"You got anything better?"

"Nope. You got a Plan B?"

"Hey, I'm still working on Plan A here. Enough with the pressure."

"Let's do it then, before people start dying."

As Matiu prepares to move, the sentry at the lookout takes a sudden step forward, clutching his chest, and drops to his knees. Matiu presses himself back against the trees and tries to get a better look at the gangster, who has something protruding from his ribcage.

An arrow.

"Crap." Matiu eases down to his belly. "Our mate Robin Hood is back."

Erica huddles down beside him. "You think he's been following us?"

"Either us, or the bikers. The point is he works for Kerr, and these guys aren't part of her plan. She must've called him in to get rid of them."

Farther away, there's a muffled grunt and another of the gangsters, silhouetted against the night sky, crumples with a fletched shaft sprouting from his spine. The dark erupts with shouts as the gangsters realise they're under attack.

"Reckon this'll work for us as a distraction?" Erica suggests.

Matiu grimaces. "Apart from the risk of running across that space and getting another arrow in me, I really wanted to blow Kerr's car up."

"Later, maybe. We might not get a better chance than this." Already, all the sentries are running south, hunting down the archer.

And then the earth slips sideways, slams and rolls.

Already on the ground, Matiu and Erica grip the shuddering earth as it rocks with the force of the aftershock, a big one. The trees around them groan, branches whipping to and fro. With a tortured shriek, the concrete paths that loop the hilltop fracture and buckle, and from somewhere nearby comes a dull roar of stone and dirt, sliding under gravity's embrace. Screams rise from the pit, a sudden panic, quickly muted by the rumble that grinds up through the rocks of the ancient volcano, Maungawhau's moan echoing around its long-dead gaping mouth. Rūaumoko, voicing his discontent with the world at large. Above them, the aurora australis shimmer and twitch, like a vast raptor flexing its wings, extending its talons, opening its beak.

Like a curtain of darkness has been thrown across the land, the lights of the city blink out.

Matiu presses himself to the ground, expecting at any moment to see the terrified Touching the Sun followers pouring from the pit in a surge of panic. But they don't.

"This is it," Matiu says. "This is what they've been waiting for. It's part of Kerr's plan."

"No-one can predict earthquakes," Erica says bluntly. "But if she's down there playing prophet, she'll be happy to say she was expecting all this. That it's a sign of the end times, why they're here."

"Come on," Matiu says, getting to his feet and yanking at Cerberus' lead, "let's go break this party up."

Erica rises to follow him and together, crouching low, they dash across the broken landscape towards the pit.

- Pandora -

"Miss, are you okay?"

Penny opens her eyes and looks around. *Oh god, oh god, I'm in a crash. No, I can't die, not yet...*

She breathes slowly, trying to calm her heart which is pounding like a Japanese taiko drum. *Breathe. Breathe.*

Still panting through her panic, she takes stock of the situation. She's upside-down. Ground level. Hanging from her seatbelt. Airbag in her face. Gritty bits of glass all over her. *Not heaven, then.* A man leans into the cab and punctures the airbag, releasing the nitrogen. He pulls the plastic out of the way. Even with the nylon cushion cleared, his face remains obscured, just the fuzz of his beanie picked out by the streetlight behind him.

Penny fumbles with her belt. "Craig! Is Craig okay?"

"The driver? He's fine. He's just over—"

"Penny. I'm here." The light goes out and then Craig is there, muscling his way past the man to get to her. *He's going to muss up the crease in his pants*, Penny thinks, and then Craig has his arms around her, holding her to him, his chin resting on her head. "Are you hurt?" he breathes into her hair.

Cradled against Craig's chest, Penny tests her limbs. She aches all over—her head is pounding from a bump on her forehead—but nothing seems to be broken. "I'm fine," she says, her voice shaky.

"Thank God. Right, let's get you out of there."

Penny wraps her arms around Craig's neck as he lifts her out of the wreckage and sets her down on the curb.

The crack in the road isn't too bad: around thirty metres long but barely more than a half metre deep. The car is a write-off though, the driver's side rear crumpled like paper and all the windows smashed. Penny's precious Breadmaker™, ejected like a space shuttle, is lying on the surface of planet-road. The sight of it jolts her to reality, reminding her why they're here in the first place.

She stands. "Craig, come on. We need to go."

But, his phone already to his ear, Craig shakes his head. "I know. I'm trying. I have to get this car off the road and find a way to bridge this crack first."

"Leave it," Penny pleads. "There's no time."

"I can't. As long as the road's blocked, the police can't get through. Besides, someone could get hurt."

She nibbles her lip. "Maybe, if they work together, the bystanders can help pull the car off the road?"

"Yeah, good idea..." He strides away to organise a posse.

Except Penny can't wait that long. She has to get to Maungawhau. To Matiu. Already, she might be too late. It isn't that far. Just another kilometre or so. She could run there, were it not for the Breadmaker™.

Dammit! She needs a vehicle.

The depot has plenty of them, but there's no point calling Carlie for a pickup. Craig's right; until the road's clear, no one's getting through. Penny casts around for a solution. The street is empty. Maybe that side street? With a glance back at Craig, Penny lopes up the road and ducks into a lane on the right. No cars here either, but there's something else. A construction site for a new townhouse development—the sort of residence with the exterior surfaces alternating between marble and glass. And there, parked in among the pallets of building materials, is a forklift. Suddenly, a vision strikes Penny like a cleaver behind the eyes; a blinding migraine haloed in brilliant white and, at the centre, Luke's forehead on the glass, his blue eyes, shock, that split-second, and then his face slackening…

Her scalp tingles. She clenches her fists, digging sharp half-moons into her shaking palms. *No. What the fuck am I doing? I won't drive. I can't. Look what happened the last time.*

Except, there's no other option. She has to get to Maungawhau. People's lives might depend on it. Charlotte. Mārama. Matiu…she can't save Luke. It's too late for that, but there's a chance she can help the people on the mountain.

She peeps back around the corner to the accident site where Craig is deep in discussion with a cluster of neighbours in their pyjamas. Penny wants to scream with frustration. This is no time to form a bloody committee. *We need to go now!* Penny crosses the road and runs across to the forklift. The new housing development might be reflective of a modernist style, but the equipment they're using is not, the battered forklift dating back to the Mesozoic. Its yellow paint is chipped everywhere, there's a ding on one corner, and a tear in the seat, foam stuffing oozing out of the crack. *Of course, it'll be locked...* She pops her head into the cage anyway. Well, there's no harm in looking…

Her heart sinks. It's fate. It has to be. Why else would the builder leave the key in the vehicle and the fork width set to narrow?

Fate. That's ridiculous. She's starting to sound like Matiu. Except, from their very first encounter with Kerr, from the day he first touched that bloodied sacrificial bowl in the warehouse, Matiu had seen this coming. Like a matakite of old, it's as if he's always known, or at least suspected that he had some role to play in this. So is her part destined too?

Stealing a forklift is written in her destiny?

Penny almost laughs out loud. Well, she wouldn't actually be *stealing* it. Just borrowing it for a bit. As soon as everything's sorted at Maungawhau, she'll drive it back. Or she'll have someone else drive it back. That is, assuming anyone lives.

Dammit!

Swinging herself into the lumpy seat, Penny clicks the seatbelt into place, and it's as if she never left. She switches on the forklift, a rare LPG model, raises the forks, and depresses the brake pedal. Puts the vehicle into gear. Then, her blood thrumming with fear and excitement, she accelerates out of the construction site and around the corner.

A cheer goes up as she roars into view. In the headlights, Craig's mouth drops open.

Beyond him, the lights strike the upturned sedan, reflecting off it like a beetle's shiny carapace. The forklift humming, Penny approaches the wreck.

But the Breadmaker™ is blocking the way. Slowing the forklift, Penny spins the forks under the machine, tilting them back until the Breadmaker's™ metal casing rests against the guard.

Then she makes a wide circle and heads for Maungawhau.

A shout goes up, then another, as it dawns on Craig's pyjama posse that she isn't coming back to help. She can't. Other people need her more. She's got to get to Mount Eden. Still, she can't help checking the rear-view mirror, feeling a stab of guilt at the sight of Craig standing in the middle of the road, staring after her. His mouth is still open, but now both his hands are planted firmly on his head.

CHAPTER 33

- Matiu -

The night falls down around this moment.

Here is Rūaumoko, angry child of the underworld, ramming sullen fists against his subterranean kingdom.

Here is Papatūānuku, her limbs skewed, her skin stretched and broken, shuddering with the memory of pain.

Here is Ranginui, flayed open and bleeding across the black, his many eyes the blind pinpricks of distant stars.

There is Erica, leaping light and deadly through the darkness, Cerberus surging ahead of her, dragging her on, the pair of them plunging towards a descent into someone else's hell.

Here is Matiu, stumbling beneath the bloody sky, tripping over that shattered earth, limping as his injured shoulder screams at him. He can't run like Erica, like Cerberus. He can't smash his fists against the earth like Rūaumoko. Can't call the mighty winds of Tāwhirimātea down around him or summon lightning to his fingertips. What in the hell did he ever hope to achieve here? He knows he's outmatched. He has no ancient sword this time, no guns. Not even the jack-knife he'd stabbed Kingi with the last time they met, when they were falling from a skyscraper roof towards certain death. He barely has the strength to stand, much less fight.

His run slows to a hobbled jog, then an agonised walk. But Penny needs him to hold them back, and hold them back he will, with his bare hands if that's all he has. One shaking step at a time.

He hears the rumble, feels the shiver beneath his feet. A tremor, yes, but not an aftershock. This is different. This isn't the wild, rocking jabs of an angry child. This is fury, rising from the darkest of places to curse the world.

He pauses, turns. A glow fills the eastern horizon. The rumble rolls on, rattling the jagged rubble and his aching bones.

Rangitoto.

The island flares. Sleeping all these long, long years, the volcano has chosen this moment to awaken and voice its contempt for the living. Its light turns the night sky a glowering shade of crimson.

All the more reason to keep moving. Matiu turns back, limps toward the crater.

Something slams into him, driving him to the ground. A rough corner of broken concrete slams the side of his head, and his vision bursts into bright burning spots. He tries to roll over, but he's being lifted by hands, many hands.

No, not hands.

Tentacles.

Flailing against the grip of more limbs than he can push away, Matiu twists in the monster's grasp. Kingi, of course. It had to be Kingi, with his twisting crown of alien flesh. Simon Kingi, who used to be his friend in another life. Something had moved on in and taken over Simon's body. Something hideous and corrupt. Now all that's left is this writhing beast.

Here is the ancient volcano sweeping by beneath them, as Kingi leaps away from the crater with preternatural strength, Matiu held over his head like a prize fish. Here is the summit marker, a narrow pyramid of steel and timber on a concrete plinth. Here are the bodies of the fallen, and the victorious.

Matiu glimpses a bloody body skewered by the wrists to the timber fascia of the summit marker, face obscured by night-vision goggles, before he's slammed into the marker himself. The pain is unfathomable, and this time he knows it's not a hallucination, not Makere messing with his head. They found the archer, and now they've found him.

He struggles to focus on Kingi, whose serpentine limbs still hold him tight. Kingi is taking something from one of the men down below, and in the same moment that Matiu registers the shape of an arrow in Kingi's hand, it's coming at him, passing through him, pinning him to the timber.

Matiu screams as fresh blood runs hot from this new wound, thrashing against Kingi's implacable grip, and he has barely drawn breath when a second arrow pierces his other shoulder. Releasing him to the arrows' hold, Kingi drops back to the asphalt.

With his hands freed, Matiu grabs at the arrows, but they're sunk tight into the timber, with all his weight pressing down on them. He can't wrench them free, can't break them off. He's hung up to bleed out, like a prize stag. Down below, the bikers watch on in amusement as Matiu's blood runs down the face of the summit marker. From here, his last sight will be a spectacular view of Rangitoto as her eruption swells, growing ever more violent.

When he looks down, the bikers have fallen back into a semi-circle, in the centre of which stands a figure who Matiu could swear had not been there moments before. Makere takes several casual steps forward, reaches out. Matiu can't see Makere's hand for a moment, but when he draws it back it shines darkly. Painted with running blood.

"You just going to stand there and watch me die, now?" Matiu manages to croak. "Is that what this is all about?"

"Course it is, bro. You didn't guess already?" Makere holds his hand up, watches in fascination as the blood trickles over his skin. "Like I told you before, it's your turn to be there, back where I've been, all these years. Your turn to watch from the shadows. I can't do that if you're still here, but it's gonna take a lot more than me just wanting it to make it happen."

"You need a sacrifice," Matiu mumbles. Just like Kerr and her sacrifices, trying to cast open the veil, let something else come through. Makere wants to open the veil so *he* can come through.

"And not just any sacrifice. Not worthless mortals with their worthless blood. I need you, Matiu. You, with the blood of Ra in your veins."

It all falls down around this moment.

Matiu sees Mārama, standing astride her waka on the rolling sea, shouting defiance at the sun cresting the horizon and the beast that breaks the waves between them. Mārama, with her visions, with one foot on the other side of the veil. Mārama, to whom this world was a hollow and insubstantial place. This is the great secret she has harboured for so long, the secret that drove her mad. The secret no-one would ever believe, not her sister, not even her son, born of that impossible union. The love she sought in places so forbidden, no-one even knew they were there.

And how would an angry god, beaten into obedience by that trickster hero now fallen to legend and myth, take to a beautiful young woman invading his realm, looking for something she could never find in the mortal world?

"You knew, deep down," Makere goes on. "You knew you were different; you knew *we* were different. Spawned of greater things. Destined for greater things. And yet you threw it away. Now your time's up."

Makere's shadow spreads out around him, flickering, curling lines of jade and ruby, a shape of nightmare. The shape of the taniwha Matiu has seen before, in that other place, when he has watched Mārama upon the waves. Makere is the taniwha. Makere, his unborn twin brother, both of them the children of Ra, the sun whose spite for the descendants of Māui knows no bounds. Makere reaches down and lifts a wooden bowl from the ground. It is half-filled with Matiu's blood, the blood of the sun.

Rangitoto thunders, and light blazes across the thick clouds of ash that now fill the eastern skyline.

"I've waited a long time for this," Makere says. "Bloody decent of you to put on some fireworks for the event." He holds the bowl out, opens his palm over it, and from nowhere, flames appear, licking the surface. "About time we made some of our own." Lifting up the bowl of burning blood, he tilts it, letting the flaming liquid pour down his face, opening his mouth, letting it cover him, fill him, etch him with curling lines of smoke and scar.

The moment falls down around them.

For a splintered shard of time which may be an eyeblink, a breath, a lifetime, Matiu hangs suspended, reality blurring around him. Like a fish caught on a hook, he is rushing through the current, ripped sideways to the flow, some grip drawing him in, more powerful than anything he's ever felt. Stronger than he can resist. Although the hour has barely gone midnight, in this other place of roaring time the sun is rising. Ra's glow is bright and angry in the east, lifting above the horizon, the eye of the god peering into this fractured world. The world that sought to enslave him.

Between Matiu's tortured frame and that glaring eye, Makere is changing. No longer bound to his shadow form, that dim reflection of Matiu which he uses to haunt the mortal realm, Makere is taking on his true shape. The further Matiu falls towards the sun, the more real Makere becomes. The shadow looms, a writhing mass, a coil of claw and wing and tooth. He will continue to grow, to blot out the moon, and he will drag the aurora themselves down to decorate his hide if Matiu lets him.

Penny needs him to hold the monsters back. This is the monster. This is the moment where if he falls, everything falls. The monster is him, everything he refused to be, the essence of Ra's hatred. It is Makere who has trodden this road, walked the path of Ra from inception to vengeance, and Matiu has walked every step of that path with him, Penny at his side from the very start to this, the moment where it all ends. He can't fail her, and all those people in the pit. He can't let Makere win, can't let him finish this journey. Not like this.

Yet he is too weak. They've beaten him down, like Māui beat down Ra in that misty mythic tale. Matiu walked into all their traps, took all their bait. Maybe Makere is right. Maybe he *has* wasted this life. Perhaps he doesn't deserve it, even with the blood of a god in his veins...

In his veins...

Makere falters. The surge shears around him, and Matiu is spinning, though he knows his blood and bones are still skewered helplessly to the summit marker. Something isn't right.

The blood in his veins...

Makere is howling now, caught halfway between worlds. The lines that thread them together are winding tighter, singing a song of imminent destruction.

"What have you done?" Makere shrieks, his voice a guttural roar drowned out by the thundering of time in Matiu's ears.

The blood in his veins is not only his. Erica gave him her blood, mingled it, tainted the purity Makere so desperately needs to work his dark magic, thwarting his desire to destroy him with her willingness to save.

Makere, half-man and half-taniwha, half-formed, half-here and half-there, his talons tearing at the fabric that holds the two worlds apart, screams. He spreads his tattered wings, draws back, and with a glint of jagged teeth, lunges at Matiu.

- Pandora -

The motor screaming in protest, Penny guns the forklift at top speed along the too-busy streets, pushing thoughts of dead boys, mangled bikes and crushed skulls from her mind. She keeps her eyes fixed on the mountain ahead, the bush-clad volcano as dark as a wedge of lime against a margarita sky. Up there, somewhere in that darkness, Matiu needs her help. Well, it's what big sisters do, isn't it? What she's always done.

All at once her mind floods with memories. There was the time she found him in the basement cupboard when she was eight and Matiu just four. He was curled up on the concrete floor amongst the coils of grey vacuum hoses, his hands over his ears, his eyes screwed up, his body trembling, and his face streaming with snot and tears. He was crying, only he wasn't making any sound. Like he hadn't wanted anyone to know he was there. Penny wasn't sure he'd known *she* was there, until she'd touched him on the shoulder.

"Matiu?"

He'd turned then, and flung himself at her, howling and screaming, *pleading* with Penny to please, please make Makere stop, to make *them all stop* because he didn't want to feel any more. On her arm, his fingers left little dents in her skin. Then she'd seen the graze on his knee, the tiny droplets of blood beading in the torn skin, and something, she's not sure what, had made her bend over and brush her lips over the graze. She'd kissed it better. Kissed the hurt away. And it had worked because Matiu had stopped crying, wiping the snot on his shoulder and giving a last sniff-in sniff.

"S'OK. Dey gone now."

He'd meant Makere, his not-so-imaginary friend, but who were the others? Penny had never thought to ask. One thing's for sure: a kiss on the knee isn't going to do the trick this time… She screams around the corner into Mount Eden Road, the forklift tipping for a second, before dropping back to the tarmac. Hillside… Hillside…Where is it? Without the GPS, and not willing to take her hands off the wheel, she can only guess. She hurtles forward, dodging cars, scanning the street signs. The mountain looms on her right now, threatening, like a bouncer at a nightclub. Rautangi Street…Batger…there. She turns, hope dying in her throat. Hillside Crescent is blocked with cars and buses. She lifts the forks and drives up over the curb, careering along the cracked narrow footpath, knocking over bins and brushing against hedges. It's no use. Kerr's acolytes have crowded the road, trying to park as close as they can to the summit. Even just half-way up, Penny can see Clark's police vehicle isn't among them. She wants to cry. She's lost her satchel, still buried somewhere in the wreckage of Craig's car, and without her phone, she has no way of contacting Clark, or anyone for that matter.

There's no point climbing any farther, so Penny makes a left onto Percy and heads back to Mount Eden Road. This close to the park's entrance, even the main road is at a standstill. Trailing stray bits of hedge, Penny crosses the road, cutting between two cars to drive onto the footpath again. Just as well the forklift is narrow enough to navigate the pavement. Since when did Auckland have so many vehicles? At least, so many not owned by Dad. She scans the patchwork of sloping roofs and peers between the hulking buses, her mind racing. Clark was coming from Auckland Hospital. If he were stuck in traffic, then he'd be somewhere on the northern side of the mountain. Penny wants to scream. How's she supposed to find Clark in this haystack? It'd be a miracle! Still, the probability gets better the further she goes up the road. She can't give up yet. Not yet.

She manoeuvres the forklift along the footpath, between the vehicle-dominoes on Puhi Huia Road, where the street winds up to the top of the mountain. Continues north. Come on, Clark. Please be somewhere. But she hasn't seen a single police vehicle. And she hasn't seen the Solaris either.

On her right, she passes the iconic tram car shelter with its pitched tile roof in bright orange, her eyes sweeping from the footpath to the road and back again.

"Dr Yee!"

Penny slams on the brakes.

"Over here!" Clark bustles out of the shelter, pushing a pram.

"I see you got my text, then," he says. "I wasn't sure because my phone's out of juice. The road is chock-a-block that way. Literally. I had to get out of the car two blocks up and come on foot." He nods at the forklift. "I guess you had the same problem."

"You brought Carlos?" she stammers, her eyes flicking to the baby's push chair. Why would Clark bring the boy here? Even without a Touching the Sun tattoo, Carlos is at risk with all the trauma he's already witnessed.

"Carlos?" For a second, Clark looks puzzled, but he quickly lifts his chin. "Oh, you mean the pushchair. I had to carry the vaccine, so I grabbed this from one of the buses. Carlos is in bed, back at the hospital." He turns the pram about, showing her two large plastic containers strapped into the seat.

"The vaccine. You got it!" Penny shuffles her feet over, and Clark loads the containers into footwell. There isn't much space, so it's not ideal, but neither of them have a bag, it'll have to do.

"Do you mind if I ride up with you?" he asks, his boot still on the running board. "I think Tanner and the boys must already be up there on the summit, trying to get the Touching the Sun fools to come down."

Penny reverses the forklift, forcing Clark to jump back. "Tanner needs to keep them there, in the crater. No one can leave."

Clark's eyes, already grey with fatigue, crease at the edges. "I don't get it. Isn't that playing into Kerr's hands? I thought that was what she wanted; to get her cult members into the crater so she can sacrifice them."

Penny looks up as the sky flashes orange. "She does like the theatre of a ritual, but she doesn't need it, not this time. I'm the one who needs them there. If we're to have any hope of saving them." She throws the forklift into forward.

Clark turns his eyes to the mountain. "You're sure about this?"

"Not really." Even with all the best methods, sometimes science is just a load of hunches.

"I'll stay here, then," Clark says at last. "Ensure any stragglers reach the top."

"Thank you, Toeva."

"Good luck, Dr Yee."

The forklift lurches forward, over the grass verge and up the hillside.

As she reaches the treeline, Penny glances back a moment to see Clark snap on his gloves and wade into the traffic.

CHAPTER 34

- Pandora -

Penny takes a shortcut, ignoring the road, too packed with vehicles anyway, and charges straight up the hill to the northern end of the crater. The cone is steep, and she almost topples the forklift twice, but, dammit, she didn't pass her forklift certificate with 100% for nothing.

She's still a hundred metres shy of the crater, her foot cramping from holding the vaccine containers firm in the footwell, when Cerberus bounds over the rim and races towards her. Her heart does a somersault. Cerberus! She's never been so happy to see the big goofball. If Cerberus is here, then Matiu has to be nearby. But instead of her brother, it's Erica who emerges from the basin. Her face red with effort, she's cradling a baby in one arm, and dragging her sister Charlotte with the other.

Her hair falling over her face, Charlotte looks as wild as Rochester's wife. She twists and yanks to free herself from Erica's grip. "Let me go!"

Erica barely manages to hold on to the baby. "Charlotte, come on! We have to get out of here. Touching the Sun are trying to kill you."

"They're trying to *save* me, Erica."

"No, that's me. *I'm* trying to save you."

Penny jumps out of the forklift and races across the paddock towards them.

"Why can't you let me Touch the Sun?" Charlotte wails. "I want to be among those who usher in the new world!"

"What's wrong with this world? What's wrong with us?" Erica screams. The baby twists sideways…

Penny dives in, scooping up the baby an instant before Erica drops her. Her hands freed, Erica snatches for Charlotte, grabbing her around the waist. "Thanks," she murmurs, while she grapples with her sister.

"No problem. Have you seen Matiu?"

Erica's face creases with worry. "He fainted, I think. Over there, on the other side of the mountain," she says, pointing to the east. "He wanted me to... I had to leave him. To get to Charlotte."

"Well, I wish you'd bloody leave me!" Charlotte shrieks. "All I want is for you to mind your own goddamned business!" Like a bull in the ring, she bucks again, forcing Erica to grab her around the neck to prevent her from slipping free. "Let go!"

Penny would help, but the baby is just as wiggly, and she hasn't had much practice. It's like trying to hold an entire sack of apples in two hands.

"I couldn't bring Mārama," Erica tells Penny, heedless of Charlotte's outburst.

"I tried to, but I couldn't make her understand, and with Charlotte and the baby, well, you saw I had my hands full. I'm so sorry, Penny. She's still down there."

"It's OK. I would have made you stay in the crater, anyway. It's the safest place. We need to tell the police; Tanner—"

"There are no police down there," Erica says, breathlessly. "Just that priest—the one from the Sedge restaurant—"

Penny jerks upright. "Kerr?"

"No, the bloke. Weis. He's got his hands full, busy anointing everyone for the second coming. Most of the cult members are already lying on the ground. They're just lying there, chanting and singing. It's fucking weird."

Lying on the ground. Penny's throat tightens. If they're already positioning themselves in the koru shape, then she and Matiu are running out of time.

"It's *not weird*," Charlotte protests. "It's beautiful."

"It's a cult, Charlotte. Can't you see you've been brainwashed?"

"Come with us, Erica," Charlotte pleads. "We're the chosen ones. Can't you see? It's the end of days. If you want to survive, you have to welcome the Sun's grace into your heart. To give yourself freely in his sacred crucible." With a massive wrench, Charlotte tears away from her sister. Long hair flailing, she dashes across the grass, abandoning her baby to disappear over the rim of the crater.

"Charlotte!" Erica wails. For an instant, she buries her face in her hands.

Penny gives the baby to Erica. "Go with her. Keep her in the crater. Keep them all in there. If Tanner arrives, Craig, anyone, tell them they have to stay in the hollow."

"But Matiu said—"

"Please, Erica. I haven't got time to explain. Bad things are coming and I don't know how long Matiu can hold them off."

Erica looks at her a moment, her stare penetrating, as if the answers to her questions are written somewhere on Penny's soul. Perhaps she finds what she's looking for because she gives a quick nod, then turns and runs after her sister.

"Wait," Penny shouts, just before she disappears over the lip of the crater. "The Solaris. Where is it?"

Erica raises a hand, making a swimming motion to the south, and a second later she's gone.

Penny flies back to the forklift, starting it up and throwing it in reverse. *Stupid, stupid, stupid.* She should've followed the road. Instead, she missed the Solaris when she took the shortcut to the summit. Hang on. She whips her head around, scanning the flattened mountaintop. Where did Cerberus go? She hasn't seen him since he emerged from the crater with Erica. Maybe he went to join Matiu, wherever that might be. Penny can't stop to look for either of them, her priority right now is finding the Solaris. She puts her foot to the floor and zig-zags through the maze of vehicles, gunning it back down to the lower carpark, finally spying Dad's wonder car under the trees. She slews the forklift to a stop, the jolt so strong that one of the plastic containers flips out of the footwell and rolls under the Solaris.

Damn.

One will have to do. She can't waste time retrieving it. First and foremost, she needs the Solaris' battery. Let's hope the wundercar recognises her voice.

"Solaris, open," she says. Nothing happens. So much for the Ali Baba approach. She tries the door. It opens! Yay for the manual override.

The tool kit is sitting on the front seat. Grabbing it, Penny sprints to the front of the vehicle. Lifts the bonnet. Where's the battery? There's nothing here that looks remotely like a battery. What had Craig said? *Rechargeable solar batteries no bigger than a ladies' handbag.* Somewhere small, then. Her hands fly over the components. Compact… What's this? She lifts a little cover, and smiles. One battery, and one space. Flooded with relief, Penny rummages in the tool kit. That explains why the car wouldn't respond to her voice command. Knowing how important the Solaris is, Matiu's disabled the vehicle. But he's also left a battery behind, and it's about the size of a ladies' handbag.

It's like he's read her mind.

If only the car's developers had foreseen the need for a screwdriver in their tool kit! Never mind: a spanner will do just the same. Luckily, when your parents own a car fleet, you learn a few things. It takes her less than a minute to disconnect the remaining cell, two to climb aboard the forklift, drop the spanner in the footwell, and gun it up the hill again. Unimpeded, she drives the forklift to the northern ridge, cuts the engine, and climbs down.

For an instant, she stares into the abyss. No wonder no one had stopped her. What did she think she was going to do? Drag them all out bodily? Only now, under the eerie glow of the australis can she discern the full extent of Kerr's empire. The crater is seething with humanity. There has to be a thousand people piled in that steep-sided crucible of hell. No sign of Kerr in the crowd. There's no sign of Erica either, but Penny knows she's in there, staying close to Charlotte with her deluded dreams of a new Eden, here on Mount Eden. Mārama will be somewhere down there too: perhaps to lend her support to Matiu and Penny, or to put an end to her anguish, once and for all. Penny wants to wade into the crush of bodies and haul her out, to rescue her from their lunacy.

Mārama, the most lucid of them all.

A sudden flash makes Kerr's puppets look to the sky, gasps catching in their throats. Penny follows their eyes. On the horizon to the east, as mesmerising as the chant that resonates in the crater, noctilucent spirals paint the sky. It's a koru, picked out in amber streaks. Then, beneath those glorious swirls, a sudden flash as Rangitoto's tongue licks the sky in a fiery whētero. The volcano is erupting, molten boulders of lava exploding on the horizon, the detritus tumbling into the ocean to sizzle and steam like a Rotorua geyser. It is as if the land itself is protesting what must surely come, Rūaumoko's earthly heartbeat booming its warning across the water.

Another flash lights the sky, this time drawing Penny's eyes to the far side of the crater where its southern lip curls into a sneer and there, at last, she spies Matiu.

The wind chills on her neck. They're crucifying him. Her brother is pinned to the summit marker, like an insect to a display board. Blood glistens from his shoulders. Penny drops to her knees, her breath frozen in her chest. From across the void, she feels her brother's pain, hot as acid in her mouth.

Matiu!

She trembles. Blinks. This time, there's no denying it. It's Kingi: a monster-once-man with tentacles emerging indolent from its back. At once grotesque and beautiful, those writhing limbs lift and fall, lift and fall, softly as fronds on the ocean. Kingi is not of this realm. He is a bottom-dweller risen from the Stygian, a shadowy wraith made substance for the moment. But there's a second figure on the ridge. Makere, Matiu's childhood nightmare, his half-brother come again to haunt him, no longer content to persist as a whisper in the darkness or a sideways glance in the mirror. Oh yes, that one has slipped through before, growing stronger even as Matiu weakens. Penny has seen his black intent, sculpted on the bitter Xeno nucleic sugars that run through his veins. No need even to check the crumpled read-out in her pocket. He is a monster. No other term describes that grovelling of gore and claw and teeth.

And Matiu is his prisoner.

There's a movement to Penny's left and the high priestess herself steps up to the rim. "I don't rate your brother's chances," Kerr says, her eyes on the horizon.

Penny looks back across the chasm as Makere draws back his blackened pinions, drool dripping from gleaming incisors. Makere lunges.

Matiu drops his head.

CHAPTER 35

- Matiu -

Framed by the fires that paint the sky, Makere plunges toward him, black eyes blazing, fangs bared, hide shining against the night. Dimly, Matiu knows Makere can't just kill him, or the baleful brother will be thrown back to the other side with no hope of ever returning. But rage is a powerful urge, and even if what can be done in an instant might never be undone, that's no guarantee Makere won't surrender to his more violent instincts. Matiu dips into his pocket and grabs the first thing his fingers close around, the screwdriver he dropped in there when he removed the Solaris battery. He grips it in both hands and thrusts it out before him as Makere strikes.

There's a flash and an inhuman scream as the shock of impact slams Matiu back against the timber. Makere reels away, serpentine neck flailing, clawed talons lashing out in all directions. His monstrous form shifts from shadow to light and back again, even as his disciples scatter or are thrown aside by his thrashing limbs. Some old western legend about cold iron being harmful to demons flickers through Matiu's consciousness, but it's a hazy thought, quickly sucked under by the need to get down off this makeshift crucifix they've hung him on. Still gripping the screwdriver like a talisman, he wraps both hands around one of the arrows skewering him to the summit marker and yanks on it. It comes free of the wood, and he swings down awkwardly, blinding pain shredding his other shoulder where the second arrow still pins him. He screams, but the sound is distant, and he grapples with the other arrow while jamming his feet against the marker and hurling himself outward, away from the boards he's pinned to.

Then he's falling, without enough time to contemplate how much it's going to hurt when he lands, and the pain when it comes hammers him into the concrete. He rolls, but not far, because there are two arrows driven through his chest, and the concrete is slick with his blood. Somehow, he's still clutching the screwdriver in his right hand, and with an effort he pushes himself to one knee. Just in time to see Simon Kingi leaping towards him.

The screwdriver won't do a thing to this creature who has survived gunshots and lightning bolts and falling from a skyscraper, but Matiu clutches it low, tight, like this is just any other knife-fight in any other Auckland alley, a final act of defiance, ready to face the demon with his last breath.

Something blurs past him. Through the haze of blood loss and shifting realities, it appears for a heartbeat like a massive wolf, with three vast heads, maws wide open to reveal yellowed, slavering teeth. A raw dog, screaming. Then the ball of canine fur and tooth and nail slams into Kingi's flank, beast and dog tumbling sideways. "Cerberus!" Matiu shouts, or tries to shout, but his throat is raw, and the battling pair roll past him and out of sight, into the dark. The dark which twists and rolls around him.

The dark which is Makere.

The taniwha surrounds him. No longer content to creep along the edges of his awareness, whispering in his ear, Makere now fills every horizon, refusing to be denied by the brother who has spent his life pushing him away. He drops his head down through the shifting mass of his coils, the once-familiar face now stretched into something hideous and hungry, the moko carved across his warped features like battlescars, the blackened lash of ancient fires that have left their mark in his flesh. Their father, maybe, in his rage? Is this what Makere is fleeing? What Matiu has to look forward to, if his brother succeeds?

Somewhere, Cerberus is yelping, a high canine whine of distress, but Matiu can barely move, much less reach the noble mutt to help him against Kingi. He's got bigger things to worry about. If the dog has any sense, he'll run. Fast.

The ground trembles, earthen fire scorching the night. Through Makere's shifting, semi-corporeal form, Auckland wavers and whimpers. Earthquakes, volcanoes, mass murder and monsters. A day in the big smoke doesn't get much worse than this.

Matiu realises he's giggling, the screwdriver in his hand weaving as if he were drunk. His legs are like jelly, and he's not sure how he's still standing, although the pain is far away now, and there is a cold settling over him, calm, peaceful. Makere, the man, steps out of the coils, standing with his fists clenched in a fighter's stance while the shadow beast whirls around them. Somehow, he is both here and there at once, and Matiu can see the koru of the rising sun paint the sky of that other world, can hear the rushing of the sea so far away, the howl of the wind on this dead calm night.

"You won't deny me this," Makere growls, stepping forward and grabbing Matiu's face in both hands, leaning in. This close, Matiu can see the fire in his eyes, can smell the burnt flesh. "I've lived too long in his light, suffering his ire. He hates me, you know. Hates us all. Hates you especially, because you slipped through his grasp."

Matiu wants to strike, to drive the screwdriver into Makere's burned face, yet he cannot raise his hand against the moko so similar yet so unlike his own. Those arcing patterns he had glimpsed now and then, in black mirrors and nightmares, assumed they were inked etchings like his own. Now he can see them, smell them for what they are: the scorched remnants of the tortures their father has delivered upon his brother all these years for the simple sin of having been conceived. How can he now turn the last of his strength against this man, his own flesh and blood, the unlucky one to have been dragged into hell when Matiu had been lucky enough to taste the light of the world? But the alternative is to let him through, and to give himself over to the beyond...

"I don't know what you did, bro, but I'll drain every drop of blood from your corpse if that's what it takes."

Erica's blood is all that saved him. Bought him some time, at least. He has to use that time. Because somewhere else, Kerr's madness is playing out as well, and at any moment there may be worse things than Makere breaking through from the other side.

Summoning as much courage as strength, Matiu raises the screwdriver. Makere's eyes widen with something akin to fear, just this side of rage. He draws a fist back and slams it into Matiu's cheek.

Matiu staggers two, three steps, then his knees buckle and he's falling backwards, the stars reeling across the sky and across his eyes, pain a blossom unfolding to shroud his skull, and it's only when the monster shrieks and he is lifted off the ground that he understands he's no longer falling. The arrows jutting from his back have pierced the taniwha, lodged there with the weight of his impact, and the enraged beast is uncoiling, taking Matiu with it. For one bright and precious moment, Matiu is on his back staring up into the aurora australis which have arranged themselves into the spiralling shape of a koru across the vast spinning vault of the heavens, and then there is nothing but fire.

- Pandora -

Stuff this.

Ignoring Kerr, Penny scrambles to her feet. Breathing deep, she rolls the Breadmaker™ off the forks and yanks open the rear casing, exposing the power converter. Kudos to the team who planned ahead and made sure the apparatus could be operated as easily in the field on a battery supply as it is in the lab. The battery may not last long, but Penny doesn't need it to. She thrusts the connectors directly onto the Solaris' battery terminals. The Breadmaker™ hums, a quiet lullaby, while on the southern breast of Eden's summit, a battle rages.

"What do you think you're going to do with that little box?" Kerr demands.

"I plan to stop you."

The priestess smiles, smug with confidence. "Oh, I think it is too late for that."

There's a good chance she's right. Maybe this time, all Penny's efforts to thwart this madwoman will come to naught. Aside from the wild dance of the aurora signalling the imminent geological shifts taking place beneath them, vaccines need time to be effective, boosting the host's own immune response to confer resistance. Plus, Penny's plan to deliver the dose could have some tiny flaws. She has no other choice. This battered box is their only hope of reversing the evil. She almost chuckles. Her name is *Pandora*, after all.

She slips her fingers into her back pocket, and pulls out the glass shard, with its smear of Makere's blood no larger than the fingernail on a child's pinkie. Opening the Breadmaker™, she drops the blooded teardrop into the cuvette.

Now for the vaccine. She jumps up and runs to the forklift for the container.

"Whatever you're doing like a busy little bee over there, you're wasting your time," Kerr drawls. She chuckles like the evil maniac she is. "Nothing can stop this now. I will have my time in the sun, like all his disciples." The priestess is so confident, so convinced she has won, that she doesn't even turn her head. "Look, already Horus heralds the Creator's arrival in the sky," she says. "Or perhaps it is your Māori ancestors who welcome him from their campfires to the south. Ra of the northern deserts, Ra of the southern oceans, they are one and the same. His eminence waned in Egypt, but only while he rested. Now, centuries on, he gathers his power to him, changing the earth's polarity in preparation for his rebirth in this humble solar temple." She giggles. "Fitting, isn't it? Since this very crater is named for secrets hidden beneath the earth. Ra will see our devotion. He will accept the sacrifices offered him—lives given freely in his service—and the portal to the new world will open."

"Not so freely. Not everyone in that crater is willing," Penny murmurs through gritted teeth.

Kerr shrugs, her eyes on the koru in the sky. "A minor issue."

Penny's bile rises. A minor issue! How can she be so glib? She's only sending a thousand people to their deaths. Not to mention the victims of this morning's massacres. And if the monsters congregating on the southern lip are anything to go by—the foul creatures currently torturing Matiu—then more will surely follow.

Penny tips the liquid into the Breadmaker™. "Of course, they have to die *first…*"

Kerr whirls. Frowning, she takes in the container, N-GenZostavax branded on the side, and her eyes widen with understanding. "You bitch!" she shrieks, flying at Penny, kicking the container out of her hands.

No! Penny dives after it, her knees grazing the stony ground. The plastic container tumbles, rolling away, precious liquid slopping out with each bounce, but Penny hurls herself forward, curling her fingers under it, righting the container before too much dribbles into the dust.

Kerr seizes her ponytail and yanks her sideways, dragging her onto her side.

Penny curls into herself and cradles the container like a newborn but, still on her feet, Kerr mauls her, frantic to pry it from Penny's grasp.

"Give it to me," she screams.

Not on your fucking life.

But Kerr lands a boot in Penny's side and her body yields, the brittle crack of her ribs inaudible over Rangitoto's booming. Penny's breath stalls in her chest. Pain explodes—white, hot, exquisite—and, suddenly, her fingers are slick with sweat. She's losing her grip. No! She can't let go. If Kerr succeeds in tipping the liquid out, Penny won't be able to save anyone, and Matiu's pain will be for nothing.

Matiu. Oh god. Is her brother still alive?

Damn you. Let go!

Blocking out the excruciating searing in her ribs, Penny hooks a leg around Kerr's and jerks back hard, upending her. The priestess grunts and thuds to the ground, her white robes tangled around her legs.

Penny gets up, taking advantage of Kerr's confusion to scramble for the Breadmaker™, but Kerr grabs her ankle and Penny goes down again, stabs of pain exploding in her side. She kicks back, Kerr gratifying her with a squeal and a moment of respite.

Taking a shallow breath, Penny rolls to her feet, the twist in her torso like a taniwha's talon slid between her bones. The ground shakes and Penny reels under a burning orange sky, although perhaps it is the pain. Already, Kerr is getting to her feet, preparing to attack again.

Swimming in hurt, Penny's mind races. Another kick could kill her, driving the cracked rib into her lungs or heart. She needs a new plan. All at once, Rangitoto sends out a burst of fire, illuminating her with inspiration. Penny clenches her teeth, pushing the burning into the background. Then she tucks the container under her arm and drives forward, legs pumping, running past the Breadmaker™ to the forklift, Kerr hard on her heels.

With ribs of glass, Penny leans into the footwell, moaning as she snatches up the spanner. Kerr is coming. Yelling. Berserk with fury and hate.

She waits…waits…her heart pounding, letting the banshee approach, not yet… waiting until she feels the woman's breath, *her spittle*, on her neck, then she spins, all her weight behind her, and cracks the spanner down on Kerr's temple.

The priestess staggers, a blue bruise already blooming on her forehead. She drops to her knee, crawls a step, then collapses.

Thank heavens.

Releasing the spanner, Penny stumbles back to her trusty benchtop DNA sequencer—more money than she's ever spent on a piece of lab equipment—pours in the remaining vaccine and closes the lid.

She throws the switch.

Then she backs away, her arm held tight across her chest and her breath shallow, making for the forklift, the nearest cover.

Will it work? Penny doesn't know. Makere's blood, his ichor, has set the machine off before. But there was more of it then, and the reaction occurred under controlled conditions. What if it needs the other reagents—DDT or proteinase—to set it off? And if, by some miracle, it works without them, will the vaccine still be viable? Will the crater act as a microcosm? What if she's too late? Penny has no way of knowing.

She sinks down, crouching behind the forklift, and looks to the south to where she last saw Matiu, her eyes clouding.

No wait. That's smoke blocking her view: pungent, acrid, rotting smoke, and it's spewing from under the lid of the Breadmaker™. It's just as well she can hardly breathe. A giggle escapes her, making her swoon with pain. Hope unfurls where the ache resides. *There's a chance...* She leans her head against the chassis of the forklift, while beyond, on the edge of the crater, putrid black bubbles boil and spit from cracks in the Breadmaker's™ casing. The machine hisses and groans. Penny smiles. Little by little, it's rejecting the ichor tainting its core. Somewhere in the distance, Penny is sure she hears Cerberus howl.

"You crazy bitch! Stop it. Stop it now. You're going to ruin it all," Kerr screams. She staggers forward, listing to one side, rushing for the Breadmaker™. "Turn it off!" She presses the buttons, desperate to reverse whatever is happening in the DNA sequencer.

It's too late.

The machine isn't made for XNA.

The metal whines. A death rattle. Penny ducks her head as the Breadmaker™ explodes.

CHAPTER 36

- Matiu -

Fire above, fire below.

Rangitoto, with her city-killing tantrum.

Ra, straining against Māui's ropes which have held him for so long.

The aurora, tendrils of flame dropping from the stars to tear at those magical flaxen braids, the powers of the cosmos wrenching against the filthy magics of that trickster demigod and his brothers to right an ancient injustice.

Auckland, the city laid out below him in a patchwork of burning dust, as his body twists with the taniwha's thrashing.

The fire in his veins, both pain and love and the hatred his father filled him with which he has tried so hard to resist, all his life. Tried and failed.

This moment, etched in his mind from the dream he had, or perhaps it was this moment remembered before it happened. The ball of fire he held in his hands as the city burned. That tiny globe cradled in his palms, like a sun, but brighter than a thousand.

Makere is not just trying to escape. He might think he is, but only because their father has allowed it. Makere is here now, in this moment, when the earth itself is shifting its weight and rewriting the laws of reality to suit itself, because only now can Ra harness the power of the aurora and liberate himself. Ra has allowed this, so that he can be free. And then he will blaze, and burn, and cast this world into vengeful ruin.

Even now, Matiu can see things moving beyond the shadows of the taniwha, things pressing against the veil from the pit, in the crater where Mārama has gone to face the collapse of all things and stand there, somehow, against it all. Creatures of writhing tentacles, blind mouths bright with teeth, nightmares of shadow and hunger. In that vortex twisting the fabric of space he can see the shape of the future, the world a shattered wasteland stalked by Kerr's blind howling monstrosities.

Yet in his hands he held the sun.

Like Māui held Ra, the sun, in his hands, and punished him.

Screwdriver still gripped tight in his right hand, Matiu reaches for his pocket with his left, finds the edge of the fabric, slides his fingers inside. Wraps them around the cool plastic of the Solaris battery. Pulls it free.

Makere, the beast, swivels its mighty head, shrieks, and lunges.

Matiu jams the screwdriver across the terminals.

- Pandora -

The boom thunders through the night, returning Rangitoto's fire, and sending scabs of fiery metal blasting for metres across the mountain top. Metal pings the front of the forklift and thuds on the sun-baked earth. Smoke and fumes choke the air.

Crouched behind the forklift, her mouth and nose covered, Penny is safe from the onslaught, as are the Touching the Sun acolytes sheltered inside Maungawhau's sloping crater. Only the priestess is still in the open. She leaps away, just as the explosion rents the air. Her howl is chilling. Desperate. Bereft.

The sound penetrates Penny's marrow, and her scalp crawls.

If this were a penalty shootout, then the priestess jumped the wrong way. Or the right way, depending on whose side you're on, because the shrapnel bursting from the exploding machine throws her backwards, the shattered pieces burying in her abdomen, her face, her chest. They sink deep into her flesh, staining her robes a violent red. The blood spreads, seeping slowly and inexorably into the fabric.

Gingerly gripping her side, Penny emerges from behind the forklift. She approaches the priestess until she is standing over her, Kerr lying spread eagle on the ground, gurgling through the piece of metal embedded in her throat.

"Help me," she slurs. Her fingers quiver. She struggles to breathe through gluts of blood and bubbles. She's dying. Penny's heart pinches, but then she remembers Jaime Sutherland and her unborn baby, butchered so this woman could practice her occult arts in preparation for this day, Carlos and his dead mother massacred this morning on Mount Māngere, poor Annie Hillsden and her beloved dog Benson, sacrificed in the bowels of the museum… She chokes back her pity.

Penny will keep her company; she'll stand by and watch over her while the woman's wairua-spirit leaves her body and makes its way to the jumping off place in the far north. Penny can do that. But there's no way she's going to feel sorry for her.

Hey. It's raining. Penny looks up. Overhead, the koru's iridescent glow lights up a fine mist falling over the crater. Not rain. It's the vaccine.

When Kerr's eyes have dulled, Penny walks to the lip of the crater and peers over the edge. Her mouth drops open. Her crazy theory is working. The cult members have stopped their chanting and they're getting up off the ground! Not all of them, but then in a large population you're always going to get variations in individual responses to a vaccine. It's enough to give Penny hope.

Suddenly, something white flashes in the bottom of the pit. Penny's eyes widen in alarm as Kerr's partner in crime, her sun priest Weis, strolls amongst the crowd in his flowing white robes and his thick glasses. Now that the intended massacre hasn't eventuated, he's searching the slopes of the crater, shoving the people out of the way, looking for something. What? A way out? Is he trying to escape? But Weis isn't heading for the lip of the crater. Instead, he's approaching one of the acolytes; a man who is still lying on the ground in the koru formation. What's Weis doing?

Horrified, Penny watches as the sun priest reaches into the folds of his robe, pulling out a curved blade. Looking to the heavens, his lips moving in that moronic chant, Weis stands over the man and lifts the blade in both hands. The steel shines dully under the glow of the aurora. He's going to kill him, and in full view of everyone.

Stop him! Penny wants to scream, but her ribs won't let her. The people nearby on the slopes are too bewildered to notice what's going on. Penny's heart pounds. She has to get down there. But even as she thinks it, she knows she'll never make it: she's too far away, and there are too many people blocking the way.

Penny's hair stands on end as a howl carries across the crater and Cerberus charges into the pit, his lips pulled back and his teeth bared. As fast as a hellhound, his eyes glowing red under the southern lights, he flies down the slopes, his growl so low and guttural that the cult members draw back to let him past. Only Weis carries on. Intent on murder, he mumbles his incessant incantation, reaching up, then swiftly bringing the knife down…

Penny gasps.

Cerberus flies through the air, his jaws closing on Weis' wrist. The priest has no time to push the blade home; the dog clamps down, closing snarling teeth, and tosses his head. Weis screams, and although she can't see it, Penny imagines the sliced veins and crushed bones. Weis opens his hand, dropping the blade. Man and dog tumble down the slopes, rolling like a crocodile in a death grip, the cultists jumping left and right. When the pair stop, Cerberus is on top, his paws on Weis' chest, and his teeth slavering at the priest's throat.

Weis throws up his hands to protect himself. The big Lab has him pinned.

Penny sighs with relief. "Good boy, Cerberus!" she shouts. "Hold him there. If he moves, I give you permission to rip his throat out." Penny has no idea how Cerberus had known it was Weis, but damn is she happy he did. Maybe he recognised the priest's white robes from that night at the Sedge, or simply sensed the man's intent. Either way, Cerberus' timing had been perfect. Who knows how many lives he saved? No sacrifices meant no portal. Now, if Matiu can just…

She turns southward, searching for her brother. He's still there, up on the rim. Facing demons. Wait, what's he doing now? Penny is squinting against the glare, trying to work out what's going on, when, all at once, the air is rent with sound, and the sky bursts with flame.

- Matiu -

There's a moment of blinding light as the battery terminals arc out across the screwdriver's shaft, then Makere's demon skull slams into Matiu's. The night cracks open, as loud and brutal as a breaking bone, and just as painful. The blazing dark folds outward around them, jaws stretching wide to swallow. Matiu and Makere are falling, the taniwha obliterated by the explosion leaving only two men, both of them dropping into that eternal gullet as the power of Ra, cunningly enslaved by human technology but no longer trapped in the battery's cells, erupts. The sun's rage was there in Matiu's hand all along, but now it is unleashed.

They're thrown away from each other, a mirror image, two souls sutured together by destinies beyond their control, their fates warped by a tragedy of love and deceit they played no part in but which, for better or worse, they will end. The veil of worlds has kept them apart, but now that veil is torn asunder, at least for a moment. Here, they are equal, as they tumble like rag dolls into a screaming white void. The laws of time and space and energy don't seem to apply to these marionettes, these children of Ra, as Matiu glimpses the shock wave expanding into the hazy realm of his own world, sees the silhouettes of men turned monstrous caught in its blossoming ring, blaze to shadow, blown to dust and ash.

Momentum is a sluggish thing, caught here in this fractured place between worlds, and both Matiu and Makere hit the ground at the same time, roll, come to a stop. All his pain is overridden by the white-hot shroud of the explosion they're caught within, and it must only be the blood of the sun in both their veins which holds the certainty of mortality at bay for a breath longer. The arrows in his flesh have been vaporised, and his clothes hang smoking on his limbs, hot with the smell of scorched leather.

Matiu stands and turns, as Makere stands and turns, their movements perfect and precise, each as exact as the other. Matiu could be looking in a mirror, if not for this impossible landscape where rippled skies cloak the muted Auckland skyline, alive with whorls and peaks from a dreamscape he has visited with Mārama, more than once.

Both their eyes flicker to the side, to the stabbing needle of darkness penetrating from yet another reality, this one speckled with black sand and distant stars and writhing with tentacles and coils and teeth. Kerr's portal.

And between them, pushing through the earth at their feet; a pulsing, heaving arc of searing light, lashed over with smoking ropes of woven flax, unspeakably hot and unthinkably vast. Ra, their father, straining to break free of the hole Māui and his brothers banished him into so long ago. Like a blot of white oil in an ocean of flame, the explosion continues to billow outwards, time choking on its own dead weight. Maybe when this tortured moment passes, the ropes binding Ra will finally fail, and the monsters will burst through.

Matiu meets Makere's gaze, both of them tensed into a fighting crouch. But beyond the raw horror of the moment, Matiu sees something in his brother's eyes he never expected to see: despair. "You prepared the way for him," Matiu accuses, stalking around the ring of fire, Makere matching his steps. "You let him get this far."

"It wasn't meant to be like this," Makere hisses. Matiu recognises the shards in his voice, blades of panic, as all his plans unspool, splinter. "Your part was to fail, like you've *always* failed," Makere goes on. "I've worked my whole life towards this, why couldn't you just break like you were supposed to?"

Matiu shakes his head, mimicking Makere's shaking head. "Bro, we might have a god for a dad, but I think you underestimate what it means to have a big sister watching over you your whole life. She's never let me fall down, never will. She's here now, you know? She's got my back. What've you got? Nothing. Just all that hate inside you. All that anger, and you haven't even got the balls, right now, to stand up and turn that all against the one who made you so fucking miserable, your whole life. You're happy to help wreck the world, when you're the one with the power to save it. Now, you've got a choice." He kneels, and Makere kneels, and together they reach out, and both wrap a hand around Māui's flaxen ropes, woven as they are with the silver light of Mārama, the moon, so they would always be cool when they were slung across Ra's fiery shoulders. Together, they strain against the ropes as eternal, infinite Ra thrusts against his prison, and the earth shudders with his violence. "It's not only the sun in our veins!" Matiu shouts, defying the father he never knew.

Matiu's brow crumples as he pictures his mother, *their* mother's face, her hands so fine, light as moonbeams in the night. If he must stand in this place and hold this rope for eternity, to keep Ra from breaking free, then that's what he'll do, for her. Because she has stood so long, not against the darkness, as he'd always thought, but against this terrible, awful light. Maybe he'll never see her again, or Penny, or Erica, but if he's failed at everything else in his life, then this can be the one thing he won't screw up. Tears spill freely from his stinging eyes and fall to cut wet lines in the ash that coats his fingers, soaking the ropes of his ancestor. "We will stand," Matiu cries, his voice a ragged flame in the chaos of the void. "We will hold this motherfucker down, until the end of the world, if we have to!"

"Brother!" Makere has no tears. Smoke boils around his hands, the smell of burnt meat suddenly sickening in the air. "Matiu!"

But Matiu's fingers, slick and wet as silver moonlight on cobwebs, are slipping, and time comes rushing back in, and the explosion claims him, lifting him and hurling him backwards, away from the pulsing orb of Ra and his smoking ropes.

The mirror is broken, the veil falling back into place, the universe refusing to be broken. Makere, still bound to the grasp of that in-between place and to Māui's ropes, recedes, shouting after Matiu, who can no longer hear his words, only the twisting of sudden terror in Makere's voice, lost in a roar which just might be the breaking of the world.

CHAPTER 37

- Pandora -

It's over. Penny blinks. She's alone on the rim of the crater. With a roar louder than cannon fire Rangitoto had erupted in a violent burst of rock and earth, and then, all at once, she was quiet, and that strident, blinding orb of light was gone, sucked back into itself.

And Matiu? In the flash that accompanied the explosion Penny had been blinded. She'd lost sight of her brother. She doesn't know what happened. She stifles a scream of panic. She can't see him anywhere. Where is he? She won't believe that Matiu is gone. She won't. Not until she sees the evidence.

And if none exists?

Thank goodness! Tanner, Clark, and Craig are coming up the road at a run. Confident one of them will relieve Cerberus and deal with Weis, Penny leaves the rim and stumbles across the mountaintop, running to the far side of the crater and down the eastern slope, her eyes blurring with tears, searching for her brother.

Matiu! Oh my god, Matiu, where are you?

She finds him curled up in the grass, his body bleeding and broken, Mārama, his birth mother, cradling him in her arms. Penny's blood drains, and her mouth goes dry. She's too scared to go to them, certain her baby brother is dead. Mārama's lips move. Surely, she is singing a tangi-waiata in honour of her son. Penny hangs back. She's not ready for this. She might never be ready for this. Her lip trembles as she imagines poor Mum, waiting on a reply to her squizillion texts.

It'll never come now.

Then, Matiu raises his hand and waves her over. "Hey, sis. You made it," he croaks.

Penny's heart does a flip. She sucks in a breath, pain flaring in her side. *Not dead, not dead!* "Yeah. I drove a forklift," she blurts.

"You drove yourself here, blew something up, *and* stopped a massacre." His eyes crease at the edges. Penny smiles too. They both know he's the one who likes to blow shit up.

"You stopped more," she says quietly.

His eyes roll back for a moment, as if he's receding into the darkness, and Penny crouches beside him, suddenly frightened. Mārama strokes his hair, pushing it back off his forehead, and after a while, perhaps coaxed back by her gentleness, he opens his eyes.

"They're gone," he says. "Ra and his demons. Maybe not forever. I…they…" he trails off. Starts over. "With Kerr and Weis out of the picture, and Kingi forced back to where he came from, Ra will need new acolytes, new conduits."

"And Makere?"

Mārama closes her eyes.

Matiu places his hand on hers. "It wasn't his fault. Makere didn't have us around to support him. Instead, he was unloved and abused by our father, tortured until he was as brainwashed as the members of Kerr's cult. But he helped me at the end. Your son, my brother. Only, I couldn't hold on and I lost him." Matiu gives a harsh laugh. "My part was to fail, he said. He *knew*. He knew and he helped me anyway…"

"Yee!" It's Tanner, the big detective striding across the grassy headland, his tan suit even more rumpled than usual—if that is even possible.

Quickly, Matiu scrubs his face with his forearm. Penny wipes away her own tears, and, assaulted by another wave of pain, resolves to keep her breath shallow.

"You OK?" Tanner asks Matiu.

Matiu sweeps his eyes over the ragged wounds, the rivulets of drying blood, and clucks his tongue. "I've been better."

"There are ambulances on the way. It's going to take a little while. Bit of a traffic jam around the base of the mountain, and we'll need all our patience to get the wheatgrass folk out of the crater and down the slopes. Believe it or not, some of them aren't too happy at being saved from a nasty death." He lowers his voice, talking behind his hand to Penny so Mārama doesn't hear. "We're trying to get the poor souls straight into psychiatric care. Have them deprogrammed." Tanner huffs and lifts his stubbled chin to the glowing ashen cloud over Rangitoto. "Guess the docs are going to be in for a busy few days."

Penny nods, thinking of Charlotte and her baby and the long road ahead. Will Charlotte ever forgive her sister for interfering? Penny hopes so. Siblings are important, after all.

Penny sits on the grass beside her brother and looks out to the horizon.

It's dawn. The sun ripples on the ocean, and Rangitoto lies spent in the bay, her fiery ire reduced now to an occasional quiet grumble. The southern lights are still shining overhead, their glow dimmer with the day's arrival, and the koru has disappeared. Even the ground beneath their feet seems subdued.

Matiu squints against the morning glare. "I suppose you've come to ask how Penny foiled Sandi Kerr and stopped the massacre?"

Tanner steps around them, into the sun, so Matiu isn't forced to squint—his acknowledgement that Penny and Matiu did a good job? "Nah, I ran into Tong on the way up the hill—looking right at home carrying Ms Pandora's satchel, he was too. Anyway, he was rambling on about how amazing Dr Yee here had been working it all out. Gave me the general gist: something about permanent state MRIs and nanobot technology and the like. I gather it was like the Darius Fletcher case, then?"

"Um, something like that," Penny replies. "Kerr was working her way up to this, trying different sacrificial rites, so she could carry out her plans on a larger scale, this time using nanobots lying dormant in the dorsal horn ganglia of the cult members which were programmed to respond to a change in magnetic…" She bites her lip. "There were some similarities."

Tanner puffs air through his cheeks, puts his hands on his hips. "Who the hell plans to sacrifice hundreds of people?"

"She believed she was creating a portal to the underworld," Penny says.

Rolling his eyes, Matiu puts his finger to his head.

"Bat shit crazy," Mārama quips, her eyes distant.

Tanner gives a cheerless grin. "Well, seems she found a way through, didn't she, and Clark has her man Weis in custody, thanks to your pooch, so that about wraps things up. Just so long as it's all explained in your report," he says.

On the southern lip of the crater, a couple of uniforms are inspecting the blackened summit marker. "Oi!" Tanner bellows, and he leaves them, marching over to ball out the hapless officers. "Careful how you handle that, you idiots. You'll obliterate any forensic evidence."

Penny glances at Matiu, who raises his eyebrows.

There won't be any trace of ichor—not given the extent of the explosion—but there is no doubt in her mind that something epic happened here on Mount Eden, something rare and significant and so surreal that even years of rigorous scientific research would fail to explain. Penny has a hunch though, because she saw it with her own eyes: one moment, Matiu was there on the mountaintop, facing down a legion of monsters, and then he was gone, vaporised, and Penny had thought it was over, that she had failed her brother, lost him forever. There's a shout, and, her nerves still on alert, Penny whirls as Erica comes flying down the hillside.

"Matiu!"

Mārama moves aside to let her in, and the way Matiu's probation officer behaves when she reaches him isn't very probation-officery.

Wincing, Penny gets up and shuffles higher up the ridge, leaving them to it. How long will it take for Matiu to admit that he's in love with her? Ha! Just wait until Mum gets wind of *that*. He'll never hear the end of it. Good. It might get her off Penny's case for a while. Mind you, when Dad finds out that Penny and Matiu have obliterated both of the Solaris' batteries, they'll never hear the end of that either. Someone isn't going to be very pleased.

"Penny!"

She turns, nearly fainting as Craig comes over the rise, her satchel slung over his shoulder and Cerberus dragging at the lead. With the prototype's batteries destroyed, Penny guesses there won't be much reason for Craig to come calling either.

"I thought you might want your satchel," he says, throwing her a lop-sided grin.

Although, you never know.

Gingerly dropping to her knees, Penny wraps Cerberus in a one-armed bear-hug. "Good boy, Cerb." He dips his head and licks the salty tear tracks from her face.

She gives him a good scratch. He deserves it. "Good boy," she says again.

After a while, Craig helps her to her feet, drawing her to him, and wrapping his arm about her shoulders. Her ribs hurt, but she snuggles closer anyway, taking unexpected comfort in his warmth. To the east, the sun bursts over Rangitoto Island in rapturous tones of pink and gold. Would it last? Had Ra the mighty sun-god really been put in his place? Penny would have to have a serious talk with her brother about that. Not today, though. Maybe tomorrow after they've all had a chance to get some sleep. Sometime when Erica hasn't got her face mashed against his.

On Craig's hip, Penny's phone rings. Using his super-spy skills, Craig follows the ringtone, lifting the flap of her satchel and fishing the phone out. He checks the screen before handing it to her, grinning. "It's your mother," he says.

Penny closes her eyes and breathes as deep as her ribs will allow. One more battle to win, then.

- Matiu -

The sky is a thousand shades of fire and blood, washed in ashen clouds lit up by the burning sunrise. Matiu squeezes Erica's shoulder and they pause, having gained the top of the rise. Penny and Craig are following, slower. Broken ribs really are a bitch to take walking. He breathes hard, looks around. Auckland lies beneath them, a city that has survived so much more on this night than she will ever know.

Standing on the path that rims the crater bowl, catching his breath, Matiu pictures all those millions of people down below, imagines them cupped in his hands, scared and desperate, most of them wanting nothing more than to tidy up the mess and get on with their lives, or get the fuck out of this place and run like hell. Like the figures inked on the sides of that bloody wooden bowl he picked up in Darius Fletcher's factory, back when it all began. Innocent, everyday folk going about their business, caught up in other peoples' nightmares, and here he is standing on the edge of another bowl, also drenched in blood. A bigger bowl, this one carved not by human hands but by the planet's violent birth, set here so they might catch the insanity of Kerr and Makere as it spilled over from those other places, containing it before it could flood the world. There's a strange sense of closure in that, even if it will only ever make sense to him.

He scans the city skyline, the needle of the sky tower dusted in ash, the serpentine hump of the harbour bridge like a sleeping taniwha. Waitemata Harbour and the Hauraki Gulf shine blinding with the dawn. Rangitoto, her anger spent, glowers sullen against the horizon, the sun at her back. Ra wraps it all in splinters of shadow and light as he limps above the sea, thick ropes of dust and mist trailing him on his course through the clouds and across the sky. Somewhere, Makere is still clutching those legendary ropes with burnt palms, crying out for his brother, bound forever to walk the path of Ra, the shadow on the face of the sun.

"You OK?" Erica asks, which is a stupid question and she knows it, but Matiu appreciates it for what it is.

"No," he says. "But I'm better than I could've been."

Erica stretches up and kisses him on the cheek. "Hey, we saved the day, beat the bad guys, you got the girl, and now you get to walk off into the sunrise. It's the best we could've hoped for, isn't it?"

Penny limps up to them, Craig Tong gingerly supporting her under one arm.

"Almost," says Penny.

"What do you mean, almost?" Craig asks, brushing a stray lock out of his face. Matiu doesn't think he's ever seen Mr Slick this dishevelled.

He gives Penny a sly look. "We're meant to be riding off into the sunset, eh?"

Penny leans into her brother, and he pulls her to him, both wincing with the pain, pain that tells them they're alive. For the moment, that's enough.

"I'll take a sunrise," she says.

"Yeah," he agrees. "Sunrise is all good."

GLOSSARY

AOS	Armed Offenders Squad (similar to SWAT)
Autōia	In Māori mythology, the third division of the underworld, dwelling place of Whiro, personification of darkness and evil
bonnet	hood of a car
boot	trunk of a car
GNS	Department of Geologic and Nuclear Sciences
hangi	earth oven, also used to describe food cooked in an earth oven
Hine-nui-te-pō	Māori goddess of night & death, ruler of the underworld iwi nation or tribe
IR googles	infrared or night-vision goggles
karakia	a ritual chant, blessing; prayer
kiri tuhi	tattoos with no cultural-tribal significance
kōrero	talk, discuss; to tell a story
koru	spiral shaped based on unfurling fern, symbolising new life, growth, strength, and peace
Mahuika	Māori goddess, fire deity
Māui	Māori folk hero, trickster, demigod
maunga	mountain, mount, large hill
Maungakiekie	One Tree Hill, a volcanic peak in Auckland
moko	traditional tattoo (with cultural-tribal meaning)
pā	Māori fortress, usually built around the peak of a hill
pākeha	New Zealander of European descent
Papatūānuku	the earth mother
patu	*coll.* broken, defective; also a club carved of wood or stone, particularly pounamu (greenstone)
pavlova	famous Kiwi meringue dessert developed in honour of ballerina Anna Pavlova's visit to New Zealand in the 1920s

pounamu	greenstone
Ranginui	the sky father
Rangitoto	volcanic island off the coast of Auckland, also volcano and scoria rock
Rūaumoko	Māori god of volcanos and earthquakes
SIS	actually NZSIS, New Zealand Security Intelligence Services
tāhu-nui-a-rangi	Māori term for aurora australis or Southern Lights
taiaha	Māori spear
taniwha	monster, serpent, also a metaphor for a chieftain
tama	son, or *e tama*, an expression of surprise
Tane Mahuta	Son of Papatūānuku and Ranginui, also an iconic northland kauri tree
Tāwhirimātea	Māori god of wind, lightning and thunder, son of Papatūānuku and Ranginui
tapu	sacred
taua	warparty, band of warriors
togs	swimsuit, swimming trunks
VMS	Video Management System
waiata	tangi lament
whaea	aunt
whaikorero	speech of introduction, detailing one's ancestry
whenua	land, homeland
whētero	provocative protrusion of the tongue during a haka (war dance)

About the Authors

Lee Murray is a multi-award-winning writer and editor of science fiction, fantasy, and horror (Sir Julius Vogel, Australian Shadows) and a three-time Bram Stoker Award® nominee. Her works include the Taine McKenna military thrillers (Severed Press), and supernatural crime-noir series The Path of Ra, co-written with Dan Rabarts (Raw Dog Screaming Press), debut short story collection Grotesque: Monster Tales (Things in the Well), as well as several books for children. She is proud to have edited fifteen speculative works, including award-winning titles Baby Teeth: Bite Sized Tales of Terror and At the Edge (with Dan Rabarts), Te Kōrero Ahi Kā (with Grace Bridges and Aaron Compton) and Hellhole: An Anthology of Subterranean Terror (Adrenaline Press). She is the co-founder of Young New Zealand Writers, an organisation providing development and publishing opportunities for New Zealand school students, co-founder of the Wright-Murray Residency for Speculative Fiction Writers, and HWA Mentor of the Year for 2019. In February 2020, Lee was made an Honorary Literary Fellow in the New Zealand Society of Authors Waitangi Day Honours. Lee lives over the hill from Hobbiton in New Zealand's sunny Bay of Plenty where she dreams up stories from her office overlooking a cow paddock. Read more at www.leemurray.info

Dan Rabarts is an award-winning author and editor, four-time recipient of New Zealand's Sir Julius Vogel Award and three-time winner of the Australian Shadows Award, occasional sailor of sailing things, part-time metalhead and father of two wee miracles in a house on a hill under the southern sun.

Together with Lee Murray, he co-edited the flash-fiction horror anthology *Baby Teeth - Bite-sized Tales of Terror*, and *At The Edge*, an anthology of Antipodean dark fiction.

His steampunk-grimdark-comic fantasy series Children of Bane starts with Brothers of the Knife and continues in Sons of the Curse and Sisters of Spindrift (Omnium Gatherum Media). Dan's science fiction, dark fantasy and horror short stories have been published in numerous venues worldwide. He also regularly produces and narrates stories for podcasts and audiobooks.

Find him at dan.rabarts.com.

CPSIA information can be obtained
at www.ICGtesting.com
Printed in the USA
LVHW042307170621
690500LV00011B/1422

9 781947 879263

CPSIA information can be obtained
at www.ICGtesting.com
Printed in the USA
LVHW042307170621
690500LV00011B/1422